FRIENDS MAKE THE WORST ENEMIES

Ashok found it ve

The crowd did

There were no favori

estly cared for the we

Devedas was beloved   ...had been seen

as a young upstart at first, because he had arrived

already gifted with one of the most powerful artifacts

in the world. Except he had gone on to win their

respect by being the most dedicated among them.

He tried one last time to get his brother to see

reason. "The Law requires me to do my best. I will

hold nothing back."

It was a grave warning, for when you fought a

bearer, you fought against the combined instinct of

every man who had ever carried that sword into

battle.

"Everyone knows you always do precisely what

the Law says, little brother." Devedas gave him

a sad smile. "It's why it's impossible to hate you."

Ashok could not feel fear like everyone else, but

he could understand it well enough in principle. He

could see that Devedas was afraid—as any sane

man would be to face an ancestor blade—yet he

was committed.

"Know that if it was my decision, I would do my

best to defeat you, but I would try to spare your

life. Only I do not think Angruvadal understands

moderation."

The duel began...

BAEN BOOKS by LARRY CORREIA

SAGA OF THE FORGOTTEN WARRIOR SERIES
Son of the Black Sword
House of Assassins
Destroyer of Worlds

THE GRIMNOIR CHRONICLES
Hard Magic
Spellbound
Warbound

THE MONSTER HUNTER INTERNATIONAL SERIES
Monster Hunter International
Monster Hunter Vendetta
Monster Hunter Alpha
The Monster Hunters (compilation)
Monster Hunter Legion
Monster Hunter Nemesis
Monster Hunter Siege
Monster Hunter Memoirs: Grunge (with John Ringo)
Monster Hunter Memoirs: Sinners (with John Ringo)
Monster Hunter Memoirs: Saints (with John Ringo)
Monster Hunter Guardian (with Sarah A. Hoyt)
Monster Hunter Bloodlines (forthcoming)

THE DEAD SIX SERIES (with Mike Kupari)
Dead Six
Swords of Exodus
Alliance of Shadows
Invisible Wars: The Collected Dead Six (omnibus edition)

STORY COLLECTIONS
Target Rich Environment
Target Rich Environment Volume 2

To purchase any of these titles in e-book form,
please go to www.baen.com.

DESTROYER
OF
WORLDS

LARRY
CORREIA

DESTROYER OF WORLDS

A Baen Books Original

Baen Publishing Enterprises
P.O. Box 1403
Riverdale, NY 10471
www.baen.com

ISBN: 978-1-9821-2546-2

Cover art by Kurt Miller
Map by Isaac Stewart

First printing, September 2020
First mass market printing, July 2021

Distributed by Simon & Schuster
1230 Avenue of the Americas
New York, NY 10020

Library of Congress Control Number: 2020023463

Pages by Joy Freeman (www.pagesbyjoy.com)
Printed in the United States of America
10 9 8 7 6 5 4 3 2 1

To Rabbit

Chapter 1

~~~~~~≈≈≈~~~~~~

Nineteen years ago

One was sixteen years old. The other only twelve. They were best friends, brothers, but not by blood. In a moment, they would duel. More than likely, one of them would die.

"I beg you, Devedas, do not go through with this."

"Can't you see? I've got no choice, Ashok!" the older of them shouted. "I have to try."

Bound by Law and tradition, Ashok couldn't walk away either. As the chosen bearer of mighty Angruvadal, he was obligated to accept all challengers, just in case the powerful ancestor blade might find someone more worthy to wield it.

How could Angruvadal not choose Devedas over him? Devedas was the best of them, stronger, smarter, and more dedicated than any of the other acolytes. He had climbed to the top of the Protector's brutal program. Officially, all were equal in status, but Devedas was the son of a Thakoor and had been raised expecting to someday rule a great house. He was superior to Ashok in every way but one.

Ashok had Angruvadal.

The mighty black steel blade of Great House Vadal had been kept from him the entire time he had been in training. The master would allow Ashok no magical edge over the other boys, so Angruvadal had been taken away. A normal man could not understand what it was like to be a bearer. It wasn't just his sword that had been lost, but it was as if part of himself had been locked away in that cold vault. For two long years he had suffered, incomplete.

Except now their trial was passed. They had crossed glaciers and fought ancient automatons. All the others had turned back as failures. Three had pressed on. Yugantar had given into fear and fled. He was certainly dead now, his body frozen up there forever. Only Ashok and Devedas had fought on. They had reached the highest peak and touched the Heart of the Mountain. Ashok was the youngest to ever do so in the entire history of the Order. They were no longer acolytes, but full members of the Protector Order, with all its accompanying status, privilege, and responsibilities.

It was one of the greatest achievements a Law-abiding man could ever hope for, yet the joy he had felt at attaining senior rank was nothing compared to getting his sword back. The normally dour masters had allowed their trainees to freely celebrate the advancement of two of their own, or to mourn the one they'd lost. All the acolytes, even the failures, were allowed all the meat and wine they desired. A rare treat indeed.

Except their celebration had quickly turned ugly.

It was plain that bitterness had consumed Devedas when he had seen the legendary Angruvadal riding upon its bearer's hip. He'd claimed it was unfair that Ashok should have such an honor, and not him. When the ancestor blade of Great House Dev had shattered in his father's hands, it had taken with it his inheritance and all his family's dignity. Ashok had tried to deflect, to once again say that it was not his choice to make, but the sword's. Only Devedas had grown increasingly jealous as the night went on. Though they'd trained together, fought together, undertaken the trial together, and nearly died upon the mountain together, none of that mattered in the moment, because Devedas' one weakness was his pride.

Accusations had been made. Youthful foolishness had led to anger. Ashok had tried to turn aside his brother's wrath. They were both tired. It had been a long journey down the mountain. Only Devedas had not relented. He had goaded Ashok to this point. Words had been spoken which could not be retracted.

"You are the closest friend I've ever had," Ashok told him truthfully. "Please do not make me kill you."

As the son of a bearer, Devedas understood the rules. A duel to see if a challenger was worthy to claim an ancestor blade did not need to be to the death, but it often was, because by their very nature black steel blades were very unforgiving.

"Better to try and fail than be a coward and never know."

The two stood in the middle of the practice field, dusted white with snow, surrounded by a circle of nervous Protectors, young and old, from the most recently

obligated acolyte, to twenty-year senior, Mindarin, who
had been one of their instructors.

That most experienced Protector was furious. "You
should stop this foolishness at once. The Order is too
small in number as it is. You're both valuable assets,
better spent in defense of the Law. However a duel
ends, the Order will be weaker for it."

"Do you order me to stand down?" Devedas asked.

Mindarin shook his head. "You know I cannot.
Your actions, though wasteful and stupid, are entirely
legal. The bearer cannot deny you, and the challenger
cannot be denied."

"Forgive me, honored teacher, for you know what
I must do." It obviously pained Devedas to disappoint
Mindarin, because he had been the acolytes' kindest
instructor, teaching by word and example. Which
was much preferred by all of them to Master Ratul's
methods, which consisted of beatings and hunger.

A man of reason rather than passion, Mindarin
did not give up so easily. "Listen to me, Devedas.
Your father is dead. Your house has fallen. Claiming
a new sword will not bring either back. Let them
go. Your life has been obligated to the Order. This
is your family now." He gestured at the acolytes who
were anxiously watching to see which of their friends
would die.

"You know I love them and the Order both."

"Yet you cannot be fully committed until you put
the Order first. Great House Dev is no more. You
were my best student, yet the one lesson I could never
get to stick with you is that you cannot reclaim old
glories. Sometimes the past is best forgotten."

Ashok found that to be a curious sentiment, coming

from the Protector who had been responsible for teaching them about history. The approved parts of history at least.

"I respect your wisdom, Mindarin, but I can't accept it. I was raised to be the Thakoor of a great house, with a black steel blade as my birthright."

"What's done is done, young Devedas."

Devedas met Ashok's gaze and gave him a sad smile. "I have to try."

"So be it then. I wash my hands of this. Angruvadal will decide which of you to deprive the Order of... Karno, summon the master," Mindarin snapped at one of the youngest acolytes, who immediately ran off to warn Ratul that his two newest senior ranks were about to kill each other.

The two of them squared off, ten paces between them. The circle of Protectors backed up to give them space, for even the ones who had not seen an ancestor blade in action knew of their deadly reputation. It was not unheard of for one of the angry things to remove the limb from a curious bystander.

Ashok found it very lonely inside the circle.

The crowd did not cheer for either of them. There were no favorites here. A natural leader who honestly cared for the well-being of the other acolytes, Devedas was beloved by all. Ashok had been seen as a young upstart at first, because he had arrived already gifted with one of the most powerful artifacts in the world. Except he had gone on to win their respect by being the most dedicated among them.

He tried one last time to get his brother to see reason. "The Law requires me to do my best. I will hold nothing back."

It was a grave warning, for though they had sparred against each other hundreds of times now, and Devedas—being bigger, stronger, and faster—almost always won, those victories were against Ashok alone. When you fought a bearer, you fought against the combined instinct of every man who had ever carried that sword into battle. A part of each of its prior bearers lived on in the black steel, as would a fragment of Ashok, as long as Angruvadal survived. It was one of the only forms of immortality in a world where the Law declared there was no existence beyond this life.

"Everyone knows you always do precisely what the Law says, little brother." Devedas gave him a sad smile. "It's why it's impossible to hate you."

Ashok could not feel fear like everyone else, but he could understand it well enough in principle. He could see that Devedas was afraid—as any sane man would be to face an ancestor blade—yet he was committed.

"Know that if it was my decision, I would do my best to defeat you, but I would try to spare your life. Only I do not think Angruvadal understands moderation."

Devedas simply nodded. It was good that he was willing to accept death. Ashok suspected that such acceptance was necessary in order to win Angruvadal's approval. Ashok did not want to die, but if he did, at least this way Angruvadal would have a worthy new bearer.

"Offense has been taken!" Devedas shouted so that all could hear the official challenge.

"Offense has been given." Ashok did not think it had, but tradition demanded he accept.

The duel began, not in a sudden burst of movement, but in absolute stillness.

The opponents watched each other, waiting.

Then Devedas shifted his weight, ever so slightly, boots crunching into the snow and gravel beneath. His strong hand moved slowly, until it was poised just over the hilt of his sword.

Ashok's hand hovered over Angruvadal. It had been two years since he had drawn the sword, but ancestor blades never lost their edge. Black steel did not rust. It was alive. And hungry. He could feel the hum of angry energy prickling through his palm. The sword wanted to know who needed to be killed.

Please have mercy on him, Angruvadal. I think this one will accomplish great things for the Law. Ashok tried his best to make his will known to his sword, but it remained a mystery if Angruvadal understood, or cared. *And he is my friend.*

There was some movement at the edge of the circle. As if from a great distance he heard someone say that Master Ratul had arrived, but Ashok's focus was entirely upon the duel.

It was cold. Thick blood made for slow hands.

The wind blew. A little eddy of snow swirled between them.

Devedas' finger twitched.

Soon.

Another involuntary twitch.

Forty generations of bearers were with Ashok. They knew exactly what would happen, they'd seen the gathering of strength, the tensing of muscle, and the sudden explosive movement thousands of times, and all of that instinct was there for the taking. It was as if there were ghosts in the black steel, always whispering.

Though legally his to use, such an advantage seemed

dishonorable. If his brother was willing to die in order to test his commitment, then so was Ashok.

No, Angruvadal. I will do this myself.

The whispers stopped. There was only the wind and the wait.

Ashok thought of nothing. There would be only action and reaction.

Devedas moved.

Eye-searing Angruvadal was in Ashok's hand, so fast it was like he'd willed the black steel into being.

They struck at the same time.

They had the same sword master, which was more important than them having different fathers. There were names for the stances and techniques they used, but in the instant, they simply *were.* It was the purest moment of Ashok's life.

There was a flash of black as the two opponents crossed.

Anyone else in the world, and Devedas surely would have been the victor. Except Angruvadal would not be choosing a new bearer tonight.

Ashok swept past Devedas, sword still rising past the cut. He saw the look on his other brothers' faces, awestruck, for they'd never seen any living thing move that fast. Protector Mindarin gaped in surprise, but Master Ratul just watched him, bemused, something calculating and cruel in his dark eyes.

As Devedas fell, the normal world came rushing back.

His opponent was down.

Ashok realized the others wanted to rush and help their fallen, but they didn't dare step into the circle as long as fearsome Angruvadal was free. Offense had been claimed. Ashok was within his legal rights to finish his challenger. But the Law was wise. *Allowed* was not *mandatory*. He looked at Angruvadal. It was somehow clean of blood, as if Angruvadal was too proud to be stained. He thanked his sword, then sheathed it, declaring the conflict over.

Ratul nodded, and that was all the instruction the acolytes needed to run over to the injured Devedas. Ashok followed them.

There was blood all over the snow. Devedas' handsome face had been sliced wide open from his chin to his right eye. Luckily the eye was still in one piece. Though the pain had to be terrible, and black steel wounds were said to burn like the sun, Devedas did not scream. Instead he ground his teeth together—Ashok could tell because they were visible through the hole in his cheek—and the only sound that escaped was the pained growl of a wounded animal. Yet Ashok could see the terrible agony in his brother's eyes. Not of the lacerated flesh alone, no . . . for though Angruvadal had spared his life it had killed his dreams.

Ashok had no dreams, only duty. Now he supposed, they were the same.

It was a good thing they had just completed their trial and touched the Heart of the Mountain, for its healing magic would save Devedas. Otherwise a wound like that would probably become infected and be the death of a normal man. The magic they had in their blood now would help him heal. Ashok was thankful for that.

"Lucky for you Angruvadal was in a kind mood and didn't remove your fool head from your stiff neck," Lord Protector Ratul said as he walked over to assess the terrible injury. He looked down at all the blood and sighed. "I swear your ambition is going to be the death of me someday, Devedas. I hope you learned a valuable lesson today."

Eyes wide and filled with agony, Devedas managed to nod his head *yes*.

"Good... Carry him to the surgeon."

But Devedas surprised even the master as he shoved the helping hands away and struggled up under his own power. Even though there was a dangling gap through the side of his face, he managed to say something that sounded like, "I'll make it myself."

"Indeed," Ratul muttered, so low that only nearby Ashok could hear. "So that's the lesson you choose to learn."

Ashok had never felt more alive, and he owed that to Devedas.

"I am honored to call you my brother." And according to the traditions of Great House Vadal, Ashok gave the deepest, most respectful bow possible, exposing the back of his neck as a sign of trust, and held it a long time as a show of admiration.

When he raised his eyes, Devedas was staggering away, leaving behind a trail of red footprints in the snow.

Chapter 2

~~~~~~~~~~

Ninety days had passed since the Capitol had ordered the warrior caste to study the feasibility of killing every untouchable in the world. This time they were not speaking of mere population control, nor the traditional method of warning and punishment, but rather the complete eradication of the casteless bloodline, every last non-person in Lok, young and old, male and female, starved, burned, thrown in the sea, or put to the sword. A morbid totality.

The warriors' report had been delivered to the Chamber of Argument that very morning. The representative of their caste had just finished testifying before the assembled judges that this task would not be nearly as difficult as some had claimed, and that it could be completed within a year, with the majority dead within one season.

The judges were assured the Great Extermination would be a simple affair.

Grand Inquisitor Omand Vokkan knew there would

be nothing simple about it. Most likely, wars would rage, millions would die, and houses would fall. However, this was the Capitol, where truth was not as important as leverage, and reality became a malleable narrative. It had actually been impressive how his handpicked warrior had been able to deliver the absurdly optimistic report with a straight face. In reality, the Great Extermination would be a violent, bloody mess that would drag on for years and crack the very foundations of the Law.

Excellent.

Through blackmail, intimidation, and bribery, Omand had made certain that the report said exactly what he wanted it to say. He'd cowed the warriors' representatives as easily as the Archivists and Historians orders before them. All the information given to the decision makers had thus far been perfectly tooled to tell the story Omand wanted told. The judges were too soft, too removed, too *aloof* to realize just how ignorant they really were about the true nature of the world. To them, the casteless were some nebulous numbers on a ledger, not beings of flesh and blood who would fight to preserve their lives, no matter how pathetic those lives may be.

From behind his golden mask, Omand watched the judges carefully as the session resumed. Even as skilled at debate as these men were, they couldn't hide their emotions. Many realized they were now seriously discussing the systematic slaughtering of the dregs of their society. Some of the judges were soft enough to think of the casteless as *people*. Not that they would dare say something so outlandish, but their revulsion was plain. Many others understood perfectly well what was being proposed, and the idea of being free of the flea-ridden garbage who haunted the worst slums of their homelands was an appealing one. Some were oblivious, for to them the casteless were little more than dangerous, dirty livestock. A few were afraid of the economic ramifications, because the poorer houses needed their labor to survive, not that they would say so here, because to do so would be a shameful embarrassment.

A handful of the judges though ... Whether they gave a damn about casteless lives or not, from their clenched jaws, and narrowed eyes, they knew exactly what was afoot, and they would not be played. They were his competition in the great game.

Omand noted each of his final obstacles. The problematic judges would be dealt with individually. He could bend some to his will, break those who would not bend, and remove those who would not break. It wouldn't take long for him to have the majority. He would win eventually, because to these men this was just another heated political issue of many, but for Omand it was the culmination of his life's work.

There was nothing he would not do, including consort with demons, or destroy the Law itself, to get what he wanted. A handful of the judges may have been adamantly opposed to genocide for whatever reason, but most didn't understand the rules or the stakes of this game, and none of them knew who their real opponent was.

As a mere servant of the Law, Omand had no vote here. Officially, the Order of Inquisition offered no opinion in the creation of Law, they simply did the unsavory work necessary to maintain it once passed. The Grand Inquisitor may have been a terrifying specter, but he was a quiet one. Omand merely observed. He rarely spoke during these events, and then only when called upon by his supposed betters.

That didn't mean that he did not have allies to speak for him.

Senior Arbiter Artya Zati dar Zarger took her place at the podium. "I would like to thank our honorable warriors, for the tremendous effort you took to conduct such a thorough investigation. I have no doubt that once our wise judges make the right decision concerning this issue, your brave caste will have very little difficulty eradicating these vermin."

The few representatives of the warrior caste allowed into the illustrious chamber sat there, stone faced, revealing nothing. Except for Omand's puppet warrior, who accepted the praise with a smile. The poor fool actually thought he would benefit from his lies once this was all over. Omand figured once everything went to pieces, the judges would need someone to blame. Better some nobody warrior than the important man pulling his strings.

Artya was a woman of notable attractiveness and rapidly increasing status. Charming, elegant, and a supremely gifted orator, the young lady had become the public face of those in favor of the Great Extermination. The play that she had produced about Ashok Vadal's violent crimes against the first caste had done much to sway opinion in the Capitol. Omand had secretly paid for the entire production, but the people did not need to know that.

As Artya launched into another impassioned speech about the casteless menace, no one interrupted her. Normally the Chamber of Argument lived up to its name. The judges were normally a verbally combative lot, but in the current climate, no one wanted to be seen as soft on the issue. The many massacres that had been recently committed by untouchables—or by Omand's agents in their name—had robbed the non-people of their regular defenders. Normally some fool would give some teary-eyed speech about the value of mercy, but even those pathetic wretches kept their mouths shut today.

At the end of Artya's speech would be presented a proposal. It would seem an innocuous enough request to the judges. Little would they realize that it would begin a chain of events which would lead to the bloodiest conflagration since the revolution that had ended the Age of Kings and brought about the Age of Law.

He already knew how this vote would turn out. The only judge he'd been worried would be shrewd enough to figure out the ramifications of Artya's proposal wasn't present. Omand had arranged a crisis which had required Harta Vadal's personal attention, so he was currently journeying north. The Vadal representative left in his place was not nearly as astute as Harta. Even though Great House Vadal had been weakened by the loss of their ancestor blade and shamed by the revelation that their greatest hero had been a casteless fraud, they remained wealthy enough to sway many votes.

The Chamber of Argument was a stunning place, improved upon over hundreds of years by the finest artisans the great houses could provide. It was odd that something so appealing to the eye could be so dead of heart. It was a vast space, filled with seats, and in each sat someone of great status and importance, blissfully unaware that they were about to vote to cause a crisis which would leave a great many of them ruined or dead. Omand found the whole thing fascinating.

"I know that many reasonable concerns have been raised. This is understandable. Though the casteless have troubled us for centuries, the Archivists have confirmed that there is no legal reason we must continue to endure their awfulness. The warriors have just told us that removing them is doable. Other reports have been commissioned to look at the economic ramifications to each house, which is exceedingly wise and prudent . . ." And that was when Artya asked for her *one small thing.* "But in the meantime, I would like to propose a practical exercise . . . a feasibility study, if you will."

"What do you mean, Arbiter?" the Chief Judge asked.

"During the time we have debated this topic, rebellion has spread over much of Great House Akershan and spilled into several other houses. While we have talked, towns have been put to the torch. Industries have been ruined. These rebels have specifically targeted our caste, killing men, women, and children of the First."

"Enough. We all know of these crimes. Specify your proposal."

"I propose that in one small part of the region afflicted by rebellion, the casteless populations be eliminated entirely. Let us pick some provinces that we have been unable to pacify. Turn loose the full might of the warrior caste in just those few, not just upon the lawbreakers, but upon those who harbor and hide them. Destroy all the casteless quarters and kill these exceedingly disobedient wretches, as they would do to us if given the chance. I propose that the Inquisition be tasked to observe this righteous correction, so that the rest of the houses can learn from the experience, and our judges will be able to make a more enlightened decision about what to do with the rest."

Another judge—who was also a secret member of Omand's dark councils—stood. "I am Faril Akershan. I second her proposal. My house will gladly volunteer the Upper Akara, the Dharvan Bench, and the North Chakma Plains for this test."

Faril had not been told why of his house's many holdings Omand had requested those in particular, but since each of them was currently unprofitable he had given them up without complaint. Omand did not choose randomly. The first two were hotbeds of rebellion, where the non-people were certain to react violently. The last province was the most important, for Chakma was not too far from the last place Ashok Vadal had been seen. If the Black Heart had survived the destruction of the Lost House, then surely a slaughter of this magnitude would draw him from his hiding place. Ideally, he'd have the real Ashok striking terror into the heart of the Capitol again, but if not, he'd simply hire one of the surviving members of the House of Assassins—now impoverished and desperate—to act Ashok's part. But vengeful Ashok would be so much better than any imposter.

The Chief Judge banged his staff on the floor. "The motion has been seconded."

The judges exchanged glances. It seemed simple enough. It was three unimportant provinces, in one of the poorest great houses, on the far side of the continent, a long way from here. Omand knew how this would go because in their own way the highest-status judges were as predictable as the no-status casteless. They could leave feeling like they'd accomplished something, while postponing facing the real problem, and it required absolutely no effort or discomfort on their part.

Of course, the proposal passed. No one bothered to argue against it. With the death sentence handed down, the chamber was dismissed for lunch.

He had been so confident the vote would proceed as expected, that Omand had already arranged for these new orders to be relayed immediately by magic. Such instantaneous communications used up whole pieces of valuable demon bone, but it was worth the expense to satisfy his excitement. This way the Akershani warriors could mobilize immediately.

In a way, this triumph was bittersweet. History had just been made, but he was the only one who realized it.

The Great Extermination had begun.

Chapter 3

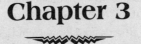

Lord Protector Devedas had crossed the frozen mountains to find the plains on fire.

It had been a long journey from the central desert, and they'd been caught in a brutal winter storm along the way. The cold had killed their horses, but it had only inconvenienced their riders. It took more than weather to stop a Protector.

His men had been miserable, but too proud to ever let it show. The other Protectors had been unlucky enough to be born northerners, where the sun always shined and the air didn't cut your face, so the journey had been harder on them than it had been for Devedas. Though they'd come from the soft lands of green grass and silk, each of them had still survived the Order's brutal program, training in the Hall of Protectors, high in the unforgiving mountains of Dev, so they had simply gritted their teeth, called upon the Heart to keep their extremities from becoming frostbitten, and marched on.

His companions had only trained in Dev. He had been born there. It had made him. His home had been slick rocks covered in treacherous snow, and ice crevasses where one misplaced boot meant they'd never find your body, where giant predatory bears—so white they might as well be invisible—lurked in wait. He'd lived beneath a volcano that routinely belched fire and molten rock, and drank sulfurous water that had gushed out of the ground steaming hot. On the southern coast, it occasionally got cold enough to freeze the air in your lungs, turning it sharp as daggers, so you'd cough up blood or drown in it.

This crossing had been pleasant in comparison.

The snowstorm had slowed them, but his small band of Protectors had pushed through the Thao passes, and then marched south into Akershan lands. Somewhere in the vast area of this great house was hidden the headquarters of the casteless rebellion, and Devedas suspected that was where they would catch their former brother, Ashok Vadal.

Ashok's fall had brought dishonor to them all, and he had murdered one of their own in Neeramphorn several months ago. No one in the Order would rest until Ashok had been put down like the rabid dog he'd become.

After the traitor was slain and his shame erased from the world, then Devedas intended to return to the Capitol, to be hailed as the hero who had stopped the most infamous criminal in generations. It was illegal for a member of the Order to seek personal glory, but the rest of the Protectors didn't know what Devedas knew. There was a conspiracy among the powerful men of the Capitol to overthrow the judges—a terrible crime—yet he had agreed to look the other way. The judges *deserved* to be cast down. A mighty change was upon them, and before it was through, Devedas intended to be crowned king.

All he had to do was find and kill his best friend first.

His Protectors had claimed new horses, tack, and supplies in the first settlement they'd come across. It was a poor place, and what they took would cause great hardship to the worker caste there, but none dared argue with the demands of four servants of the Law. Riding was better than walking, and his men had breathed sighs of relief, as it was all downhill from there.

They had been riding along the banks of the Akara River for two days when they saw the plume of smoke.

Akershan was notorious for having wildfires that could stretch for miles but there was still snow on the ground, so it was unlikely that this was natural. Plus, in the two decades he'd served the Law, Devedas had put many buildings to the torch, and the smoke always had a certain color when it was someone's home that was burning. From the amount, several structures were on fire, perhaps even a whole village.

"Let us investigate," Devedas told his men.

"Hopefully it's the rebels attacking again." Abhishek Gujara was obviously excited at the prospect of a fight. They'd endured weeks of hard travel, hunger, and discomfort, so a good battle against lawbreakers would certainly cheer them all up. Protectors could be a grim bunch, but they never lacked for enthusiasm when it came to applying their trade.

"If we're lucky they'll be led by the Black Heart

himself," Jamari Vadal stated flatly. "And we can get this over with."

They pushed their horses hard, but these were herding mounts, not used to carrying men in armor. It took them a while to get close enough to ascertain the cause of the smoke.

It was a settlement of maybe three hundred people in total. Only a handful of homes belonging to the higher-status members of the worker caste were made of wood, the rest were the tent homes common to these lands, round to survive the constant winds, with walls made of hide or gray felt. Most of those were untouched. However, across a small stream was a separate, smaller living area, crowded and muddy, and currently entirely aflame.

Devedas slowed his horse to a walk so he could better assess the situation. The others followed his example. He used the Heart to sharpen his vision, until distant things became clear. There was at least a full paltan of fifty warriors there. The banner they were flying consisted of vertical green stripes on a tan flag. The symbol of Great House Akershan was supposed to represent the grass on the plains, or some such nonsense. Devedas had always struggled to pay attention during Master Mindarin's lessons on heraldry.

"They're burning that casteless quarter," Abhishek muttered. "I wonder why?"

"It's their house's property to do with as they wish, so it's none of our concern, but if it's because they've been caught aiding the rebels I want one alive to interrogate." Devedas thumped his horse with his heels and forced it into an awkward gallop.

Surprisingly, these casteless were fighting back,

and from the looks of it, had achieved a tiny—albeit temporary—bit of success. The warriors must have been surprised to meet actual resistance, but they were warriors, and casteless were casteless, so it appeared to have quickly turned into a massacre. There were a couple obviously dead warriors lying in the mud, but for every dead warrior, there were ten dead casteless. Their rough weapons—mostly repurposed farm tools—were still in their hands, but there were a few splintered spears and stolen swords among them, and it was illegal for the non-people to possess arms.

So it was the rebellion then. *Serves them right.*

There were still pockets of resistance between the burning tents, but the warriors appeared to have the matter well in hand.

"Who is in command here?" Devedas shouted.

The warriors had been so focused on their mission, that they'd not heard the Protectors approach. Several of them immediately pointed toward where their flag had been planted into a pile of straw. The risaldar in charge of the butchery seemed shocked to see silver armored Protectors riding up to him. One of the mightiest enforcers of the Law was a rare sight, four was unheard of.

"I am." And then the officer saw that Devedas wasn't just wearing the fanged visage of the Law on his chest, but also the special insignia that marked him as the head of that entire fearsome Order. The color drained from his face as he meekly asked, "How may I serve, Lord Protector?"

Since Devedas held the power to declare almost anyone in the world a violator of the Law, and then immediately carry out their sentence, he was used to such reactions. It was good this risaldar knew his place.

"What's going on here?"

"Orders direct from the Capitol to our Thakoor earlier this week. We're to put all the casteless here to the sword."

From the looks of things, they were being rather thorough about it. Non-people were being struck down left and right. Spears were thrust into fallen bodies to make sure they weren't just faking. A few non-people were crying and begging for mercy, swearing that they weren't aiding the rebels, but not too far away could still be heard the sounds of battle, proving them liars. If they weren't rebels, they were at least collaborators.

"Odd. Why would the Capitol even know of or care about this one village?"

"My apologies, Lord Protector. I didn't speak clear enough. It's not just these here, but *all* of them. Every quarter across the north, from the Akara to the eastern Nansakar is to be burned. We're to spare none of them."

As Devedas watched, a casteless child ran from one of the burning tents, but a warrior caught her by the hair, and hurled her screaming back into the fire.

"Every single untouchable... Not just those who are rebelling?"

"This is the third quarter we've struck in two days. The first two didn't even know what was happening until it was over." The risaldar seemed haunted as he said that. This certainly wasn't the glorious battle that young warriors dreamed of, that was for sure. "I know they're not really people and the Law has spoken but..." Then he realized he was on the verge of saying something that could be construed as subversive and stopped. "The Capitol's request will be carried out expediently, I assure you."

"That's a vast area. There has to be a multitude of casteless there."

"Tens of thousands, Lord Protector. Here..." The officer reached into his uniform and pulled out a folded letter. "So you know I speak the truth."

Saddle creaking, Devedas leaned over to take the orders. At some point the risaldar had left bloody fingerprints on the paper, now dried. He read carefully. The order was legitimate, lawful, and stamped by a senior arbiter. His horse began to shake nervously beneath him, nostrils flaring as the thick smell of burning flesh and hair reached them.

"It'll get more difficult as we go. Word has already spread that we're coming, so they'll go into hiding, or be like these fools and actively try to stand and fight. I don't know if the Capitol understands there are a lot more non-people in this province than there are warriors."

The Order of Census and Taxation surely knew the exact population down to the last casteless and goat, which meant the judges knew and simply did not care. Trying to kill all the casteless was madness. Previously, he'd made the mistake of voicing his disgust in the Chamber of Argument, as the clueless weaklings and sheltered fops had debated such a bloody scheme. If Omand wanted a crisis sufficient to shake the Capitol, he was about to get one.

"You have the Law on your side," Devedas said as he handed the letter back. "I'm sure your Thakoor will give you whatever support you need."

Devedas turned back to look at his men. The youngest among them was Abhishek, but even he was a five-year senior. None of them were strangers to this kind of grisly business. They might not be as unfeeling about carrying out their darker duties as Black-Hearted Ashok had been, but the Law required Protectors who would do what was necessary and not flinch. If any of them objected to what was happening here, they were careful not to show it.

Suddenly there was a loud noise, like a crack of thunder. It made Devedas' poorly trained horse rear back, frightened. As he got the beast back under control he demanded, "What was that?"

"I don't know," the risaldar said. "Excuse me, I must see to my men."

The sound had come from inside the flaming casteless quarter. Two warriors came running out, dragging a third between them. That one was dangling limp, with a small wound on his back, and drizzling blood from a gaping hole in his chest. Whatever had struck him had punched a hole through his armor, front and back, and clean through his torso. They were carrying him to aid, but as the Protectors watched them go by, it was obvious that nothing would be able to save him.

"Curious," said Abhishek, right before his head exploded.

Blood hit Devedas in the eyes as the sound of thunder washed over them. Abhishek toppled from the saddle as his horse bolted.

Devedas' horse nearly threw him as well, but moving faster than any normal man could, he was able to dismount and jump aside to land smoothly.

Perplexed, Devedas wiped the blood from his face with one hand. Abhishek was lying in the mud. The top of the young Protector's skull was split open as if it had been hit with a war hammer. Bone and brain were visible to the light of day and spread upon the ground. His eyes were open and staring. Even with the Heart of the Mountain to sustain their lives through terrible injuries, that blow had been so sudden, so devastating, that death had been instantaneous.

"What manner of witchcraft is this?" shouted Jamari as he ran to Abhishek's side.

"Fortress magic," Devedas snarled as he drew his sword. "Find the wizard!"

He ran in the direction the thunder had come from, leapt high over a burning tent, and landed on the other side in a clank of steel and rattle of chain. He moved through the swirling smoke, searching. Bits of burning felt were drifting into the sky. Then he saw a figure holding a strange device, still shrouded in a gray haze. Since warriors were running from him, that had to be the wizard. Furious, Devedas shoved the terrified soldiers out of his way.

But the wizard's deadly magic had caused the casteless to rally. One of them charged him with a pitchfork. Devedas kicked the tines aside, slashed the thigh to the bone, and kept moving. Another threw a hatchet at him. Devedas caught it and hurled it right back, striking the casteless in the throat. He collapsed with a gurgle.

The wizard was wrestling with his strange device. It was about a foot and a half long and appeared to be made of metal and wood. He saw Devedas coming for him, and the look upon his soot-stained face was one of pure terror.

Devedas darted between the terrified casteless, rapidly closing the distance. The wizard pointed his device, but Devedas called upon the Heart to give him all the speed it could. A terrible roar and shower of orange sparks erupted from the wizard's device and he felt something hot move past his cheek. Immediately behind him a casteless woman was knocked off her feet.

The magic must generate a great deal of force, because the device was lifted high, nearly torn from the wizard's grasp, but he managed to bring it back down. It had produced even more of the odd white smoke. The lawbreaker reached for something tied to his waist—the horn of a bull—but whatever evil magic he intended to work with it, he never had the chance.

Devedas' sword was forward curving in the southern style, made for removing limbs. He stepped through the haze and struck. The device went bouncing across the dirt, along with the wizard's hand. Devedas kicked the wizard in the chest, launching him back ten feet. He landed on his back and slid away.

As he moved forward to finish the job, Devedas saw that this was no powerful wizard. He was filthy, terribly thin, and dressed in rags like the rest of the non-people. The kick had broken multiple ribs so he let out an agonized wail. The wail became even more pathetic when he realized his hand was missing, and began thrashing around, trying in vain to stop the gushing of his stump.

The other two Protectors caught up a breath later. Behind them was a pile of dying rebels who'd been foolish enough to get in their way.

"Secure the prisoner. Tie off his arm so he doesn't bleed out. I want this one alive."

Furious, Devedas walked to the device and picked it up. He had to shake it until the severed hand fell off. It was a curious thing, steel, with bits of moving brass on it, far heavier than it looked, and the metal part he was holding was hot to the touch. It didn't seem so dangerous up close, but then he looked back toward the casteless woman who'd been struck by it instead of him. It had blown a hole clear through her guts. It was a ghastly and fatal injury. She may have only been a non-person, but Jamari bent down and quickly cut her throat anyway, mercifully ending her screaming.

They walked out of the burning quarter, Devedas with the killing device, and his men carrying their would-be wizard. Around them, the slaughter resumed. Now that the warriors knew there had been deadly Fortress magic hidden here, their savagery increased. Not that there had been much mercy given before, but it was an impossibility now. Warriors who trained their whole lives were especially offended by magic which could make pathetic non-people their equals in combat.

"Torture what you can out of him. I want to know where the rebels hide, and I want to know where he got this thing. I'll be along shortly."

Devedas stopped and knelt by Abhishek's body. He had been a good man, reliable, and a loyal servant to the Law. They'd just spent months cold and hungry together, and it was easy to become fond of someone who suffered beside you. Now he'd have to strip him of his valuable armor and arrange for the locals to deal with his corpse.

They had an incredibly dangerous job, and it was rare for one of them to live long enough to complete their entire obligation and return to their house, yet every single death under his command seemed a great personal offense. First Ishaan, and now Abhishek. There would surely be many more to come. That thought pained him. For though Devedas was an ambitious man, he was not a disloyal one.

"Forgive me, Abhishek. I didn't expect this. You deserved a better death."

Talking to the dead was absurd. The Law declared there was nothing beyond this. Their lives were a temporary spark clad in flesh and bone, and when it was gone, that was all. Devedas reached down and closed the dead Protector's eyes anyway.

As he walked away from the massacre, Devedas held the strange device up to the sun to study it. From the soot around the metal parts, it was obvious which was the dangerous end. It even had a strange and distinct smell, a mix of sulfur, charcoal, and urine. A Protector had senses which allowed them to see arrows coming and the reflexes to dodge out of the way. Even as fearsome a combatant as Abhishek was, he'd never even had a chance against this thing. If the casteless in this province had many more of these hidden, things could turn very ugly, very quickly.

"Pardon me, Lord Protector Devedas? Is that you?"

He turned to see the snarling face of the Law, and growled at the Inquisitor's mask, "What do you want?" The last thing he wanted to deal with right now was the Inquisition.

"I was just informed of your arrival," the Inquisitor said. "I've been ordered to observe this paltan as they participate in the test, in order to write a report about the results for the Capitol."

He didn't know this Inquisitor from any of the others, but he felt like he understood everyone in his rival order well enough. They were malicious, sneaky, liars without honor, the lot of them. The Inquisitor had even worn his fine metal mask, usually reserved for holidays and important events, instead of the more practical and comfortable cloth kind they were issued. He supposed in a way, today probably was a holiday for them.

"You can tell your master, Omand, that once the casteless who escape across the river into Dev or across the mountains into Thao tell the rest about this bloodbath, word will spread until every non-person in the world decides they have nothing left to lose. When they panic and rise up against their overseers, he's sure to get that crisis he wants."

The Inquisitor gave him a small bow. *Another northerner then.* "I don't know what you speak of, but I will be sure to record your opinions on the matter and pass them on." Then he nodded toward the device in Devedas' hands. "If I may see that, please."

"It killed one of my men."

"My apologies, Lord Protector, but the Law is clear in such things. Seized illegal magic, especially items believed to have originated from the island of Fortress, are to be turned over to the Inquisition as soon as possible." He held out one hand expectantly. "I will have it rushed back to the dome for study immediately."

Devedas mulled over just killing the annoying man where he stood. That would be one way to end his report to the judges . . . But he was correct. The Law was clear. And more importantly, Devedas had made an arrangement with the Grand Inquisitor that greatly benefited them both. It would be unwise to jeopardize it over something so petty.

"Take it." He smacked the mysterious weapon hard against the Inquisitor's open palm. "And hope these rebels don't have too many more of these."

"That is doubtful, Lord Protector. Fortress seems to like annoying us by letting some of their craft out into the Law-abiding world, but they are too insular, too isolated, and the rebellion too poor to actively trade." He took the device by the wooden handle. His eyes could be seen through the holes in his mask, and he seemed impressed by the thing. "We've found these before, but never one so compact. This would be easy for a rebel to conceal... Now, may I ask what brings you all the way out here?"

"It is none of your concern. I have other Protectors already on assignment in this region. Do you know their current location?"

"I do not. I can send for—"

"That will not be necessary." Devedas began walking away.

"May I inquire if you are here searching for Ashok Vadal?"

Devedas didn't bother to answer. He knew his former brother better than anyone else alive. From what he'd seen today, if Ashok had truly joined with the rebellion, he wouldn't allow this carnage to continue unopposed. Anything Ashok considered a crime he would be compelled to stop. The object of his devotion might have changed, but Ashok never would.

The Inquisitor called after him. "Ashok Vadal hasn't been seen for months. He could be hundreds of miles away."

It wouldn't matter if it was a thousand, Devedas knew that Ashok would be drawn here soon enough.

Chapter 4

The wild men of the swamp marked the end of the year with a vast bonfire.

As spring had drawn near, every member of the tribe had constructed for themselves a little doll out of hide, sticks, and vines. Each doll was given a name, like *returned from the hunt without a kill,* or *fell asleep on watch*, or *failed to tend the crop.* Then on the night they called Dahan the entire village took turns tossing their dolls into the great fire. Together, they watched their guilt and failings blacken and twist into ash.

The many other lands that Ashok Vadal had visited had all celebrated the arrival of spring with festivals of color, singing and dancing, feasting and drinking, but this outcast tribe kept their own odd tradition, which they claimed was based on a ceremony that predated the Age of Law.

Religious rites were forbidden. Such a brazen display of Law breaking would have angered him a year ago, but since this isolated people had scraped out an existence in the unforgiving swamps of Bahdjangal, where demons prowled the fog, only a few miles from the shores of hell, the bonfire seemed appropriate.

It made a certain sense that a grim people would hold a grim celebration.

"Where's your doll, Ashok?" Thera asked, as the two of them watched the spectacle from a polite distance away. "If anyone has some sins to get rid of, surely it's you."

There weren't sticks and vines sufficient in the world to build a doll big enough to absorb all his transgressions, nor a fire hot enough to burn them away. He would have to build an army of sin takers, and give them names like *casteless who unwittingly claimed honors beyond his station* and *murderer of honorable men*. Yet Ashok would never give up those burdens. He'd own them until death, because forgiveness was a myth. However, the two of them had many conversations while wintering here, so he knew Thera meant no offense. Blunt and abrasive speech was simply her nature.

"I have no use for foolish superstition. Where is yours, Thera?"

"I'm a criminal. What would I know about guilt? It's you Law-abiding types who are constantly plagued with it, not me."

"Guilt is the natural result of violating the Law. It is a warning that we have strayed from our place."

"You keep telling yourself that, Ashok. Most of the Law is just smug proclamations from men who think they're better than everyone else. You often still sound as much the religious fanatic as Keta, only your god is made of paper."

"And yours is made of glowing noise."

She snorted. "Fair." Though one of the old forgotten gods had chosen her to be his prophet, Thera wasn't particularly devout. In fact, she didn't care for her god at all. It was an odd combination. "Regardless, these folks seem to take some comfort and strength from the spectacle."

The tribe of swamp dwellers had pledged themselves to Thera and joined her rebellion. "They will need to be strong. Yet they've managed to survive in this inhospitable place, trapped between wizards and demons for a very long time. However illegal their customs, I cannot deny their effectiveness."

"Maybe I should've made a doll..." A deep melancholy grew in Thera's voice, and he suspected she'd have named hers *led many fools to their demise.* "But I don't think I could've stitched together one with these hands."

Ashok glanced over. She had her arms crossed and her hands tucked inside her coat. Most people would have taken her stance to mean that she was simply chilled and trying to keep her extremities warm. A reasonable assumption, given that even at the edge of spring this place was still wretchedly damp, and they were too far away to receive any warmth from the bonfire, but Ashok knew that stance had become a habit for Thera so she could hide her damaged hands from view.

He struggled with the concept of kindness, but never with honesty. "Severe burns take a long time to heal, and then rarely heal completely. You've recovered far better than I expected when I first saw your injuries. Wielding the Forgotten's magic charred your palms so badly you are fortunate your fingers still work at all."

"Yeah, lucky me."

They went back to watching the ceremony in silence. The villagers had painted their faces, but unlike the bright and colorful festivals in the rest of Lok, the only pigments available here were black, white, and the grays in between. Their clothing was dark furs and tattered weavings, better to blend in with the hanging moss of their decaying swamp. They played simple instruments, drums and flutes, as the tribe's headman, Toramana, called each of his people forward to burn what troubled them. Ashok noticed that while most of his troops were watching from the sides as he was, a few of the Sons of the Black Sword had joined in with the villagers and made their own sin dolls.

The Somsak especially seemed to have an affinity to the Wild Men. One group was from the mountains and the other the swamp, but both were barbaric in their nature. In this place, the Somsak had found a kinship. Perhaps long ago their houses had been distant cousins? On the other hand, the Sons of the Black Sword who hailed from the great houses of Thao, Kharsawan, and Akershan seemed to be uncomfortable with the whole thing. They came from lands where an open show of faith in illegal gods would bring a swift death sentence from the Inquisitors or Ashok's old Order. So they were used to practicing their beliefs in secret, not with giant pillars of fire. Their prayers were whispers, not beaten on drums.

"You know, I think Toramana is telling the truth and this ceremony really did come from the Forgotten back in the old days," Thera muttered.

Ashok looked toward her again, but her face was lost in the shadows beneath her hood. "Why do you say that?"

"It's his style. I was a vessel for his failures, and then he threw me in a fire to burn up..." She pulled her hands from her coat, slowly unclenched her fists, and stared at her scarred palms. "I'm merely the doll."

He had no response for that.

Once the last of the hideous dolls had been consumed, Toramana raised his voice and addressed the village. Of great stature, and physically powerful, he was used to giving commands. The headman spoke from the chest loud enough so that even their guests standing at the periphery could hear him clearly.

"Into this fire we have fed all the evil things which have collected in our hearts. This is a new beginning. Let the smoke rise to the gods above, to their mansion on Upagraha, as our spirits shall rise when our bodies return to the mud, so that they can see we are good. On this holy Dahan we are especially blessed for the gods have gone to war!"

The Wild Men gave their victory shout. It was like the barking of the wild dog packs which prowled their swamp.

Toramana waited until the sound died down. When there was only the crackling of flames, the headman began again, "The Mother of Dawn told us the servants of the old gods would come to us and kill the great evil within the graveyard of demons. They drove the wizards from our land and destroyed the assassins' house. Tonight the People of the Woods are one with the Sons of the Black Sword. Tomorrow we will travel to the secret kingdom spoken of by the Prophet Thera, a paradise, where water is pure and food plentiful, where there are no castes, where the people rule themselves, and are not slaves to the Capitol!"

Ashok stiffened at the cheering that brought about. Though he'd become an enemy to the Law, his conditioning still made him ache to see such division. These people were descended from the refugees of a house the Capitol had scrubbed from existence. For that, they still held an animosity that burned hotter than their bonfire. They'd been joined over the years by captives who'd escaped from the House of Assassins. Those captives had come from all across Lok, but they'd been stolen from their homes as children, so they retained no real memory of the Law. To this tribe, the Law was distant and abstract, but every bit as despised as the wizards who had tormented them.

Thera must have mistaken what Ashok's reaction was about, because she whispered, "Paradise is an exaggeration, but the rebellion's hideout in Akershan is much nicer than this demon-infested mud pit."

But the blighted status of their home was exactly why these people's hatred of the Law still burned hot. Over the last few months he'd explored the flooded forest and seen the partially sunken ruins for himself. House Charsadda had once been a marvel. The Wild Men knew that their ancestors had lived in splendor, but because they had been condemned for the transgressions of men who'd been dead for a century, the Law still forced them to hide in squalor.

"Blessed are the People of the Woods, for we are the ones who gave shelter to the Forgotten's prophet! We are the ones who dug the Forgotten's warrior from the rubble that would have been his tomb. We are the ones who fed the Forgotten's servants while they were ill. And now we are blessed to join them in this great war! This *holy* war!"

Ashok whispered to Thera, "Once we march these people to your hideout, you, Keta, and the voice in your head should forget all this talk of war."

"I'd be happy for them to just farm in peace for the rest of their lives, but that's up to the Capitol now isn't it?"

Sadly, Ashok knew she was right.

"Powerful is the god who made the trees and the rocks! Powerful is the god who gave us the rivers and the cows. Tomorrow is a new year, and a new beginning for our people!" Even though they were standing in the shadows, Toramana somehow knew where they were, and he looked right at Thera. The headman made a great display of going to his knees and slapping both his hands against his chest. "Oh, Prophet of the Forgotten, accept these humble servants. We've prepared ourselves since the Mother of Dawn gave us the prophecy. With arrow and spear we will serve you. Our lives belong to the Forgotten."

Thera sighed. They'd already negotiated this all out in advance when Toramana had started pestering her about his tribe joining the Sons of the Black Sword a month ago. There had been logistics to work out. You can't just pack up an entire village, cross the mighty Nansakar, and then walk across the Akershan plains on a whim. All the real decisions had already been made. This part was a show for Toramana's people.

"I accept these brave servants," Thera declared, acting far more formal than was her regular rough manner. "I humbly thank you for taking us in this winter. We've eaten your food, shared your fire, and you've given us a place to heal from our wounds. This kindness will always be remembered. Together we will bring freedom to all the people of Lok."

Ashok found her diplomatic reply ironic. *Now which of us sounds like Keta?*

"The prophet has spoken! We shall journey to paradise where the Keeper of Names shall add all of us to the great book!"

The tribe barked and howled and pounded away on their drums. This wasn't just another new year, tomorrow was a new adventure. A great journey into the unknown. Ashok suspected that once the full might of the Capitol was turned against their little rebellion, these people would wish that they'd stayed hidden in their swamp.

All of this carrying on, and it wasn't even really the New Year yet. In the rest of Lok, that was still a week away. Only the Wild Men didn't follow the standardized calendar mandated by the Capitol. They declared it spring based upon when certain types of local flowers bloomed. Way out here it was almost like the Law had never existed at all.

They watched the party for a time. The Sons who hadn't participated in the ceremony had no qualms about drinking the village's alcohol or dancing with their women. Hopefully no jealous swamp man would start a knife fight with a Son for fancying the wrong one. So far that had not been an issue, because life was so dangerous for their hunters there were more females than males in the village.

"We've got a long journey ahead of us tomorrow." Thera sounded weary, but becoming responsible for the safety of a large number of people had that effect. Or at least it did on any leader with a conscience. "I'm going to sleep."

She began walking away, but then she paused and looked back toward him as if she wanted to say something else. Thera was just a shadow in front of the fire, but somehow Ashok could tell what was going through her head. A terrible burden had been placed upon her, she was afraid, and worse, alone.

Tonight, she didn't want to be alone.

"Good night, Thera."

She gave him a polite nod. "Good night, Ashok." Then she walked away.

He watched her go.

The village children ran up to Thera and surrounded her, laughing and giggling, broad smiles on their white-painted faces. At first they'd feared her, because their parents had warned them that the very voice of the gods was their guest, but she'd treated the little ones with a gentle kindness the entire time they'd been here—an attitude totally different than the abrasive one she used on adults—so now the children loved her. To them, Thera was a marvel of the outside world.

Ashok noticed that with them, she didn't try to hide her hands, and she patted each on the head as she passed by.

Despite being a criminal, Thera was as brave as anyone from the warrior caste, and cunning as an Inquisitor. Over the last few months he'd watched her as she'd healed. That recovery had been a grueling ordeal. Every day for weeks as the village women rewrapped her bandages they'd come away covered in blood and blackened skin, but she'd faced it with stoicism worthy of a Protector. By a miracle in this damp place they had avoided infection, and her palms and fingertips had eventually healed to angry red scar tissue.

Once Thera could grasp something without too much pain, she'd immediately gone back to practicing throwing knives. She'd mastered the skill growing up among the proud warriors of Vane, who were widely considered to have the keenest eyes and best throwing arms in all of Lok, and been furious when her partially deadened fingers had proven clumsy and near useless for that task. Yet every sunrise since, she'd been out there futilely hurling knives at the same stump.

He found such stubborn determination intriguing. If life had been different, and he'd not secretly been born casteless, and she'd not been chosen by an illegal god to be its voice, Ashok would have been honored to have his arranged marriage be to someone like Thera.

"What in the oceans is wrong with you?"

"What?" Ashok turned to see Jagdish approaching.

"You see the way she looks at you." The risaldar had obviously been drinking his way through the celebration. Normally their officer would not set a bad example in front of the men, but the drink the Wild Men made from fermented potatoes was incredibly potent, so it didn't take much to leave one a little too talkative. "I didn't know Protectors took a vow of chastity."

"First, the Protector Order does not have such a rule. Protectors may not wed until after their obligation has been fulfilled, but the services of pleasure women are allowed. And second, I'm not a Protector anymore."

"So as I said, what the hell is wrong with you? Aside from some mystical gods living inside her head, that's a fine and lonely woman."

Ashok couldn't deny that the thought had crossed his

mind with increasing regularity over the long winter. As Thera had recovered, she'd become impatient with hiding. Despite the Wild Men's protestations that it wasn't safe, she'd demanded to get out of the village. Not being able to draw back a bowstring, she couldn't hunt, but she could forage like everyone else. Of course Ashok had insisted that he would be her bodyguard during such ventures. Since they were worried about attracting demons, foragers seldom spoke to each other, so they had spent many silent hours together.

It was odd, but spending all that time together, digging up roots, he'd been content.

Ashok was not used to such things.

"I am obligated to serve her. To form such a bond would be inappropriate."

Jagdish laughed at him. "You're the most wanted criminal in the world! That's pretty bloody inappropriate already! And despite you being such an ass toward her—"

"How much have you drank?"

"Not near enough! Let me try again. Despite you being so damned awkward and cold toward her, you still crossed half the continent to rescue her from wizards, and even a pragmatic girl appreciates such a gesture. Especially one who grew up a warrior."

"That is not—"

"I'm not done!" Jagdish was one of the only people in Lok who could cut Ashok Vadal off and get away with it. Such were the indignities of friendship. "Then the whole time we've been hiding in this awful place"—he gestured theatrically around the small village—"you've been damned near the only person she's confided in."

That was because Ashok had demonstrated beyond

any doubt that his vow to serve her was sincere. Most everyone else here either worshipped or feared her, whereas Ashok had only ever worshipped the Law and feared nothing. He had simply treated her with the respect that she had earned by her deeds.

"I suspect that she enjoys my company because we are both anomalies in a Law-abiding world. Yet Thera is my master. I'm sworn to serve her."

"And you're plenty bitter about that," Jagdish snapped. "Oh, don't deny it. You know I'm right. You won't say a word about whatever your mysterious vow's about, but I was the one who delivered those high-status men and the Grand Inquisitor himself to your prison cell, before you all of a sudden went from eagerly awaiting your execution, to running off to join a rebellion. Just because I'm warrior caste doesn't mean I'm stupid—"

"Of course not." The last thing he needed was for Jagdish to take offense. "I will not argue for or against your conclusions." Though Jagdish was right. It had been Grand Inquisitor Omand who had given Ashok his final obligation—and punishment—to serve the worst of criminals for the rest of his days.

"Of course. Because the way I figure it, next thing I know you've pledged your life to someone none of us had ever heard of, and the only way you'd do that is if the Capitol had ordered you to. Going outside the Law's the worst punishment someone like you could ever face, so of course you're bitter. Even though you know the real Thera now, and she's not so bad, you're still angry at the criminal they made you swear to protect."

Ashok frowned. Jagdish was far too perceptive. "An interesting theory."

"Well, that's because I've had nothing to do for a while but be sick and wait for the roads north to thaw. It gives a man time to theorize." Jagdish had been eager to return home after completing his mission of vengeance against the House of Assassins, but like many of the Sons, he'd come down with a fever that had left him ill for several weeks. The swamp was an unforgiving place, but luckily none of them had died.

"I hold no animosity toward Thera."

"You say that, and since you're so painfully honest, you probably even believe yourself, but don't you dare blame her for your punishment. She's not the Inquisition or the judges. They wanted to hurt and shame you. If it hadn't been this rebel, it would've been someone else. You could have ended up sworn to some mad bandit king or merciless tyrant. You should be *thankful* you got sworn to the likes of her."

Ashok started to respond, but caught himself. He could never reveal the truth of his orders.

"Come on. After all we've been through together, you can admit I'm right."

"I cannot." So Ashok tried to change the subject. "Do you still plan on leaving us tomorrow?"

"I do." Jagdish paused, probably realizing that he'd lost his initial argument before it had really begun. "Gutch and I will head north to Guntur, take the trade road to Warun, and then home to Vadal. Once I tell them of my deeds, I'll either get a hero's welcome, or they'll hang me. Either way, it's what I must do. I was born in Vadal, and I intend to die there."

"Death will come sooner rather than later once Harta finds out that you've been serving as his most hated enemy's second-in-command."

Jagdish gave him a lopsided grin. "I can handle Harta Vadal, the fop, I know him from my time in the Personal Guard. He can spin some pretty words, but our house's new Thakoor isn't near as tough as his mother was. Besides, I'll come bearing gifts."

"Sacks of demon bone may be valuable, but they're not nearly enough to make up for the loss of their house's ancestor blade." They'd had this discussion many times, and Ashok knew that he could not shake Jagdish from the path he considered most honorable, but he still had to try. "The Sons of the Black Sword will be lessened by your absence."

"I've trained them hard. They sure won't miss all the drills I put them through, that's for sure..." It was no exaggeration. Even while the men had been weak with the swamp fever, their risaldar had made them train. Even dizzy and sluggish contact drills were better than none at all. When they'd been too weak to stand, Jagdish had made them lay upon the grass while he'd lectured them on battle strategies. "Take care of my boys, Ashok, and I know they'll do you proud."

Ashok was the far better combatant, but he knew that he'd never be half the commander Jagdish was. Some men were simply born to lead other warriors into battle. One of Ashok's greatest shames was that his fall had brought dishonor upon someone who was such an exemplar of everything the warrior caste should strive to be.

"I will do my best."

"Unlike most, a promise from you really means something, I know. They may be fanatics believing in idealistic foolishness, but they're good men. I've been proud to lead them. Even if I get my old rank back and am given fifty of Vadal's finest warriors, I don't know if they'll be able to compare to the Sons."

"If they survive, it will be because of what you taught them."

Jagdish grew solemn. The crafty warrior hadn't been quite as liquored up as he'd first acted. "I've thought upon the offer to stay on as your second, many times... But I've come a long way to redeem my name, and still have a long way to go before I get home. I know it might all be for nothing, but more than anything else I just want to see my wife again. I hope it doesn't make me seem weak to admit I miss Pakpa. I was lucky to be given her as a bride. She was pregnant when I left. Imagine that. By the time I get home I'll have a child...Surely, a son! A warrior needs a good woman to come home to... Speaking of which, with you and Thera both outside the Law, it isn't like you'd even need an arbiter to arrange a marriage."

"Such tenacity. You're not going to let that go until I demand a duel, are you?"

"Ha! No, I've not had nearly enough to drink to work up that much courage. I'm just saying, Ashok, to the oceans with the Grand Inquisitor and whatever his mysterious orders were. You're on your own now. This is your life, make the best of it... Now I've got to go make arrangements for tomorrow. These villagers have shown us their hospitality, so I'm going to make sure the Sons pay them back by keeping them safe all the way to the fanatics' hidden kingdom." Jagdish gave Ashok a deep bow. "Good luck in the south, my friend."

Ashok returned the respectful gesture. "Good luck in the north, brother." He'd not even intended to use that honorific. It had just slipped out, as if it was the old days, and he'd been speaking to a fellow Protector.

Jagdish seemed moved by that. "Don't worry, I'll put in a good word for you with Harta."

Ashok rarely laughed, but he couldn't help it when the sheer absurdity of that idea struck him.

Jagdish left to have a few last discussions with the men. Their risaldar would be sorely missed by the Sons. They had killed a demon together and lived to tell about it. That was a bond that transcended house or caste.

Ashok leaned against a tree and watched the village for a long time, until the bonfire was dying down, the musicians done, the dancers spent, the fog came creeping back in. Most of the villagers were going to sleep or leaving to make last minute preparations. In the morning these people would abandon the only home they'd ever known and join their new cause. The Sons of the Black Sword had turned into something somewhat resembling a small army, only it was made up of warriors, workers, casteless, freed slaves, and an outsider tribe, all led by a fake Protector and a reluctant prophet.

It was a very strange thing they'd built.

Though it was their last night here, and ostensibly a night of celebration, the Wild Men still set guards in each of their tree-stand towers. They lived in a perpetual state of alert. Demon incursions were rare, but always a possibility this close to the sea. Several of the deadly creatures had been killed at the House of Assassins—including the biggest one anyone had ever heard of—yet over the ensuing months they'd found fresh signs of other demons while out hunting.

By these people's standards, the secret place Keta had built really might be a paradise.

In the silence, Ashok mulled over Jagdish's words. The warrior had guessed right about the Grand Inquisitor's orders. Making a man whose very existence was based upon the Law live out as his days as a criminal was the worst punishment he could imagine. Yet, what if instead of this particular criminal, he had been charged to be in the service of a mad raider like Nadan Somsak? Or a merciless assassin like Sikasso? Mighty Angruvadal had been destroyed, but it had been destroyed stopping an abomination, not aiding one. What foul deeds could a leader like those have accomplished with the greatest swordsman in the world at their command?

The prophet he'd sworn to serve had been revealed to be a woman who—despite being a criminal—retained a certain sense of honor. His obligated master didn't want to destroy the world, she just wanted to be left alone. Thera was no power-hungry conqueror, just someone who had been forced into a role not of her choosing... Just like he had been.

It could have been so much worse.

Perhaps he owed Thera an apology.

The rest of the newcomers had been crammed into various buildings for the winter, but the villagers had given Thera her own hut. Being religious fanatics, they had been so excited at having a real prophet in their midst that the headman had given up his own home, which was by far the biggest in the village, though still humble by the standards of even the poorest in the rest of Lok. Ashok walked to it.

The young warrior, Murugan Thao, was guarding the entrance. He had been assigned to be Thera's personal bodyguard during the battle for the House of Assassins and had been solemnly fulfilling that assignment ever since. "Greetings, General."

Ashok hated that archaic title, but since it had been handed down by their supposed god, all the men insisted on using it. "I need to speak with Thera."

"My apologies, but that's not possible." Like most of the Sons of the Black Sword, Murugan was obviously intimidated by Ashok. Even in a band that was attempting to do away with castes and status, when you could fight a small army on your own, you still received greater deference. "I mean no offense, but she told me that she's retired for the evening and not to be disturbed."

Thera called through the deer hide curtain that served as a door. "It's fine, Murugan. Let Ashok in before he gets grumpy and tosses you into the trees."

"I would not have done that," Ashok assured him. "I will watch over her tonight. You are relieved of duty. Be elsewhere."

Murugan obediently stepped out of the way as Ashok climbed up the small ladder. Every hut in the village was elevated because of the occasional flooding... He couldn't imagine living on top of water. Riding on a barge was one thing, but having malicious water creep beneath your home while you slept was a terrible feeling. This truly was a dismal place.

It was rather dark inside, but Ashok called upon the Heart of the Mountain so his eyes could gather more light. The rough wooden walls were decorated with the biggest antlers from Toramana's many hunts.

Thera was sitting up on the pile of soft furs atop straw that served as the headman's bed. Apparently he had interrupted her in the process of undressing, as the ties of her shirt were undone. She didn't even bother to close it, though she surely knew by now he could see in the dark when he felt like it.

When they'd first met, he'd found her decent looking enough—for a criminal—but it hadn't been until they'd been silently digging up tubers from the mud together, that he'd glanced over and it had struck him that Thera was truly beautiful. It was odd, how perspectives changed.

"What is it now? Did we forget something about tomorrow?"

"No. Our preparations have been thorough. I'm here because I believe I may have inadvertently given offense."

"You're like a never-ending river of offense." She undid the cord that was holding back her long hair and shook it free. "What makes this particular one special?"

"I have come to apologize." Then Ashok realized he wasn't really sure how to proceed. He could never tell her of Omand's final command, but he needed to get this off his chest. "I wish to say, that of the many different criminals I could have pledged myself to, you are probably the least offensive of them."

"Really?" Thera was perplexed. "Was that supposed to be a compliment?"

He thought about it for a moment. "In a manner, yes."

"That's good, I suppose." She sat there, waiting, with the curve of one breast peeking out from around the fabric of her shirt.

It had been a very long time since he had been with a woman. Trying to recall, it had been before prison in Vadal, before traveling to and from the Capitol, before his assignment to Gujara even... His mind had been trained to remember everyone he'd ever killed, but he couldn't recall the last time he'd shared a bed with another. That was something a Protector simply did when the mood was upon him.

"Anything else, Ashok?"

There was an awkward silence. His assumption had been that she had wanted company for the night, but perhaps he had interpreted that incorrectly. He was a man of accomplishment by any measure, able to read an opponent and predict their moves long before they made them, who had traveled many times from one end of the continent to the other, and had even died and come back to life, but the basic whims of the female remained a mystery to him.

"That was all. I will leave you now."

"Hang on..." Thera seemed incredulous. "You barged in here to tell me that? That's it? That wasn't even proper flattery to try and get beneath a girl's skirts. What is wrong with you?"

"A great many things, I suppose."

"Maybe I was just caught up in the moment, a new year, a new beginning, and all that. Maybe I was a fool to think there could be something more... Are you afraid of girls, Ashok?"

"You know that my ability to feel fear was taken from me by magic."

"That's not what I meant."

"I am familiar with such matters. Wherever Protectors go, the local authorities are quick to provide all manner of gifts to show their loyalty, but you are not some mere pleasure woman, whose feelings don't matter. You are far more than that."

Thera cocked her head to the side. When she did the cloth slipped from one shoulder, leaving the skin bare. He suspected she might have done that on purpose. "What am I to you then?"

It was a good question.

"You're the one I've sworn to obey. If you ordered me to wade out into the ocean, I'd do so without hesitation. Yet I also know of your suffering. You were driven from your house, lost your family, your people, your very caste, and that you have been crushed beneath the weight of great responsibility ever since. You've been through much but know there is more to come. I would not complicate this burden any more than it already is. You are the one who regardless of where your path leads, I will be there by your side. That is who you are to me."

"Oh."

He was not an eloquent man, but he needed her to understand this. Ashok went to the edge of the furs and knelt close to her. "I can protect your life. I'm very good at that. That is my duty. Only I don't know how to protect you from your own sadness. That is not my obligation, but I would like to try."

Thera seemed at a loss for words.

"Did I give offense?" he asked.

"No . . . I just didn't expect that. For a man who almost always says the wrong things, sometimes you say something surprisingly . . . decent. You honestly care about me?"

"I do."

Apparently, their last night in Bahdjangal wasn't going how either of them had expected.

Thera placed her damaged hand against his neck, and then realizing what she'd done, immediately snatched it away, embarrassed. But Ashok caught her hand, and gently pressed it back against him. Her fingertips were hard with scar tissue, but he didn't care. He had plenty of his own scars, inside and out. She'd earned those injuries *destroying a demon god*. That made her even more beautiful to him.

Ashok discovered that a kiss was an entirely different experience when it wasn't merely a transaction. Together they sank down onto the furs.

It was good to not be alone.

Chapter 5

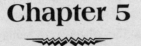

In the morning, the Wild Men said their final goodbyes to their village. That included tearful farewells to all the guardian spirits they claimed lived in the trees, and to their ancestors who supposedly had watched over them all these years. If you counted all the invisible imaginary things which supposedly lived here too, it was a very crowded place. They were truly an odd people. It was amazing how only a few generations cut off from civilization was enough time for a group to make up all manner of crazy superstitions.

Ironically, it was Thera who would be providing them with new ones.

She just shook her head at the absurdity of her life and went back to practicing. She hurled another knife at her target. Like the vast majority of her previous attempts, the blade twisted in her clumsy fingers before release, and clanged off the wood sideways.

But that one had felt *close*.

So Thera walked over to the stump and retrieved

all the knives. Not too long ago she would've had to wrench each one out, because they'd have been reliably planted deep, right where she wanted them. Now it was all about bending over and picking them off the dirt. For a child of Vane, that was downright degrading. But House Vane had two things in great abundance, pride and stubbornness, so she walked back to the line she'd set at fifteen paces to try all over again.

Even though the village was being busily broken down, no one interrupted her. A month ago she'd lost her temper and snapped at one of the warriors who'd come over to pester her, asking some annoying questions about the will of the gods or something. Lucky for him, when he'd failed to take the hint to shut his mouth, the knife she'd thrown at him had gone sideways and bounced off his boot. But the message had been received, and ever since then they all knew to leave their prophet in peace while she practiced.

She may have been the Voice of a god, but that didn't mean she knew a damn thing about their inscrutable will. So she wished people would quit asking her about it. Keta was always quick to come up with an explanation for everything, whether it rained or you got stung by a bee, Keta always had some reason why that had been the will of the gods, and he actually believed it.

Honestly, the gods' motives remained a mystery to her. People were asking for her to do things like bless their crops, or heal their sick children, but in her experience all the gods did was meddle and complicate. To hell with making the garden grow, all the gods had gotten her was kidnapped by wizards or into a fight with some hellish nightmare being left over from the rain of demons.

The next knife bounced off the bark a foot away from target.

"Oceans," she muttered.

The sun was rising over the swamp. Soon they'd begin the long march to the Creator's Cove. She could only hope that Keta had made it back there safe and sound before winter had gotten bad, and that the place was still in one piece. Her worst fear was that they'd cross the plains only to discover that the Inquisition had found the rebellion's home, and all that would be left of her adopted people was buzzard-picked bones.

Everything of value these people owned was being taken with them, on their backs or in a handcart. The Wild Men—as the Sons called them—or People of the Woods—as they called themselves—were a hardy bunch, but they didn't need to carry that much, because they were rather poor.

Well, they *had* been poor. After butchering the demons they'd killed and salvaging what they could from the smoking wreckage of the House of Assassins, her humble group of refugees were probably per capita the richest bunch in Lok. Every single one of them, man, woman, and child, would be carrying at least a few pounds of demon flesh and bone, rich with potent magic, and incredibly valuable on the black market.

They'd taken the Lost House's jewels and banknotes too. And whatever they couldn't carry, they'd hidden in a cave so that they could come back and claim it later. Including the bones of the great demon that were so heavy it would take teams of oxen to carry them back to civilization. If they could ever sell all of it on the black market, the rebellion would suddenly be rich as her old house.

That thought amused her greatly. Her next knife hit the target, but her release had been timed wrong so it landed handle first... But hard enough to make a dent, so that was an improvement. She used to be good enough to pin a running rat to the ground, so it was incredibly frustrating to fail over and over again, but her father had always said that a warrior needed to be realistic about assessing his abilities. So she was still a miserable frustrating failure, but an *improving* miserable frustrating failure.

"Are you attempting to bludgeon it to death?"

She hadn't heard Ashok approach. If she'd been able to move as quiet as a Protector, she would've been far more successful as a thief. She didn't intend to greet him with a smile, but she couldn't help herself. "The goal is to stick it, but I'll take what I can get."

Her hand flashed to her belt, and the next knife hit solid, but edge first instead of point. It actually stuck, though shallowly embedded.

"You are improving greatly."

"It's not good enough yet." Thera shook out her fingers. It was hard to get the release right when most of the feeling was gone. Actually sticking a living, moving opponent in combat was a dubious proposition—often more of a distraction than a killing blow—but the warriors of Vane loved to do it anyway. It was tradition, and if she was being honest, normally a rather relaxing pastime. One that she really wanted back.

She looked over at Ashok. He was just standing there, tall and imposing, unreadable as usual, as if nothing had changed between them. Perhaps to him, nothing had. No one else was near enough to hear them, so she said, "You were gone when I woke up."

"I thought it best. I did not wish to complicate matters for you."

"You didn't want these people to know their so-called prophet is a woman of flesh and blood? It might ruin my image as a pure vessel of the gods?" She pulled out the next knife and turned back to throw.

"I doubt even the most idealistic of these fanatics assumed you were that pure."

That time she missed the stump by a several feet, and the knife went sailing off into a bush. "You fish-eating bastard!" She turned back to him. "You distracted me with all your charm."

Ashok gave her a curious look. "You are being sarcastic."

What an odd, damaged man, yet loyal and stronger than anyone she'd ever met. It was strange in a way. Ashok was so infamous as a Law-enforcing executioner that he was known across the continent as the Black Heart, yet despite being so named he was still a far gentler man than her former husband. The last time she'd seen Dhaval, he'd been trying to kill her. Perhaps Ashok only seemed like a good choice because her previous experiences with men had been so bad?

"Obviously. So how goes it?"

"I came to tell you it is almost time to go."

Ashok seemed like he wanted to say something else, but this recent change was as strange for him as it was for her. She didn't want to talk about it. She was no idealistic girl reading poems. Life had kicked her too many times for her to be naïve enough to believe in love. The gods—or whatever they were—had thrown them together, they were just making the best of it.

"If you're worried about complicating things, Ashok, don't. It is what it is. I was married once before and it didn't end well."

"You've not spoken much of your past. Death or divorce?"

Thera laughed. "We attempted a little of each."

"Among the First they simply get an arbiter to dissolve the arranged marriage contract, but from your tone I take it yours was bad even by warrior caste standards."

"If you genuinely want to know, I slashed him across the eyes with a knife while he was trying to throw me off a cliff into the ocean. It's a long story. But since I'm telling you my secrets, don't worry about last night. My husband had children from a previous wife, but he never got me pregnant. I think because I was sick for so long when I was young, the bolt left me near dead for a few seasons, I think I can't ever have a baby."

Usually Ashok did a much better job of hiding his emotions, but from the look on his face it was almost as if his brain had tripped over the idea. He had never even considered having a child before. She considered his discomfort payback for what he'd just said about her perceived virtue.

"I had not thought of that possibility."

"In the moment men rarely do. But it was fun."

Ashok looked uncomfortable. "Do you wish to speak about what happened?"

"Not particularly."

"Good." The man was no poet, but she appreciated his directness.

"Go on. I'll join you shortly."

Ashok simply nodded and returned to work.

Thera pulled out her last knife, wondering once again what she'd done to end up in a situation like this.

Three hundred people were counting on her here, and nearly a thousand more back at the Creator's Cove. Not to mention all of the foolish casteless scattered about Lok who'd heard Keta's sermons and taken hope from them. She didn't give a damn about the gods who'd cursed her with a bolt from the sky, but as much as she hated to admit it, their believers had begun to matter to her.

She looked at the target, mostly unblemished after months of practice, and asked herself once again why she bothered.

This knife was a simple tool, four inches of polished steel. It was no less effective than before, but the hand that wielded it had become damaged, clumsy, and unfeeling. She'd learned to use these knives because she'd been born into a warrior house, to a father who'd treated her as if she'd been a firstborn son. Practice had continued even after she'd been married off to a beast because it had made her feel in control. Honestly, she had her own army now, and fanatics who'd lay down their lives for her. She didn't need to be able to fight with a humble knife when the most dangerous man in the world had pledged himself to fight on her behalf.

But she'd keep practicing so that someday she could feel in control of something again.

Her arm flashed, the motion smooth, and the knife flipped toward the target.

It hit the dirt right in front of the stump.

Today would not be that day.

Chapter 6

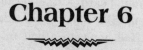

It would take their ragged band a few days to cross the Bahdjangal, and with luck, they would encounter no demons along the way. A slow-moving column like this, with children and elderly among it, would surely be a delicious snack for a sea demon.

With his superior senses, stamina, and speed, Ashok decided it would be best if he spent the journey ranging back and forth, scouting around the main body of the group. The Wild Men knew their swamp well and moved through it comfortably, always able to pick out solid ground from the treacherous muck, and they were seldom surprised by the venomous snakes or crocodiles that lurked within. Yet as good as they were, they were nothing compared to Ashok. That was not pride speaking. It was a simple fact.

He would run ahead, find a good vantage point, and then watch and listen, using the Heart of the Mountain to heighten one sense, and then another, until he was certain there wasn't any danger. Then he would move to a flank and check there, and then run to the rear of the column to make sure no curious demon had picked up their trail. Throughout the day he repeated the process, and would continue to do so until they reached terrain less suitable for concealing demons. That activity meant that he had to cross three times as much ground as the rest of them, and at a much faster pace. It was tiring, even for someone who had touched the Heart of the Mountain, but he didn't mind. It gave him time alone without anyone calling him *General*.

While he waited in a position of cover, observing and catching his breath, he caught glimpses of Thera's *army* through the trees. On point were always Toramana and his Wild Men, because only they could easily navigate the treacherous paths. As long as they stuck to the trails the hunters knew well, the livestock they were herding wouldn't flounder into the mud and get stuck.

Occasionally someone would find an isolated group living unnoticed somewhere outside the control of the Law, but those groups tended to be sickly and dim-witted. The Wild Men were robust and clever. Ashok assumed it was because they'd had a bigger population to start with. Inbreeding made for weak and stupid children, which was why arbiters checked genealogical records before arranging marriages. The occasional escaped prisoner from the House of Assassins who joined them had brought fresh blood as well.

It was surprising how many of the tribe had come from the Lost House over the years. The wizards made at least a cursory attempt to catch their runaways, but if they made it very far at all it was easy to declare them dead from exposure or eaten by demons in the unforgiving swamp, and give up the search. If anything, the haughty wizards had probably assumed their neighboring barbarians would kill any escapees they found, not take them in and offer them shelter. With nowhere else to go, far from homes they couldn't really remember because they'd been kidnapped as children, most of them had been glad to be adopted into the Wild Men. From what Thera had told him, the wizards had been a cruel and nefarious bunch of plotters. Better to live a simple life in a swamp.

The tribe's hatred of the wizards was palpable. It had taken Thera's direct intervention to keep the Wild Men from murdering their lone wizard prisoner, Waman. Both groups had been of the same house once, but after the Capitol had broken the dams and flooded their lands, the wizards had left the lower-caste survivors to fend for themselves. Knowing that the wizards had only spared their lives because rumors of a savage tribe living in the Bahdjangal helped keep their house a secret, had made the Wild Men even angrier at their wealthy cousins. Last night Toramana had said it was the prophecy of Mother Dawn that had told them to move to Thera's paradise, but Ashok suspected the biggest reason the Wild Men had been so eager to join them was because with the House of Assassins destroyed, they had no one left to spite with their survival.

Satisfied that there was no significant danger ahead of them, Ashok leapt up and ran east toward the sea. For speed and stealth, he was dressed like the swamp hunters, shirtless and barefoot. The suit of Protector armor that they'd found in the House of Assassins—which Gutch had repaired and fitted for him over the winter using the Wild Men's meager blacksmithy—was packed with their baggage.

At the flank, Ashok positioned himself between his obligation and hell. But today the distant waves were still. The meanest predators they faced now were the mosquitos. From his hidden position, he watched the column pass.

Even though Jagdish had left them that morning and gone north, the Sons of the Black Sword were still following their risaldar's last orders. Warrior and worker both—from several different Great Houses, their divisions forgotten—had placed themselves protectively around the women, children, and animals of the Wild Men.

They were called the Sons because their organization had been born with the destruction of Angruvadal. Though for Jagdish, it was more like he was their father, even though he was barely older than they were. Jagdish was a fine officer, and Ashok would do his best to lead them as Jagdish had, though he knew he would fall short. Some men—like Jagdish—were born to lead others into battle. Ashok was battle incarnate. Where he led would be the death of a normal soldier. But he would try to keep these alive.

Scattered among the crowd were the dozen slaves they'd freed from the House of Assassins. Thera had told him about how the wizards kept their numbers up by stealing magically gifted children from all over Lok. Those who developed the proper skills and mindset would eventually join the ranks of their captors, while those found unworthy had their minds scrubbed by magic and were made into slaves.

The simpletons were easy to pick out, because the former slaves needed to be guided along or they'd wander off. They were really only good at simple repetitive tasks, and anything that required much thinking left them befuddled. Ashok found that their presence made him uncomfortable, so he had avoided speaking with any of them too much. Perhaps it was because what had been done to them sounded similar to what the wizard Kule had done to him as a child. The difference being that Ashok had been carefully reconstructed afterward into a perfect servant of the Law, while the Lost House slaves were left broken and simple.

It was unknown if their minds would ever recover, like the one who had set fire to the Fortress powder at the Lost House had seemed to somewhat. Waman, their captive wizard, had denied knowing the answer. However, regardless of their condition, Thera had declared that they were to be treated well. Life was cheap in Lok, but not in her camp.

As for their wizard captive, Waman had not survived the winter. Thera had wanted to keep him alive in case she could think of a use for him. Except even a prophet's authority only extended so far when it came to a wizard prisoner being held by a tribe those same wizards had hunted for sport. They did not know which of the vengeful Wild Men had snuck into the prisoner's hut and slit Waman's throat late one night. Finding that answer was not worth testing the tribe's loyalty.

However, the wizard's presence had one lasting effect. In the weeks before he'd been murdered, Waman had testified to everyone who would listen about how he'd seen Ashok return from the dead and lift himself off the meat hook that had gone through his heart, a feat that should have been impossible, even with black-steel magic. The tribe may have despised the wizard, but they believed his tale about Ashok, and since Ashok would never deny the truth—and he truly had died and come back—his legend grew.

Though Ashok had lived among them for a season, most of the tribe talked about him as if he was a supernatural being more than a man. Luckily their reverence was not too galling. One could hardly worship the Forgotten's warrior as some high and mighty being when he went hunting or foraging with them every day.

Ashok moved to the end of the column.

As he crouched there, waiting to see if they were being followed, an odd thought occurred to him. For a few months, life had been uncomplicated. This had been a brief glimpse into a mundane existence of survival and labor. He knew it was naïve, but he could almost picture himself and Thera living out their days in obscurity, tilling the soil like workers, not leading a futile rebellion to certain doom.

He had never been allowed thoughts of a *future*. That had always been a nebulous concept at best. There had been only obligation, and when his service to the Protector Order was done, then surely there would have been new duties assigned by his house. There was no longer a plan. He did not have a place. Was it possible? Dare he make his own?

Only Thera had an obligation from the gods, and he had an obligation to her. In a few days they would be back within the civilized world, beneath the unflinching gaze of the Law, and in all likelihood their lives would be short, and never simple again.

He was going to miss the swamp.

Chapter 7

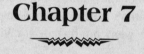

The snow in the mountains was beginning to melt, so the Nansakar was running high, fast, and cold. It would have been madness to try and swim this group across—especially since none of the higher castes could swim—but Thera had thought ahead. Before she had sent home the casteless who had delivered the Sons of the Black Sword here, she had gotten them to drag one of their barges safely inland and leave it behind.

It had actually been Jagdish's suggestion for them to stash a barge for future use. It was a good thing too, since Thera had been in too much pain at the time to think much beyond her burns. The Lost House had still been smoldering, Ashok was buried in the rubble, and she had only just met the small band of fanatical warriors who'd come so far to save her.

Of course, when she'd agreed she had only been thinking about how to get herself back to the Cove, not a whole village worth of people, two milk cows, several goats, donkeys, and two carts full of squawking chickens.

They found the barge right where Jagdish had told the casteless Nod to hide it. Luckily it had survived the winter and was still intact. The plan was simple. They tied all their ropes together and then Ashok and a few of the Sons had poled the barge to the other side of the river to attach their line to a sturdy tree. They had to battle a fierce current that wanted to carry them toward the ocean the entire way. They'd pushed so hard that Thera had been afraid their poles would snap, and then they'd be carried off, but they'd made it across.

Once their line was secure, the real work began. The process took an entire day, from dawn to dusk, with their strongest men taking turns poling back and forth across the rushing Nansakar. The casteless barge wasn't very big. They could crowd at most fifteen bodies on at a time. If it flipped, or anyone tumbled over the edge, they'd surely die in the freezing water. If a demon were to come from below—and they weren't too many miles from the sea—everyone aboard was as good as dead. Occasionally a massive log would float by, big enough to upset the barge, and they would have to time it to avoid the impact. For the passengers, the trip across the Nansakar was one of white-knuckled terror.

Ashok was aboard for every single trip.

Thera watched him, curious why he'd been so quick to volunteer for such a duty, because she knew how much he despised being on the water. In a land where anything deep enough to hide your legs from view might conceal a demon, everyone was distrustful of water. For Ashok it was more than that. To him water was the source of evil and the home of hell, because the Law declared it so. And though he'd learned to tolerate *some* criminals, the rivers, lakes, and seas would always be beyond his control.

Yet he remained out there, going back and forth across the white froth and tearing currents, pulling on the rope like an ox pulling a wagon. And when they'd land, and the shaking nauseous warriors fell into the grass, and new volunteers took up their poles and got aboard, Ashok just stayed there—soaking wet, surely chilled to the bone—and off they'd set again.

When one of the Wild Men's cows panicked halfway across, kicking and thrashing, threatening to swamp the barge, Ashok had calmly stunned it with a fist to its thick skull, and then simply gone back to pulling the rope. They'd rolled a thousand pounds of unconscious beef off on the other shore, and Ashok had immediately gone back for more people.

Once half their force was on the south bank, it was Thera's turn. Their prophet was precious cargo, and they wanted her on whichever side had the majority of the warriors. Since she'd been a smuggler, she'd spent more time on the rivers than anyone else here, but even for her this was the roughest water journey of her life. Churning, bouncing, and crashing, it was far worse than it had looked from the shore. The river was so turbulent and dark with silt that there could be a demon right beneath them and she'd never know. The rocking made her stomach clench. Water washed up over the sides, and spray soaked her clothes. The wind was so sharp it cut right through her damp coat. The shivering began immediately.

Children cried. Goats screamed. Men vomited over the side. Despite the wind and the water, Thera found that she could smell her own sweat, cold and fearful.

Through it all Ashok remained as relentless as a machine in a worker's factory. He had the rope, because that was where he could exert the most force. She watched the powerful muscles of his arms and back tense each time he pulled. Ashok was a tall, lean man, yet hard as iron. House Vane was the home of some of the most physically imposing warriors in Lok, but she had never seen anyone near as strong as Ashok. Each time he pulled she could feel the force through the wood beneath her knees.

It was his will versus the might of the river, and Ashok was winning.

"Our last barge trip together was far calmer."

Ashok grimaced as he tugged the rope again. "I drowned that time."

So much for conversation. They made the rest of the crossing in silence.

It was a violent journey, but with an effective rhythm, so they made good time. The grinding of their wooden planks against the sand of the south shore was the most welcoming sound Thera could imagine. The waiting warriors waded out to secure them, and then the other passengers stumbled off. To her, this shore appeared to be the exact same kind of terrain as the one they'd just left, but from the tribe's whispers of wonderment it might as well have been a whole new world to them. The Wild Men rarely ventured out of their swamp. The Nansakar might as well have been the edge of the world.

Though beached, Ashok still held onto the rope, only now it was to keep himself upright. He looked exhausted, wrung out as if his body was a rag and strength made of water. She didn't understand what manner of magic it was which made Protectors so tough, but Ashok must have temporarily let go of it once he was certain they were safe.

"You should rest, let someone else take your place at the rope."

He shook his head. "It is better if I do it."

It wasn't just the physical strain that was making him weary, it was how much the river weighed on his spirit. Thera could have ordered him to stop, to stay on land with her, to let someone else bear the burden for a few trips, but she wouldn't force him to. It would be better to order the river to flow uphill. He might not care for these people, but he would protect them, no matter what. With Ashok, words were irrelevant, all that mattered was deeds. He would always do what he thought was correct. The man who had sworn himself to her would never ever quit.

It was one thing to know something. It was something else to truly see it in action. Thera tilted her head in respect.

Eyes heavy lidded from exhaustion, he just looked back at her. Ashok probably didn't even grasp the magnitude of the realization she'd just had about him.

Or maybe, he did... As Thera gathered her pack and began to get off the barge, Ashok reached out and caught her by the sleeve. "Wait."

"Yes?"

"Our last time on a river together, I may have drowned, but you brought me back."

She had saved his life, putting her mouth on his and forcing her air into his lungs, and then pushing on his chest like they were a bellows, until he coughed up water and started breathing again. "The casteless who work the rivers call that trick the breath of life."

"I don't recall if I ever properly thanked you for doing that."

"On the contrary, you woke up ready to murder us all and accused me of witchcraft."

"I regret that now."

It was because she'd interrupted his plans. He'd wanted nothing more than to die, and he'd continued living only because he was obligated to. She was afraid to ask if that had changed.

"It's fine..." Then Thera lowered her voice to a conspiratorial whisper so the fanatics wouldn't hear. "Though I'll say the second time our lips met was much more entertaining than the first."

Ashok raised an eyebrow.

"Prophet! You made it. Excellent," Toramana shouted. The leader of the Wild Men was a thickset man, and the entire barge shook as he climbed aboard. "Come, come, we've built a fire. Warm yourself and dry your clothes before you get sick."

As Toramana began to usher her away, she glanced back at Ashok. "I'd like to see how the third time goes."

"Is that an invitation?"

"It is."

It was unusual to see Ashok smile. "Then I have further motivation not to drown."

"Huh?" Toramana had no idea what they were whispering about as he placed some furs over Thera's shoulders. "This way, Prophet, let's get you warm. My hunters on this side have already caught a deer, two rabbits, and a snapping turtle. We are very skilled like that. We'll eat well tonight. The gods are blessing this journey already."

Most of her band weren't staying close to the river.

No sense in tempting demons. Their fires had been built on a rise two hundred yards inland. As the latest arrivals walked along on still wobbling legs, she couldn't help but glance back over her shoulder.

With rested men aboard to take over the poles, they started back across the river. Ashok wasn't even looking at her, he was once again focused on the rope with that single-minded determination of his. As she watched them shove off, a strange feeling came over her. Since her marriage had ended, she'd been with a few other men. When you lived as a criminal, you had to do whatever was necessary to survive. It was a lifestyle that required you to be harsh, ruthless, and mercenary, or you'd end up as prey. Women had few advantages. Sometimes that meant seducing a strong man just to have an ally.

She just wasn't used to actually liking them.

Chapter 8

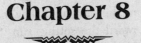

Their second day on the Akershan plains, they came across the scene of a massacre.

It had been a small settlement, just five of the gray homes that were common here, but the casteless knew how to pack a great many bodies into a small living space.

Tattered bits of fabric whipped in the wind. The felt walls had been slashed open, their inhabitants dragged out and put to the sword. Ashok stood in the packed dirt circle in the middle of the homes and counted the dead.

It was mostly women and children, all casteless. They'd been thrown in a pile for the buzzards, right atop the fire pit where they'd cooked their meals. From the look of the bodies, they'd been killed recently, in the late afternoon.

"General." Shekar Somsak ran up to Ashok. "I've got the trail."

Shekar had been with them since Jharlang. Like

all the Somsak raiders, his body was tattooed to commemorate his many battles. Since Shekar had been the most cautious and strategic of that hot-blooded house, Jagdish had appointed him to be one of his two havildars. However, more importantly to Ashok right now was that the Somsak were excellent trackers.

"Report."

"It was about fifty on horseback who did this. They came from the east, and they're headed west." He gestured toward the setting sun. Since the Wild Men also practiced the art of tattooing, Shekar had a new demon taking up most of that arm, celebrating the Sons' victory in the swamp. The skin was still red and healing.

"Was this the work of warriors or criminals?"

"From the uniform horseshoes and the matching boots from the dismounts, I'd say regular cavalry soldiers."

Why would Great House Akershan send a full paltan to slaughter this isolated group of casteless? But more importantly, if warriors were actively patrolling this region, how would his slow column be able to avoid them? According to Thera's directions they were still weeks from Keta's hideout at their column's plodding pace.

"Alert the others. Tell the prophet that I need to speak with her. We have to change our plans."

Shekar immediately complied, sprinting off through the tall grass. Grass was the only thing this poor land had in abundance.

Ashok went back to examining the settlement. He'd done this sort of work before, killing whole villages. He'd taken no joy from such duties, but he'd still done it because the Law had required it. He wondered what crime these non-people had committed that had been so great it had required all their deaths? There were no men of fighting age, which suggested they were probably off getting into trouble. Had Thera's rebellion been the cause here?

There was a noise from way out in the grass. He'd assumed there had been no survivors, but that had sounded like a moan. Hand on his sword, Ashok began walking in that direction. He found grass which had been bent as if someone had crashed through it. He spotted droplets of blood dried on a flat rock. Apparently, the warriors had missed someone. Ashok was no Somsak, but he could follow this haphazard trail easily enough. The injured man had run, bleeding, until he'd fallen, and then he'd crawled for a time.

Akershan wasn't nearly as flat as people from the other houses commonly believed. It was because as you looked out over the endless grasslands you couldn't really see all the swells and gullies that crossed the land. Only at sunset or sunrise could you see the terrain features by the shadows they cast.

He found the man lying at the bottom of one of those gullies, on his side, in a puddle turned pink from blood. Surprisingly, he was in a warrior's garb, and had the insignia of Great House Akershan on his sleeve.

At first Ashok thought that maybe this one had been wounded by the casteless, and then left behind by his companions, but that made no sense. The arrow stuck in his back was obviously of quality, more likely from the warrior caste than something unskilled non-people could make, but that didn't mean a rebel couldn't steal a bow and a quiver ... Take his own Sons of the Black Sword for example. They were rebels and rather well equipped.

The warrior moaned again. So he'd not bled to death quite yet. Ashok walked over to him.

The injured man heard Ashok's boots splashing through the puddle and jerked awake. He grasped instinctively for his sword, but the scabbard at his side was empty. The sudden movement must have shifted the arrow, for he winced against the pain.

"Calm yourself. I mean you no harm." He knelt next to the warrior, who was quite a bit younger than Ashok, but it was hard to tell with his face so swollen and cut up. In addition to the arrow, he'd also received a severe beating. From the look of him, Ashok guessed that he'd been shot in the back, and then several men had stomped and kicked him, then left him to die. He must have come to and tried to flee after that.

"What happened here?"

"I couldn't do it." The warrior had gone gray from lack of blood. Ashok knew that feeling, sinking into a cold fog.

"Couldn't do what?"

"Kill them. Kill them like that." Eyes wide and terrified, he was near the endless nothing, and he knew it. "They did no harm. But kill 'em all. That's orders. But these were babies. Just babies."

"You disobeyed your orders?"

"Weren't gonna spear no babies." Surprisingly, the warrior began to laugh, but it was more of a soft wheeze. "I punched that Inquisitor right in his mask."

Law-breaking disobedience still offended Ashok to his core, but recently he'd started finding the idea of harming Inquisitors amused him. Hopefully this defiant one would live, and not just because Ashok wanted to interrogate him. Upon inspection, it was obvious the arrow had struck the shoulder blade, and from the amount of shaft sticking out, it had ground out on the bone. If any vital organs had been pierced, he'd already have bled out.

"What is your name, Warrior?"

"Rane."

"I'll help you, Rane Akershan, but I need you to answer my questions."

The warrior was weak and wheezing, but he was focused now. "To the oceans with Akershan. I was obligated to them from vassal house Garo. That's why they treated me like this."

"Your orders were to kill all the casteless, why?"

"Kill 'em all they said. The whole province full."

That made no sense. "All of them?"

"Every last one. Great Extermination the masks called it. Every warrior available is being sent here to fight... But most of us didn't want to. This ain't war, it's butchery."

"Your paltan, where were they headed?"

"We were to clean out Dhakhantar in the morning. There's supposed to be three or four hundred untouchables there."

Ashok unwound the sash from his waist. "Last question. Akershani arrows, are they broadheads or points?"

"For hunting casteless, they told us to pack our cheapest iron bodkins. Why?"

"Pulling out a flesh cutter can cause more damage."

"Wait—"

From experience he knew it was best to not give them too much warning. Ashok grabbed hold of the shaft and yanked it straight out of the warrior's back. This caused a scream, which was justifiable, considering the narrow point had been lodged in the bone. As the warrior faded back into unconsciousness, Ashok used his sash to staunch the bleeding. Then he hoisted him out of the mud, threw him over his shoulders, and ran back toward the others.

The column was drawing near the casteless camp. As Ashok approached, he saw that Shekar had already spread the word, because they were preparing to fight. The Wild Men were readying their bows. The Sons of the Black Sword were donning their armor. The young and vulnerable were being herded toward the safety of the center.

"I've got a wounded man here. Fetch the surgeon."

Some of the hunters ran off to get the tribal healer. She was more of an insane witch doctor than a proper surgeon, but he'd seen her work in the swamp. When it came to stitching wounds or setting bones, she was competent enough.

His arrival drew a curious crowd. A pair of hunters took the warrior from him.

"Watch it. He's got a puncture wound to the back."

Eklavya Kharsawan was his other havildar, and the serious young man looked worried. Where the Somsak were natural raiders always itching for a fight, the warriors of Kharsawan tended to be cautious and defense minded. Jagdish had liked getting wildly divergent perspectives from his junior officers.

"Shekar told us there're patrols around. Your orders, General?"

"It appears you're already doing the correct thing. Where's Thera?"

"She wanted to see the massacre for herself."

Ashok started back toward the settlement, and then he paused. He had to ask himself what a proper military leader like Jagdish would do in this situation. "Tell them no fires in the camp tonight. In this terrain they can be seen for miles. Gather all the Sons who come from Akershan lands. Make sure they're willing to shed their brothers' blood. If not, place them with the noncombatants. If they are willing to fight, then they need to tell us everything they can of their house's tactics."

"Right away." Eklavya began shouting names as Ashok walked away. Those that could hear his voice came running, and the rest were passed down the line.

Ashok found Thera amid the gray homes, standing in front of the corpse pile. She had her head down and one hand pressed tight over her mouth.

Murugan and another of the Sons were guarding her, and both of them looked grim. "Leave us for a moment," Ashok said. They immediately did as they were told.

He couldn't see her expression because her long hair was whipping in the wind. He went to Thera's side, unsure how she would react to such slaughter. Would it be grief? Shock? But instead he found her with teeth clenched, staring at the bodies with narrowed, furious eyes. Of course. He should have known. She had been raised warrior caste.

"Was this because of the rebellion, Ashok? Is this because of me?"

"I don't know their reasoning yet, but the Akershani

warriors have been dispatched to kill all the non-people in this region."

"Don't call them that! These were people! Just like us. Just like the great-house families. I don't give a damn what the Law calls them. They say they aren't real, so they can justify sending men like you to treat them like this!"

Ashok merely nodded.

"Never call them non-people again," she muttered as she knelt next to the corpse of a little girl. "Please."

"As you wish." Even knowing he was one of them, even after coming to know many of them as real flesh-and-blood beings, with feelings, wants, accomplishments, and flaws, it would be a difficult habit to break. There was a power in words.

"They really intend to kill them all?" Thera whispered.

"I have no reason to doubt the injured warrior I found. The paltan who did this is riding in the same direction we are. Even on horseback they're only a few hours ahead of us, but they'll need to camp for the night. If we want to avoid them—"

"Avoid them?" Thera snarled. "I want you to *kill* them. I want you to punish them for *this*."

She was normally more calculating than that. Something here had affected her deeply. "That wouldn't be wise."

"All those years you were murdering everyone who even looked at the Law crossways, did you ever stop and care about the *wisdom* of it?"

"Not really. I was expendable. But if this paltan does not arrive at their destination, more will be dispatched to check on them. It is not my safety I'm concerned about."

No matter how much righteous anger she was feeling, it wouldn't spare the lives of her followers from the warrior caste's wrath, and she knew it. Thera took a deep breath. "This isn't right, Ashok."

It may not be right, but it was *legal*. And that thought made Ashok deeply uncomfortable. As a Protector he'd never given much thought to what happened after his grisly work had been done. In a way, he wanted nothing more than to chase down these cowards and let them face an opponent who could actually fight back, even if it wasn't prudent.

"I did this," she said.

"It's not your fault."

"Isn't it? Why is this pile just mothers and children?" She had noticed the same thing he had. "It's probably because the ones who can fight have run off, inspired by the Voice. Inspired by those damnable prophecies. They're off picking fights they can't win, because they believe in Keta's fairy tales." Thera used her damaged fingertips to brush aside a lock of hair that was covering the little girl's face. "This is my doing. I caused an uprising, and now they're getting stepped on like bugs."

He couldn't argue, because she was probably right. The Law had very little patience for rebellion. "I don't know what caused this, but if you send me to collect heads, then you will be responsible for the repercussions. An attack will surely bring a response."

"Saltwater," Thera muttered. "We're still a long way from the Cove."

"A very long way, and we weren't expecting this much activity in the region either. They might catch us even if we try to remain unnoticed. They might even find us if we turn back and flee for the swamp. Our trail is impossible to hide and will look like casteless fleeing for the border."

"So we're damned no matter what."

"Before you make a decision, you must know the warriors who did this will be striking another casteless quarter tomorrow."

"How many live there?"

"I was told that one is home to a few hundred. But if the warriors are truly coming for all of the casteless in this province, that's only a fraction of how many will perish in all."

Thera was silent for a long time. The only sound was the buzzing of flies. Finally, she stood up and dusted her hands off on her coat.

"You know, Ashok, I've always looked out for myself. Nobody else was my problem. I survived because of that. When there was trouble I'd vanish into the crowd and never look back. How did I end up responsible for all these people? Was the bolt from heaven random, or did the Forgotten pick me for a reason?"

"I have no answers." It was hard to know the will of something they couldn't even begin to understand.

"Because if it was just chance that it hit me, then I'm not special. It could've picked any unlucky fool. I should do what I've always done. Run and hide. You know, the two of us could just walk away right now. Forget the gods, forget the Law. Leave the casteless to their fate. Let the fanatics have their rebellion. We could disappear and let everyone assume we're dead. It would be so easy."

The idea sounded appealing. He had thought of it himself a few times. Yet he doubted the gods had chosen her randomly, any more than mighty Angruvadal had chosen a little casteless blood scrubber to be its bearer on a whim.

"If the Forgotten picked me for a reason, then he wanted a child of house Vane. Vane, who once conquered the entire west, who are still the fiercest warriors in all of Lok. Not only that, he wanted the firstborn of Andaman Vane, leader, hero, *rebel*, who always did what he thought was right, no matter the cost." There was steel growing in her voice now. A decision had been made. "If the Forgotten chose such a woman to be his Voice it can only be because he desires a war like nothing the world has seen before."

"Have you started to believe your own prophecies then?"

"Maybe. Or maybe I'm just tired of running. But if the prophecies are true, that means the Forgotten also delivered to me the most dangerous man alive to be my sword. If I'm truly the voice of the gods, then I declare *I've had enough.* I want to see you treat these murderers like you used to treat lawbreakers. I want them to feel as powerless as the casteless have. I want the Black Heart to strike fear into the real criminals."

Ashok looked again at the bodies, and he too saw them as *people*. "So be it."

Thera turned to him and gave a command that would change everything.

"Ashok, go to war."

Chapter 9

Ashok twisted the sentry's head around so hard that his spine snapped like a twig. As he quietly lowered the body back into the tall grass, he saw the other sentry be engulfed by two Somsak raiders. They were ruthlessly efficient. A hand was clamped tight over his mouth so no warning could be shouted as knives rose and fell in the moonlight. Then that one too was gone from sight.

As the warrior beneath him shuddered and died, one leg twitching, Ashok sharpened his hearing and waited. There was no one else moving on this side of the encampment. From the sound of it, most of the others were asleep.

They'd not stationed too many men on watch, and most of those were on the opposite side of the camp, guarding the valuable horses. Their overconfidence had been expected. They were on a mission to exterminate vermin. Who was going to threaten them inside their own borders? The casteless? They'd probably laughed at that idea. Who needed sentries when you could smell them coming?

Their lack of discipline further angered Ashok. Didn't they know this was war?

Well, they would soon enough.

The big moon Canda was full and bright, so the Sons had used one of the sunken gullies to approach unseen. When they saw the sentries go down, the others rose from their hiding places and began skulking forward. They'd fought demons and wizards together, but tonight would be the first time they fought against other warriors. If all went according to plan, it wouldn't be much of a fight at all.

Toramana and his hunters were on unfamiliar ground, but they still moved with lethal silence, bows strung and arrows nocked. They spread out to engage the remaining sentries the instant the alarm was raised.

Satisfied everyone was ready, Ashok stood up, and walked directly into the warriors' camp. The Sons followed.

Shekar had estimated fifty by the tracks. Ashok had brought thirty. He would make up the difference through surprise and overwhelming violence.

The air was chilly, but there were only two small campfires going. From the smell, they were mostly burning dried dung they'd gathered along the way because wood was scarce. They cast little light, but many flickering shadows. All the better for their quick and grisly work.

There were only a few small tents, probably for the comfort of officers and the higher-status men, but most of the warriors just slept in bedrolls under the stars. Most would be deep asleep. He knew from personal experience that a day of hard travel and massacring villages tended to be tiring. Well, not Ashok, but he'd often seen the weariness among the warriors obligated to help him, and the distant stares as they tried to forget what they'd done.

Ashok drew his sword, slow and quiet. He went to the first bedroll, where a warrior was asleep on his back, and jabbed the sword directly into his heart. The warrior never woke up. He simply stopped breathing. The next was on his side, so Ashok cut his jugular. The noise he made was probably mistaken for wet coughing by anyone who was still awake.

The Sons fell upon the sleeping warriors as well. This wasn't battle. It was murder.

Ashok continued his murder walk all the way to the command tent. Behind him, the silent culling continued.

There was one junior nayak posted at the front of the command tent. He must have heard something, because curious, he stuck his head around the corner. Ashok promptly struck it from his shoulders.

The horses had smelled the blood and begun to whinny nervously. Some warriors woke up and immediately shouted an alarm, only to be immediately stabbed, slashed, or bludgeoned by the Sons who were already next to them.

The instant the sentries on the perimeter turned their heads to see what was going on, a dozen bowstrings thrummed.

Ashok stepped over the headless corpse and ducked inside the command tent. There were two men in here, and they must have been important enough that they'd even brought cots for them to sleep on. The Heart sharpened his vision. One of them had the look of an officer, middle aged and gone to fat. From the mask dangling by cords from the edge of his cot, the other was an Inquisitor. Ashok killed that one immediately.

The risaldar woke to the noise of his traveling companion gurgling and gasping, and then shrieked like a child when he saw the hooded form of Ashok looming over him. He grasped for his sword, leaning against the cot. Ashok simply yanked his sword from the Inquisitor's ribs and used it to slash the officer's fingers off.

"Quit your screaming," he ordered. Not that his were the only screams in the camp now that actual battle had begun.

The risaldar struggled to get off his cot, but Ashok kicked his ankle out from under him, hard enough to shatter the bone. Then he reached down and picked up the wailing man by his hair. If this one had ever been much of a fighter, he'd forgotten how long ago.

"Who are you?" the officer gasped as he clutched his ruined hand to his chest and tried to stand on one leg.

"I am Ashok Vadal."

The risaldar lost control of his bladder. "Spare me, Black Heart, please. What do you want?"

"I've come to take your horses, supplies, and lives. Order your men to surrender and I will remove the last one from my list."

By the time the sun rose, there were over thirty dead warriors in a pile—larger—but not too different from the pile they'd found yesterday. Higher status, but they'd taste the same to the birds. The remainder had been stripped of their uniforms, and were standing in a line, naked, barefoot, and shivering. Most of them were injured to one degree or another. Standing twenty paces behind them were the Wild Men with their bows, ready to dissuade the foolhardy.

Ashok walked in front of the line. Word of his identity had spread. The majority of the prisoners were afraid to meet his gaze, and instead they exchanged terrified glances. They knew of his reputation then. Good. That would save time.

"I'm willing to spare you, but in exchange you will return to your Thakoor to inform him that the casteless of this land are now under my protection. This indiscriminate killing of those who've broken no Law ends now."

As Ashok walked down the line, he found that most of the warriors were scared to death, but a few were seething with anger, the will to fight still in them. He thought about just killing those now to save him the effort in the future, but honestly, their rage meant they were the most honorable ones in the bunch.

"Tell your brothers that I have no quarrel with Akershan, but any warrior who raises his sword against the innocent from now on becomes my enemy." He stopped in front of one of the proud warriors until that man worked up the courage to look Ashok in his cold dark eyes. "Those, I will show as much mercy as they have given to the casteless."

That warrior looked down.

When he got to the end of the line, the officer he'd crippled was sitting in the dirt, hand wrapped in a bloody rag. He looked like he'd spent the rest of the night weeping.

"Warn your Thakoor that if he continues to harm these casteless, I will come for him personally, and visit carnage upon his house in measure equal to that which he has bestowed upon them. Now go and tell him."

The risaldar actually seemed baffled by that sudden command. "But you've left us no rations. We'll starve."

"You can graze like the sheep you are."

"You took our horses, took our boots even! You expect me to hop on one bare foot all the way to the great house?"

"If your men respect you, they will carry you. Unless you are the incompetent coward I suspect you to be, then they'll leave you for the buzzards and tell their rescuers you perished by my hand." As he said that, he looked back toward the brave ones, and from the subtle glance they shared, he bet this risaldar would be dead the instant the Sons were out of sight.

Ashok went back to the middle of the line. "As honorable warriors, you are obligated to obey the Law. I understand the difficult position this places you in. I have no easy answer for you. Start walking."

Most of the warriors did. A few, it took a moment for the reality of their situation to sink in. One who'd been bashed over the head by a club must have been having a hard time thinking at all, because he didn't move until he got shoved by a surly hunter. One warrior grudgingly helped up their officer.

There were two warriors of Akershan among the Sons of the Black Sword who had participated in the night's raid. Their uniforms were faded and worn thin after wintering in the swamp, but Ashok had asked them to wear them still. He'd wanted the prisoners to see that there were men of their house and caste among their enemies. Let them worry about how many more there might be.

One of the Akershani Sons had covered his head with a scarf, hiding his features in case he might be recognized, because he still had family in these lands, and didn't want them to be held accountable for his crimes. But the other was an orphan, siblings dead of a plague. With no loved ones left to be tortured by the Inquisition, he stood there, proud, as his former brothers marched past.

"Traitor," the officer snarled.

"You abandoned your gods and lick the Capitol's boots, butchering unarmed women on behalf of the Inquisition, while the Sons of the Black Sword have battled wizards and demons and won. Which of us is the real traitor?"

"There's no such thing as gods, you fool. What's your name, boy, so I can sic the masks on you?"

"Ongud Khedekar dar Akershan, and I no longer fear your Law, you son of a whore." The young warrior raised his voice so all the prisoners could hear. "Heed me, brothers. The Forgotten has returned. I've heard his voice. I've seen his might. We are the Sons of the Black Sword! You can either join our cause or stay out of the way. If you don't, Ashok Vadal will end you all!"

Ashok scowled. He would have to say something to the men about using his name in such a manner. It was one thing to kill the enemies of Thera's god, but it was another thing to be used as a recruiting tool for him.

As he watched the defeated depart, Ashok was joined by his two junior officers.

"We should've killed them all when we had the chance," Shekar muttered.

"Perhaps." That had been his initial inclination. Ashok wasn't used to explaining himself to anyone, but if he was killed, then it would fall on them to finish the mission. "Yet Thera wished for this house to taste fear. By the time these survivors are found crossing this sea of grass, they'll be sunburned, dehydrated, with feet blistered and bleeding. Let these proud warriors be seen made into pathetic wretches."

"And even with that, they'll be seen as the *lucky ones*," Eklavya chuckled. "Assuming they don't come across a casteless mob they've chased from their quarters along the way, because then they'll never be seen or heard from again."

"I've no love for the non-people." Shekar spit on the ground. "But that would be a downright poetic end for this bunch, getting their throats cut by fish-eaters."

Eklavya gaped at him. "How can you insult the chosen people? The Keeper of Names had declared the casteless to be the true descendants of mighty Ramrowan. They're the ones who'll eventually defeat all the demons!"

"Then they'd better step up and start acting the part, buncha weak-armed cowards. I'll gut whoever the general says needs gutting, but if we're to bleed for the fish-eaters, they'd better be willing to bleed for themselves."

"One of the prophecies says that when the time comes, the Forgotten will deliver weapons into their hands, sufficient to overthrow the Capitol."

"Enough," Ashok said. Keta and Thera could hammer out their doctrine and leave him out of it. He had no time for legends of heroes falling from the sky when there was work to be done. "We'll take their horses, but leave a few hunters to guard the captured supplies and pack animals until the main column catches up. We've work to do."

"Where to next, General?"

He was no tactician. Protectors normally worked alone, or in small units, and even when they were functioning as part of a larger force, they usually roamed about doing whatever they felt like. Yet, he recalled the lessons of Sword Master Ratul. *The best time to inflict damage upon your opponent is before he knows you are there.* An army was bigger, but the principle remained the same.

The Inquisitor's orders had been left in the risaldar's tent. Ashok had read them and studied the map. On the afternoon of the twenty-eighth of Phalguna, today's date, three paltans were to converge on the slums of Dhakhantar. It was one of the bigger towns in the region, with a large casteless quarter that had grown up around their coal mines. Since it was notorious for harboring rebels, the warriors had wanted to surround and then strike with overwhelming force. This paltan would not be arriving, but that left two more to be dealt with.

The Sons had marched all day, then run until midnight to catch up with these warriors. They were tired, and would be outnumbered three to one, but they wouldn't have an opportunity like this again.

"We ride for Dhakhantar."

Chapter 10

~~~~~~~~~~

They crested the eastern rise and found the town of Dhakhantar spread across the valley floor below them.

Ashok signaled for a halt so the rest could catch up. Most of them were from the warrior caste and were fine riders. However, those from the worker caste had been abused by the pace, and the poor swamp hunters had never been on a horse before. For them the morning had been a terrible experience atop unfamiliar beasts. Toramana had already fallen off his mount twice.

The casteless quarter was easy to pick out. It was the shanty town on the north side of the valley. It had sprung up below the gaping holes in the hillside that had to be the coal mines. Luckily they'd made good time, so the quarter wasn't on fire yet.

Between the casteless quarter and the town itself was a bustling worker district of factories and brick buildings whose purpose was a mystery to Ashok. Smoke belched from tall stacks as the workers went about their industrious tasks.

On the west side of the valley was a warriors' camp, only it was far bigger than the one they'd just raided. There had to be over a hundred soldiers already there. The other two paltans had arrived. They had just been waiting for this one before beginning their attack.

"Ongud, to me," Ashok called.

The Akershani warrior rode up beside him. Ongud was a round-faced and squint-eyed young man, who seemed possessed with great enthusiasm. "Yes, General?"

"Have you been here before?"

"I've only passed through. Those of us from Akershan who joined the Sons are from a vassal house to the south."

"It'll have to do. Does this city have warriors stationed in it?"

"Only a handful to keep order. The main barracks are out of Chakma, a city a few days from here. This is mostly a worker town, only exists because there's a mighty lot of coal here. The number of warriors stationed here might've changed since last year though. Word is this place hides many of the faithful."

Being infested with rebels was why the warriors had sent three full paltans to handle it. Ashok stared at the opposing force on the far side of the valley. Someone of great importance had to be leading it, because they'd erected a rather impressive command tent. Easily five times the size of the humble one he'd invaded last night. He could see a commander's flag atop it but wasn't familiar with the heraldry.

"Whose symbol is that?"

Ongud squinted. "I'm sorry, General. I can barely

see the tent from here and it's big as a house. They've got to be a mile away."

"The flag is three red stars over a green field."

"The gods have given you the eyes of a hawk!"

"The gods have given me nothing. What I have in sight I lack in patience. Who is it, Nayak?"

"Sorry. That's the phontho of the Chakma garrison himself."

A high-status man made a valuable hostage. "Excellent."

"He'll be traveling with a reinforced paltan, probably seventy or eighty men, heavy cavalry, lance and bow, all very good on horseback. We destroyed Chakma 3rd Paltan. So the other one will be the 2nd or 4th, horse infantry. Sorry, in the Akershani warrior caste that means they ride to battle, but usually fight on foot. They'll be spearmen more than likely."

"Then we'll engage them inside the casteless quarter." Then Ashok grew curious why a lowly junior nayak would know so much about an entirely different garrison. "What was your obligation?"

"I wanted to be cavalry, like my father, but there was some suspicion that I was a believer in the Forgotten... Which was correct, but—"

"Spit it out, Ongud. There's no shame in any obligation. Every man has his place."

"I was a mere logistics clerk, sir. All I did was keep track of storehouse inventories and supply lines."

Akershan was a vast place, but resource poor. Soldiers can't eat grass and armies ran on their stomachs. Ongud thought of himself as less because his caste had put him in a position with little chance for glory. Only he knew all about their enemies' most vulnerable systems. The *gods* hadn't given him superior vision—that had come from the Heart of the Mountain—but maybe they did give gifts after all.

"We will speak more about this later. Your knowledge is extremely valuable. Try not to die during the coming battle."

Ongud swallowed hard. "Yes, sir."

Their poorer riders had finally caught up. The swamp hunters looked terribly uncomfortable. They were going to hate this next part.

"Shekar, raise the banner."

Being a rather straightforward sort, Ashok wasn't inclined to deception. But that was what he had Somsak for. It had been Shekar's idea to fly the stolen banner of the paltan they had just defeated. Their enemy was expecting another force to join them. He'd give them a force all right.

A cold wind was blowing through the valley. It made strange patterns in the grass. He waited until he saw a commotion in the other camp. They had been spotted. Surely a phontho would have someone with a spyglass, so they'd be able to make out the banner of 3rd Paltan.

"Sons of the Black Sword." Ashok raised his voice so all of them could hear him over the wind. "The enemy is under the mistaken impression that we are their reinforcements. The phontho will expect us to wait for his signal before beginning our attack. Instead, he will see us charge directly into the caste-less quarter. He will believe that we're trying to steal the honor of striking first and will rush to catch up. Warriors of such status do not like being insulted by upstart risaldars."

"They'll be running into something a whole lot worse than insults!" Shekar shouted.

"They're expecting casteless, not men who've slain a demon," Eklavya said. "We'll trounce them so hard that Risaldar Jagdish will hear about our victory all the way in Vadal and smile with pride."

"From atop his pile of treasure!" Shekar finished for him.

The men laughed. Despite the odds and their exhaustion, they were in high spirits. That was good. Ashok wasn't used to taking into consideration the morale of others, but he was trying.

"We will be waiting for them. Casteless quarters are packed tight. Dismount, let your horses run free to add to the confusion. Use the terrain to funnel their superior numbers. Do not attempt to follow me. You will not be able to keep up and you'll only get hurt. Stick to your havildar. Follow their commands. Archers on Shekar. Armor on Eklavya."

"Try not to fall off until we get there," Shekar told the flustered Toramana.

"We will not let you down, Warrior!" Toramana shouted back. "The gods will keep my ass seated upon this animal, or I am not chief of the Wild Men!"

"Give no quarter. Break them utterly. Ride, Sons!" Ashok kneed his already exhausted mount, but it still leapt forward. *Ride!*

Down the hill and across the plain, the Sons tore toward Dhakhantar. Soft earth was thrown high by their hooves. Akershani horses were fast and eager to run. As cavalry mounts they were second only to the massive black beasts of Zarger. Their charge made a sound like thunder. The warriors bellowed their war cries. The workers and hunters just hung on for dear life.

Across the valley, the other camp burst into activity. Considering the time of day, their arrival had probably interrupted the phontho's lunch. As they closed the distance, he could see the enemy soldiers rushing about, grabbing weapons and saddling mounts. They thought they were in a race for bragging rights. They didn't realize they were about to enter a fight for their survival.

He nudged his horse straight for the center of casteless quarter. The untouchables must have realized something bad was happening with so many soldiers camped outside, because there was no one in the open. Many frightened eyes were peering through doorways or tears in the fabric of their walls. They were all hiding inside so as to not draw the warriors' ire, and they immediately ducked down when they saw Ashok looking their way.

As soon as the Sons were between the ragged gray homes, Ashok leapt off his still galloping horse, skidded to a stop, and bellowed, "Bring me the overseer of this quarter!"

The Sons rode in behind him and dismounted. His havildars took in the layout of the quarter, and then began barking orders. Horses were slapped on the rump and sent running. Depending on how the battle went, there would either be plenty of spare mounts around at the end of this battle to claim, or they wouldn't be needing rides at all.

The place smelled like coal and shit. A hushed silence had fallen over the quarter, but in the distance, the workers' district sounded of hammering and steam whistles—they were too industrious to stop their labors just because a small army was camped nearby.

Then a horn sounded. The enemy was on the way.

"Come out, overseer. Time is short. We're not here to kill you. We're here to protect you."

A tiny casteless man ran around one of the tents with a long pole in his hand. "For the Forgotten!" He went to one knee and pointed the pole toward Ashok. The end of it was capped in metal, and from the way it was wobbling around, it must have been very heavy.

"Are you the overseer here?" Ashok wasn't sure what the little casteless was doing, so he started walking toward him.

There was a sharp *crack*. The puddle next to Ashok's boot suddenly erupted in a geyser.

Ashok didn't even need to say the word. Both the Sons of the Black Sword and the Wild Men had fought wizards before. They simply reacted. Several arrows and crossbow bolts flew through the haze of white smoke to pierce the casteless. He flopped into the mud with a splash, pierced in several places.

As the droplets rained down on him, Ashok thought, *Fortress magic?* Such things were a terrible crime. Its presence also meant the warriors were right and this place was infested with rebels. That made Ashok annoyed, and tempted him to leave these fools to their fate.

But he had orders... They might be fools, but they were his fools now. So he raised his voice loud enough the entire quarter could hear. "I am Ashok Vadal, you imbeciles. I am here to save your stupid lives. Warriors are coming from the west to kill you. Stay out of my way so I can kill them first!"

He heard their panicked whispers as they spoke his casteless name. *Fall.* At times it seemed like every untouchable in the world knew about him, though in their version he was one of them who'd taken an ancestor blade, and then been raised up by the gods to be their avenger. But once the reality of his words sank in, a multitude sprang from their hiding places and began fleeing in every direction.

Ashok drew his sword and started across the quarter. From the sound of hooves, the warriors were in the process of charging across the valley. In the open, they would have the advantage in mobility and massed archers, but in the cramped and disorderly confines of the casteless quarter, chaos would reign.

He shouted at his havildars. "Let them enter, then engage."

Shekar was right behind him. He was grinning from ear to tattooed ear. "Was it like this when you went to fight us in Jharlang, General?"

"I had an ancestor blade then. Now I have you."

"Not a good trade, that!"

"Take the archers, fall back behind Eklavya's men. Look for targets of opportunity. Hit and run."

"That is what we do best." The Somsak signaled for his men to follow him as he broke away.

The quarter didn't have streets. There were no straight lines in a place like this. The casteless either lived in the round felt tents, and these were the soggiest, dirtiest, ragged things he'd ever seen, or they lived in huts made of whatever building materials the workers had thrown out, like cracked mud bricks and discarded sacks. Filthy streams ran through between the homes. Chickens clucked and pigs squealed.

Eklavya Kharsawan was beside him in the red lamellar plate of his house. Every man with him was wearing at least leather and chain, and even the worker-caste Sons were wearing armor they'd looted from the Lost House or the stores of Chattarak. In addition to the swords at their sides and shields on their backs, they were carrying spears, battle axes, or war hammers. And they'd spent the last few months being trained relentlessly by Jagdish and sparring against Ashok. The Sons were certainly not the feeble and half-starved opposition the warriors would be expecting.

Most of the untouchables were fleeing, but a few of the brave ones were staying in place. They watched the Sons march by, and some began to chant, *Fall, Fall, Fall.* Ashok saw them picking up tools that could be used as weapons, like hay scythes and shovels. Then they got in line behind the Sons. They were wide eyed, terrified, and out of their element, but the Forgotten's warrior was here. Why wouldn't they fight? How could they lose with the gods on their side? The whole situation made Ashok very uncomfortable, and they'd only just begun to violate the Law today.

There was a great deal of noise and furor as the Akershani warriors entered the opposite side of the quarter. Ashok could feel the vibration through the ground. In their eagerness to strike first, the heavy cavalry hadn't bothered to dismount. Casteless screamed as they were crushed beneath hooves. Arrogant, they intended to boldly crash right through the whole slum. They would meet here, halfway through the quarter, in terrain which would most favor the Sons.

Ashok lifted one hand and made a motion for his men to take cover. They immediately complied, ducking into tents or crouching behind crumbling walls. The casteless *volunteers* were too dim to know what that sign meant, so he snapped, "Hide, fools!"

As the Sons spread out and prepared their ambush, they could still hear the angry shouting of warriors, and the death cries of the casteless. Many would perish because he'd chosen to stop here, but all of them would die if the Sons were defeated.

Then the warriors of Akershan were upon them.

Even deprived of the ability to feel fear, Ashok could fully understand why heavy cavalry were so intimidating to a man on the ground. They shook the world. They used the strongest horses, dressed in barding which made them look even bigger, and the warriors atop them were armed with lances which gave them incredible reach. With such an impressive thing thundering toward them, it was no wonder that even the most fanatical gods-inspired rebels turned and ran.

And the warriors gave chase, riding right past the hidden and waiting Sons. He waited until several of them had gone by.

"Now!" Ashok roared as he stepped from around a tent and swung his sword at a horse's leg.

If he'd still had mighty Angruvadal, he could have removed all four of the animal's limbs in one blow, but the blade of regular steel merely sheared through flesh and clipped one thick bone, but it was enough for the speeding beast to trip. Horse and rider went down, crashing and sliding into a felt home that crumpled around it. Immediately Eklavya stepped around the animal's thrashing legs and punched a hole through the downed rider's helmet with the spike on the back of his hammer. Blood squirted from around the cap.

Five riders went down fast. The ones behind them realized too late that they should've dropped their lances before entering the tight confines of the casteless quarter, when they couldn't turn to meet the Sons who were rushing at them from all sides. Horses reared and kicked as their riders were speared or hooked and yanked from the saddle by pole arms. One Akershani stood up in his stirrups and began shouting a warning to the riders behind him, but a Wild Man's arrow struck him in the mouth.

"Hound them from the quarter, but do not chase them into the open," Ashok ordered Eklavya. "I must go." Then all he could hope was that Jagdish's lessons had stuck, and his havildars would know what to do, because in a situation like this, Ashok was far too valuable a weapon to be wasted giving commands. He needed to range ahead, spreading chaos.

Ashok picked a narrow path and ran, using the Heart of the Mountain to give him incredible speed, leaping over debris and cowering casteless. He paralleled the path the heavy cavalry had taken. There were more spears and the plumes of helms poking above the shacks to the side, and once he reached a spot where the warriors seemed unafraid and unaware, he vaulted over the roof of a shack, launching himself at the enemy.

The first rider never even saw death coming. It was as if Ashok had fallen from the sky, like Ramrowan of old. The horse went galloping off, headless body still in the saddle.

Ashok hit the muddy ground, rolling, and came right back up to his feet to meet the next surprised warrior. That one tried to ride him down, but Ashok sidestepped, called upon the Heart to provide inhuman strength to his limbs, and struck the animal in the head with his fist. The thin metal chanfron designed to protect the horse's face bent around his knuckles.

The animal collapsed. The rider was flung down. Ashok stepped over the struggling man and jammed his sword deep into the warrior's back. With a twist the spine was severed, and another died.

He heard dismounted soldiers moving a few alleys over, the metallic clank of weapons, the creak of armor, the splashing of boots in mud, and then the screams as casteless were yanked from their pathetic homes. Ashok ducked into the felt tent which separated him from his next victims. It was dim and musty inside. There was a woman and casteless children huddled in the corner, terrified that he'd come to massacre them. He knew that look well, because he'd seen many faces like theirs before, thin, dirty, and afraid. Only this time he was here to save them, not destroy them.

Before they began pleading for their lives and crying, he whispered, "I am Fall." Then he put his finger to his lips. "Shhh."

The young mother nodded fearfully.

The opposite side of the tent lifted as an Akershani warrior stuck his head inside. He glanced over the huddled children dismissively, but when he saw their mother, he grinned and began to move inside. "Hello, little lamb." Then he caught sight of Ashok crouched there, waiting, and before he could cry out, a sword tip was driven through his eye socket and deep into his brain. The only sound he made was a pathetic squeaking noise, before Ashok wrenched the steel free and dropped him in an unmoving heap.

"Stay down. It will be over soon," he assured the casteless family as he moved past the corpse. He slightly parted the felt with his free hand, saw a multitude of warriors rampaging, and picked his next targets.

"Risaldar!" An Akershani warrior approached at a run. Blood was running down his sleeve. "There's resistance ahead."

"They're only casteless," a man out of Ashok's sight snapped back. "Just kill them."

"The vanguard was ambushed and are being slaughtered! These are real warriors."

Ashok was pleased. The phontho's heavy cavalry had been prideful. They'd thought they would be able to ride down starving casteless with impunity. Instead they'd found themselves in a twisted maze of shacks, where their horses made them clumsy, and their height made them easy targets for lurking archers.

Before the puzzled officer could formulate new orders, Ashok came out of the tent swinging.

Chapter 11

〰〰〰

The phontho was confused and displeased. "Give me that." He snatched the spyglass from Bharatas' hand and put it to his eye. "Why are they flailing around like that? What are they doing down there?"

"It appears our men are retreating, sir."

"I can see that, but why? Are they reforming? I told them to push straight through that slum until they came out the other side. Damn that upstart 3rd Paltan, stealing my glory."

The phontho didn't see it yet, but Bharatas did. What was happening below wasn't orderly. It wasn't maneuvering to a superior position. It was a rout. It was death and defeat. The scattering men and riderless horses fleeing the casteless quarter were bloody and afraid. *How?* They were fighting fish-eaters. This hadn't even been a mission worthy of warriors. This made no sense, but they were clearly losing.

The phontho's eyes had gone blurry in recent years, so even with the spyglass it would take him a minute to realize the awful truth, which was a minute they might not have.

So Bharatas caught the attention of the other bodyguards, and then gave them a few silent raider hand signals. They would be prepared to retreat from the camp or counterattack, whatever the phontho willed once he grasped the situation. He dared not say it aloud though, because the phontho was a prideful and angry man, and he didn't like when his subordinates came to conclusions faster than he did. Which was often now, since he'd become doddering in his old age.

It was only the command and support staff left in the camp. Most of the warriors had ridden, fast and disorganized, into the quarter at the phontho's hasty orders. Their illustrious leader himself had stayed behind with his personal bodyguards. Truth be told, their leader should have retired a long time ago, because riding a horse at anything faster than a trot made his back ache for days so badly he could barely walk, so he'd ridden in a cart all the way from Chakma to get here. Which for a warrior of Akershan was downright shameful, but Bharatas wasn't of status, and the phontho was of high status, so nobody cared about one bodyguard's opinion, even if he was one of the most accomplished killers in Akershan.

"What is Risaldar Odgerel doing?" the phontho muttered. "Why is he riding back here by himself?"

Bharatas looked at his commander. The spyglass was shaking badly in his thin, bony hands as the old man squinted through it. Then he followed the path of the glass, until he saw a lone rider heading their way, galloping hard through the tall grass. The only reason the phontho's watery eyes had been able to identify Odgerel's horse was because the 2nd Paltan's risaldar rode a magnificent white stallion so tall and muscular it stood out from the others. Odgerel came from a high-status line, so he had access to the best stables in Akershan.

"May I, see that, sir?" Bharatas risked the phontho's wrath by reaching for the brass tube, but he had an obligation to protect the old bastard, so he needed to see for himself. It took him a moment to find the rider on the white stallion again through the narrow, magnified field of view. "Oceans."

"What is it? Is Odgerel injured?"

"That's not Odgerel." What their phontho hadn't been able to see was that the rider atop Odgerel's stolen horse wasn't wearing the armor of Great House Akershan, but rather a drab worker's coat, painted fresh red, and the blood-soaked maniac was heading straight for them. "Sukhbataar, Artag, intercept that rider."

The other bodyguards were already atop their horses, so by the time he handed the glass back to the phontho they'd begun riding downhill toward the interloper. Each of the phontho's personal guards was an extremely proficient combatant, chosen for his skill with horse, bow, and sword, so this wouldn't take too long.

But just in case . . . He put one gentle hand on his commander's sleeve. There was almost no meat left beneath the fabric. It was just gristle over bone. "Perhaps we should go to your cart, Phontho."

"What?" he sputtered. "How dare you? No real warrior would ever flee from non-people! They're starving in rags and don't even have swords! They don't even eat meat, but subsist on wheat gruel and are covered in fleas! And—"

"Of course you are right, sir." Bharatas sighed. Since he'd already stood in as the old man's proxy in four duels since he'd been picked for this obligation, he knew how quickly the phontho was to declare that offense had been taken. "However, if you stand atop your cart, the added elevation will give you a better view of the entire battlefield."

"Oh . . . Good idea. Very well then."

Bharatas signaled for the last remaining bodyguard to escort their illustrious leader to his cart and to hitch up the horses. Then he turned back to the crisis below.

By the age of thirteen Bharatas had been considered one of the finest swordsmen in Chakma. By fourteen he had survived his first raid into mountainous Dev. By fifteen he had earned an award for valor during a raid deep into Kharsawan territory. There had been a dozen more medals and ribbons since, and his chest wasn't wide enough to wear them all. He was only twenty now, but already the highest ranked among the phontho's handpicked bodyguards, and deadly enough that the older men never questioned his instincts. The phontho kept picking stupid duels, but Bharatas kept winning them, which meant he would be trapped in this obligation until his master died of old age, because the old fool would never retire.

Truthfully, he didn't mind the duels, for Bharatas was a gifted killer.

Right then his instincts were telling him that something was terribly wrong.

As Sukhbataar and Artag closed on the lone maniac charging their camp, they split wide, one going left, the other right, both of them readying their bows. All Akershani horseman knew how to shoot on the move. Most of them were as familiar with the feel of the animal beneath them as their own legs, so it wasn't even challenging. *Mobility and accuracy.* That slogan was embroidered on the bottom of the Chakma garrison's flag.

The poor suicidal fool coming at them on the stolen stallion didn't even have a bow. With nothing but a sword in one hand, he wouldn't even have a chance... Except Odgerel was a very accomplished combatant, second in the garrison only to Bharatas, which begged the question how had this maniac gotten ahold of his horse?

Akershani bows were short, but made of laminated horn and required great strength to pull, which generated great velocity. Once they closed within seventy yards, Sukhbataar let fly. The rider simply ducked. When Artag launched his arrow the rider spun his sword and knocked it from the air.

Surely that was a fluke.

They continued to close the distance. Two more arrows flew, one right after the other, both aimed at the horse this time, but the rider stood in his saddle, smacked one aside, and then lightning quick, turned and cleaved the arrow on the other side in two.

"How..." But Bharatas quickly overcame his hesitation and shouted in the direction the phontho had been taken. "Get the commander out of here! Wizard incoming!" And then he ran for where Khurdan was hitched nearby.

While Artag wheeled his mount about and spurred it to run for camp, Sukhbataar drew his sword, let out a mighty battle cry, and charged directly at the rider. *"Akershan!"*

They thundered at each other. Sukhbataar raising his saber overhead, the intruder leaning way over in the saddle, sword held out to the side, like some Zarger trick. The stranger suddenly rose in the stirrups. Blades flashed as the horses passed, less than a foot between them.

They parted. Bharatas couldn't tell what happened. But then Sukhbataar's sword arm *fell off*. His horse reared as its neck was suddenly drenched in hot blood, and it wasn't until Sukhbataar fought to not be thrown from the saddle that he discovered his hand was missing and began to scream.

The rider was still coming.

Artag turned back in the saddle, drawing his bow to fire at his pursuer, but the rider had closed some of the distance. This time when the arrow was launched it was effortlessly struck aside again, but in the same smooth motion, he let the sword fly from his hand. Bharatas watched in horror as the sword spun through the air and impaled Artag through the back.

That was impossible.

His friend seemed surprised to see several inches of steel sticking out his chest, but then he toppled from the saddle, dead. He landed on his face, the hilt of the sword sticking up from the grass like some manner of burial marker. The rider didn't even slow as he leaned down to snatch the sword from Artag's corpse as he galloped by.

What manner of witchcraft is this? But Bharatas pushed his fear aside, jumped onto his horse, and turned her to meet the demon shaped like a man. "Defend the phontho!" he shouted to the warriors remaining in camp, already knowing that since most of them were the political appointments of a vain man, they would be useless in a fight. If anyone was going to stop this madman, it was him.

The rider pulled on the reins, slowing as he entered camp. Though dressed as a common worker, this was obviously no tiller of the soil. He was tall and strong, with a stare sharp enough to cut the grass, cruel as the plains, and covered in fresh blood. He had to be warrior caste, and not just born into it, but molded by its very precepts, into something hard as iron. The stranger saw Bharatas, a proud and obviously skilled combatant waiting to challenge him, and didn't seem concerned in the least. Instead, he shouted so that all could hear, "You are already defeated. Blow your horn. Sound your retreat. Save what lives you can."

"Never!" Bharatas bellowed. "Identify yourself, Warrior!"

"I am not warrior caste. I am Ashok Vadal."

It was like an icy hand reached into his body, grabbed hold of his stomach, and twisted. Everyone in the world had heard of Black-Hearted Ashok and his sword that could murder armies. He wouldn't have believed the man was who he claimed to be, if he'd not just seen him effortlessly drop two of their house's finest. Bharatas suddenly felt cold and ill.

Their leader was rolling away in a cart. His command staff didn't know what to do, and none of them showed any inclination to rise to the occasion either. The camp was quiet, except flags whipping in the wind.

As his stolen horse danced nervously, Ashok reached up and wiped the blood from his face with one sleeve. But there was too much blood. Vainly smearing it around only made him look even more terrifying.

"Sound the horn, young Akershan. I've killed enough of you for one day. Though your attack has already failed, isolated pockets of your men still fight within the quarter. They will continue butchering casteless until they are stopped, and that I cannot allow. The casteless are under my protection now."

Bharatas didn't know what to do. He'd trained his whole life, and fought in many duels and battles, but how did one prepare to fight a legend? His body wanted to run, except surrender was for cowards, and Bharatas was warrior caste, where death was preferable to shame. So he kneed Khurdan into a charge.

"Or do not. It is your choice." Ashok thumped his stirrups against the stallion and clicked his tongue. "Go."

Across the grass, they rode toward each other. Both horses were bouncing, throwing up tufts of soft earth behind them. Bharatas knew his steed so well that he steered Khurdan with only the gentle pressure of his legs, guiding her toward their target. Once his saber was in hand, all his fears were forgotten. There was only the movement and the moment. That was why he was the best swordsman in Chakma.

Only as they got closer, Bharatas realized something. Ashok was looking through him as if he wasn't even there. The expression on his face was detached. Bharatas' defiance didn't even rate anger from the former Protector. It wasn't that Ashok couldn't see him, but rather that he was just a minor obstacle in pursuit of his goal, like a stump to be ridden around as part of a much longer journey. Bharatas would be dispatched without thought.

That unnerved him. And then it offended him.

They passed. He struck. Ashok reflexively brushed

the attack aside with the flat of his blade, and Bharatas grimaced as Ashok's sword turned into him. He felt the impact through the leather armor over his side, hard enough to lift him in the saddle, and nearly hard enough to fling him from Khurdan's back.

But he hung on, and with one easy hand guided Khurdan to wheel about to continue the fight. He stayed calm because that kept Khurdan calm. Ashok was turning back as well, but since he was on an unfamiliar and angry horse, was having to wrestle with Odgerel's fierce beast.

Fighting on horseback was different than fighting on foot. On the ground, you were in control, but in the saddle you had to depend on your horse to understand your will. You were partners. Khurdan had been Bharatas' primary mount for two years now, and they worked well as a team. She sensed his will. He pressed this advantage.

Yet even on an erratically bucking stallion, Ashok was such a good swordsman that it was no advantage at all. Their swords crossed again as the horses circled, trading blows, but dueling the Black Heart proved to be as much the nightmare as the stories made it out to be. Bharatas kept attacking, bringing his saber around in an arc, and then back the other way with the twist of his wrist, but Ashok avoided the steel as if it was nothing.

It was only by pure instinct that Bharatas flinched back to not get his throat cut by Ashok's counter. It was so close that the razor edge shaved the hairs from the bottom of his chin. But Khurdan bounded away, and there was a small bit of distance between the combatants for a moment.

"You are very skilled." Ashok seemed mildly surprised that his opponent wasn't dead yet.

Oh, he has noted me now. In any other context, having the greatest swordsman in the world give such a compliment would have been a warrior's proudest moment, but right then Bharatas was simply trying to stay alive.

Odgerel's horse had always been an aggressive one. He didn't even seem to care that he'd switched sides, just that he had gotten a chance to fight. He snorted and wheeled about, kicking wildly, bringing Ashok closer. The stallion crashed into Khurdan's flank, making the smaller mare stumble.

Ashok used that opportunity to knock Bharatas' protective saber down, and in a blur of steel that was too quick to track, the pommel of the Black Heart's sword came back up and hit him in the side of the head. It was the worst pain he'd ever felt, like lightning through his cracked skull. The world spun about, sky and grass, and then Bharatas landed hard, bouncing across the dirt.

Khurdan ran away. Thankfully both boots had come free of stirrups or he would've been dragged, a terrible, yet common way to die on the plains. All he could hear was a ring, like the vibration of a bell that refused to end. Bharatas tried to rise, but ended up flopping over on his side. Even though he could tell he was on the ground, everything seemed to still be spinning. He put one hand to his temple, and discovered that not only had his conical helmet been knocked off, but that his head was leaking blood. There was something dangling from his hair. He tried to pull it off, until he realized that the thing he was tugging at was a bit of his scalp come up from his skull, so he mashed it back down.

By the time he crawled through enough of the tall grass to see the camp, most of the command staff were already dead. And Ashok was dragging one man by the neck to where the phontho had left their paltan's horn. Bharatas still couldn't hear, but it was obvious from the puffed lips and crying eyes that the warrior gladly sounded the tones ordering a retreat.

He couldn't hear the sounds, but words were exchanged. The surrendered warrior pointed one trembling finger in the direction the phontho's cart had gone. It was said the Black Heart was without mercy, but he spared the life of the wretch who'd complied with his request, and simply left him there. Ashok climbed back onto Odgerel's horse and rode after their phontho, either to kill or capture him, Bharatas didn't know, and frankly, right then, was in too much pain to care.

Barely clinging to consciousness, Bharatas crawled deeper into the grass to hide before slipping into the dark.

Chapter 12

It only stood to reason that the farther one got from the Capitol, the fewer Inquisitors one would encounter. The foul masked agents of the Order of Inquisition were uniformly awful people, who had terrorized her, intimidated her into breaking the Law, hounded her from her home and her beloved Capitol Library, and forced her to live in hiding in the most dreadful of circumstances.

Thus Radamantha Nems dar Harban had been glad when Protector Karno had told her it was time to travel north.

Rada believed the reason the Inquisition sought to capture her was so that she could be used as leverage against Lord Protector Devedas, who loved her and planned to marry her once this mess was sorted out. Devedas had kept her in the dark about his plans—for her own safety of course—but she knew whatever vile plots the Inquisitors were up to would result in no good. She'd been snuck out of the

Capitol months ago, hidden at an awful stinking goat farm, and narrowly avoided being captured by bounty hunters only because Devedas had dispatched mighty Karno to watch over her.

She couldn't even begin to speculate how much harder they would search for her once they learned that she had in her possession something else that the Inquisition dearly wanted, an ancient artifact of black steel.

Senior Historian Vikram Akershan had told her the thing was called the Asura's Mirror, but it filled her with such a general sense of unease that she had trouble thinking of it as anything other than *the thing*. Black steel was the most potent magical substance in the world. Weapons forged from it could obliterate armies and cleave demons in half. Tiny fragments of black enabled wizards to do terrible and seemingly impossible things.

And the material it was made out of wasn't even why she was apprehensive about the thing, but rather what it *did*. Its original mission no one knew, but in the one brief demonstration she'd had of its power she'd seen that *something lived inside it*.

Intellectually, Rada knew that wasn't quite true. It wasn't a cage. More of a window, or a portal, or some such thing, but to where or who or what or how, she knew not. She'd never read about anything like this in the Library!

And if that wasn't bad enough, when Protector Karno had found out Vikram Akershan had given her the thing, he'd warned her to keep it well hidden, because if word got out that she had in her possession an item of such value, there would be no shortage of thieves who'd gladly murder them both for it.

So here she was, skulking toward Apura with a mysterious black-steel device stuffed into a satchel slung over her shoulder, hiding from Inquisitors and robbers and bounty hunters and who knew what else.

This was all Vikram's fault. The crafty old man was the one obligated to care for the cursed relic, not her. She was a valuable Archivist, not some over-rated Historian. To the oceans with that entire stuck up order! But Rada couldn't be too angry at him. The Inquisition was looking for Vikram too. They wanted to secure the mirror for themselves for some unknown, yet surely nefarious reason. Since their two rival orders were about as friendly as the cobra and the mongoose, the Inquisitors would never expect someone from the museum to entrust one of their artifacts to someone from the library.

Originally Vikram had asked her to take on his obligation should he be killed, but when he had been informed by his Astronomer friends that a great force of angry Inquisitors and their drafted warriors had shown up at the observatory demanding Vikram's whereabouts, he had rethought his original plan. Vikram and his family had fled one way, and she and Karno had gone the other. Karno had offered them his protection, but the Historian had said that he had other plans which he would not divulge.

"I've never been to Apura before, Karno."

"No offense intended, Librarian, but I'd assumed that you've not been many places besides the Capitol."

Rada sniffed, but it was in fact a fair assessment. Her father was the head of her Order. Her family seldom had a reason to leave the confines of the finest city in the world. She'd never wanted to live a life of adventure and would've been content to stay in the library the rest of her days.

Karno Uttara was slightly ahead of her, astride a truly gigantic horse. It looked like a pony beneath him because Karno was quite possibly the biggest man she'd ever known. Not fat though, not in the least. Karno was made of meat so solid he was more like a bull than a man. It seemed to her that he'd have been better off riding around on an elephant than a horse, but when she'd suggested an elephant to be a suitably impressive mount for the Protector, he had laughed aloud, and told her that her book learning did not always translate so well to the logistical issues of the real world. This had caused Rada's cheeks to flush, but she'd held her tongue, because yes, she had in fact once read a library book about the care and maintenance of elephants, so should've known better.

"Apura is a busy place," Karno told her. "Too many eyes for my taste. I don't intend to enter the city itself. Tonight we will camp. Tomorrow, we will skirt around the edge, avoiding checkpoints, and then take one of the trade roads north."

It was illegal to cross great-house borders without getting your traveling papers stamped, but Karno had already done similar sneaky things to get them out of the Zarger desert and into the hill country of Thao. As a Protector, all he had to do was flash the symbol of his office, the fanged and leering face of the Law, and he could go wherever he wanted. But people inevitably talked about encountering one of the rare Protectors, and word would surely get back to the Inquisitors.

"Though I understand the need and agree with

your caution, I'd been hoping we'd be able to stop in civilization, and eat a meal not killed by you immediately before. A real bath would be wonderful. I smell worse than my horse. I've not slept in an actual bed since we left Vikram's estate."

"Sleeping on the ground builds character," Karno said.

"It builds back aches and tick bites." As a daughter of the first caste, Rada had lived a life of comfort. The last few months had been painfully educational. She was actually rather proud of how many indignities she'd bore on this journey without complaint—she'd tried especially hard never to whine since Karno was so taciturn and stoic—but Apura *was right over there*. There were still too many trees in the way to see it yet, but she could hear the faintest sounds of civilization echoing through the hills. In fact, it sounded like . . .

Could it be? "Karno, is that music?"

She didn't know how, and neither Karno nor Devedas would ever share their order's secrets, but somehow a Protector's hearing, sight, and sense of smell were supernaturally good at times. Karno lifted his shaggy head for a moment, and then nodded. "Yes. You're probably only hearing the drums, but a great many bands are playing. There are hundreds of voices in song, probably in the streets from the echoes. Hmmm . . ." He looked back at her. "I had forgotten today's date."

"It's Holi!" Rada exclaimed. She had been riding across the miserable desert and then the chilly hills for so long that she'd not even realized the new year was upon them. Holi day was the biggest celebration in Lok. The Law granted every member of the three castes two days away from their obligated labors, one to prepare, and one to enjoy. Every Great House

celebrated it differently, but it was always a colorful festival of feasting and dancing. Even Rada, who
was normally very uncomfortable in the company of
people, enjoyed Holi.

However, the part she found most appealing right
then was the mandatory hospitality, which meant there
would be wonderful food everywhere, and she'd be
able to finally eat something other than whatever poor
animal Karno had managed to brain by throwing his
hammer at that day. "Karno, think of the food. We
must go into Apura."

Karno nodded toward their pack horse, where a
dead rabbit hung. "We have sufficient for tonight."

If she ate one more stringy, unseasoned hare, she
would simply die. "There will be cakes."

"It would not be prudent."

"There will be sweet yogurt." But she already knew
she was trying to tempt the untemptable.

Karno just frowned at her. Or she assumed he
frowned. His beard was so bushy after weeks without
care that she could only assume the expression by the
further squint of his already narrow eyes.

Rada sighed. She'd always thought of herself as an
unsociable and untalkative person, but she didn't hold
a candle to Karno. Over the last month she could
count their not immediately pertinent discussions on
the fingers of one hand. In the rare times he actually
engaged in idle conversation she learned that Karno
himself was a straightforward creature of pragmatism
and duty. Devedas, his lord—her lover—had commanded Karno to keep Rada safe, so that was what
he was going to do, no matter how terribly uncomfortable it might be.

They rode for a while down the trade road. She'd wondered why they'd seen so few other travelers all day, but it made sense now. They were all celebrating the new year. As their horses plodded along a vast lake came into view. This had to be the infamous Red Lake, which she'd read about in the history books. A great battle had once taken place upon these shores, and the lake had turned red from all the blood. She'd not realized just how much blood that indicated until she saw the real thing. Despite the grim name it was a never-ending blue, with brown mountains capped in white rising up all around it. The sight of so much water frightened her.

"It is like the ocean."

Karno chuckled. "It is nothing like the ocean. There hasn't been a demon this deep into the interior in a very long time. Allow the animals to drink and let's fill our canteens."

Of course Karno would be jaded. He was from a peninsula surrounded on three sides by hell and it was his Order's job to fight demons. Rada was from the Capitol, which had been built as far from the corrupting sea as possible. All of the Capitol's water came from mighty aqueducts. This was the biggest body of water she'd ever seen. As an educated woman, she knew that water was just an element, not the embodiment of evil as believed by those who followed an extremely literal interpretation of the Law. It wasn't water's fault demons lived in it. Still, she was so nervous that even her horse could tell, and the mare paused, hesitant to continue.

"It's fine, girl," Rada told her, even though she herself couldn't shake the feeling of unease which had come upon her. She dismounted—something she'd become exceedingly skilled at in recent weeks—and led her down the sandy bank. Despite her assurance to her steed, Rada still let her horse drink first, just in case a demon came exploding out of the depths.

Because the sun was setting, the reflection on the rippling surface made it so that she couldn't see the bottom more than a few feet away, yet no giant sea demons leapt out to consume them. Rada knelt down and filled her canteen. It was then that she realized she could see buildings farther down the shore. The outskirts of Apura were less than a mile away.

Karno knelt next to her, scooped up the icy melt, and drank from his cupped hands. He also saw what she was looking at. Karno may have been a stern man, but beneath that, he was not an unkind one. "I know these months have been difficult for you, Rada. If it were up to me, I would take the fight to the corrupt Inquisitors and end this once and for all."

"Only Devedas asked you not to."

Now it was Karno's turn to sigh. "I know not why. I've no head for the politician's games. But Devedas is my commander, so I obey. And he is my friend, so I trust him. He asked me to keep you safe. So I will... If it were not for this oath, I would go into Apura and bring you back a sack full of treats."

"I know, Karno. You keep me miserable, but only out of a sense of duty, like a kindly prison guard."

He chuckled. "Thank you." While the animals drank with great gulping sucking noises, Karno sat on a nearby rock. Even though they were close to the shore and it was nearly sundown, Rada was glad to sit for a moment. She'd read books about horsemanship, but books were insufficient to teach you just how sore riding made your legs and buttocks.

Large insects buzzed over the surface of the water. Karno must have decided the moment called for one of his rare conversations, because very surprisingly he said, "You know, I believe Devedas loves you very much."

It was not like Karno to speak of frivolous things like love. She thought Devedas truly did, but it was nice to hear it confirmed from an impartial witness. "As I love him."

"I told him it was foolish. Do not make that face at me, Librarian. It is not an insult to you. It was an insult to him. He let love get in the way of his obligation, which is why we suffer now. We are not supposed to become emotionally attached to those we protect for good reason. Yet, he is a man with few flaws. If a man must have flaws, I suppose loving a beautiful woman is a most understandable one."

Rada blushed. "I see once again why they call you Blunt Karno." But then she was curious. "You said few. What do you think his other flaws are?"

"Hmm... It is not my place to say."

"Karno, please. Once he retires from his obligation, we plan to marry. If he's a secret monster I'd rather know now." Not that she would believe Karno if he told her that anyway. Her experience with the opposite sex wasn't exactly exhaustive, but she'd found nothing in Devedas' character to suggest that he was low or mean.

"Nothing of that sort. He will surely treat you kind. Like most of us, he is only cruel toward those who break the Law, and that's not because he enjoys it, but because it is required." Karno cleared his throat and spit on the ground. "No. Devedas' problem is that he's ambitious. He tries to hide it, but Devedas has a desire for achievement that is rare even among great men."

"Why? That's not a bad thing at all."

"Determination itself is not. Young Devedas lost everything. His house. His family. The ancestor blade which he believed would eventually be his, broken, and his father driven mad from shame, hurled himself off a cliff into the sea. Devedas' only inheritance was a bad reputation. No house wanted a child of bad omen, so he was given to the Protectors, where he worked his way to the rank of master, a rare achievement indeed."

"Then his ambition is a good thing."

"The Law says every man has his place for a reason. On a fundamental level, Devedas is unable to accept this. By his nature, he will never be content with his current station, no matter how vital it is, but instead will always be looking for more. That is how he earned his scar." Karno ran one finger across his face.

"Devedas was cut by the black-steel blade of Ashok Vadal! There is no shame in losing a duel to an ancestor blade," Rada said reflexively, trying to defend her man's honor.

"Of course not. The shame comes not from losing that duel, but from the desire which caused it. I was there. A new obligation, only a boy, but I watched that fight. That prideful, pointless, inevitable duel. Ambition can make a man great. It can even make him the Lord Protector, but too much ambition blinds a man to dark paths..." Karno trailed off. "Enough. I will speak no more ill of my superior. We are all imperfect somehow, especially me. Despite his flaws, Devedas is one of the two best men I have ever known."

"The second?" Rada was afraid she already knew the answer, and that the man she loved was hunting him now.

"Ashok Vadal. Though such a statement of fact is not a popular one to make nowadays, it remains true. He saved my life many times. But I misspoke. Ashok is no man."

"Of course not, he's a casteless criminal!"

"No. Ashok is a force of nature. He was the Law made flesh and bone. We all aspired to be like him, and any Protector who claims otherwise now is lying. What Ashok has become? I don't know. The only thing I do know with a grim certainty is that Devedas will find him and kill him."

"Good," Rada snapped.

"Perhaps."

The two of them were silent for a long time, as the sky turned orange, the lake glowed, and the music of a new year's celebration drifted across the water. In a way the view was calming. It was nearly enough to make her not fear the water.

Karno changed the subject to lighter fare. "Before I was obligated to the Order, back in Uttara, on Holi my mother would make sweet milk balls."

"How do you make a ball of milk?"

"You fry it. I mean it's like cheese, but golden and covered in syrup. Very good. Protectors are not supposed to serve in their homeland, to prevent bias in our judgment, so I've not had one in a long time. Eighteen years I've been a Protector, but I can still remember the taste... Or at least I imagine I do. Should I ever return, I wonder if the real thing would live up to the memories?"

Since she'd never before heard Karno sound nostalgic, Rada decided to try swaying him again. "You know, you might be a foot taller than everyone in Apura, but I'm not. I'm so dirty they'd think I'm the poorest worker. If anyone asks, I'll say I'm a farmer of goats. I'm practically an expert on that subject now. With all the strangers sure to be in town for the parties, I could sneak in and—"

He held up one big hand. "I will save us both time and stop you there." Karno abruptly stood, his weekly allowance for idle conversation used up. "Come. I remember a good place nearby to set up camp."

They led their horses away from the lake, which made Rada breathe a little easier, and up the hillside toward the trade road.

Unexpectedly Karno stopped. "There's eyes upon us."

Rada looked around. The shadows were deepening. There were a thousand places someone could be hiding behind trees or rocks. "Where?"

Karno didn't answer the question. Instead he took his war hammer from where it hung on his saddle and placed it over one broad shoulder. "Rada, get on your horse."

"What's—"

"Do as I say."

She got her foot in the stirrup and climbed up, noticing as she did, that her horse was being oddly skittish all of a sudden. The mare had sensed something as well.

"Be silent. Follow my orders without question."

Karno never got upset. His voice remained calm, yet for the first time since she'd met the fearsome man, she detected an unfamiliar emotion. This was a hero who'd taken on assassins armed with only an armful of books, who'd she seen fell a Zarger warhorse with a casual hammer toss. What in the world could make Karno *afraid*?

"If I tell you to ride, ride as hard as you can into Apura, then dismount and try to disappear among the crowd. Find a place to hide until I come for you. Do you understand?"

Rada nodded vigorously. Any unseen thing that made Karno nervous was enough to leave her utterly terrified.

Karno then walked with purpose up the road, and planted himself in the middle, staring at a particularly dark thicket of trees and bushes. She couldn't tell what he was looking at... *There.* A high branch shook, as something leapt soundlessly down from it. No man could have climbed that high unseen or dropped without breaking their legs.

What was stalking them? To worry Karno so, maybe it was a demon? Only the lake was to their backs. Were they standing between a demon and its home? Rada held onto the reins with both hands, knuckles white, ready to jab her heels into the flanks.

But it was no demon that strolled confidently out of the bushes, but rather a *tiger.*

Rada had seen a tiger before. There was a zoo within the Capitol which held many animals from all over Lok for the amusement of her caste, only those had been sickly and weak compared to this sleek beast. Books had told her that tigers were common in Gujara and Vokkan, and scarce everywhere else. But reading about a wild tiger or seeing one while separated by iron bars was nothing like facing one a hundred feet away.

The tiger made no sound whatsoever. Paws padded across rocks and sticks without so much as a whisper. It was so silent that Rada wondered why it had showed itself at all. She'd read that they were ambush predators. If it meant them harm, why not wait until they were on the road and then jump down on them from a branch? Its actions made no sense.

As their horses whined and stamped, Karno took his war hammer from his shoulder and laid it across both hands. "Greetings," the Protector said, as if he were speaking to a man rather than a great cat.

The cat stopped fifty feet from Karno, and stood there, looking at him. Its manner so incongruous that Rada thought perhaps she'd lost her mind. She expected it to leap at him. Only then there was a terrible blurring, a black sear that made her blink and shield her eyes, and when she looked again, the tiger was gone, and there stood a man.

He was of average height, of dark complexion, clean shaven except for a mustache and narrow goatee, dressed in the baggy clothing preferred in the Zarger desert, and he wore a curved sword on his belt.

All Rada really knew about wizards was that they scared her to death.

"Hello, travelers," the stranger said, cold but cordial. "Merry Holi."

"Merry Holi to you as well," Karno replied, not seeming the least astounded at seeing a tiger turn into a man. "Inquisitor."

"Witch hunter," the stranger corrected him.

Rada had to stifle a cry as he identified himself, for the witch hunters were the near mythical elite of the Order of Inquisition. She'd heard rumors of them, everyone in the Capitol had, but never read anything about them, because every reference to that secretive group had been long since scrubbed from the Capitol Library.

"Identify yourself, travelers," the witch hunter demanded.

"I am but a humble man of the worker caste, journeying with my wife to Apura for the festival." Blunt Karno was a terrible liar.

"A humble worker, eh? Which is why you do not quail before the tiger form, and why you stand there with a war hammer, overly confident."

"Workers have hammers too. They're remarkably versatile tools. How may I help you, witch hunter?"

"Leave the false identities to my order, Protector. Lies do not suit you."

Karno's silver-inlaid armor was hidden in the bags on their pack horse, and the token of his office was on a chain hidden beneath his shirt, but there was no use denying his identity. "Very well. How may I help you, witch hunter?"

"I am Khoja. I seek a fugitive. A woman." He gave Rada a sly look as he said that.

"And I am Protector of the Law, eighteen-year senior, Karno Uttara. And you should move along, for I have no fugitive here."

"Radamantha Nems dar Harban has been summoned to the Inquisitor's Dome. It would be a grave violation of the Law for her to ignore such a thing.

Even the Protectors must honor the summons of the Inquisition."

The Inquisitor took another step forward. Karno tightened his grip around the well-worn shaft of the war hammer, fingers so strong his callused skin made an audible creak like leather. The Inquisitor paused.

"These are perilous times for your Order, Karno Uttara. You are not currently favored in the Capitol, as we are. Ashok Vadal has shamed you all. The judges doubt your loyalty. Should you stand against my lawful summons, word will get back to the Capitol. You may be doing great and irreparable damage to your Order. Think carefully on this, Protector."

"I was just telling my friend here how I have no head for politics."

"You are making a grave mistake."

Karno grunted. "This would not be my first. Now do your little tiger trick and scurry off. I tire of your threats."

"Forgive my overfamiliarity. I've been tracking you for weeks so I feel as if I know you." The witch hunter spread his arms, a mockery of an apology. "When I was given this assignment I was warned that Karno Uttara was an unsubtle brute, but second in ferocity only to the Black Heart, which is why I brought a few of my brothers along to help."

"Saltwater..." Karno muttered as something orange and white slunk through the brush to their side.

"Your reputation is also why I used up a precious fragment of black steel, to muffle the approach of our Inquisitors and the fifty warriors we drafted to aid us in Zarger." The witch hunter snapped his fingers. The change was abrupt. Even Rada's normal human ear could suddenly hear the sound of hoofbeats, out of sight around the bend, but closing fast. It must have sounded like thunder to Karno's ear.

"Ride, Rada!" Karno bellowed. "Go!"

Her horse had leapt forward before she'd even had a chance to thump it, and she took off down the road. All Rada could do was hang on.

"Get the librarian!" the witch hunter shouted.

Seemingly out of nowhere, there was a flash of orange ahead of her. Another tiger! The mare stuttered to a halt, reared back and screamed, and Rada screamed as she was nearly thrown from the saddle.

The tiger slunk toward her, eyes glowing with a greenish black light, teeth bared. It leapt!

Karno's hammer smashed it out of the air.

The tiger went bouncing and rolling down the road in a cloud of dust.

Karno appeared next to her. He grabbed her horse by the bridle and with a display of incredible brute force dragged the kicking animal down with one hand. Then he scooped up his hammer from the ground, and turned back to meet the witch hunter, who had drawn his sword and was charging their way. "I said ride." He smacked her horse on the rump. She started to run.

Another tiger pounced.

Rada had not seen this one coming at all, but Karno had. Its claws nearly sunk into her, before they stopped inches away, seemingly frozen for an instant. *Karno had caught it by the tail!* She had enough time to see an almost human look of surprise on the beast's face, before the Protector spun it around, and hurled it at the charging witch hunter. They collided violently, and man and tiger both were sent hard to the ground.

"Yah!" Rada shouted, though her terrified mare needed no urging. They ran through the grass, going wide around the crumpled form that had been hit with Karno's hammer, which was now in the shape of a gasping man clutching at his broken ribs, and then they bolted for Apura.

Rada risked a look back over her shoulder just in time to see the mob of horsemen appear, dozens of them, swords raised, their mounts whipped into a lather, thundering down the road in pursuit of her.

Between them stood lone Karno, blocking the path.

Chapter 13

"Faster! Go!" Rada urged her mare as she imagined tiger claws sinking into her flesh at any moment. She didn't know who was more terrified, her or her horse.

Karno was tough, but there was no way he could survive against so many warriors, and sure enough once Karno was occupied, some of them went after her.

She lowered herself in the saddle as Karno had taught her. Though she'd gotten a lot of riding practice in recent weeks, she'd never gone this fast before. Despite that, each time she looked back, the horsemen had closed more of the distance. Their animals were the muscled black animals of the desert warriors, and they were much stronger than her mare.

When she looked again, her pursuers were close enough for her to see some of them wore gleaming, fanged masks. *Inquisitors!*

The Protector had distracted most of them, but the witch hunter had still sent five of his men to run her down. Karno had given her a proper dagger to use in case of an emergency, but she was no fighter. If they caught her she wouldn't have a chance against one of them, let alone five!

The city was near. Forests turned to pasture and farms. Instead of trees along the side of the road there were low stone walls to pen in livestock. It was getting dark, but there were people on the road ahead, wagons of goods, and farmers pushing carts, all of them heading into Apura, probably late arrivals to sell their goods at the festival.

They didn't see her until Rada flew past them at a gallop. "Sorry." Men had to leap out of the way, spilling their baskets and bundles. "Excuse me!" A cart overturned. Melons rolled as a woman cursed her. "Sorry!"

She had an idea, and as she passed by she reached out and smacked her hand against an ox's backside. "Boo!" That startled the drowsy animal, and in response it bellowed and lurched, pulling its wagon off to the side. The merchants rose off their seats to shake their fists at her.

Luckily the chaos she caused bought her some time, as the Inquisitors rode right into the snarl. They roared for the workers to get out of their way.

Karno had wanted to avoid the travel checkpoints, but she was heading straight for one. There was no fancy gate on this road, just a small shack for the comfort of the warriors who manned it while they stamped papers and collected taxes. If she slowed down and tried to talk her way through, the Inquisitors would surely catch up enough to yell for the warriors to detain her. So all she could do was stay low, hug her horse tight, and hope that the road guards weren't alert enough to immediately fill her body full of arrows.

The warriors were busy checking someone's papers by lantern as Rada flew right past them. One of them had time to shout, "Hey, stop!" but luckily he didn't throw his spear at her.

There were three roads, so she picked the middle. Or more like she'd completely lost control of her frightened mount, and she just kept running straight. They rode hard into Apura, and Rada hoped she would be able to put some distance between her and the checkpoint. Travelers had to rush to get out of her way. The crowd thickened. There were people everywhere, men, women, and children. Her mare began to twist her head from side to side, suddenly blocked by bodies and unable to run.

"Damned drunken fool!" an old woman shouted at her.

"Slow down before you trample someone, idiot!" Someone had the audacity to throw a vegetable at her. It missed.

Rada looked back. Lanterns were moving around the checkpoint. An Inquisitor was shouting at one of the guards and gesturing wildly. Another Inquisitor saw her atop her horse, because she stuck out above the crowd, and he pointed and yelled for his companion's attention.

She couldn't stay silhouetted up here, so Rada dismounted. "Run away, girl." It filled Rada with despair to see the confused horse trotting off with her saddlebags containing most of her worldly possessions, but then she turned and began to push her way into the mob. All Rada had left was the rough-spun clothes on her body, the knife Karno had given her, and the satchel which contained her two most valuable things, the black-steel Asura's Mirror, and her reading glasses.

Though terrified, she knew she had to keep her head. It was escape or the dome.

The Inquisitors were heading her way, so Rada kept moving, pushing and shoving against men who were far heavier than she was. There were so many bodies pressed together here that the spring chill turned a damp warm. People were laughing, singing, and prancing about. A crowd of dancers created an opening for her, and she ducked between them, putting more bodies between her and the masks. There were so many people jostling around that her rudeness went unnoticed.

The people of Apura were dressed much like she was, most of them in the simple garb of the average worker, but they were all stained with colors tonight. Brilliant reds, blues, greens, and yellows.

Rada gasped as she was hit in the face with a blue cloud. The pigment dust got in her nose and made her want to sneeze.

She'd forgotten about that part of Holi. They didn't make a mess like this in the Capitol. Everything was bright and decorative there every day, and no first-caste woman would allow one of her fine silk dresses to be stained with indigo or turmeric. But Rada had read that the poor worker caste lived a drab existence mostly, so it made sense that their holidays would be extra colorful to compensate.

The buildings in Apura were short by Capitol standards, only two or three stories tall, but they all had balconies, and on every balcony someone was either playing an instrument, or tossing handfuls of colored pigments toward the ground. So much of the colorful dust had been thrown already tonight, that the farther she pushed into the city, the thicker it became in the air. It hung like a pink swirling fog. And Rada was thankful for this small miracle, because it would make it much harder for the Inquisitors to see her.

A parade of drummers was making their way down this particular street. The noise drowned out the shouts of the wolves snapping at her heels. Risking a glance back, she saw them, giving orders to the warriors they had just taken command of by virtue of their office. But she didn't think they saw her. They were easy to spot because of their terrifying masks, so their presence was drawing the people's attention, and then fear. Unfortunately, as she watched, one of them shouted a command, and they all removed their masks. Now they looked like normal men, and one woman. They would blend in and she would never see them coming.

Karno had told her to hide. The Inquisitors were brutal, but she was smart, and more importantly *educated*. She'd once read a memoir about a Vokkan spy's exploits in Vadal City, and she did her best to recall its lessons. She had to blend in. She could not attract the hunter's eye.

On the road the Inquisitors had seen a dusty woman dressed in a gray coat and desert scarf. So she wadded up her scarf and dropped it on the ground. Rada was of average height, and Vadal women tended to be tall, so she didn't stick out that way. They wore their long hair down and loose, so she undid the band she'd used to keep her hair out of the way while riding and shook it free. Vadal women were renowned for their beauty, and in previous years that would've intimidated her, but due to her affair with Devedas, Rada had decided she was no slouch herself. However, it appeared all Vadal women could dance, twirling and swinging their hips with perfect rhythm. On that front, Rada was completely out of luck, trying to emulate them would make her look like a clumsy duck among swans, so she just kept walking.

Reaching an intersection of five points Rada realized she needed to change her route. The Inquisitors would have to split up. She took the second right, toward the city center, and luckily it appeared that street was even busier than the first.

It was common for the youth of the worker caste to engage in water fights on Holi, and a big one was going on here. So Rada gladly stepped in front of the giggling children throwing buckets of colored water. They seemed rather gleeful that an adult would jump into their game. She was quickly drenched, half purple and half green, but with wet clothes even more of the dry pigments were sure to stick to her. She'd be as camouflaged as the tigers had been in the forest. She glanced back, couldn't spot anyone following her, and kept walking.

Rada was unsure how long she wandered, trying to disappear among the masses, but the farther she got from the violated checkpoint, the better. She passed by stands of delicious food, though so tempting earlier, now her stomach was so restless that the thought of eating made her nauseous. If found, she'd be taken to that most dark and terrifying place that loomed over the Capitol . . . *the dome*. The shadow it cast on Mount Metoro warned everyone in the Capitol to behave or else. There were tales of underground dungeons and torture chambers, and many who were summoned there were never seen again. The fear made her chest ache.

She reached an open area, which on normal days must serve as some sort of park or city gardens, but during Holi it was filled with huge tents belonging to performers. Men stuck torches to their lips and breathed out balls of fire. Acrobats leapt, flipped in the air, and rolled on the grass. There was even an elephant which did tricks, and a tiny man who balanced upon its trunk.

Between the noise, and the colorful dust clouds, there should have been no way for the hunters to track her. She didn't see anyone she took to be an Inquisitor. There were warriors, but they weren't searching for her. They were with their families, relaxed, and enjoying themselves. So Rada leaned against a wrought-iron fence and tried to catch her breath. She'd not realized how hard her heart was beating.

Karno had said that he would find her, except he was probably dead. *Oh no. Karno.* He was powerful, but there was no way one man—even a Protector—could fight fifty warriors and survive. The first time they'd met, he'd knocked her down and set his hammer on her chest because he'd thought she was an assassin or a witch, but they'd become friends. The thought of him dying made hot tears come to her eyes.

Karno would not approve of tears. Get yourself together, Rada. What would that spy have done?

He wouldn't get complacent. That was for sure. So Rada dried her eyes, wiped her nose, and kept watching for threats...Which was when she noticed the woman looking right at her.

Everyone else was watching the elephant, the fire-breathers, or the sword-swallowers. The young men were watching the female acrobats. But this woman had definitely been studying Rada. There had been a female among the Inquisitors. Was this her? It was hard to tell now, because like Rada, her face was also smeared with pigment. In her case, a ghastly red.

Their eyes met. The woman didn't look away. Instead she began walking toward Rada with great purpose, roughly shoving children aside. Rada pushed off the fence and began walking along the park. The woman walked faster. Rada increased her pace. So did the woman. Rada ran. The Inquisitor gave chase.

Rada fled as swiftly as she could, but she was a librarian, not an athlete, and the Inquisitor closed the distance quickly. Watching her pursuer instead of where she was going, Rada crashed right into someone. Since he was much heavier than she was, physics made him stumble, but put her on the ground.

She'd bumped into a warrior, and this one wasn't here to celebrate, but was rather obviously on duty. He was wearing armor, the steel plates painted that distinctive Vadal gray-blue, and intricately decorated with rings of bronze. He wore no helm, but had a spear in one hand, which he carefully kept upright so as to not poke the crowd.

A look of mirth crossed his face. "Careful. I know the acrobats are a sight, but don't break your neck."

There were two other warriors right behind him, similarly armed and dressed. Rada didn't know much about their caste, but their armor was artful, more like what she'd expect to see in the Capitol than some common place like Apura. These were men of status, or more likely, servants of a man of status.

Rada saw that the Inquisitor was nearly there, and quickly blurted. "Help me, Warriors! A fiend is trying to murder me."

The man she'd bumped held out one hand to help her up. He hoisted her from the ground. The expression on his handsome face indicated that he thought this was all some manner of holiday-related foolishness. "How much have you drank tonight, girl?"

But one of his companions was more alert. This one was older, with a scar that split his chin, and he recognized Rada's genuine fear. His eyes quickly snapped up, scanning for threats. He spotted the oncoming Inquisitor and put one hand on his sheathed sword. "Halt!"

The red woman stopped. "Turn her over to me," she demanded, imperiously. "Now."

The Inquisitor sounded so used to people immediately doing as she commanded, she must have forgotten that she wasn't wearing her mask.

"What's going on here?" asked the first warrior.

"She's a maniac, trying to kill me," Rada exclaimed.

The older warrior glanced between the two women, and then snapped at the third warrior. "Warn the palanquin there's a disturbance I must investigate."

That soldier immediately complied, and ran off, armor clanking.

"This is none of your business, Warriors," the Inquisitor snapped.

The handsome one standing next to Rada must have still thought that he'd interrupted some worker's spat.

"If it's in the borders of Great House Vadal, then it is our business. So watch your tone, woman."

"Identify yourself," demanded the older, because he recognized from the Inquisitor's bearing that she was no mere worker.

Rada hurried and answered before the Inquisitor could. "I'm Senior Archivist Radamantha Nems dar Harban of the Capitol Library, and this woman is an assassin!"

Either these warriors were exceedingly devout patrons of the library—which she doubted—or they were particularly sensitive to the accusation of *assassin*, because their reaction was immediate and extraordinary. The handsome warrior shoved Rada violently aside, and in the same movement his spear whipped around, aimed at the Inquisitor.

"Wait!" said the Inquisitor as she raised her hands revealing that she had palmed a stiletto, and had been keeping the long thin blade concealed along the inside of her forearm.

"Knife!" At the sight of the readied weapon, the handsome warrior punched his broad spear right through the Inquisitor's chest.

There was an odd look on the woman's face, almost dumbfounded, as she was shoved back until she hit the fence. With a brutal twist, the spear was wrenched free. She tried to say something, but only blood came out. She went to her knees, then flopped over on her face, to lay there, limp.

Rada cringed. It wouldn't just be powder staining the streets tonight.

The party around them had paused as the revelers realized something had gone horribly wrong. Then they saw who had done the stabbing, and that the victim looked as low status as they were, so no one said a word of complaint. They either went about their business or stopped to gawk.

Rada felt something cold against her neck. Cautiously, slowly, she looked down to find that the older warrior had her on the end of his sword.

"I—"

"Not a word until my superior arrives." He said that to her, but his eyes were nervously flicking over the rest of the crowd. "There's nothing for the rest of you to see here. Move along."

Rada didn't dare nod because she feared she'd cut her own throat. These warriors were clearly not the hesitating type.

The younger one used his boot to nudge the knife away from the dead Inquisitor's hand. "The edge has been coated in something green and oily. Poison for our charge most likely. That's a weapon for quiet murder if there ever was one."

Rada knew that they wanted her alive. The "poison" was more than likely a drug to cause sleep or befuddlement, and the Inquisitor had intended to prick her with it, so they could sneak her away without notice, as she'd read about in her book of spies. Not that she was going to tell them that, for the presence of that substance seemed to confirm to the warriors that they'd done the right thing.

The young one used the butt of his spear to roll the body over and knelt down next to begin checking through her clothing.

"Careful," said the elder. "If she's one of the assassins we've been warned of, she'll have demon on her."

"No, but I've found traveling papers." He was near a pole where an oil lamp hung, so he held the stamped forms out to better read. "She's from the Capitol." Then he went back to searching, and his face fell. "Oh, this is not good."

"What?"

He held up an Inquisitor's mask.

"Saltwater!" The old warrior flinched so hard Rada felt the sword edge rub against her neck.

"How was I supposed to know? She was acting like a threat. I was doing my job!"

"Do you think they're gonna care? Hide that thing before anyone sees."

The young one hurried and stuffed the mask beneath his arm. It was probably a futile gesture, since despite the admonition for the crowd to move on, quite the opposite had happened, and more people were coming closer to see what was going on. When they'd seen the mask they began to mutter. Inquisitors were feared, never loved, but pity the poor bastard who angered that order.

The way she was being held at sword point Rada figured everyone would assume she was a criminal. If she wasn't so worried about her imminent murder, she'd have been rather indignant about that.

Rada noticed a familiar face coming through the crowd. It was the witch hunter, Khoja. He was walking with a limp, and was also stained red, though she feared his wasn't from powder, but rather the blood of noble Karno. The fact the tiger man was alive didn't bode well for the safety of her friend. Khoja saw the dead Inquisitor and a look of fury came over his face. Rada knew she was doomed.

"Here he comes," the senior warrior warned, but he wasn't talking about the witch hunter. He was looking in the opposite direction. The spearman moved away from the body and stood at attention.

She could tell Khoja wanted to snatch her by the hair and drag her from this place, but he stopped, obviously fuming, but not possessing the prideful stupidity of his predecessor. He pointed at her with two fingers, elbow bent, then mouthed the words so only she could see. She thought the message was *you are mine*, but she supposed it could just as easily been *you are dead*. Rada couldn't really read lips, but either way the message was bad.

A great excitement went through the assembly. There was a rapid spread of awed and fearful whispers such as, "It's really him," and mothers warning their children, "Bow your head!" Rada was afraid to turn, but out of the corner of her eye she saw the colorful crowd parting, and more warriors in the same ornate armor approaching. Behind them was a magnificent palanquin, carried on poles by eight burly workers. The curtains of embroidered silk had been pulled aside, so that the rider could enjoy the spectacle of the festival, while remaining in complete comfort and relative isolation.

With a word from their master, the workers stopped, and then gently lowered the palanquin's hardwood and carved-ivory compartment to the cobblestones. The armored warriors spread out, forming a protective circle around it.

The man who got out was truly notable, wearing the finest robes of the Capitol and a sash of Vadal gray. Around his neck was a chain bearing a ruby the size of a baby's fist. He had a neatly trimmed beard, gone just enough gray around the edges to make him look distinguished and wise. He lifted one hand— every finger bearing a golden ring—and waved at the crowd. They *all* bowed. Rada could tell that half of them adored him, and the other half were scared of him, and that seemed to make the man happy, for he smiled at the people of his house like a patient father and gestured for them to rise.

Rada recognized this man, for she'd heard him speak in the Chamber of Argument. He was supposed to be one of the greatest orators in the history of the Capitol, though she had no ear for such things. Any important new change to the Law she'd filed at the library, odds were his signature had been upon it. Her father—who followed politics rather closely—believed him to be one of the favorites to be obligated as the next Chief Judge. While Devedas had warned her that he was a venomous snake, never to be trusted, for though he couldn't prove it, Devedas believed that this man had been part of the conspiracy to conceal Ashok Vadal's true identity from the world.

It was Harta Vadal, the Thakoor and ultimate ruler of Great House Vadal.

"Greetings, Apura."

The crowd went wild. Love him or hate him, it was rare for people in a place like this to actually lay eyes on the man who quite literally owned their lives. Their Thakoor's presence was obviously unexpected.

Harta had the orator's ability to speak from the chest, to make his words clearly heard even though all around them the city was still filled with music. "It has been my great pleasure to partake of your hospitality this Holi.

Apura is one of the finest cities in all of Vadal, the most blessed of all the great houses. Let it be known that I am proud to be your leader..." They cheered. "Thank you, thank you. Return to your festival and know that Great House Vadal loves you. That I, Harta, love you."

As the cheering continued, Harta walked over to the warrior who was still ready to slay her. He lowered his voice and went from pleased to annoyed very quickly. "What's all this, Girish? I was told of an assassination plot against me."

"Luthra and I were approached by this one here, claiming to be of the first caste, my lord. She warned that the other, the dead one there, was an assassin. When she flashed an assassin's blade, Luthra dispatched her."

"I knew I was right to increase the numbers of my Personal Guard." Harta scowled at Rada. "Who are you supposed to be?"

"Senior Archivist Radamantha Nems dar Harban of the Capitol Library, your honor."

"Nems of the library... Durmad's daughter?" Harta snorted as he looked at her purple-stained face. "Bloody unlikely. I was told the daughter of Durmad is a charming young lady of breathtaking beauty."

She was sopping wet, covered in clumping dyes, atop clothes filthy and stinking from travel, but still Rada had to try really hard not to take offense at that. "That would be my sister, Daksha. But you've seen my name. I'm the one who prepared the report for the judges about the legality of casteless genocide."

"Ah, yes." Harta nodded thoughtfully. "I do recall that particular Nems now." The way he said that however, Rada didn't know if it was a good thing or bad.

"There's, uh, one problem, my lord." The younger

warrior—apparently called Luthra—came over and handed his Thakoor the dead Inquisitor's mask. "This was upon the dead woman."

"What?" Harta took it in his hands, brows furrowed, and he stared at it for a long time.

"She wasn't wearing it when I killed her, I swear."

"This particular Order is already a source of great consternation for me. You'd better hope this is a forgery, Luthra."

And that was the precise moment that the witch hunter Khoja decided to approach. "It is no forgery." He had put his own golden mask on, accentuating his fearsome office, and hiding his face from the people he was supposed to spy on.

Some of the warriors protectively stepped between their Thakoor and the witch hunter.

"What do you want?" Harta asked, sounding bored.

Khoja bowed in the northern style, respectfully low. "We are in pursuit of a fugitive."

"Her?" Harta asked incredulously. "Is the library supposed to be a hot bed of rebellion now? If so no one informed me."

"No, noble Thakoor, it is her alone." While the last who'd tried to take her had used threats and bluster, Khoja used honeyed words. "The death of my associate was an unfortunate misunderstanding. She was after this fugitive, and meant you no harm. Though I can understand why your guards reacted as they did. These things happen, and I will be sure to personally tell the Grand Inquisitor that the Personal Guard of Great House Vadal did absolutely nothing illegal."

"Oh really? How magnanimous of you." Harta's words dripped with sarcasm.

Khoja's mask hid his expression, but Rada suspected he was grinding his teeth. "The librarian has been summoned to the Dome. She needs to come with me."

"Interesting . . . And why does the spider Omand require her in his web?"

Khoja paused. It must have been rare for him to find someone brave enough to openly speak ill of the Grand Inquisitor. He was probably used to being able to push people around, but nobody pushed around a Thakoor inside the borders of his own house.

"Apologies, your honor, the Grand Inquisitor's reasons are not mine to question. I merely fulfill my obligation and do as I am told."

Harta studied Khoja for a moment, and then looked back to Rada. "You don't look like much of a heretic."

Rada spoke carefully, because the old warrior, apparently named Girish, had not yet removed his sword from her throat. "I've done nothing wrong. There is a conspiracy among the Inquisitors to break the Law and lie to the judges and—"

"Enough." Harta held up one hand. He thought it over for a moment. "Lower your sword, Girish."

Rada took a deep and thankful breath after the steel departed.

"Please, Lord Vadal. It is of utmost importance that I return this fugitive to the Capitol."

"I was just in the Capitol myself recently. I'm on my way home because there's business which requires my personal attention in Vadal City. It is by happenstance that we stopped in Apura to rest for the holiday. But since I am here . . . Set my mind at ease, Inquisitor. If this woman has been summoned to the dome for questioning, then surely you have the proper paperwork to show me. I am curious to know which of my fellow judges signed this warrant."

Khoja was silent for a long time. "Apologies. I do not have that on my person."

"Unfortunate. The Inquisition cannot just snatch a member of the highest caste off the street without a warrant. That would be unseemly. I've heard rumors of Omand doing such things in recent years, but I had always dismissed such claims as outlandish rumors. Surely the Grand Inquisitor would not do something so clumsily illegal."

The masked man had no response. Rada doubted the Inquisition had ever issued any such official thing. That was why at first they'd sent bounty hunters after her in Zarger.

"I'm afraid that as the Thakoor and supreme arbiter of the Law in this land, I would be remiss in my duties if I allowed the Inquisition to trample upon the rights of our visitors. Convey to your master that I will take this... Radamantha, is it? I will take her into my custody. Once Omand gets his paperwork sorted out, he may *officially* send for her. She will be a guest at my estate in Vadal City. You are dismissed." Harta began walking away.

"You are making a mistake!" Khoja shouted. "I obligated an entire paltan of Zarger warriors and have tracked her for weeks. The Inquisition will remember this!"

Harta stopped, back turned, but from the hunch of his head and way his hands clenched into fists, it was obvious that the witch hunter had just crossed a very dangerous line. Khoja hadn't just called him out, but he'd called him out in front of his witnesses. Regular people, who would surely talk. When Harta looked back, the smiling orator was totally gone, replaced with a steel-eyed *ruler*. The first kind gave flowery speeches. This one ordered men killed.

"I am Thakoor here. Thus I cannot make *mistakes*. Anything I say becomes true, because of the act of my saying it."

Khoja must have realized he'd gone too far. He glanced furtively to the side, and Rada noticed that a few of the gathering watchers might be the Inquisitors who'd been chasing her. Was this witch hunter bold enough to challenge a Thakoor? Luthra must have noticed that a few of the people in the crowd were acting out of place, because with a nod of his head, another armored warrior moved in that direction to block them. Harta traveled with a seemingly immense number of bodyguards, not to mention there were many regular warriors here as well who would gladly leap to their Thakoor's aid. The Inquisitors would be ripped to shreds.

"What's more, you brought Zarger dogs into Vadal? Which of my foolish arbiters signed off on this, this, *incursion*?" When no immediate answer was forthcoming, Harta said, "I thought so. Girish, summon the local garrison. Have them find these desert scum and annihilate them. Hound them to the border. Do not stop the chase until they cross it. And then notify the Thao, who I am sure will be equally as furious about the Inquisition casually bringing illegal invaders into their lands."

"Yes, sir!"

"Did you hear that, Inquisitor? The festival will buy you some time for my warriors to assemble.

Consider that your head start. You are lucky I have such great respect for the Law or I'd just have you killed here and now."

Khoja, knowing that he was defeated, gave Harta a small bow, and then walked away. Many of the locals, having overheard this exchange, started to boo, and then the drunker ones began throwing fruit and even rocks at the retreating Inquisitor. They seemed gleeful about it too. It was as if the presence of their offended Thakoor granted them temporary license to mock an organization they were terrified of, and the chaos of the colorful crowd gave them the anonymity to get away with it.

Rada felt an emotion somewhat akin to relief, but only briefly, because then Harta grabbed her roughly by the arm. "Come."

"I was traveling with a friend—a Protector—when they attacked. He might be dead or captured—"

"I don't care," Harta snapped as he shoved her toward the palanquin. "All that matters to me is that for Omand to be so brazen, you must be very important to him. But he's not the only one who can play the great game. If the Grand Inquisitor wants something so badly, then that is reason enough for me to take it away. You are property of Vadal now, Librarian."

Chapter 14

It had only been a day since Thera had commanded Ashok to go to war. She'd not expected him to conquer a town already.

The so-called Voice of the Forgotten had been sitting next to a humble campfire made of old grass and dried dung, when her so-called general had ridden up on a giant white horse to deliver his full report. If the story had come from anyone other than always-truthful Ashok, she might not have believed her ears. The casteless quarter of Dhakhantar spared, three paltans of warriors utterly defeated, twenty hostages taken, including the phontho of the Chakma garrison, and the Sons had only sustained minor injuries in the process.

Thera had never led an army before, but her father had led many, and she'd practically memorized all his stories. The idea of what was basically a small raiding party crushing three paltans without losing a single man wasn't just unrealistic, it was absurd. As Andaman Vane had always taught, no matter how good you were, or how lucky you were, bad things happened in battle. A group of warrior castoffs, workers, and swamp men who'd never ridden horses before shouldn't have been able to take on such a superior force at all, let alone win. And without great cost? Impossible.

Keta would surely give all the credit to the gods, but Thera needed to know what had really happened. "How?"

"Surprise, terrain that favored us, and a prideful adversary," Ashok said as he dismounted. One of the workers immediately rushed up to take the reins from him. "Take good care of this animal. Make sure he is cleaned and fed. He did well today."

"Yes, General!"

Thera still couldn't get over how eager the religious fanatics were to serve anyone their god hung a title on. Only Ashok had spent most of his life as one of the highest-status men in the land, so he was probably used to such things. Though right then he didn't look like any first-caste man, being filthy, covered in dried dirt and matted blood, and stinking of sweat, both his and the horse's.

"It appears our numbers have grown," Ashok muttered as he looked across her mob.

"We've been coming across refugees all day, caste-less who've fled ahead of the warriors sent to murder them." Most of the newcomers were thin, sickly, and weak. Some of them had hacking coughs. Many of them were weeping or in shock, because their loved ones had just been put to the sword over recent days. It was a motley bunch.

Ashok just scowled.

She knew what he was thinking. This was a lot of slow feet and hungry bellies. "They fell in with us. What else was I supposed to do? Turn them away?"

He had only just arrived, but already those who'd come from the swamp were telling the newcomers about how the man before them was the mighty Fall. It was long after sundown, and everyone in their hasty camp who hadn't been given some other pressing duty began gathering around the fire to hear their returning legend speak. Only Ashok didn't seem to care for their attention. Instead he sat down on the ground next to her, and simply said, "I need food."

One of the women they'd freed from the House of Assassins immediately rushed to ladle him some stew from the kettle placed over the fire. The magically befuddled slaves still didn't communicate, but they seemed eager to serve when given the opportunity. If this camp was to survive, everyone would need to pull their weight. So even though it made her feel guilty to do so, she'd ordered them to work. They were rather proficient at preparing food and caring for the livestock, which made sense, since that was what their wizard masters had forced them to do.

The slave gave Ashok a bowl of their stew—made from every edible shoot, mushroom, or root they'd come across, and any animal that had been unfortunate enough to blunder into the path of their column that day. It was hearty, but Thera didn't know how long that would last.

Ashok stared into the fire as he ate, the exhaustion plain on his dirty face. Even the strongest man could become worn out. Thera passed Ashok a jug of water that had been resting next to her knees, and he immediately gulped down half. Then he stopped, ever practical, and asked, "What is our drinking-water situation here?"

"Plentiful. There's a clean stream nearby."

"Good." Then Ashok dumped the rest of the jug out over his hair and used his least dirty sleeve to try and scrub the caked blood from his face. It made a small difference. Then he looked across the crowd of curious and hopeful faces. "What are they staring at?"

"Their hero," Thera explained. "Who the gods sent to avenge them."

Ashok snorted. She thought it was absurd too, but if the belief kept these casteless orderly, she'd use it.

Thera had spent the whole day's march worrying that in her anger she'd sent Ashok and the Sons off on a mission of certain doom. Seeing the scene of that massacre had infuriated her, but as her calm had returned, she'd begun to think through all the terrible ramifications of her hasty command... Yet it seemed none of those worries had come to pass. If Keta was here, surely he would proclaim this as a sign that the gods were really on their side, as he did every stroke of good fortune, which usually sounded like childish superstition to her. But frankly, for this she didn't have a better explanation.

Ashok continued his report between spoonfuls. "We ran all night, assaulted a camp, rode all morning, and fought a battle. The Sons needed to rest. They've taken the warriors' encampment outside Dhakhantar. I left Eklavya in charge and warned Shekar not to loot the town. Looting seemed inappropriate. I returned alone to warn you."

"Warn me of what?"

"We were lucky today. The warriors did not expect such resistance in their own lands. They will not make this mistake again. A great many warriors escaped. Word will spread. Now that they know there's an enemy force here, they will be searching for us." As if to accentuate the dire situation, Ashok pointedly glanced around the camp. "A group like this will be easy to track, easy to find, and far too slow to evade pursuit. It will take several days for the Great House to get word and a few more to mobilize all their forces, but after that the whole army of Akershan will come after us."

His grim assessment delivered, Ashok put the bowl to his lips and began to shovel in food.

"I thought of that after I sent you off to provoke the entire warrior caste." Thera wasn't the type to sit and fret about problems. As a criminal, she'd needed to think fast to stay ahead of trouble. She tried to tell herself this was similar, only now she was planning for a great number of people rather than just herself. Small gang or big gang, same principles, just with more potential executions if she mucked it up.

"Do you have any ideas?"

"Out of our whole band, we had one man with a head for military tactics, and Jagdish is walking back to Vadal beside a fat merchant and a donkey train full of demon parts. So in his absence, I asked myself, what would Jagdish do?"

Ashok shrugged, as if to say he wasn't sure either, and continued chewing.

Thera continued, "We need to get these people back to the hideout, but without the Akershani following us and finding the secret entrance. Only this many feet leave quite the trail and the way this damnable grass bends, even a blind man could follow us. Normally warriors wouldn't bother with a column of casteless refugees, which is surely what our sign will look like, but according to that injured man you found, the warriors are supposed to hunt all the casteless down, every last one."

"The letters I found in the defeated camps confirm that all of them are to be exterminated. It seems your rebellion has greatly angered the Capitol." Ashok must have been starving, because he handed the swiftly emptied bowl back to the woman who was still waiting to serve him and said, "More."

"But the rebellion is how we're going to slip away. You know what leaves an even bigger trail than us?" When Ashok didn't immediately answer her riddle, Thera proudly declared, "Cows."

"I do not understand the significance of *cows*."

"Of course you wouldn't. First casters never have to concern themselves with mundane things like where their food comes from. Keta told me of a family of fanatics who live near here, worker caste, but secret believers in the Forgotten. They are drovers and occasionally supply the rebels with meat. This land doesn't have much besides grass, but it's great for grazing. And the workers here move vast herds of cattle back and forth as they eat down the grass. They winter them on the plains, but it's normal to move them up to the mountain valleys to feed after the snows melt. That's the direction we're heading."

"You intend to order the cow people to drive their animals behind us, to obscure our passing."

"I don't know much about cattle, but they're hardly

graceful. All that stomping and pooping is sure to obscure our trail."

"This seems reasonable." Ashok nodded. "Clever."

It was interesting that when dealing with a man who was so frugal with praise, when praise was given it meant more. "Thank you, Ashok."

He paused inhaling his stew long enough to say, "But it will not be enough."

"What do you mean?"

"Hooves may destroy your tracks, but not hide all these bodies from the eyes of a scout. After suffering a defeat at the hands of such low-status foes every warrior in Akershan will be offended and eager to avenge this insult. The plains are big, but not big enough to avoid them for that long." Ashok leaned forward and used his finger to draw in the dirt. "We are here. The Sons are here in Dhakhantar. That's where the warriors will be converging, but they'll have a large number of scouts roving ahead. You need to head west toward the mountains, but there is no way you'll make it past unseen. However, if I take the Sons to threaten Chakma—a valuable prize—it will surely draw the warriors' attention and your path will be clear."

Thera frowned. His plan made sense, but it also placed the Sons, and Ashok himself, in great danger. "I don't think it's wise to split our forces again."

"Understandable. You'll need the Sons to protect this mob. Then send me alone. I should be a sufficient distraction."

Thera looked at Ashok like he'd gone mad. After all that they'd been through together, was he still trying to kill himself to be free of his obligation to her?

She started to snap an angry response, but then realized that there were a great many eyes on the both of them. To these people, they weren't Ashok and Thera, fallible individuals who got tired and made mistakes, they were the Forgotten's warrior and the Voice of the Gods. And many of these people had just fled from their homes, narrowly avoiding death. They'd lost everything they had, and members of their families too. All they had left was faith in their cruel and illegal god, so the last thing they needed to see was his representatives bickering.

"An interesting idea, General, but let's discuss this privately so we can seek the wisdom of the Forgotten to see which way he wants us to go."

Ashok gave her a curious look. He knew very well her low opinion of the Voice and its *wisdom*. Of course he didn't understand her desire for privacy, because he probably spent even less time considering their followers' feelings than the feelings of their supposed gods, but she was his sworn master, so he said, "Very well," and stood up.

The two of them walked away from the fire, out into the tall grass, until she was certain they were far enough away nobody would be able to overhear even if she got angry and raised her voice. "You'd go to Chakma by yourself? Are you truly that desperate to be rid of me that you'd rather commit suicide?"

"Dying is not my intent."

"It's the most likely outcome. You don't have your magic sword. You're not a one-man army anymore. And you said yourself how angry the warriors are going to be."

It surprised her that it was Ashok who ended up

raising his voice. "Then you should have thought of that before you ordered me to attack them! Blood has been spilled, Thera. I can't stuff it back in their veins."

"I know." She looked up at the sky full of stars and sighed. "You're right."

The two of them stood there for a long time, quiet. It was still cold, but the wind had tapered off to a slow breeze. Canda was full, and its white light gave the endless sea of grass an almost fuzzy glow. The second moon, tiny Upagraha, was barely noticeable making its swift line across the sky. Back in the camp, a child laughed. It was an odd sound considering their circumstances, but it just went to show that moments of happiness could be found in the strangest circumstances. It would've been a nice night, if they weren't drowning in troubles.

"I volunteer, not because I wish to die, but because it is my duty to make sure you live."

She believed him. And though it made her feel worse to recognize the truth, it made her feel better to hear him say it. "There's got to be another way."

"In the morning we will rendezvous with the Sons. Perhaps we will come up with a better plan by then." Surprisingly, it appeared that Ashok was trying to *comfort* her. "In the meantime, do not regret your command to avenge the dead casteless, for it saved many lives today. The casteless quarter in Dhakhantar would've been slaughtered if not for you. They will probably still die before this is over, but for now they have a chance."

He may have been trying to comfort her, but he was terrible at it. "I never wanted to decide who lives and who dies."

Ashok nodded. "When you are a leader it falls on you to make difficult decisions. My sword master always told me that every choice has consequences, but once committed, you must see it through. Hesitation leads to defeat."

"Ratul told me basically the same thing." It had come as quite the surprise, during a conversation back in the swamp, when they'd realized the same man had instructed both of them. Ratul had taught one of them how to be a Protector, and the other how to be a prophet. It was odd, how the same man could teach both the most legal and the most illegal trades in the world. Though Ratul had much more time to teach Ashok—and much better luck getting his lessons to stick—than he had with her. At times it seemed like Ashok was the paragon of relentless perfection, while Thera felt like she was drowning in water over her head, blundering about, trying to survive, clumsy as her scarred-up hands.

"He was a maniac, but with good advice. Sometimes."

"Good old Ratul," Thera muttered.

"Good?" Ashok snorted. "He was anything but good. That crazed fool kept it a secret from the entire Order that he thought the gods were whispering in his ear. Then he found you and abandoned the Law to help a rebellion."

"And now you've taken his place...So who is the crazy one?"

Ashok just shook his head. "The gods do not whisper to me."

"Though on occasion, they shout." It pained her to show weakness to anyone—especially to him—but it needed to be said. "Listen to me, Ashok. I need you. I need you with me."

"Do you say this as the prophet, or as a woman?"

She couldn't discern his expression in the moonlight. Amid all this suffering and strife, deep down, did he also wish for a normal life? Was he even capable of such thoughts? Or was that just her own wishful thinking? And in that moment, Thera hated herself for being weak, and for briefly allowing herself to have dreams.

"Either. Both. It doesn't matter. I've survived a lot on my own, but I can't do *this*. We were both forced into these roles against our will, but here we are. It is what it is. These people are counting on me. I'm counting on you to get us to the Cove. There we can be safe. For a while at least."

Even as she said it, deep down Thera wondered if the gods or the Law would ever grant them that small mercy.

Chapter 15

"The sun rises. Thus begins a new day in the merry journey of the warrior Jagdish, his loyal companion Forge Master Gutch, and their team of hardworking pack animals." The big man sat up, stretched his arms, and then twisted his head back and forth to pop his neck. He groaned. "Ah, I never thought I'd miss sleeping in a swamper's hut, but deer skins make for a softer bed than this hard ground."

"It's not been so bad since it quit raining on us," Jagdish replied as Gutch wandered into the bushes to relieve himself. "Walk further out. You'll scare the donkeys."

"Only because I piss like unto a mighty waterfall," Gutch shouted back. A minute later he wandered back into camp, yawning and taking in the trees around them. "What a beautiful day."

Jagdish looked up from the breakfast he'd been preparing over their small campfire. He'd taken a small copper frying pan from the Wild Men, and it had proven remarkably useful. There was a surprising amount of food available in this region, once the Wild Men had taught him where to look for it. "You're in a fine mood this morning, Gutch."

"Despite having pointy rocks sticking me in the kidneys and spine all night, that's because by the light of dawn this place looks to be far more forest than swamp, which means we're that much closer to civilization. I tell you that civilization is a damn fine thing when you are wealthy men, as we shall both be as soon as we sell all that." Gutch gestured to the giant pile of sacks and saddlebags they'd stacked against a tree trunk the night before. "There's enough demon parts there to keep us in wine and pleasure women until the end of time."

Jagdish chuckled. He knew where his stubborn traveling companion and partner in crime was going with this, because they'd already had the same argument every single day of their journey. "Do with your half as you wish, Gutch. But you know what I intend to do with mine."

"Donate it to Harta Vadal in the vain attempt of restoring your name, right before he has you publicly executed for riding with Ashok the Black Heart? A fine plan, that." The worker walked over to their fire, and then sat down on a fallen log across from Jagdish. "What's for breakfast?"

"I found a nest full of eggs while I was on watch."

"Bird or lizard?"

Jagdish shrugged. He was assuming grouse, but it could go either way out here.

"Who am I kidding? There could be baby demons inside and I'm still hungry enough to eat them..." Gutch trailed off. "Do you suppose demons lay eggs?"

"Why would they do that?"

"They live in the ocean, like fish. A casteless told me fish lay eggs. Casteless even eat those." Gutch shuddered. "Fish lay eggs in water, so it just stands to reason demons would too, Risaldar."

That wasn't the kind of philosophical pondering he'd wanted to start his day with, but it beat Gutch pestering him about his plan to return to his Vadal homeland. "Well, we've now harvested more demons for parts than anyone else alive, and I still couldn't tell you one way or the other how their insides work. Besides the bones and the general outline, they're nothing at all like a man or any animal I've ever seen."

"Eggs then," Gutch declared. "Demons must lay eggs."

"Hold on now. I didn't say that. You declare them to be like fish because they live in Hell, but if Keta and the old stories are to be believed, demons aren't from the sea originally."

"As if anyone sane would believe a word Keta said about anything, with his tales of mighty Ramrowan riding a black-steel ship down from the heavens." But then Gutch stroked his bearded chin as if he were an arbiter reasoning through a fine point of law. "By that logic though, the histories say demons fell from the *sky*. You know what else lives in the sky? Birds. Which lay eggs."

"You have me there, Gutch. Eggs it is." Jagdish didn't know how the monstrous things worked, he just fervently hoped he never had to fight one again.

They consumed their breakfast in silence. Gutch was a giant of a man, barrel-chested, and solid, but like Jagdish, he too had fallen ill with the swamp fever.

He'd lost quite a bit of weight, so wasn't nearly as ponderous as he had been. Living off what you could forage while walking all day didn't give a man much opportunity to be fat. Though surely Gutch would remedy that situation as soon as they were back in the Law-abiding world. He often said as much himself during their daily march, as he listed off the many items which would be on the menu for the great feast celebrating his return.

When they were done, the two of them gathered the donkeys they'd taken from the Wild Men and started piling the cargo on their backs. Toramana had not been eager to send so many of his tribe's precious livestock off with two northerners, but one stern glance from Ashok had settled the debate. Gutch and Jagdish had taken a disproportionate amount of valuable demon, but they'd all had more than they could carry anyway. They had so much weight in magic that unloading so the poor donkeys could rest, and then reloading them to begin their journey anew, took quite a bit of time and labor, but the two men had worked out a system. They took good care of the beasts, because losing one of them didn't mean just losing an animal, but also leaving behind a fortune in magic.

"You know, I bet I could find some trustworthy workers in Warun, put together a proper expedition, and go back to gather the bones of that giant fella we left hidden in the swamp. Forget enjoying civilization. With those big old bones we could *buy* civilization. You don't need to appease your old Thakoor, Jagdish. With this much money, you could *be* a Thakoor."

"That's not how it works. A warrior can't just buy rank and status, Gutch."

"Oh, really? And what exactly are you doing way out here in the middle of bleeding nowhere with the world's most valuable donkey train then?"

"This is different."

"Is it now!"

Jagdish frowned as he cinched down another sack that probably had enough demon inside to pay the living stipends of fifty warriors for a year. "I'm not buying anything. I earned my place through blood and sweat. I'm using these riches to get back the rank that's rightfully mine is all."

"Men of honor are a rare and dying breed, my friend. Probably because you're all busy dying stupidly while more pragmatic men rise to the top." Gutch grew serious. "I am begging you, Jagdish. Don't go back to Vadal. I can find us buyers in Warun. You can build an estate in Kharsawan or Sarnobat. We'll get you forged traveling papers for whatever destination your heart desires."

"My heart desires my home."

"Then your heart is filled with foolish sentiment."

"My wife is there. My child I've never met is there."

"Get new ones!"

Anyone else, Jagdish would've punched them in the teeth for that, but after traveling across a third of the continent, battling smugglers, demons, and wizards together, Gutch was basically his brother, so Jagdish just laughed at the foolishness.

"I'm not inclined to. I'm rather fond of mine." His arranged marriage had been a lucky one. Normally when a disgraced warrior was married to a worker girl to seal a contract, you couldn't expect much. But wise, supportive, beautiful, and kind, Pakpa had turned out to be his treasure. Jagdish happened to love his wife very much.

"Then create a new identity, settle elsewhere, and send for your baker's daughter. Pakpa is the same caste as me. We workers are practical! Trust me, she'd rather live in a manor in Kharsawan than a widow's shack in Vadal."

"I'd rather die than give up my caste. My son's going to be raised as a warrior."

"No problem. You want a command again? No other house is going to turn down an experienced officer who shows up on their doorstep with enough banknotes to fund his own garrison."

"I don't want to buy a new name. I want my old name back. I'm no traitor to my house."

"Ah! Why have loyalty to a house that had no loyalty to you? The instant Great House Vadal needed someone to blame they tossed you, a blameless man, beneath the wagon wheels. Harta will take your demon, say thank you very much, noble warrior, by the way I heard you've been serving as the right hand of the man who cut my mother's face off, now right this way to our gallows. They're the finest gallows in all of Vadal."

Jagdish groaned. "For the thousandth time, they'll not execute someone who avenged the murder of the Cold Stream guards and brought back an incredible treasure for his house in the process. I intend to dump a bag of bones and the seal of Sikasso on the throne room floor and declare that offense has been satisfied. That's what I'll do, or I am not the warrior Jagdish."

"Bravo." Gutch started to clap as if he'd just enjoyed the finale of a play. The noise even spooked one of the donkeys, who brayed at him in consternation. "They'll be so impressed they'll certainly hang you with a chain made of gold."

Deep down, he knew much of what Gutch was saying was valid. Depending on the mercy or wisdom of a politician was suicide. Perhaps the worker was right. Perhaps the honorable path only led to a bad end.

Jagdish just shook his head. "You're not a warrior, Gutch. I don't expect you to understand."

It was going to be a long walk back to Great House Vadal.

Chapter 16

〰〰〰

Ashok had ridden ahead to scout for danger and stopped on the hillside overlooking the coal town of Dhakhantar. It pleased him to see that his blood-thirsty Somsak had managed to not burn it down in his absence. That must have been difficult for them, as the Somsak had raiding in their blood.

Half a mile away, the Akershani warriors' tents still stood, though they were now occupied by the Sons of the Black Sword. The flag bearing the three red stars over a green field had been pulled down, and in its place hung a ragged strip of black fabric. He called upon the Heart of the Mountain to sharpen his vision. It appeared his men had been busy, as a large number of horses had been gathered. It looked like they had also stolen a few wagons from the town's workers as well. It simultaneously offended him that his gang of criminals had taken property they had no right to claim, and made him glad that they had shown initiative, because wagons would be useful to haul their supplies and the weakest of their marchers.

Even setting a brutal pace, it had taken Thera's pathetic army nearly the entire day to walk to Dhakhantar, and by the time they got there their number had swelled to nearly four hundred. The plains were like a never-ending parade of casteless fleeing ahead of the warriors' extermination, and Thera seemed determined to keep taking them in like they were homeless pets.

Ashok was highly annoyed by this, because every sickly casteless who fell in with them made their column that much more vulnerable. Their meager supplies wouldn't last. Hunting or foraging food sufficient for such numbers would only slow them down more.

Yet in another respect, Ashok found that he was actually impressed by Thera's deep sense of responsibility for others. It was a noble trait, though one she normally kept well hidden beneath a hardened shell of self-preservation. Either the visions she'd received in the graveyard of demons had put a crack in her selfishness, or more likely, she was driven by guilt because the rebellion she'd inspired was the reason the Capitol had ordered all of these casteless butchered.

Regardless of her motivations, her mercy toward the casteless was certainly making his obligation to keep her safe more difficult. It was his job to make sure her newfound kindness would not be the death of them all.

It was curious how you could take someone with a sense of duty and honor, and difficult circumstances could turn them into a criminal. But when given an opportunity, some criminals could still try to do the right thing... Maybe not the legal thing, but the *right* thing—there being a difference between the two still being a new and uncomfortable concept—but it was enough to make him question the multitude of executions he'd carried out over the twenty years he'd been a Protector of the Law. Were all those criminals as deserving of death as he'd thought they were at the time? Or like Thera, would they have tried to do good if given the opportunity?

Foolishness. Ashok cursed himself for letting his mind wander. Leisurely philosophy was for the judges. Ashok was a criminal, and he had criminal duties to attend to. Satisfied that there wasn't an army of angry warriors waiting to greet them, he kneed his horse and set off back toward the column.

The white stallion he had claimed yesterday was always eager to run. He was truly a magnificent animal, easily the equal in strength and stamina to a mighty Zarger warhorse. He must not have cared much for his previous rider, because he had given Ashok little trouble all day.

"Good job, Horse." That name would do, because Ashok had never been creative in the naming of his steeds.

When he got back, he found Thera marching at the head of the column, red faced and sweating. Their last few miles had featured a gradual but steep climb into the hills around Dhakhantar. In fact, since they were traveling from a swamp by the ocean to the edge of the mountains almost every day of their journey had been, and would continue to be, uphill to one degree or another. Such were the joys of marching. Even though Thera could claim the highest status of their odd band, she was carrying a pack as heavy as anyone else.

Thera's ever loyal bodyguard, Murugan, was walking

beside her with a bow in his hand. He saw Ashok approaching and shouted, "The general returns."

For security, Thera should not have been at the front of the column, but rather in the middle, where it was safest. Ashok had told her that a few times already. Surely Murugan had insisted as well but debating with that woman was about as useful as arguing with a wall. Only the wall was more likely to give.

"The camp is just over this rise. The Sons await us. Why are you on point?"

"Somebody needs to set the pace for this lollygagging gang of imbeciles!" Thera shouted back.

As Ashok got closer he realized the color on her cheeks wasn't from the exertion, but rather from frustration. "You appear angry."

"Of course I'm angry. Some of these damned fool idiots won't listen. I've had two men get into a fight over a woman, and two women get into a fight over who was the rightful owner of a chicken. It turns out that every casteless jealously despises all the casteless from the next village over. They slow us down with bickering and whining, I break them up to make peace, they're terrified of me, and while I'm there it's all heads bowed and *as you wish, Prophet,* until I go to fix the next problem and they go back to squabbling."

"Do you wish for me to kill some as an example?"

"No!"

"I already offered, sir," Murugan said helpfully.

"As you should have." A good bodyguard tended to unpleasant tasks so that the higher-status person they were protecting didn't have to worry about it. As for how to deal with this issue, he knew very little about the management of casteless beyond what he'd seen their overseers do. The casteless bargeman, Nod, had taught him that whipping them only made the casteless go slower, but then again Ratul had certainly known how to motivate Protector acolytes. "Perhaps a few beatings then?"

"Tempting as that is, they're scared and upset, Ashok. Hurting them more won't fix that. They're refugees. They need something to believe in. Something to hope for. Keta would've had them singing songs by now."

Ashok might not understand much about life among the other castes, but he did understand discipline. "If you treat them as children, they will remain children. You must impose order on them. Every man must have a place."

"Don't quote the Law at me, while we're actively rebelling against it."

"You have said yourself, you don't hate all of the Law, merely the parts you find unjust. Then I would suggest adopting the parts which suit you, and quickly, before your disorganized rabble gets us all killed... But I did not ride back here to discuss the politics of the casteless." He held one hand down toward her. "Ride with me to the camp. The column can catch up."

Thera seemed torn as she looked at his extended hand. "They're a mess. I'm afraid they'll fall apart without me."

"If they can't make it the last few miles on their own then they do not deserve you, and they should die alone on the plains."

Thera bit her lip as she thought it over, looked at Ashok's hand, and then back toward her ragged mob, obviously torn between duty and annoyance.

So Ashok provided her an honorable way out. "You

need to decide what to do about the town and the hostages. Such decisions are not mine to make."

"In that case..." She took his hand.

He effortlessly swung her up behind his back. Horse snorted and stamped, as if to say that he'd never agreed to *two* riders. "Whoa."

Thera had one last command to give. "Murugan, you're in charge of the column. Let it be known I've declared if any of them cause any more holdups, you'll leave them on the side of the road."

"It will be done gladly, Prophet."

Ashok nudged Horse into a quick walk. Once they were away from the column, he said, "I have no doubt your bodyguard will fulfill that particular command with great enthusiasm."

"He's a good kid. Murugan's as faithful as Keta, but only half as obnoxious about it. He's like my shadow when you're not around. I'm still getting used to the idea of warriors being willing to sacrifice their lives for mine, but I've no doubt that boy would take a blade meant for me in a heartbeat."

When the Sons of the Black Sword had encountered the demon in the swamp, it had been young Murugan who had become frightened and ran, attracting its attention. Though Ashok couldn't himself feel fear, he'd faced enough sea demons to understand why a normal man would be terrified of them. They were pure lethality, bound in near impenetrable flesh walking on near unbreakable bones, and Murugan had panicked. It had only been temporary, and he'd returned quickly to the battle, and from all accounts fought well, but as warrior caste, he'd be forever shamed by that lapse. Ashok wondered how much of Murugan's devotion to his prophet was due to faith, and how much was compensating for his earlier failure... Ultimately, his reasons didn't matter, as long as he did his job.

"That warrior you found who'd punched the Inquisitor and caught an arrow for his trouble will be fine," she told him. "Disobeying orders to murder casteless doesn't mean he wanted to join a band of them though, so I had him dropped off at a farmhouse we passed along the way."

"Good," Ashok said. Because even though it was illegal, the idea of striking Inquisitors amused him. It seemed incongruous how he could now simultaneously respect someone for keeping one part of the Law, while flagrantly violating another, but it was what it was.

It seemed getting away from the refugees had greatly improved Thera's mood, because she said, "Come on, Ashok, you can tell this stallion wants to run. Let him run!"

"I didn't cross half of Lok to save you from wizards, to have you break your neck falling off a horse."

"Cram your obligation. I'm a daughter of House Vane. I can probably ride better than you."

He doubted that very much. "As you wish."

Horse needed very little coaxing. Thera had to wrap her arms around Ashok's waist and hold tight. He found that he didn't mind the closeness.

After half a mile at a fierce gallop, feeling the wind on his face, he heard a surprising and unexpected sound. Thera laughing. It was an honest sound this time, not the sardonic, weary noise that she usually made indicating mirth. He glanced back over his shoulder, and found her actually grinning, carefree, while her dark hair whipped in the wind.

It was a good moment.

But all moments pass, and as they neared the camp, Thera's laughter trailed off. He glanced back and noted that she composed herself, and put on a stern face, a commander's face. It wouldn't do for the fanatics to see the Voice of their god being unserious. She hadn't needed to try, because when she saw the buzzards circling over the corpses piled outside the casteless quarter, Ashok could tell it brought reality crashing back, abruptly ending whatever joy she'd felt along their ride.

He slowed Horse as they approached the camp. It was better not to startle a weary guard and have an arrow launched their way. A couple of Somsak rose from the tall grass where they had been waiting in ambush. Even Ashok hadn't noticed their hiding places. Their vigilance pleased him.

The camp was in good order. There were a few spots where blood had turned the ground to mud, but the solders Ashok had killed here had been carried down and thrown upon the corpse pile. The Sons appeared upbeat and had gotten some rest. Their prisoners looked battered and surly, their wrists bound and tied to stakes driven into the ground. There were several strangers present, wearing insignia of various status, their expressions ranging from fearful to curious.

"General," Eklavya Kharsawan came out to meet them. "And the prophet! Welcome."

"How goes it, Havildar?"

"All is well here, Prophet. The Sons are ready to serve."

"Good." Thera didn't wait for a hand to be offered, and instead just jumped off Horse and landed lightly

on her feet. Ashok suspected she liked to remind the
Sons that she too was warrior caste, and not some
pampered Firster. "We've got much to do. The column
will be here soon, and it's now four hundred strong."

Ashok resisted the urge to shake his head at the
use of the word *strong*. "I see we have some guests."

"Yes, sir. Representatives from the various worker
councils in Dhakhantar, come to beg for mercy so
we don't pillage their town, then some others saying
they are part of Keta's rebellion."

"Have you confirmed they are who they claim to
be?" Thera asked, which was a good question, considering how crafty the Inquisition was with their spies
and infiltrators.

Eklavya spread his hands apologetically. "Sorry. I've
no idea how. I only knew the Keeper of Names for
a few days. So I hid them and told them to keep
quiet until the general got back. But, they're not
what I expected."

"Meaning?"

"They're whole men, not non-people." The havildar
caught himself, but too late. All of the Sons had been
told of Thera's declaration that the casteless were
human too. Only Thera didn't seem to notice his
mistake. It was one thing to insist on their person-
hood right after they were the pitiable victims of a
terrible massacre, and quite another thing after a long
day of the casteless annoying her with their frivolous
squabbles. "I mean they're men of status, supposed
secret leaders of the rebellion who've been funding
the faithful in secret."

Ashok knew very little about the real nature of
Keta's rebellion or its participants, so that made

him curious. These were far better at keeping their identities secret than most of the rebels the Law had required him to deal with over the years.

Thera must have been thinking the same thing. "I know many of the rebels Keta has worked with, at least by name, but he kept most of them secret even from me. Ratul told him to keep things compartmentalized."

Of course a Lord Protector had known a thing or two about hunting down criminals. "It takes longer when each captive you torture can only give up a couple of others rather than the whole conspiracy," Ashok explained.

"I'll speak with the rebellion first, take the town's tribute second, and then we'll talk about what to do with the hostages last. We'll need privacy." Thera glanced over at the command tent which had belonged to the phontho of the Chakma garrison. "Anyone using that fancy thing?"

"Not anymore." Ashok had already noted that the previous owner was among the prisoners. One of the Sons must have taken pity on the frail old man, because a cape had been put up on a few poles to provide him with shade. The phontho was so elderly he'd hardly even put up a fight when Ashok had captured him. The same could not be said for his bodyguards, who had fought valiantly. Killing them seemed an unnecessary waste of honorable lives, but such was war.

"The big tent's where I told the rebels to wait for you so they could stay out of sight. I figured if we are going to ransom back these prisoners, it's no use them seeing our allies' faces," Eklavya said. Jagdish had seen great potential in the intelligent young man, which was why he had picked him to be one of the Son's leaders. Such wisdom indicated that Jagdish had been correct in his assessment.

"Good thinking, Havildar." Thera started walking toward the command tent. "General, would you accompany me?"

"Of course." Ashok dismounted Horse and turned the reins over to one of the Sons. It would be interesting to see what manner of lunatics Keta's preaching had attracted this time. Also, he needed to be there in case one of them turned out to be a secret Inquisitor who'd try to put a knife in the woman he was obligated to protect. "Please do not introduce me."

"Why? Is the great Ashok Vadal still ashamed to be seen slumming it with criminals?"

"If they are assassins, I would prefer for them to be surprised when they learn I am no mere bodyguard."

"Oh... Good point."

The interior of the captured command tent was entirely too nice. Soft rugs had been rolled upon the grass. There was a circle of pillows for the officers to sit on as they planned their strategy, and a wicker chair for the phontho that was throne-like in its proportions. The incense and perfumes were thick enough to drown out the stink of horse soldiers. It was more like entering a fine home than a tent, so much so that the waiting fanatics had even reflexively taken their shoes off at the entrance. There were two pairs of sturdy work shoes, and a pair of slippers decorated with bits of ivory.

"Living in such comfort, no wonder that old man was so easy to capture," Ashok muttered as they walked inside.

"I've missed comforts." Thera gave a low whistle. "I say we keep it."

"Such opulence is unbecoming your warrior caste."

"I'm in my own unique caste of one now. It stands to reason religious figureheads should have a fancy tent."

Ashok studied her curiously. Apparently, she was being serious. "The Keeper constantly preaches about the unfairness of the high status having all the wealth while the lesser get nothing. What would Keta say about that?"

"Right now I don't rightly care. That's his thing. I want to sleep on pillows again."

Ashok shrugged. He knew Keta was just making up all this religious nonsense as he went along anyway. However, he did not like the idea of claiming this tent. Even outside of the Law, Ashok still preferred things to be *consistent*, but it was not his decision to make.

She raised her voice to address the waiting men, who had not noticed them come in. "I am Thera Vane."

"The prophet!" Then all of them immediately went to their knees, bowing like she was the Thakoor of their house, the bearer of an ancestor blade, and the Chief Judge, all rolled into one.

Ashok could see now why Thera had tried so hard to keep her identity a secret from adversaries and sycophants both. With so many followers it was no longer an option for her, but such piteous, fawning behavior would quickly become tiresome.

"I can tell this is going to be a long day." Thera sighed as they kept their eyes averted. "All right, enough of that. I've got no time for foolishness. Stand up already."

As the men did, Ashok assessed them. Two were

of the worker caste, the insignia on their sleeve that symbolized their particular duties were a mystery to him, but their rugged clothing was clean and new. The last, surprisingly, was of the highest caste, and had the insignia of a tax collector upon his colorful silk robes. Of course the fanatics had worn their finest to meet the Voice of their god.

It was unknown what manner of tales these men had been told about Thera, but they seemed awestruck to be in her presence. When they came to their senses, they began babbling introductions, and then launched into the typical story of conspiracies and prophecies and how they'd known all along the gods would return, so on and so forth. Their manner seemed sincere, except witch hunters were supposed to be phenomenal actors too. Despite that Ashok's gut told him he would not be needed to prevent any assassination attempts during this particular meeting.

Regardless, he took up a position just to Thera's side, where he could immediately place his body between her and the fanatics. There he waited, scowling.

To her credit, Thera managed to keep the surprise from her face, though it was obvious that she had not expected to find a member of the first caste here. In Lok it was instinctive, reflexive even, to be submissive to your betters. Even defiant Thera, who had long since disregarded the Law, obviously experienced a moment of trepidation before speaking to someone born of higher caste so as to not give offense. Even if this one was little older than a boy, thin and gangly, with a wispy excuse for a mustache.

Regardless, rebellion was rare among those born to such lofty stations. That was probably why she let her visitors rattle off their introductory speeches before she cut them off.

"Yes, I am the Voice." Though admitting it seemed to pain her. "I am honored by your greeting, and I'm glad to hear that those who've heard Keta's teachings have remained faithful. Only I've not come to save you from the injustice of the Capitol right now. I'm just passing through with a column of refugees."

"We understand, mighty Prophet. It is we who have come bearing gifts for you," the tax collector proclaimed. "We were warned to be ready for the day you came here, and to have it prepared for you."

"Warned by who?"

"Mother Dawn," said one of the workers.

Now that got Ashok's attention. The odd woman who knew too much and traveled too fast always seemed to be preparing the way ahead of them in places they'd never intended to go. She'd appeared to Eklavya and the Sons who had met them on the road to Haradas, and warned Toramana and his Wild Men that someday they would need to shelter the Voice, years before Thera had even heard of the House of Assassins. To the workers the Mother of Dawn appeared to be a worker, to the warriors a warrior, and when Ashok had met her in Jharlang, she had been a casteless.

Thera looked to him, eyes narrowed. She was even more suspicious of the mysterious woman, or wizard, or creature, whatever she may be, than Ashok was. Thus far Mother Dawn had aided them, but her ultimate purpose remained a mystery.

"What manner of gift did she tell you to bring me?"

"Five hundred rebel fighters in position and prepared to seize the walls of Chakma at your signal."

Chapter 17

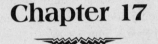

A vulture pecking at his bloody head woke him up.

"To the ocean with you," Bharatas tried to say through cracked lips and a mouth dry as sawdust. All he could manage was an angry whisper. "Go away. I'm still alive."

The vulture seemed unsure of this claim, but it waddled off. After all there was no shortage of easier carrion to feed upon nearby.

Bharatas found himself lying in the weeds. But better to be hidden in the grass than dead or a prisoner. He felt nothing but pain, until the memories of his brothers being killed one by one came rushing back. He had fought Ashok Vadal, and like a thousand men before him, lost. His head hurt where the Black Heart had split it open, and a throbbing pain went out in a circle around the wound every time his heart beat. His helmet had saved his life, but the blow had rendered him useless. Upon checking the injury with one shaking hand he found that the only thing holding a flap of his scalp down was dried blood.

It was unknown how long he had been out. From his terrible thirst and muscles too stiff to move, hours? A whole day? More? He'd never been struck like this himself, but he knew from seeing it happen to others that it was hard to tell what a head wound bad enough to make a man's brain swell up would do to them. Ignoring the agony and dizziness he managed to get to his knees so he could see over the grass. An experienced raider, he kept his movements slow so as to not catch a sentry's eye.

Except there was no one left to hide from. It appeared they'd broken camp and moved out. Any faint hope he might have held that his people had turned things around and claimed victory was dashed when he saw the pile of bodies wearing the tan and green uniforms of Great House Akershan. Weary, he sunk back down, and even that movement made him nauseous. If there'd been any water left in his body he would've vomited.

Bharatas knew he was a good swordsman. Perhaps one of the very best in all of Akershan, yet he'd been nothing but a temporary distraction to Ashok Vadal. None of them had. And when Bharatas thought of his dead brothers an angry determination filled him, and he began to crawl.

Ashok's men, whoever they were, had looted the Akershani camp, taking the food, weapons, tents, horses, and tack, and probably carried it all off in the cumbersome wagons their elderly phontho insisted on bringing. As much as he disliked the old man, his safety had been Bharatas' obligation, and now he was either dead or a hostage. Anger turned to fury as he dragged himself through the dirt by his fingernails. This insult would not stand.

Bharatas found that though the enemy had stolen most of their gear, they'd not taken all of it. The wine skins had been drained and discarded, but he found a canteen on the belt of a dead man that was still half full of water. He drank it slowly, lying there and plotting his revenge, until the dizziness passed enough for him to stand.

On wobbly legs he could now see that Dhakhantar hadn't been put to the torch, but neither had the caste-less quarter. He needed to get to Chakma, to warn the rest of the garrison about Ashok's rebels but he'd never make it across the plains on foot in time. He had the status to go down there and demand the workers lend him a horse, but he'd be sure to be seen by the fish-eaters, and he doubted his caste was very popular in Dhakhantar right now. Surely the non-people knew that they were all supposed to have been killed. They would be in a bloodthirsty mood. In his current weakened state even the skinniest casteless could take him.

From the bloat and flies on what was left of his friends and colleagues Bharatas realized he'd been unconscious for a day and a half. Odds were that Khurdan had been seized too, or she'd run off thinking him killed, and was long gone. But now that his lips were moist enough it was worth a try, so he whistled for his horse.

When there was no response, Bharatas cursed and set out toward Chakma, knowing that he would more than likely never make it. He was dehydrated, hungry, had lost too much blood, and as the sun fell the temperature would drop. Except Bharatas was no quitter. His burning hatred for Ashok Vadal would have to sustain him.

He walked and walked, falling occasionally because of feet that didn't want to work right. Whenever he fell down, he would tell himself that he was merely stopping to rest, because to admit otherwise was weak. Whenever he got back up, he would look back toward Dhakhantar to see how far he'd gone—not far enough—then give a sharp whistle in the vain hopes that the winds would carry the familiar sound to wherever Khurdan was, before going back to his march.

Once he fell, and must have passed out, because when he woke up again it was dark. This time it wasn't a buzzard's beak on his face, but rather a vast, soft nose.

As a Law-fearing man, Bharatas did not believe in miracles, but he did not have any other word sufficient to describe seeing Khurdan standing protectively over him.

Bharatas rode for three days though he barely remembered them. It was a blur of grass and sun. He spent most of the journey semiconscious in the saddle, but Khurdan knew the way back to her home pastures. Occasionally he'd wake up on the ground, having fallen off, unsure how much time had passed, with his noble horse waiting patiently for him. She probably even kept the buzzards and wolves away. She was a good girl, so loyal that if he died here she'd probably wait there until there was nothing left but his skeleton before sadly moving on.

His saddlebags had supplies for the journey. If she had been captured, Ashok's rebels hadn't even had a chance to pick through his belongings before she had heeded his call and escaped. Or perhaps she had simply gone off to graze until he'd needed her? Either way, there was naan, dried strips of goat meat, and a wine bladder full enough to get him part of the way back to Chakma. He'd also had a small bottle of potent sunda, but rather than drink it to dull the pain, he'd used it to make the pain worse, by washing the gash on his head in the hopes the alcohol would keep it from getting infected. Then he'd wrapped his head in bandages to keep the flies off it and hoped for the best.

Long ago his uncle Vikram had been obligated to the Historian's Order and promoted to the first caste. When he had come home to visit family, Vikram had seen in young Bharatas a sharp mind and intense dedication, and thus tried to recruit him for service in the Capitol. Only Bharatas' father would have none of that nonsense. They were riders of the plains, not guarders of the walls. Proud and swift, and his son was intended for greater things than guarding a museum!

He'd not even been able to guard a crusty phontho from criminals. If his father could see him now he'd kill himself because of the shame. He should've taken Uncle Vikram up on his offer.

There were a great many more warriors in Chakma. They were supposed to watch the casteless there, but not make a move against them until the phontho returned to personally oversee the extermination. He hadn't wanted anybody else to be able to claim any glory. Bharatas had been forced to hide his disgust at the time. As if there was glory to be found in killing helpless fish-eaters... Well, at least they'd all thought they would be helpless, until they'd somehow routed some of Akershan's finest.

This was all Ashok Vadal's fault. Bharatas vowed that after he warned the rest of the Chakma garrison, and he was well enough to travel the great distance to MaDharvo he would personally tell the Thakoor about Ashok's crimes and ask for the aid of the bearer of their ancestor blade. Ashok was good, but he would be no match for the legendary sword Akerselem, which was said could take all four legs off an armored horse in one swing. Bharatas felt no shame in losing to a bearer. It would take another ancestor blade to beat an ancestor blade.

Come to think of it... ancestor blades were supposed to be made of black steel that devoured the sunlight and stung the eye to look at. Though the fight remained hazy in his mind, Bharatas didn't remember seeing anything like that. Even though it had been lightning quick in his hands, Ashok had been using what appeared to be a regular sword. And if he was that terrifying of an opponent *without* an ancestor blade the man was a monster.

Bharatas was a fighter, not a tactician, so he'd never paid much attention to the lesser duties of the logistics corps until he needed them, but he always memorized where the supply station was in the region he was serving. There was one between Dhakhantar and Chakma, where he would be able to get his head stitched up and refill his saddle bags. Khurdan was doing fine. There was plenty of water from the spring runoff, and she grazed whenever he passed out, which was often.

Except when he found the station it had been ransacked. The water tank had been punctured and drained. The rations had been stolen. Whatever the raiders couldn't carry, they'd burned, including the haystacks. Judging by the lukewarm ashes they were at least half a day ahead of him. The handful of warriors who were supposed to be manning the place were missing. Judging by the tracks they'd been quickly overwhelmed and captured by a group of about thirty horsemen. It angered him that there wasn't even any blood spilled. They'd not even put up a fight.

It was a slight detour off the main route to Chakma and located in a gully so it wouldn't have even been visible over the horizon. How had the rebels known about this place? Had they found it by accident? Unlikely on the vast plains. Or had someone betrayed them? There had been talk about Akershani warriors joining the rebel's cause, but Bharatas had dismissed those rumors as foolishness. Now he was not so sure. The idea that some of his people would fall in with fanatics disgusted him. No. It was more likely the local casteless had known about it. They were idiot savages but they weren't blind.

He'd not cared for their orders. Slaughtering casteless seemed like a pointless waste. Yes, there were rebels among them. Bharatas had fought criminals before, but he knew most of the casteless were too stupid and lazy to rebel. Killing such defenseless wretches was beneath their dignity, and most of his brothers felt the same... But the arrival of the Black Heart would change everything.

That would be a proper war. Even though he was injured, delirious, and had just suffered a terrible defeat, the thought energized Bharatas. Regardless of how low his rebels were, the army that defeated Ashok Vadal would become legend. If their bearer wouldn't kill Ashok, then Bharatas vowed that he would find a way to destroy the Black Heart himself.

"Faster, Khurdan. To Chakma."

The next day he found his home city at war.

Chapter 18

~~~~~~~~~~

"I will cut a path!" Ashok bellowed at the Sons of the Black Sword. "On me!"

Shoulder to shoulder and three ranks deep, the Akershani heavy spearmen filled the entire street, their weapons leveled and ready as they quick marched forward. Their armor was made of chain and green lacquered plate, their footsteps in practiced time—they made for an imposing force. Nothing at all like the loose clusters of surprised warriors they'd cut down to make it this far into the heart of Chakma.

The Sons of the Black Sword ran to keep up as Ashok charged the center of that steel wall. The soldiers seemed surprised, surely wondering what manner of madman would willingly impale himself on their spears. The closest two thrust with an accuracy that would've caught any normal man in the ribs, but with the inhuman strength stolen from the Heart of the Mountain, he smashed the attacks aside. Poles splintered. He dodged another point and rolled between the shafts, swinging his sword. That hit, clean beneath the helm. A warrior fell, blood spraying from his neck. Ashok turned into the next and kicked, shattering a knee. As that spearman dropped, Ashok vaulted over him and struck at the next.

He'd made a hole. As the second rank tried to plug it, the howling, battle-mad Sons rushed to exploit it. Ashok made it wider for them.

Outside a few feet a spear made for a fearsome weapon. Inside that radius however, its length became a liability, so Ashok went to work. Laying about him with his sword, he kept pushing, staying as close to the enemy as possible, crashing into them, denting helmets with his elbows or cracking skulls with his hardened fists. Anyone he knocked down would be easy to finish by the Sons behind him.

He could not feel fear, but he could recognize it on the faces of other men. From the look of these poor warriors Ashok must have made a terrifying figure. Per Thera's command—to do his best to remain alive—he had worn the Protector armor that Gutch had repaired and fitted for him. Except Ashok could not stand the indecency of a criminal like him wearing the symbol of the Law, so he had removed the face, and rather than shame the proud colors of his former order, he had blackened the silver with soot and ash, so that instead of a shining beacon of the Law he had become darkness incarnate, black as a demon.

The tall brick walls had fallen before the city had even known it was under attack. The rebels had seized the towers and flung open the gates for them. The Sons had ridden inside as all of Chakma had descended into chaos. The rebels were fighting house to house, getting revenge against any who they'd felt had wronged them. And from the amount of bloodshed in this place, that had been a great many wrongs indeed.

All this Law breaking disgusted him, but he had a mission to complete. Seize the first-caste district and the government house to force their surrender.

Ashok caught a spear in his free hand an instant before it would've impaled him. He sidestepped and yanked the spear forward, jerking the warrior off balance. The handguard of his sword broke jaw and teeth. Another warrior was battling one of the Sons, and Ashok took advantage of that temporary distraction by slicing a leg out from beneath him. A moment later the Son smashed a mace down on the fallen man's head.

Most of the city's warriors had been taken by surprise, but the paltan stationed at their garrison nearest the first-caste quarter had come out ready to fight. Rather than blunder out in small groups to try and stop the rampaging rebels like most stationed here, this risaldar had taken the time to organize, armor up, and stick together. They'd marched to the street that allowed entrance to the estates of their highest-status men. Now that same sharp risaldar was behind his heavy infantry, riding back and forth on a horse so his men could see him, shouting for them to hold the line even as the Somsak kept launching crossbow bolts at him. There was already one bolt that had failed to penetrate sticking out of his breast plate, but he still refused to dismount because his men needed to see him. Ashok knew they would probably have to kill that officer before this was over, but in the meantime, he had earned Ashok's respect.

The Sons kept pushing into the gap, swinging

swords, axes, and hammers. They took advantage of the violence Ashok caused even as he spread far more, darting between the defenders, slashing and striking.

Though they'd fought wizards and demons and ambushed many soldiers, this was the Sons' first stand-up battle. They did not disappoint. Jagdish would have been proud of his fanatics. All Ashok could do was fight as hard as he could to keep the Sons alive.

Steel rebounding off his lamellar plate, he crashed forward, spreading chaos among the ranks, shoving armored warriors into each other, keeping them off balance, bounding back and forth, preventing them from organizing a good defense, and killing, always killing. Each time a warrior slipped, Ashok took advantage of it and another man died.

If he'd still had Angruvadal, they'd all be dead already.

The Sons flowed in around him, stabbing and crushing. There were tall buildings on both sides of them, and as the Sons took the middle the spearmen's ranks were cut in half, and each half was pressed against the walls. Jagdish would have yelled at them for that because it meant they were now surrounded on three sides, but this had degenerated into something so savage that there was no real strategy at all. The enemy risaldar was screaming for his back rank to drop their spears and draw their swords, but then a bolt hit his mount in the neck and horse and rider went crashing to the stone.

They were winning, but Ashok saw that reinforcements were running up behind the enemy. These weren't even real warriors, just a mob of sepoys, worker-caste militia who could be called up and issued weapons in the direst emergencies. They were unarmored and unskilled but numbers could make the difference.

Eklavya was at Ashok's elbow, battering the enemy with a war hammer. The young man was obviously frightened but in the moment, too determined to feel it. There was a flicker of movement, the briefest of warning that any normal man would have failed to see, but Ashok reached back with his free hand for the spear that had been flung at his havildar, and caught it with only inches remaining between the blade and Eklavya's spine. He swung it around, broke the shaft in half over a warrior's head, and then hurled the rest end over end into another man's chest.

Ashok knew he should not have been able to react so quickly on his own. Once again, it was almost as if Angruvadal was still with him, whispering. Did the shard lodged in his heart still live?

There was no time for such idle ponderings though. So he grabbed Eklavya by his shoulder plate and spun him around. "Havildar."

"Yes, General!" The wide-eyed warrior didn't even know that Ashok had just saved him from being paralyzed from the neck down.

"Break down those doors, send archers up the stairs. Fire down into the enemy."

"Yes, sir!" Eklavya ran back, shouting commands.

Ashok returned to the fight. The faster he could beat these warriors, the sooner the city would fall and Thera could order the rebels to stand down, the more lives spared. Though he was unsure if once released, the rebels' bloodlust could be so easily stopped. As if to accentuate this thought, there was a sharp crack of thunder, as somewhere nearby a rebel unleashed illegal Fortress magic.

Backs to the brick, the Akershani warriors fought desperately, but it wasn't enough to stop the brutal assault of the Sons, and the enemy began to fall apart.

Above them curtains were flung open as the archers of the Wild Men took up position. On this flat street, beyond the line of colliding and moving men, their targets had been limited for fear of hitting their brothers. With a bit of elevation however, their choices must have seemed endless. Bowstrings thrummed. More Akershani warriors fell.

The sepoys ran forward, carrying cheap short swords that must have felt unfamiliar and clumsy in their hands. The blades were even speckled with rust, probably because they'd been long forgotten and locked up in some storage room. Normally when the bell rang to summon these workers it was to fight fires. Being handed a sword instead of a bucket must have confused and frightened them. It almost made Ashok sad to have them killed.

Ashok broke past the last of the warriors and launched himself directly at the sepoys. A few of them yelped, turned, and fled when they saw him. The brave ones kept coming. Ashok simply cut the leader's head off. The body managed to run a few more feet past him before falling over and dumping what to the workers must have seemed a ridiculous amount of blood.

The workers skidded to a stop. The head landed between them.

"Flee, or I will kill you all."

The drafted workers must have believed the terrifying, blood-soaked, black-clad apparition because they all turned and ran for their lives.

That problem solved, Ashok turned back to the battle. The Akershani were overwhelmed and crumbling. One of their havildars was shouting for a retreat. Shekar of the Somsak leaned way out one of the upstairs windows to launch a crossbow bolt directly into that warrior's head. The command had caught the attention of many of the warriors and having the word *retreat* punctuated with its issuer's immediate death broke them. Men fled. Others tossed down their weapons and begged for mercy. Swords and hammers were raised—

"Let them live!" Ashok bellowed. The Sons heard him. Mostly.

Something warned him to turn and lift his sword. Sure enough, the enemy risaldar was coming at Ashok, curved sword moving in a blur. Ashok met it, steel on steel, then swiftly turned into the man to violently shoulder him to the ground.

There was no mistaking it that time. That blade should have struck him in the back. That instinct had been Angruvadal's gift. Like during the duel against Bundit or bringing him back to life on Sikasso's meat hook, it was plain now the shard in his heart intended to keep him alive by once again granting him the instincts of all its previous bearers.

That was huge. Amidst all the carnage, Ashok laughed.

There was not time to ponder on the ramifications of Angruvadal's gift, because the warrior was getting back to his feet.

"Surrender, Risaldar. You are defeated."

"And let you rebels destroy Chakma? Never!"

Ashok could have easily killed him on the way up,

but he did not wish to. "We will not raze this city. Nor will we execute your men. You have my word."

The risaldar extended his sword before him, ready to attack. "What worth is the word of a criminal?"

"When the criminal is Ashok Vadal, it is worth everything."

The risaldar flinched. "Ashok Vadal?"

"I am."

"Better to swordfight a wildfire." The warrior looked like he was ready to die and would go to the great nothing without a regret—as befitted his caste—but then he looked to his men and saw their sorry state. It was easy for a warrior to think of his own glory, and harder to set it aside for the safety of others. This one was brave, but their battle was lost. Best to save who he could.

"Do you promise you'll let my men live?"

"They will be ransomed back to your house when your Thakoor agrees to spare the casteless." It was what Thera had decided to do with all the other prisoners they had taken so far. Ashok saw no reason why she would decide differently here. "Until then you will be bound, but neither starved nor tortured."

He glanced toward the impressive government buildings behind them. "What of Chakma's first caste?"

"Their fate will be theirs to decide. They can be proud, or they can survive."

The offer was fair, the stakes high. It was a difficult choice, but the wiser one was made. The risaldar nodded in submission and then placed his sword on the ground at Ashok's feet.

Chapter 19

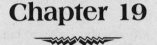

Taking the city had not proven that difficult. However, keeping the victorious rebels from burning it down was.

When the rebellion's leaders had told Thera about their plan—which had been put into place at the mysterious Mother Dawn's urging—she had seen great opportunity. Thera had never been a raider or played any political games herself, but her father had, and she'd learned much from Andaman Vane.

The rebels had been smuggling men and weapons—both mundane and Fortress forged—into Chakma for months. With most of the city's garrison deployed across the region to exterminate the casteless, it was an ideal time to strike a fearsome blow against the Law, or so they had assured her. They intended to seize the city to use as a bargaining chip.

Their plan made strategic sense, but Thera wasn't Keta. She had no grand illusions about throwing off the chains of the Capitol and creating a free house where all people could live as equals. She didn't want to capture territory. She just wanted to be left alone. Only the extermination order against the casteless had changed everything. Thera had no desire to meddle in anyone else's affairs, but whenever she closed her eyes she was still haunted by the images of those dead children on the plains. If there was a way to stop such horrors, and she didn't act then she would be every bit as cruel as the judges who'd signed the order.

Thera was a pragmatic survivor, but that did not make her a coward. Mother Dawn—whatever manner of being she really was—had laid the groundwork for something impressive here. It stood to reason that if the casteless genocide became too costly to continue, then the Thakoor of Great House Akershan would have no choice but to call off his warriors. Losing control of the little coal town of Dhakhantar was one thing but losing the valuable market city of Chakma would be a costly embarrassment. It would be difficult for him to continue dispatching paltans to murder casteless if the First was demanding all the warriors stay in their cities to protect them.

The opportunity was too great to pass up.

However, Thera had also seen the madness that accompanied war, especially illegal war, and didn't want to bring that hell down upon these people. The Law allowed for raids and disputes between houses. In fact that was how her father had become so rich and respected. The judges knew that low-level violence between rivals was inevitable, so the Law included a code of appropriate behaviors for raiders. Stealing was fine but needed to be kept within limits. That way valuable trade could resume as soon as possible.

No salting fields or destroying factories for example. Death on the battlefield was expected, but torturing captives was not, so on and so forth.

These rules enabled her old caste to conduct their bloody business without too much disruption to the others. They were often so good at it she'd even heard rumors of border villages that had changed hands so many times that the worker caste who lived there didn't even know who they belonged to until it was time to pay their protection notes.

When warriors weren't good at it, innocents died, crops were burned, people starved, rats feasted on the fields of bodies, and plagues spread. Whenever raids threatened to spiral into full-blown house wars the Capitol would step in and send their dreaded Protectors to restore order. Thera figured the judges only cared because dead workers couldn't be taxed.

As if by a miracle, Thera had been given an army. Only this army had no code of conduct. They had not been raised to understand honor between foes. Her forces consisted of the bitter and oppressed, the grudge holders, the criminals with nothing to lose, and a few she suspected simply wanted to start fires and hurt people. She had long since been forsaken by her caste, but the teachings of Andaman Vane remained. Thera would use this gift army, but she'd be damned if she'd let them run wild in the process.

So when she had agreed to the rebels' plan, she had sent them back with a message. They would take the city at her signal, but afterward there would be no revenge killings, no unorganized looting of the city's store houses, they would take prisoners, and above all, no rape. Thera had seen her husband's forces do that during the house war in Makao, and the memories still filled her with disgust and revulsion.

Thera had met many rebels and fanatics over the years, and most were good people done wrong, or true believers, but very few of them were as high-minded as Keta or as faithful as Ratul, and unfortunately she knew many of them were simply opportunistic scum. The ones who had faith that the Voice was really divine would obey, but she suspected a few would not. So to accentuate her commands she had warned them that anyone who failed to obey their prophet's commands would be dealt with by Black-Hearted Ashok himself.

Though inscrutable as always, Ashok had not seemed to mind his name being used to strike fear into the disobedient. After twenty years of collecting heads for the Law, he was probably used to it.

Ashok dragged the criminal into the command tent by his hair. His squealing and crying annoyed Ashok, but worse, the noise interrupted Thera's meeting with the rebel leaders. Since he had been inside the walls of Chakma all day putting out fires—sometimes literally—Ashok did not know what he had missed, but from the raised voices he'd heard though the fabric and the angry looks he could see now, Thera had upset these men somehow.

This was not a surprise to Ashok. She had a knack for infuriating people. He had simply become used to her obstinate ways. The rebels had just met her.

"Ashok has returned. Please join us." Thera clearly noted he had a prisoner, but chose not to say anything about it. "We were just discussing our next move."

It was plain that whatever she had declared that

move to be, the rebels had not agreed with it. They had taken a city, which was quite a triumph, only they seemed angry, rather than happy. There were a dozen men assembled inside their spacious stolen tent. The bodyguard Murugan was standing right behind Thera, looking extremely nervous. Among the rebels was Pankaj Akershan, the first-caste man they had met in Dhakhantar.

When Pankaj noticed Ashok's captive he exclaimed, "That's one of my servants. What are you doing with him?"

"Master Pankaj, please don't let them kill me," the criminal begged.

Ashok kicked him in the stomach hard enough to send him rolling across the fine rugs. "Be quiet. You will be judged shortly." He turned back to the council as if he'd never been interrupted. It was plain Pankaj did not like his man being abused, but Ashok did not care.

"Why are you treating one of my servants like this?"

Thera held up one gloved hand to silence the tax collector. "How goes it in the city?"

Ashok noted that she stopped the rebel abruptly, reflexively. She was settling into her role as a commander, but she was a stranger to the subtle manipulations of the highest caste. The young man seemed angrier at being cut off than his man being treated poorly. Thera didn't seem to notice, but the First tended to remember such sleights.

"It is disorderly, Prophet," he reported. "The rebels bristle at the code of conduct you have set for them. Their desire for revenge has made them stupid. There have been retribution murders, looting, and arson. A riot has broken out in the market district. There have been attempts on the lives of our hostages."

"What? The fools. We need those warriors so we can ransom them back to their house."

One of the rebels spoke up. He wore the insignia of some kind of high-status worker. "It's because the warriors in Chakma have been cruel, taking what's not theirs, and abusing their authority. The phontho here was an old fiend who let his men do whatever they felt like. My people's anger is a righteous one."

"They'll have to get over it," Thera said. "I need to trade hostages for the lives of the casteless."

As she said that, Ashok noted that though they had provided most of the bodies to the fight, there were no casteless among the rebellion's leadership. It was ironic that even among those who brazenly defied the Law, they still instinctively followed its divisions.

Other than Murugan, Pankaj was probably the youngest one in the tent, but he was clearly used to throwing his weight around and getting what he wanted. "If we let the warriors go, then they'll simply return to fight us again. We must execute them at once."

Pankaj was not incorrect. Except Ashok had given his word to the men he'd captured that their lives would be spared. He would not violate his oath, even one made to someone who'd be dead shortly thereafter. Having already explained the circumstances of their surrender to her, Ashok looked to their reluctant prophet.

"No," Thera said, in a tone that said the matter was settled.

"Before letting them go we could cut one of their hands off at least," one of the workers suggested. "That will render them useless in a fight. And the presence of so many cripples among the warriors will remind them not to trifle with us! The Law will be too scared to come here."

A few of the rebels nodded in agreement.

Ashok had to restrain himself from speaking out of turn. These fools did not understand that the Law did not forget any trespass. They could remove the limbs from every warrior in Akershan and there would still be hell to pay for what they had done here.

"At least let us cut off their thumbs," said a rebel. "Can't hold a sword without thumbs!"

But Thera was having none of it. "There will be no torture. That's final."

The high-status worker spoke again, but with the tone of a sullen child. "Very well. I will tell my men to leave those prisoners alone."

Ashok did not tell the worker that his word would probably be unnecessary now, since Ashok had already killed the ringleader when he had refused to stand down. The mob had watched Ashok do it, and an example had been set. Then he'd left Toramana and his archers to watch over the prisoners just in case. He rather doubted it would be an issue again.

"The rioting continues, but it is contained to one district for now. The Sons are in place to keep it from spreading. The workers blame the casteless for this battle. The casteless seem content that they are not being exterminated, but they are afraid. Word of our refugee caravan has spread, and many of the faithful wish to join."

"They cannot leave!" Pankaj exclaimed. "We will need them here to defend the walls if we are to hold Chakma."

"I've been trying to tell you, if the warriors lay siege to this place, it will fall," Thera said, and from her exasperated tone, Ashok now knew what they'd been arguing about before his arrival. "They'll surround it and camp until you starve, or if they're in a hurry they'll build siege engines and tear these feeble walls down."

"That will not happen. We have proven ourselves strong! I will declare myself the rightful judge of Chakma and open negotiations with the Thakoor. He will grant us autonomy." Pankaj gestured at the workers. "Their demands about pay and working conditions will be met. The non-people will be allowed to live. And the faithful will be granted leniency so they may worship freely."

Ashok couldn't believe his ears. It turned out a first-caste fanatic could be just as delusional as the lowest of the low. He tried to warn Pankaj. "Your Thakoor will not agree to any of that. As long as the Capitol stands, the Law will never abide such dissent. The Protectors will come for you. They will make an example of this place."

"How do you know this? Did the gods tell you?"

"Your gods tell me nothing. I know that is what they will do, because it is what I would have done in their place."

"The gods should be guiding us!" exclaimed another worker. "Only we've seen no evidence this girl is the true Voice. Mother Dawn told us to watch for a prophet, but all this one has done is keep us from taking what is rightfully ours and stopped us from killing those who deserve it."

When several of the leaders murmured agreement,

Murugan actually spoke up. "Don't you dare speak ill of her. She's the Voice. I've heard it with my own ears."

"Lies!" the worker shouted.

"It's the truth." Murugan moved his hand to the hilt of his sword. "If you want, I'll demonstrate my conviction."

The worker glared at Murugan, but though the worker was a tall, fit man, he wasn't stupid enough to try the young bodyguard. That was wise.

"I've seen it as well," Ashok stated flatly, because even though he thought the gods were foolishness, he would not withhold truthful testimony which might aid the woman he was obligated to protect. Thera seemed thankful for him speaking up for her, though the fanatics remained belligerent.

"Then why haven't the gods spoken to us? This girl wants to go and hide in the mountains, when we just conquered the jewel of the plains. Why live in a cave when every one of us here can claim our own mansion? Mother Dawn's prophecies came true, but we've seen nothing from this one. While we took the city, she was outside the walls, doing nothing."

"What is your name?" Murugan asked the worker.

"I am Rohit the Miller."

"And the man you disrespect is Ashok Vadal, twenty years a Protector, who once bore mighty Angruvadal, who has killed more than a thousand men in battle, who came back from the *dead* to serve this woman. Whose testimony is worth more? Rohit the grain grinder or Ashok whom the gods chose?"

Ashok just scowled at the bodyguard. That description was true for the most part—though it was more the Grand Inquisitor who had put him here than the Forgotten—but he did not care for the way the Sons had built him up in their heads. It still seemed inappropriate to flatter a criminal.

"Enough, Murugan. They simply don't realize that the Forgotten only speaks when he feels like it, he's a lot like Ashok in that way." There said that last bit with a lighter tone that was obviously intended to break the tension and calm the belligerent leaders. "The Forgotten will make a pronouncement when he's good and ready. Until then, you may not know me, but many of you know Keta and trust him. You've heard his sermons. He's prepared a place for the rebellion to be safe. You believed him before."

Pankaj shook his head. "Chakma hasn't seen the Keeper of Names for a long time. He abandoned us. We've had to figure out things on our own, and we have, accomplishing more in the last day than Keta has in years. You can't just use his name and expect us to obey. We have claimed a position of authority here. We will not throw it away."

"I think you are wrong," Thera said.

"But do the gods? Rohit brings up a good point. We placed our faith in you, but what has it gained us?"

"A way out of this death trap," Thera snapped. "The rebellion has survived by hiding and using hit-and-run tactics. These walls may look safe, but so does a turtle's shell, until the bear flips it over and eats its soft belly."

Rohit was growing furious. "So you have warned, but in your own voice, not that of the gods. I've seen no vast light, no words that sound like trumpets in our head as Keta's stories have claimed. You say the Forgotten speaks in his own time, but our time is now, and you have offered nothing. We built an army sufficient to take a mighty city, and all you brought was a bunch of starving non-people."

Ashok knew that he and the Sons of the Black Sword had defeated more warriors than the rest of the rebels put together, even though the rebels were far more numerous. The locals had opened the gates, but without the Sons to intercept and defeat them, the organized warriors would have crushed any resistance. To say they had brought nothing was a terrible personal insult, but Ashok held his tongue.

"We got our hopes up expecting divine intervention, and instead we received a woman with a cripple's hands and a coward's heart!"

Thera gasped at the brazen insult. But before she could respond, before anyone else could react, Ashok crossed the entire tent to grab Rohit by the throat. He choked the man's air off before he could utter one more disgusting lie.

The other leaders all flinched and stepped away from their unfortunate comrade.

"Ashok, put him down!" Thera commanded.

In his anger he had not realized that he had lifted Rohit, so that his feet were kicking a few inches above the ground. The miller's eyes were popping out of his head. His mouth was puckering as he tried to desperately inhale. He slapped futilely at Ashok's arms, but he could do nothing against the iron grip.

"Offense has been taken," Ashok growled. It was the official challenge for a legal duel, and from the reaction of the rebels, the most frightening thing that could be uttered by a man of Ashok's dark reputation.

"Offense has *not* been taken," Thera insisted. "I'll

decide when I am offended. He insulted me. Not you. Rohit misspoke. We need to work with these people, not against them. Let him go, Ashok. Please."

"As you wish." Ashok dropped the terrified worker on his ass. He had acted inappropriately and overstepped his bounds. It was his obligation to protect her life, not her feelings. But for some reason the insult against her had meant far more than the one against himself, so he addressed the rebels. "Let it be known that Thera has more courage than all of you combined. Those scars on her hands were earned fighting a battle against an evil beyond your comprehension in the graveyard of demons. If you ignore her counsel, then you are fools, and will perish like fools."

A few had the sense to feel shame. The others were a combination of angry and afraid. Rohit was coughing as he crawled away. But sadly, Ashok could see that proud young Pankaj took his henchman's embarrassment personally. The young man may have been a true believer, but he also retained his caste's exaggerated sense of importance. Thera had been trying to keep the rebellion in one piece. In his anger, Ashok had unwittingly sabotaged her. Pankaj would not, could not, back down now without losing authority in front of his men.

Pride had made Pankaj blind to the future, but brave in the moment. "Enough of this. I am not some fish-eater to be bullied and led around. Mother Dawn came to me. *Me.* She said I was special. I risked my life and my name. I organized the rebels of Chakma. I bought weapons and hid them until it was time. I have the greater force. Those who fought here today are loyal to me. I will not be disrespected and offered scraps. You forget who this city belongs to."

Ashok did not understand these fanatics. Pankaj had seemed so hopeful when they'd first arrived. Perhaps the young man had imagined the prophet would simply tell him what he wanted to hear?

"Pankaj, please reconsider," Thera began. "Let us work this out."

"If the Forgotten is displeased by my decisions, then I am certain he will tell me himself," Pankaj snapped. "Where is he?"

Thera's eyes narrowed dangerously. She had been trying hard to be polite, and she was an impolite contrarian by nature. There was no controlling the Voice, but if she could, Ashok had no doubt she would've made it appear right then in order to smite these stiff-necked idiots.

With their alliance falling apart, Pankaj tried to assert his dominance. "Now that Ashok's report has been given, I *demand* to know why my loyal man is lying there with his hands tied."

"I did nothing wrong!" Pankaj's servant wailed.

Ashok walked back over to him, grabbed the man roughly by his shirt, and hauled him to his knees before Thera. "He is a rapist. One of my patrols heard the screaming and found him and his men having their way with a woman they'd dragged into an alley."

The captive tried to plead his case. "She was a warrior's wife. We caught them trying to sneak out the gate in disguise. We killed the man, just as we should have. She tried to run and we caught her."

"And then brutalized her next to her husband's dead body." The Sons had put arrows in the other participants, as per Thera's orders not to tolerate such things, but they'd not known what to do with this one when he'd started crying about his high and mighty office with his pants still around his knees.

"So what?" Pankaj demanded. "She was of lower caste and deserved it. This man is of my household. His family is wealthy and influential. He should be treated with more dignity than this."

Several of the workers gave their self-appointed ruler the side eye as he said that. There wasn't much profit in rebelling against one overbearing ruler just to trade him for a new one.

"I can think of nothing more disgusting than excusing evil just because the perpetrator has important friends," Thera said. "My instructions were clear. He did not heed them. For that, he deserves execution."

Ashok pulled back the captive's hair with one hand, exposing his throat, as he drew a knife with the other.

"No, wait, please, I beg you! I did nothing wrong!"

"Stop this madness at once," Pankaj said. "How dare you? This man is obligated to me. He's been a loyal servant during our plots against the Law. He is valuable to the rebellion and necessary for the defense of this city. I will not tolerate such an insult. You need us more than we need you. I have an army of brave men and twenty Fortress rods. You have an army of refugees. Without what I bring, you have nothing."

There was an edge of anger slipping into Thera's voice. "I said *my instructions were clear.*"

"You will heed my words this instant!" Pankaj shouted. "Kill this man, and our arrangement is finished. You will be cast out of Chakma. You will receive no further aid from us. Your sick and weak will die on the plains."

Ashok went to kill the criminal anyway, but before the killing strike was delivered, Thera said, "Ashok, wait..."

Knife pressed against the rapist's neck, Ashok paused, genuinely curious. Would she back down in order to keep the rebellion unified?

She met Pankaj's eyes with a cold, level gaze. Thera stared him down, unblinking. "I don't want to get blood in my new tent. Do it outside."

"As you wish."

Ashok dragged the criminal across the rugs, as he kicked and thrashed and wailed, "No! No! Please, no!" through the furs that served as a door and into the night.

A few of the Sons were standing watch. They saw their beloved general pulling the pathetic wretch along but said nothing. Once he was far enough away to not get arterial spray on the fabric, Ashok jammed his knife beneath the rapist's ear, and then yanked it out in a spurt of blood. The pathetic mewling died off as he flopped over, clawing at this wound. Ashok wiped his knife on the dying man's shirt, then left him there to water the grass.

"Like us to carry the body off after he quits twitching, General?" Gupta asked.

"No. Leave him so as our guests depart they can see what happens when one does not follow the rules." Ashok reasoned it was good for the Sons to see this as well. Though faithful thus far, they had been growing in numbers and it would be good for them to be reminded the value of maintaining discipline. He sheathed his knife and went back inside.

The leaders were dead silent. Pankaj was seething with rage. Thera had just folded her arms and was standing there, as if daring him to complain. The only sound was a large moth beating its body against the glass of an oil lamp. After a quiet moment, Thera walked over to a small table of refreshments.

As she poured herself a cup of wine, she said, "To those of you with any sense, ponder on what you wish to serve. Your god's voice, or a petulant man-child's pride."

Pankaj stomped toward the exit. "You have until dawn to leave this city."

"And you have until I finish this drink to get out of my tent."

Thera took a drink.

Chapter 20

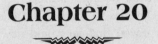

When Devedas heard about the fall of Chakma, he rode there as fast as he could. Akershani warriors had already surrounded the city but not yet attacked. Each time scouts had approached the walls they had been fired upon by terrifying Fortress weapons. No one had been hit, but the warriors were rightfully worried about the thunderous things, and it was unknown how many the rebels had inside. There wasn't enough good lumber around the cursed windy place to build proper siege engines to shatter the gates or smash holes in the brick walls, so the warriors had formed a perimeter to keep the rebels from escaping, and then waited.

What was their plan? Were they shipping in logs, or sitting around hoping for trees to grow? Perhaps they were waiting for the city to run out of food, content to let the Law-abiding trapped inside starve along with the guilty. Devedas had not known, nor cared what their plans were. All that mattered to him was that

Ashok Vadal had been seen inside that city. He was told that a few residents had snuck over the wall to escape. When they'd been caught at the perimeter, they'd claimed that Ashok Vadal was still inside, a terrifying specter in blackened armor who served as the vengeful right hand of the false prophet, who ruled over the city as a blood-soaked tyrant, purging all who would not obey his whims.

It pained Devedas to think of his once brother, so fallen and depraved that he would now serve such a foul creature. Ashok needed to die for a multitude of reasons, but in a way Devedas suspected killing Ashok would be doing him a favor. It was time to end this.

So Devedas had taken command. The phontho in charge had been dispatched from a garrison to the south to deal with this mess and was eager to give up responsibility for the siege. The Akershani warrior caste had been embarrassed enough already. Their Thakoor, safe in distant MaDharvo, would be enraged when he found out that some of his lands had been taken over by lowly fish-eaters, and would need someone to curse. The phontho was happy to let the Protectors be the ones to take the blame for a while.

Only Devedas was not a patient man. Word of the rebellion claiming an actual city had drawn every Protector in the region like crows to a corpse pile. You did not need siege engines when you had ten Protectors at your disposal.

Thirty days after the city of Chakma fell to criminals, Lord Protector Devedas liberated it.

The Protectors crept up to the city in complete darkness with eyes like owls. Kushal and Usman scaled the wall first. They were both mountain born, able to climb like monkeys, and that had been before they had been given the incredible strength and dexterity that could only be bestowed by the Heart. The rest of them were wearing their silver armor hidden beneath thick gray cloaks, but Kushal and Usman were dressed in nothing but dark silks, so they could make their way up the weathered brick in complete silence. At the top, they smoothly knifed the nearest sentries, then sent down ropes.

Once they were atop the battlements, the Protectors made their way toward the gatehouse, silently killing as they went. Just because the Order normally worked in the open, as a gleaming, unforgiving example of the Law's ultimate authority, that didn't mean that they couldn't be stealthy when necessary. The gifts they were given by the Heart of the Mountain made them fearsome hunters. It could only help one thing at a time, but in turn they could sharpen their hearing, heighten their sense of smell, improve their vision, and then give their bodies incredible power and speed. Even without the magic in the blood they had far more experience than their foes, the finest training in the world, and a dedication that these savages could never understand. The sleepy casteless manning the walls never stood a chance.

Devedas took half his men down a ladder into the interior. They made it all the way to the gate before one of their victims managed a scream before dying, but by then it was too late. Shrugging out of their cloaks, they fell upon the rebels at the entrance and hacked them to pieces. Most of the rebels never even got a chance to wake up. Ranvir and Broker increased their strength so that they could move the iron crossbar that would normally take half a dozen men to lift, while far above them Kushal lit a torch and began waving it in a predetermined pattern to signal the warriors it was time. The gates of Chakma were open.

Not too far away a rebel began to bang on a drum. They had made sufficient noise that the alarm had been raised. No matter. Across the distance the plains lit up as hundreds of torches were struck. The warriors had begun their march.

"Smash the hinges so they can't close them, and let's go." Killing criminals was always a rewarding business, but they were here for more serious matters. It was time to end Ashok's life.

They made their way toward the government house which the escapees had said the false prophet had claimed as his palace. They remained together. Normally in a situation like this the Protectors would break into smaller groups to move ahead of the less-capable warriors, spreading fear and removing choice targets, but for Ashok, Devedas wanted superior numbers to make sure the job was done.

It was a rare event to have this many Protectors working together. Any one of them was an incredibly lethal combatant. Ten of them were concentrated destruction. They sprinted through the city in a loose knot, killing anyone who got in their way.

Men rushed out of their homes, ready to fight, only to be promptly sliced to ribbons by a silver blur before they even understood what was going on. Devedas had warned his men about the Fortress magic that had killed Abhishek Gujara, so half of them were armed with bows. Whenever a head appeared in a window or peeked over a balcony, it was immediately stuck full of arrows. Considering how fast a Protector's reaction times were they probably killed several innocent bystanders that way, but Devedas could not risk losing any more men to that despicable Fortress magic. To best mighty Angruvadal he would need them all.

There were rumors that Angruvadal had been broken, and Ashok had not used it in Neeramphorn—otherwise three Protectors would have died there instead of just one—but Devedas was still prepared for the worst. Each of his men was ready to face the deadly fury of a black-steel blade.

They passed bodies impaled on stakes, surely belonging to those who had resisted the tyrant's rule. There were a great many of them, male and female, old and young, their caste unknown because they'd been stripped of their garments and their skin flogged to ribbons. This was cruelty, but it did not seem Ashok's flavor of cruelty. Their brother had down terrible things in service to the Law—they all had—but he struggled to imagine Ashok lowering himself to this barbarity in the name of a false master. Such tortures seemed . . . petty.

What have you become, Ashok?

There was a semiorganized force of twenty men guarding the government house. Despite the fact they were wearing armor and carrying proper swords, they were obviously workers wearing stolen and ill-fitting gear. Two of them had the strange wood and metal poles that spewed illegal Fortress death. The guards had heard the warning drums and the approaching screams, but still hadn't fully prepared themselves for an attack. Even if the walls had been breached there should have been no way an enemy could cover this much ground so quickly. Only Protectors were no normal enemy.

Devedas was in the lead. Jamari Vadal was to his right. Broker Harban to his left. As the ones with the Fortress staffs were riddled with arrows, the three lead Protectors crashed into the remaining guards. The Lord Protector's sword was designed for chopping, and excellent at removing limbs, so he took two arms and an ankle by the time he bounded up the steps. Certain the job would be done, he left the remainder to his men. They'd trained together. Fought together. He had complete faith in their performance. So he leapt up the ten steps without looking back.

The government house had a heavy door made from a single piece of oak—a lavish display of wealth in a land without trees—but Devedas kicked it into splinters.

He stepped inside the government house and roared, *"Face me, Ashok Vadal!"*

It was a large room, probably for public meetings, only now a multitude of fanatics were camped inside. Probably the false prophet's most loyal troops. They had been woken by the alarm, but Devedas' sudden appearance still took them by surprise.

The rest of the Protectors rushed in behind Devedas, and immediately formed a cohesive line. Devedas scanned the room but there was no sign of their former brother. "Kill them all."

The line moved forward like a worker's scythe as the government house filled with blood. As Devedas killed his way across the room he noticed a gaudy mural had been painted upon one wall. It showed a man in golden robes preaching to an adoring crowd as a faceless armored figure with a black sword stood behind him like a menacing shadow. It was very amateurish and looked to have been painted recently.

A throne had been erected in the room, but it was empty now. There were stairs behind it, surely leading up to the regional arbiter's personal chambers and offices. As his men slaughtered the last of the nearly helpless rebels, Devedas went upstairs. *"The Law is here, Ashok! It's over!"*

Without saying a word, Jamari and Broker were at his side again, and directly behind him were two more Protectors with arrows nocked.

There were several doors on this landing, but only one had a man guarding it. His armor had been stained black, and in his hand was a *black sword*. Devedas felt a surge of conflicting emotions, fear, anger, eagerness, and then . . . *disappointment*, because that was no Ashok.

That still didn't stop his men from putting two arrows in his chest.

The false Ashok crashed against the wall. Jamari cut his sword hand off and Broker shattered his femur with a mace. The fake ancestor blade hit the floor. Devedas looked at it in disgust. He'd never forget the real Angruvadal that had forever marked his face. At times when he closed his eyes he could still see the searing darkness. This sword had merely been painted black. The imposter stared up at him in lip-quivering fear, and with a snarl Devedas smote his head off.

Devedas went into the arbiter's bedchamber. A young man was there, naked and thin. Three women were huddled in the corner, mostly without clothing. From the odor, they'd been smoking an obscene amount of poppy.

"I am King Pankaj, Voice of the Forgotten, Ruler of Chakma, and I wish to negotiate—"

Devedas broke his nose with one fist. The false prophet landed on the bed and got blood all over the sheets. "Search the place," he told his men, then turned back to the idiot.

"You can't do this. I'm of the first caste!"

"Where is Ashok Vadal?"

The king was holding his face and sobbing. "You killed Rohit," he said when he saw the headless body in the hall. "I made Rohit my Ashok because every prophet needs a servant to strike fear into the hearts of the wicked. With no Ashok they wouldn't respect me like they respected her!"

Devedas sheathed his sword and grabbed hold of Pankaj's hand. Then he took up the pinky finger and snapped it. "Where is Ashok?" Then he broke the next. The king screamed. His concubines screamed. "Where is Ashok?" He broke the next. And the next. "*Where?*"

"They left." He managed to get that out through the sobbing. "To the mountains! To the west!"

Devedas had just come from that region after a futile search. He might have even passed them on the way. "When?"

"I don't know. What day is it?"

Devedas snapped the thumb.

"Since the city fell! They left the next morning!"

"A *month ago*?" A cold rage descended upon Devedas.

"They took the hostages and half my faithful betrayed me and went with them," Pankaj wailed. "Couldn't they see I was the one Mother Dawn chose to save this city? The gods will smite you for this!"

"I've heard that threat many times but have yet to meet one of these supposed gods. They must be afraid. I'd love for them to come out and fight."

Protector Jamari rushed back into the bedroom. "Building's secure, sir. No sign of Ashok."

"This imbecile says they went to the mountains a month ago. Question the other survivors and see if you can confirm that. I want numbers, direction, and any possible clues to their destination." Jamari left. Then he turned back to Pankaj. "Where in the mountains did they go?"

"I don't know. Some secret hideout the Keeper of Names found years ago. It was once the Hall of the Marutas, the storm gods. Runaways built a whole town inside, but only the Keeper knows the secret way in."

As long as Ashok lived, his Order would be shamed. As long as Ashok lived, Omand would keep the crown from him. As long as Ashok lived, Rada would have to remain in hiding. As long as Ashok lived, Devedas' destiny would go unfilled.

As long as Ashok lived . . . And he had just missed him by twenty-nine days.

Devedas let go of the hand. Pankaj held the ruined thing to his chest and cried, "You can't do this to me. I'm a king."

"You're no king." Devedas drew his sword. "Lok will know a real king soon enough."

He slashed Pankaj across the belly and dumped his guts on the rug.

Chapter 21

～～～～

"Here we are. This is the entrance," said Thera.

She had never told Ashok how to get to Keta's hideout, and Ashok had never asked. His obligation was to her, not these criminals, so there was no point to knowing how to get inside without her. Yet as Ashok looked around, he could see absolutely nothing that looked like an entrance to a secret rebel kingdom—or frankly anything else of interest at all—and that made him a little curious. From the way Keta had talked the place up, it was like he had a hidden fortress full of industrious people, free of the Law, toiling happily together beneath the smile of a benevolent god. All Ashok saw was rocks. Lots of rocks.

Though rocks were still a welcome change from the seemingly endless plains. For weeks their lumbering column had crossed the grasslands. For the last few days they had been following a stream of freezing cold runoff through the foothills and up into the mountain valleys. This particular valley appeared to be a dead end. Before them was a narrow lake, surrounded by pine trees. On the other three sides of the lake were rocky cliffs. Beyond those abrupt walls stretched the extremely steep, snowcapped mountains of western Akershan.

"Where?" Ashok asked.

"Right here. You'll see."

Ashok sharpened his vision, but even his heightened senses could discern no path up the cliffs. Calling upon the Heart, he might be able to scale them, but the others would be trapped. "What do we do now?"

"We wait for Keta to open the door for us." Thera turned her mount and began walking back toward their column.

Horse flicked one white ear, annoyed. Ashok patted his neck. "I hear you, boy."

Thera's army, now numbering nearly eight hundred men, women, and children, was waiting in the valley below them. They were mostly casteless who had fled from the warriors' purge, but there were also a surprising number of workers and even some warriors, who had been among the faithful in Chakma. They'd brought along their livestock, seed, and their most valuable tools. All that cargo meant that they had made terrible time. The only reason they'd not run out of food was that Ongud had known about every warrior supply cache in the region, and he'd sent the Sons out to loot them all.

Ashok drew alongside her. "Does Keta really have room to house all these people?"

"He does. It's actually rather impressive."

"And somehow feed them all?"

"For the thousandth time, yes, Ashok. I've not just

led them all up into the mountains to die of exposure. I don't expect them to eat pine needles or turn to cannibalism. I'm no idiot."

"True. You are not."

"Thank you, silver-tongued Ashok, master of compliments. Just trust me."

"I am obligated to do so."

Thera laughed. "Admit it. By now, you would trust me anyway."

He gave her a grudging nod. She was correct.

"However, if I've drastically overestimated Keta's abilities, there is that vast herd of cows being driven along a day behind us to obliterate our trail. We could eat them."

"While faithful to your silly gods, I do not think those drovers would appreciate you depriving them of their livelihood." Ashok knew that the lesser castes did not enjoy having their property confiscated. That had never mattered to him as a Protector, but it did now.

"I'd make it fair. We could always trade them some demon parts for their herd. We've got piles of the stuff and no wizards to use it."

"What would cow herders do with magic?" he asked suspiciously. "It is illegal to sell or possess without a license."

"Oh, Ashok. It's endearing how you still honestly think anyone out here cares about the Law."

"And I think you underestimate how much regular people fear attracting the attention of someone like"—Ashok caught himself, he'd been about to say *mē*—"a Protector."

The two of them rode along in silence the rest of the way down. It was a warm day. The sky was clear and blue. In Thera's company it was almost...pleasant. They had formed an odd relationship. He was her guard, her enforcer, and now her lover, but had also become something more than that. This feeling of *partnership* was an unfamiliar thing, and not one that Ashok had ever before experienced in his life. He did not mind it, but Ashok was unused to such thoughts and was happy to return to his duties. Duty, even an illegal one, was easy to understand.

"You're much better at being loud. I need their attention," Thera told him as they stopped on a small rise overlooking the column.

Ashok raised his voice. "Your prophet speaks!" Everyone stopped what they were doing and looked his way. "Heed her words and relay them down the line."

Thera stood up in her stirrups to be a bit taller. In the preceding weeks she had gotten quite a bit more comfortable with her role as a figurehead, so she spoke with confidence. Even Ashok could not tell if this confidence was real or feigned. She had given these people no signs beyond keeping them alive, yet they followed her. The Voice had not come upon her since the graveyard, but truthfully, Ashok thought she was better off without its meddling.

"Our long journey is almost done. In a few hours we will be able to enter the Creator's Cove. There, we can be safe. There's only one small part left, only a few miles, but it will be...different. Right away I need everyone to fill all their canteens and water the animals. Then I need you to find dry wood to make torches."

That too was curious. Thus far they had not marched at night. And it was only lunchtime, they still had quite a bit of daylight remaining. Perhaps they were going underground? There were many caves in Lok. Since they were a popular place for smugglers or criminals to hide, he had been inside several cave systems over the years. Only Ashok could not imagine there being one big enough for the population of a town to live in, and even if there was a cavern so gigantic, surely the residents therein would become sickly without the sun.

"One torch for every five or six of you should do. Now come on, get to it," Thera ordered.

A month ago, they would've milled about stupidly, a few would have even argued with her or murmured about being forced to labor. Now, they simply hopped to and did as she said. There'd been no miracles on the plains, but Thera had been a consistently good leader the whole time, addressing their problems, while keeping them moving, motivated, and fed.

"I think Keta would be pleased with how you have done," Ashok told her.

"He'd better," she said smugly. She clicked her tongue, and her horse began descending the rise. "I'm not too ashamed of this bunch myself."

Ashok had to admit that they had accomplished far more than he'd expected. Taking Chakma and then leaving it in Pankaj's prideful hands had caused a far greater distraction than anything he would have been able to accomplish by himself. His scouts reported that every warrior they came across had been heading toward Chakma or hunkering down to protect their home garrisons from attack. The order of casteless extermination was so neglected, it might as well be forgotten. As for the casteless, most were staying in place hoping that this threat would pass, but many others were fleeing the region. Apparently, it was only in the northern provinces of Great House Akershan that they'd been ordered killed. What would happen to the casteless in the future he did not know, but for now they were still alive because Thera had directed him to take action.

The slaves came to take their horses and left them with some freshly cooked rabbit on a skewer. Thera had declared the silent people to be free, but since they were still doing the exact same things for them that they'd done for the House of Assassins, Ashok had a hard time thinking of them as anything other than slaves. If the magical pattern that had broken their minds was weakening, the process had been too gradual for him to notice.

They sat together on a fallen tree. "Meat on a stick while sitting on a log... I do miss my glorious command tent." Thera had abandoned the ostentatious thing on the third day of their long journey. It simply took too long to set up and take down and required several animals to lug it about. She had kept a few of the pillows though.

While he and Thera ate, a shout went up at the back of the column. *Riders incoming.* Ashok had left a string of spotters trailing behind them to relay warnings of danger. He tensed, but then relaxed when he heard some shout that Toramana's expedition had caught up with them.

Thera couldn't sharpen her hearing like he could, so she looked to Ashok. "What is it?"

"The Wild Men have returned."

"Excellent. I can't wait to hear how our *diplomatic mission* went."

"You sent the barbarian chief of a gang of lawless swamp dwellers to deliver prisoners and an ultimatum to the most delicate members of the first caste. It was doubtlessly the least diplomatic thing imaginable."

"Don't underestimate Toramana, Ashok. Keeping his people alive beneath the wizards' shadow made him rather cunning. I told him to try and look like a frightening savage, I'm certain he delivered."

"Do you think all his men painted their heads to look like skulls again?"

"I certainly hope so."

A short while later the returning Wild Men were greeted with great enthusiasm as they made their way up the stretched-out column. From the smiles on their faces their mission had been a successful one. Sure enough, they had covered their faces with white ash and black charcoal around their eyes to create pits and lines across their mouths to create the illusion of fangs. *War face* they called it. Ashok found the habit odd. Personally, he had never needed to try and look intimidating. He was intimidating simply by existing. But then again, these were the same odd people who thought burning eerie sin dolls made for a fine celebration.

The contingent of Wild Men rode toward Thera, proud in their furs and feathers, waving to their wives and children and all the adoring refugees. They were popular among the camp because to the Faithful the Wild Men were the ones who had saved the Voice from the wizards and dug the Forgotten's warrior out of the rubble. To the not-so-faithful, they were a fearsome bunch of archers who could be nearly invisible when they put their minds to it. The Wild Men were still awkward horsemen, but they had improved greatly over the last month. They had, after all, gotten a seemingly endless amount of practice.

"Greetings, Chief Toramana."

"Hail, Prophet." Toramana dismounted, almost graceful now, for such a large man who seemed chiseled from a brick of muscle. "I hope all is well."

"Better than well. You caught up to us right as we were about to enter the Cove."

"Then the gods have smiled upon us," Toramana shouted. His men made the repetitive, deep bark that they used as a cheer. The fanatics seemed to love that.

Ashok was uncertain just how much Toramana actually believed in the gods, and how much of his loyalty to Thera was based on pragmatism, but he was nonetheless an effective leader dedicated to making a better life for his people. Hopefully Keta's secret kingdom would live up to their dreams.

"It was slow getting there, but swift as the wind to return to you. The gods blessed us with good timing, but it was the Voice who had the wisdom to send us with a guide who kept us from getting lost on those awful, featureless plains."

Ongud Khedekar dar Akershan approached. "It's only confusing if you're not from here." The young warrior had left behind his uniform and had dressed to blend in with the swamp people, though he'd not bothered to smear ash on his round face. There was only so much indignity a civilized man would bear. "There's plenty of landmarks when you know what you're looking for."

"Grass, grass, and more grass," Toramana said. "Occasionally, a stick."

"It beats swamper directions like turn left at the alligator," Ongud responded.

"Ha! Accurate." The chief slapped the much shorter warrior on the back, nearly knocking him over.

"How did you fare in Kochar's Pass?" Thera asked.

"We delivered all the hostages, warrior and highborn both, alive and mostly in one piece. The perfumed sissies living there didn't really know what to do with all of them."

The location had been Ongud's suggestion. The palace at Kochar's Pass only had a tiny garrison stationed there. It was best known for its artisan's school, renowned for the sweeping vistas where the first caste could practice their painting and be inspired to write bad poetry, and not much else. It had also not been too far out of their way.

"I made your ultimatum clear. These lives were a gift to the Akershani chief. A showing of respect. We let these warriors live so that he would be moved to let the casteless live. I said our prophet only wants to be left alone. There was no need to hunt for us, because they would never see or hear from us again. Unless they came again against the casteless, because then Ashok Vadal would return to kill more of his men and capture more of his towns."

"How did they take that?"

Toramana gave her a sly grin. "The ones I told this to were feeble, girlish men, who stank like they'd rolled in flowers. Their perfume made my nose itch. I think they were very frightened of me, but better to remember it that way. Their chief will get the message."

"And you were not followed?" Ashok asked.

"We're clear, General," Ongud replied. "I'm certain of it. The swampers got a little exuberant."

"We stole all that garrison's horses," Toramana explained. "But do not worry. There was a village a day's walk from the pass... In the wrong direction, but we'd already made the prisoners walk so far already, what's another day?"

"Fantastic work, all of you," Thera said. "Now go see your families and get some food in your bellies. We should be moving out in a couple hours."

"There's one other thing," Ongud said. "On the way to the pass we encountered some merchants fleeing south. They said the warriors had laid siege to Chakma, but when the Protectors got there they just climbed the walls and ripped the place apart. The Protectors executed many men."

For a moment Thera looked stricken. The news wasn't surprising, but Ashok knew she had felt guilty about how things there had turned out there. "Pankaj's pride killed them. Not you."

She sighed. "I tried to warn them. Only if they'd not been there like a big defiant beacon drawing every warrior in the country, then we might not have ever made it this far unseen."

Toramana grinned. "I like to think just as Mother Dawn picked my people for our courage and skill, she picked that tax collector precisely because he had such a swollen head. Perhaps this was her plan all along. She is plainly a divine being sent by the gods, able to see into the future. We should be thankful that she has been preparing the way."

"That sounds absurd," Ashok said.

"Yet she appeared in my swamp and told my people

to expect you," Toramana replied as he spread his hands apologetically. "Long before you ever thought of traveling to the Bahdjangal, as you said yourself."

"And she told mine when to be on the road to Haradas so we could join you," said Ongud. "But regardless of what the Mother really is, the merchants said all the rebels and suspected collaborators in Chakma were put to the sword by a Protector with a big scar on his face."

"Devedas," Ashok muttered. "This is dire news."

"You know him?" Thera asked.

"The Lord Protector of the Order, who was once my brother. I am the one who gave him that scar."

"There's a story there I'm sure," Toramana said.

"There is. Though I will not tell it."

"But this Devedas won't find us now," Thera said. "We're a long way from Chakma."

"Distance does not matter. Underestimating him is a fatal mistake. Devedas is perhaps the most dangerous man in the world."

Thera was incredulous at that claim. "Even more than you?"

"What I accomplished with an ancestor blade he did nearly the equivalent by strength of will alone."

Ashok's ever truthful nature was now well known to all, so Toramana and Ongud shared a nervous glance. There were many fearsome combatants among the Sons, and Ashok rarely gave praise. For him to speak so highly of an enemy...

"How long ago did the Protectors take the city?"

"Six days, General."

Protectors would move with far more swiftness than this cumbersome mob. Ashok looked to Thera. "Then if you have a way to make Keta open the door faster, I suggest you do so."

"Don't worry." She pointed toward the nearby stream. It took Ashok a moment to realize that the water level had dropped nearly a foot while they'd been standing here. "It's already started."

Chapter 22

The small mountain lake was now less than half its original size. By what mechanism the flow into the lake had been stopped, Ashok could not tell. The remaining water was waist deep and clear enough that the rocky bottom could be seen all the way across. They wouldn't even have to worry about demons. Not that there should be any this far into the interior anyway, but with the creatures of hell, you never knew.

Havildar Eklavya was standing nearby, and had been studying the situation for quite some time. Jagdish had said the clever young warrior had a mind for fortifications. Apparently, his love of engineering extended to drainage systems as well, because he seemed rather fascinated by it all. He'd been tossing sticks in the water to watch where the current took them.

"See that shadow beneath the water back there?" Eklavya said to the other Sons. "A banknote says that's the secret entrance."

Nobody took Eklavya up on his bet.

"I'm guessing there's a reservoir above us somewhere, and it was draining downhill enough to keep this lake full. They shut if off somehow. The entrance to the Keeper's secret kingdom will be revealed soon."

Ashok would have asked Thera if Eklavya's theory was correct, but she was busy using the time to give instructions, riding her horse back and forth along the shoreline as her people crowded close to hear. "We'll have to lead the animals. It's dark in there so don't spook them. The water should only be about ankle deep, but there are a few lower spots where you'll have to carry your little ones. It's not that far. Don't be afraid. It's safe."

"Are we going to live under the ground?" asked a casteless child. "I don't want to live in the dark!"

"Don't worry. We're only passing through the mountain to what's on the other side. We're not going to stay under it for very long."

"What if it falls and smashes us flat?" cried a woman.

"The tunnel's not going to fall on us," Thera assured her anxious mob.

Gupta was one of the Sons of the Black Sword who had once been a miner in Jharlang. "Eh, with tunnels, you never know." But thankfully he kept his voice low so only the other Sons around him heard. They laughed nervously, but warriors weren't about to show apprehension in front of these people.

Only Thera overheard Gupta, and she asked him, "Have any of your mole holes in Jharlang lasted a thousand years?"

"No, Prophet, I don't think so." He looked down, embarrassed. "Sorry."

"Then this is a bit better. They knew how to build

things back in those days." Thera went back to the
adoring crowd. "As I was saying, there's no need to
fear. I was nervous the first time I came here too.
While we wait for the water to go down, I'll tell
you the story of this place, as it was told to me by
Ratul, who was the Keeper of Names before Keta. It
was Ratul who discovered this secret path. Like our
General Ashok, he had also once been a Protector
of the Law."

Many of the fanatics grimaced or spit when Thera
mentioned his old Order. That annoyed Ashok to no
end. Even though he was nominally on their side
now, and the Order's primary goal was his death, it
remained a struggle to see such flagrant disrespect for
something he'd devoted most of his life to.

"Ratul did a great many terrible things, hunting
down the faithful or anyone who didn't follow the
cruel and often senseless commands of the Law. But
he learned the truth, that the gods still lived, and
so he began to prepare for this day in secret. Ratul
always did what was necessary, no matter the danger.
Once, I was thrown into the ocean by a wicked man,
and I was about to be eaten by a demon, but Ratul
dove into the ocean to save me. He fought the demon
and scared it away."

Her audience gasped.

"That's right. Ratul was very courageous."

And possibly insane, Ashok thought.

"He knew that our uprising would need a place to
be safe, beyond the reach of the Law."

"Like Fortress!" shouted one of the workers helpfully.

"Sort of. But those on the frozen island are no
friends of ours. Not really. They'll sell us powder and

weapons, but in their own way they're just as stuck-up as the Law. The Keeper knew we'd need our own land for the faithful to build homes and grow crops. Ratul learned of this place from one of the forbidden books in the Capitol Library, so he went looking for it. It's older than the Law. Older than the kings. It was here before the demons fell from the sky even."

The people seemed confused. Since the Law had done such an excellent job erasing and rewriting their history, most of the people had no idea what Thera was talking about beyond vague associations with their illegal stories that had been passed down in secret. To most Law-abiding people, Lok was as it always had been, and if you wanted to know about what came before, you needed permission from a few specific orders to learn about it. The secret fanatics may have had long memories, but they were blurry ones.

"Look, I'm really bad at explaining all this. But Keta's really good at it and you will be able to speak to him soon enough. Just bear with me a little longer and he can explain it to you. Once Ratul got close he said that he could feel this place calling to him, almost as if it was singing. We have to pass beneath this mountain, but on the other side is the Cove, and it's a fine place to make a home."

"What if we don't want to go down there?" someone in the back of the crowd shouted.

Ashok already knew the answer to that. Thera was hardheaded, but she was also kindhearted, though she did her best to hide that aspect beneath a mask of sardonic pessimism. If someone really wanted to leave, she would try to talk them out of it, but would ultimately let them go.

As for Ashok, most of Lok called him the Black Heart and that name hadn't been earned because of his mercy or patience. He would always do what needed to be done. With Devedas on their trail they could not afford to let anyone who knew of this place be captured. To do so would be to utterly fail in his obligation.

Ashok caught Shekar's eye. "Bring up the rear," he whispered.

Shekar nodded in understanding. All of the Sons had differing beliefs as to the true nature of the Forgotten. The Somsak's version was merciless, direct, and practical enough that he would have no issues with removing liabilities. Shekar would keep an eye on that complainer.

"You're committed," Thera said. "There's no going back. The Law knows about all of you now. The Protectors have Chakma and Dhakhantar. Anyone they even vaguely suspect of believing in the old ways has already been killed."

"The Law knows your name," Ashok warned. "The Law does not forget."

"Thank you, Ashok..." Thera turned back to the murmurers. "Look, I understand you're afraid, but the Cove is a rich and bounteous place, where there are no castes determining how you can live, where the faithful are free to worship openly, where the gods have given us resources beyond our dreams. There's plenty of room. There will be a roof over your head. There's wood to burn and grass for your animals to eat. The water's clean to drink. Keta called the place the gods' holy mountain."

Even though Ashok knew Thera did not believe very

much of Keta's nonsense she was doing a good job selling it here. Either she was starting to believe her own propaganda, or she'd overheard Ashok's orders and didn't want the Somsak to have to murder any stragglers.

"All right. We have faith in you, Voice," the man who had been worried called out. "We'll follow you through the dark!"

Shekar looked slightly disappointed at that change of heart, but they'd be on the lookout for deserters anyway.

"Thank you." Thera glanced toward the receding water. "It's almost time. I'll lead the way."

Their prophet got off her horse and passed the reins to one of the Assassins' slaves. Murugan had lit a torch for her and handed it over. It was just a stick with a head of tightly wrapped dead moss, but she'd said they'd not need to last long. Thera took the torch and held it high. "Follow me."

There was probably some imagery there intended to boost the faithful, but Ashok had no mind for such things. On that note, he didn't like how some of the fanatics had started wearing little metal hooks as jewelry, as a reminder of when he'd come back to life and lifted himself from Sikasso's meat hook.

Ashok placed himself at Thera's side. Even though she declared the journey to be a safe one, that did not make it so. Foul creatures lurked in the dark corners of Lok, and who knew what manner of beast might have moved in here since Thera's last visit?

"I need to be in front," she whispered at him. "It's *symbolic*."

"Of course." But he stayed close enough that if she fell, he could catch her.

Water crept in through the holes of his worn-thin boots as they waded across the lake. It was surprisingly warmer than expected. Runoff from the melting snow should have been shockingly cold, but the almost comfortable temperature suggested that whatever was feeding this lake from above was volcanic in origin. It was common for hot water to seep from the ground in Dev, but not so much here. It still made him uneasy though, because no matter what Keta proclaimed to the contrary, Ashok knew that whenever water collected into large bodies it became a potential source of evil. Water was necessary to support life, cleanliness, and commerce, but it was still made from the same stuff as hell.

The tunnel into the mountain was clearly visible. It was bigger than Ashok had expected, being a good twelve feet across, and probably ten feet tall, leaving plenty of room to spare even for their wagons. The rectangular shape marked it as clearly man made. The material appeared to be rock, but it was so coated in slimy plant life it was impossible to tell.

The temperature dropped significantly as they left the sun behind. Having been recently filled, fat droplets of water rained from the ceiling. The ones that hit the torches disappeared with a hiss. The column trudged along obediently after them. Some of the livestock balked at being led into the water, but the silent slaves were remarkably skilled at animal handling and got them soothed without so much as a word.

They went deeper and deeper into the tunnel. A slick green ooze had grown on every surface. The water was now up to their knees. If Thera was worried, she didn't let it show. Ashok looked back, and could see a line of torches stretching back to the shrinking rectangle of daylight. The fanatics were worried, and it was plain on their faces. Even some of the Sons were unable to hide their emotions.

"This is a strange place," Murugan said. "It's unnatural."

"It's a fascinating construction," Eklavya disagreed. "The engineering behind this had to be rather impressive. There's got to be some manner of device up ahead to divert the water, and from the volume necessary it must be gigantic."

"What happens if they open it back up while we're stuck in here?" Murugan asked.

"That would be . . . interesting."

"Keta's not going to do that," Thera said.

"Assuming Keta is the one in control," Murugan muttered. "If this place has fallen to the Inquisition, it would be a simple way to drown hundreds of rebels at a time."

"Calm down, boys. I've seen what happens when they turn it back on. It's not a rushing wall of water. It takes hours for the lake to fill back up. Worst case we'd make a slightly damper retreat. Keta's got lookouts all over the peaks above. They saw us as soon as we entered the valley. Once they decided we were friends they shut the valve. It doesn't make for convenient travel in and out, but it's secure."

"What if the valve breaks off?" Murugan asked.

"Considering the size of the reservoir above us, if it all let go at once . . ." Thera thought that over. "Our bodies would probably get washed clear back to Chakma."

It was a much different setting than where the

Heart of the Mountain was hidden, but Ashok had no doubt this place had been built in the same era. Ashok knew almost nothing about the time before demons, but the people who had lived back then had certainly liked to build things. In his travels across Lok he had come across the remains of many great and mysterious structures. These discoveries were often of interest to the Capitol. In order of descending importance, any images or icons deemed to be religious in nature were destroyed by the Inquisition. Anything relating to stars or constellations went to the Astronomers. Artifacts would go to the Historians or to the Order of Technology and Innovation. Anything with writing became property of the library. If there was a device with writing on it, well...he had actually seen Historians and Archivists take offense and get into duels over which order claimed what. Fortunately those duels had been mostly bare-handed and ineffectual since neither of those orders could fight worth a damn, and usually ended with one first-caste man getting a black eye while the other order got a new treasure to hide in their vaults.

It was unclear how far they had gone, but the sun behind them had vanished. Once their way was lit only by torchlight, the fanatics became somber. The moist walls seemed to absorb sound. Even the chickens and goats were quiet.

"Is this the only way in?" Ashok asked.

"If there's others we've not discovered them yet. Maybe someone like you could climb over the mountains, or a wizard could change into a bird and fly out, but for normal people this is it. Once inside, leaving is a big enough of a production you'd better have a good reason for going out. The lake stays warm enough not to freeze, so you can even get in during the worst part of winter. The Keeper has a group of rebels he trusts, and he'll send them out a bunch at a time on various errands, but most folks are happy to stay inside. You'll see why soon enough."

Ashok had to grudgingly approve. It was no wonder his brothers hadn't been able to find the rebels' hideout. "If this place was submerged, how did Ratul find it?"

"He swam all the way up this tunnel."

Ashok shuddered. His old sword master was full of surprises.

Thera looked at Ashok conspiratorially. "I didn't tell everybody, but in those ancient books where Ratul learned about this place, they declared this place to be cursed. Or haunted. Probably both. That's one reason it stayed empty for so long."

"Foolishness." Though he had himself spoken to entities that some would refer to as *ghosts* and his sword had been imbued with the memories and emotions of all its previous long-dead bearers, he had been taught that there was no such thing as a haunting, because if there was, that would mean there was some manner of existence after death, and the Law did not allow for that.

Now curses on the other hand were very much real. All that required was an illegal wizard, some demon parts, and a grudge, but he'd never heard of one strong enough to linger for centuries.

They reached a point where the water was almost entirely gone, so each of their footfalls only made a little splash. There was enough airflow that the tunnel didn't become choked with smoke. For the most part the floor beneath them was level, but there were a few holes. Hopefully none of their cows would break a leg.

As their feeble torches began to die off, the tunnel became darker. Each time a torch was extinguished, cries or curses could be heard.

"We're almost there," Thera shouted.

Ashok was unsure if she believed that or was merely trying to comfort them. There was no way to actually tell where they were by the featureless walls. The distance was uncertain, but if Ratul swam this far there was no way he could have held his breath that long. He must have used the Heart of the Mountain to keep him alive. Ashok had figured out that same trick fighting Chattarak in the river Nansakar. That experience had been awful, but brief. He could not imagine sustaining it long enough to make it through this tunnel, especially not knowing what would be on the other side. Ratul had been as dedicated in his religious fanaticism as he had been to his swordsmanship.

After a time, Ashok's heightened senses felt a change in the air pressure, and his improved vision saw a faint light far away. "I believe that is the sun."

"Told you we're almost there." Thera turned back and shouted. "You hear that everyone? Ashok sees the sun!"

"I should run ahead and make sure it is safe."

"No, Ashok. These people have been through a terrible upheaval. I need to be the one to lead them into the promised land. I didn't want this stupid job, but it's mine now. They've still got challenges to face. They need something to believe in."

Getting others to believe in you, when you didn't even believe in yourself? Ashok found that curious.

"It will do your followers no good if their Voice walks into an Inquisition ambush. You have your obligation to them." He nodded back down the tunnel. "My obligation is to you. Let me keep it."

"Fine. Just don't make a big deal out of it."

He addressed Murugan and Eklavya. "Stay by her side." Then Ashok called upon the Heart to give him speed. To those behind them it was if he disappeared from the circle of torchlight in the blink of an eye.

He ran the last mile of featureless tunnel in a few minutes. Imagining covering this distance while submerged made him feel a grudging new respect for his old sword master. He had loved Ratul once, like the harsh replacement for the father he could not remember, but he had lost that love when Ratul had betrayed their Order. Now that Ashok was the despised traitor, he could understand his predecessor a bit better.

Ratul had also been gifted with the ability to sense magic. What was it he had felt on the other side of this tunnel that had caused him to risk his life in the darkness beneath?

Ashok slowed as he neared the exit and listened carefully. There were people waiting just out of sight. From the sounds of leather creaking and metal clanking, they were armed. If this place had been found by the Inquisitors, better to face them directly and get it over with. Ashok walked into the light.

He squinted and held up one hand to block the sun. The tunnel opened into a now empty lake bed. The entire area had been hewn from stone and then rounded by time. On the side opposite the tunnel was a vast gray wall, in the middle of which was a metal square, big as an elephant. That must have been the valve Thera had spoken of. When it was lifted this basin would fill and flood the tunnel.

There were also several men waiting in the lake bed with sword, hammer, or spear, but they looked to be Law breakers, not Law keepers. Ashok looked up and saw that there were men and women atop the wall with bows and what were probably Fortress poles. He looked behind him and saw that rocks had been stacked above the tunnel, the avalanche being held back with only a wooden fence. It would be relatively easy for the rebels to hold this narrow position and bury it if they needed to fall back.

"What's the password?" one of them demanded.

Thera had not told him of such a thing. She had left this place a long time ago though.

"My password is lower those weapons before you annoy me. Tell Keta that Ashok Vadal has arrived."

There was a happy laugh from up above. "I knew it! I knew it! Praise the Forgotten, I knew you would come!"

Ashok was not given to frivolity, but hearing that familiar voice caused a faint smile to cross his lips. "Hello, Keeper."

"Do as he says and put down your arms, my children!" There was a path that led upward out of the lakebed, and a short, balding man came running down the bank with near giddy excitement. "Before you stands the one I've been telling you about, the Forgotten's chosen warrior himself! Ashok Vadal is here!"

"I am."

"I knew you would live." Keta reached him, and surprisingly enough, grabbed Ashok by the arms and shook him, as if to make sure he was not an illusion.

Ashok just stood there, awkwardly. The last time he had seen the Keeper of Names they had drank together as friends, but that did not mean Ashok was good at such business.

"It is good to see you again, Keta."

"Did you find Thera?"

"She's right behind me."

Keta was so filled with joy it appeared he might start to cry, but thankfully he let go of Ashok's arms. "Of course you have her, because you declared you'd walk out into the ocean if you couldn't save her, and Ashok Vadal is a man of his word! I knew she was still alive and I knew you'd bring her back to the faithful." He turned back to his people. "Rejoice everyone, for the Voice has been returned to us at last! All will be well."

The rebels seemed overjoyed at the news.

"Hurry, Ashok. Come with me before she gets here. You need to see this. You need to know what you've been fighting for this last year."

He had been fighting because he had been ordered to protect a criminal, nothing more, but Keta seemed very excited and proud to show off what he had built, so he followed the Keeper up the hill.

"Behold, the Creator's Cove."

Only a fool named a place something related to the sea, but as he reached the top and looked inside, Ashok actually felt surprise, for it was not at all what he had expected.

At first Ashok thought the thing stretching before them was a regular mountain valley, surrounded on all sides by giant forested peaks, though the valley was uncannily *round*. They were standing at the edge of a circle that stretched for several miles, almost as if a great scoop had come down from the heavens and cleaved a hole in the rocks.

To each side, entire buildings had been *carved* from the walls. Blocky, with circular windows, they were gigantic, and surely the work of the ancients. And with a shock, Ashok realized that there were dozens, maybe hundreds of the structures stretching all the way around the circle's rim. Many of them were crumbling, but most seemed solid.

"What was this place?"

"The people who came before built it for us as a gift, and now we have claimed our birthright."

"Meaning you don't actually know."

"I can only guess, as I count myself fortunate to live amongst its bones."

Ashok walked toward the edge to look down into the valley, but then he had to reassess his terms. It seemed more of a crater, like the graveyard of demons. though this was *far* larger, and there was no sign of what spectacular impact must have dug the massive thing. Far below was a white lake, and from the steam rising off the surface, it was a hot one.

The sides of the crater might have once been smooth, but terraces had been cut into it all the way down. Upon many of those, crops were growing. Upon others, fences had been erected along the edges and animals grazed inside. They were all connected by a wide road that wrapped like a corkscrew down the interior. Ashok realized the stone wall with the metal gate he had first seen was a dam, because a multitude of concrete pipes stretched from it down to feed the terraces.

"I thought you were prone to exaggeration, Keeper. I was not expecting something so . . ."

"Impressive? I told you it was wonderful. The one thing we have been missing is the Voice of the gods and now you have brought her back to us. I had faith that the Forgotten picked you for a reason."

Ashok wanted to argue against that superstitious foolishness, but there were more pressing matters at hand. "Thera also picked up a few hundred followers along the way."

A glimmer of some other emotion crossed Keta's face, fear? Worry? But whatever it was, he quickly shoved it aside and put his happy face back on. "We saw the great mob camped below, but don't worry, as you can see we have plenty of room. We will find shelter for all! Everything will be fine now."

"We have spent far too much time traveling together for you to deceive me, Keta. What troubles you?"

"Nothing insurmountable, Ashok. The gods brought our prophet back. I'm sure they'll provide a way through our current difficulties as well."

Keta had been thin since they'd first met, but he was nearly emaciated now. There were dark circles beneath the Keeper's bloodshot eyes. Before him was a man who had been pushed to his ragged edge. Then Ashok looked over at the rebel guards, and he noted that all of them appeared pale and weary as well. One of them atop the dam coughed, and it was a wet, painful hacking sound.

"There is sickness here," Ashok said.

"An illness has come upon us, yes, but the Forgotten was merely testing our mettle. I'm sure now that the prophet has returned everything will get better."

The words were hesitant, as if Keta did not wish to speak freely in front of his men.

Ashok was obligated to keep Thera safe. Exposing her to some plague was the opposite. As he took Keta by the arm and roughly steered him away, he whispered, "Be forthright, Keeper. Lives are at stake. How dire is your situation here?"

Keta was stricken. "It starts as a weakness, a trembling in the extremities, and fits of coughing. Some of us develop sores on the body, armpits, thighs, and a few start bleeding from their nose, ears, and finally eyes, but all who've gotten to that stage died shortly after. The rest get a little better but remain weak. We've lost nearly a tenth of our number this winter. Of the rest, half of us are still ill. These men here are the strongest I have left. And it's taken everything in my power to keep them from running away."

"It is good you did. They only would have spread it across Akershan." Though he himself was immune to all diseases, Ashok had witnessed a sickness with those exact same symptoms rip through a community before, though he had never heard of it appearing this far south. "It is the Gujaran Blood Eye."

"Is there a cure?"

"No. It will only get worse."

Keta did indeed have a great amount of land here, but it would only be useful for burying their dead.

Chapter 23

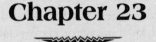

Spring was a good season for travel, so Jagdish and his wagon full of illegal demon parts had made excellent time. The trade roads were well maintained from Gunter to Warun and even better on to Vadal City. The Kharsawan were so orderly that he didn't get accosted by a single bandit in their lands. Of course, a few fools had tried to rob him after he'd crossed into Sarnobat. That place was known as the land of the wolf for a few reasons, rampant banditry among them. Most of workers who needed to cross the northeastern-most house joined forces, formed caravans, and those who could afford to do so hired warriors to ride with them. When some criminals had seen Jagdish's wagon passing through all by itself, they took him to be an easy victim. He'd only had to cut one down before the rest of the cowards had fled.

Those bandits must have spread the word to their peers that he was not worth the trouble, because he'd had no issues since. If they'd only known what was in his wagon, every wolf in this Law-forsaken house would have come for him.

The hardest part of his long journey was pretending to be a merchant. Dressing like a member of the worker caste wounded his warrior pride, but it was the only way he could smuggle hundreds of pounds of magic through other great houses. If any of the warriors he met along the way came to suspect what was really hidden beneath the rolls of cloth in his wagon, they'd kill him, seize his precious cargo, and then hold a feast in his honor because he'd just delivered them more riches than they could loot in a hundred border raids.

Whenever Jagdish stopped at various inns along the way he constantly had to remind himself not to be who he really was. Workers talked different. They even stood different. If they possessed any pride, they'd best only show it around their betters. And they for damned sure didn't maintain direct eye contact and make a smart remark while being grilled by a Sarnobat border guard while getting his traveling papers stamped. That mistake had nearly earned him a duel before he'd managed to apologize his way out of his inadvertent offense.

Of course he should've known offense would be taken. Workers who were licensed to carry swords for self-defense—and he'd been sure to get Gutch to forge one of those papers for him—were looked upon with sneering disdain as uppity amateurs by the superior warrior caste. Only in this instance that guard would've been in for quite the painful surprise if he'd not accepted Jagdish's apology.

Yet, Jagdish had come to marvel just how much

leeway workers got to generally travel about unimpeded. Warriors were only supposed to cross borders when they were ordered to. But workers, as long as they had the paper for it—and Gutch's forgeries were excellent—could go where they wanted. *Conducting business* they called it. Well, some workers at least. The unlucky ones ended up obligated to spending their whole lives working in the same mine shaft or plowing the same field. They were just as much victims to rank and status as his own caste in that respect.

He had discovered that playing pretend was a great deal harder than it looked. But the stakes were high, so he made do. There was already a lot of shame heaped upon his name. According to accepted narrative, he'd failed to protect Great House Vadal from the Black Heart *twice*. If he got caught with all this demon, he would end up giving an incredible amount of magical power to one of their rivals. It would be a long time before anyone in Vadal named their child Jagdish again! So he kept his head down and spoke to as few people as possible.

It was lonely upon the trade road, and he missed the loud and boisterous companionship of Gutch. Though Gutch had tried his best to nag Jagdish from this honorable path, the risaldar was a hard man to sway. So while Jagdish had continued on toward their homeland, Gutch had remained in the city of Guntur. They'd divided their treasure, fifty-fifty. Gutch hadn't even tried to rip him off by weight, which was a remarkable testament to their friendship considering Gutch's general inclination toward thievery. Before they had parted the smuggler had educated him on which checkpoints to avoid and who to bribe if necessary.

Magic smugglers often left marks or graffiti in a secret code around border checkpoints so their fellows would know who was willing to take a bribe, or which official to avoid because they were thorough in their searches. These lessons had been greatly appreciated. It wasn't as though honorable warriors like Jagdish had much experience in such things.

It had been with great solemnity that Gutch had said his good-byes. It was plain on the big man's face that he believed Jagdish was delivering himself to his own execution. Come to think of it that must have made it even harder for Gutch to resist the urge to try and steal Jagdish's share of the demon, since it was probably just going to get confiscated anyway. Bluster to the contrary, Gutch was a true friend.

Sarnobat reminded him of a wilder, untamed version of Vadal. Less populated too, but that was mostly because he'd taken a route designed to avoid most of the major towns. During the warm days he'd drive his team of oxen, and by the cool nights he'd lay in his wagon, dreaming of his reunion with Pakpa and their child he had never met. But his sleep was often fretful, as his dreams turned to unease, and dark thoughts about how his return would be received. For though Jagdish had accomplished great things, he'd done so in the company of their house's most infamous criminal.

And then one glorious morning Jagdish found himself approaching the border of Great House Vadal. When he saw the distant blue-gray and bronze flag flapping in the breeze, an involuntary smile crossed his face.

"At long last, I am home."

Tensions must have still been running high between

Sarnobat and Vadal, because there was a full paltan of warriors set up in a temporary camp here. Yet there must not have been any recent raiding because the men looked so bored they could barely trouble themselves enough to notice yet another worker's wagon.

That simply would not do.

Jagdish had been thinking about this moment for months. He could risk smuggling his illegal cargo across another border, and though he liked to think Vadal soldiers would be more diligent in their duties than the other houses and catch him, he knew they probably wouldn't. He could continue pretending to be a merchant all the way to Vadal City and the great house itself... But such a discreet entry would make it very easy for Harta Vadal to simply make Jagdish disappear.

However, if he made a grand entrance, a proper *warrior entrance*, then word would spread, and his whole caste would hear about the deeds of Avenging Jagdish, bringer of treasure, killer of wizards and demons. It would be harder for a Thakoor to execute a hero than just another dishonored scrub.

Gutch had not needed to worry so much. Jagdish certainly wasn't a politician, but he was not stupid. A grand entrance it would be.

"Whoa." Jagdish pulled on the reins until his lumbering team of oxen came to a stop, still a few hundred yards from the checkpoint. Once the four obedient animals were content, Jagdish climbed back into his wagon and pulled out the fabric he had purchased in Guntur. The dyes lacked the depth and vibrancy of true Vadal colors, but it was as close as he was going to find in a lesser house. His real uniform had been lost in Neeramphorn, but this would have to do. After tearing off the worker's insignia—that felt good—Jagdish tied his improvised Vadal colors around his chest as a sash.

His obvious delay stopped in the middle of the trade road had made the soldiers curious, and a few more had approached the checkpoint to see what this odd merchant was up to. When you were stationed in the field, any activity out of the ordinary was interesting. By the time Jagdish got back on the bench there was a small crowd waiting. *Excellent.* He put the sack of treasure he'd picked out special on the seat next to him and flicked the reins. "Go."

The oxen complied, pulled, and the wagon began to roll, toward legend or infamy Jagdish did not yet know.

The soldiers shared an incredulous look as he drew near. "What's with the sash, Merchant? Are you trying to play dress up?"

"Perhaps he wants to look like he belongs to a real caste," said another.

"Surely this fool knows it takes more than wearing our colors to be a warrior of Great House Vadal."

"Whoa." Jagdish got his oxen to halt. These soldiers plainly thought he was just some merchant mocking them, and thus about to catch an educational beating, but it felt so good to cross the border he couldn't help but grin. "Hello, warriors of Great House Vadal. You have no idea how happy I am to see you."

The highest-ranking man there was only a senior nayak, but he must have been the one actually manning this duty station, because he held up one hand to silence his friends, and then loudly and officially declared, "Prepare your papers, Merchant."

"I have no papers for you, Nayak, but I bring more treasure to this house than this checkpoint will collect in taxes in a million years." Then Jagdish leapt down from the wagon, got on his knees, and kissed the ground. That was the dirt of his homeland. It was theatrical and silly, but he enjoyed doing it. Then he laughed, raised his hands to the sky, and announced, "I am home, brothers!"

"Good for you, but you're not my brother," muttered the senior. "Now hurry it up, worker."

"I am no worker," Jagdish stood. "Fetch your commanding officer, Nayak. He will want to hear this."

Now the soldiers were really curious. A couple of them chuckled. "I think this merchant's been in the sun too long!" But someone did go to get their leader.

Anything shiny enough to catch the attention of a few warriors would eventually gather a crowd. That was just the way of things in camp. More men ambled over, probably thinking the merchant was about to try and sell them something, but Jagdish waited until an officer approached. The risaldar's uniform appeared squared away, and like all proper professional soldiers, he seemed annoyed that someone was wasting his time with nonsense.

"What's all this?"

"This worker claims he's not a worker, sir."

"What is he then?"

Jagdish suddenly used his command voice so all the camp would hear. "I am Risaldar Jagdish, warrior of Great House Vadal, formerly of the Personal Guard, and last commander of the Cold Stream garrison."

From the confused looks apparently none of them had ever heard of him. But they were way out on the eastern border so that was no surprise. It was a long way to Vadal City.

"Cold Stream is one of the places that got massacred by the Black Heart," said the risaldar suspiciously.

"It was, but that crime was not carried out by Ashok Vadal, but rather by a gang of evil, shape-shifting wizards. I spent the last year chasing down the real killers across half of Lok. I return now, having exacted revenge for this insult against our caste." When Jagdish reached for the sack, several hands moved to their swords, but their risaldar waved for them to calm down. He wanted to see where this show was going.

Jagdish took out a golden symbol hanging from a chain. "This is a trophy from Lost House Charsadda."

"Who?"

"A powerful gang of magical assassins, the lot of them. It was they who spilled Vadal blood at Cold Stream and Sutpo Bridge. They lived in a secret fortress far away, between the Nansakar and the sea, but they are broken now, dead or scattered, and their house reduced to rubble. I saw to that." Well, he'd had a lot of help, but Jagdish didn't want to get into the details quite yet.

One of the junior nayaks snorted. "A likely story."

"Oh, but I didn't just kill illegal wizards, my friends. There were many other battles along the way." Jagdish reached back into the sack.

"I don't care what your tall tale is, worker or warrior, if you want to cross this border, you're gonna show me some tax papers or—"

Jagdish held up a skull, big as a melon, with a splintered hole in the top. With the razor-sharp teeth and no eye sockets, it was plain what it was, and still terrifying even stripped of flesh. The soldiers were shocked into silence when they beheld the demon skull.

Jagdish simply dropped the precious item in the dirt. An act so nonchalant that it seemed to surprise them even more. It rolled over to bump against the boot of the risaldar, who instinctively flinched away.

"Impossible..." said one of the soldiers. "He must have just found that on a beach somewhere!"

"No. I beat that head in with a mace myself. As I said..." Jagdish reached into the sack again. "I saw a great many battles." He held aloft the second skull, this one half smashed by a blow from Ashok's war hammer.

The soldiers gasped. "Oceans!"

He dropped that one too. And then they stared at him in awe as he reached into the sack once again, unbelieving, as Jagdish produced a *third* demon skull. This one had belonged to the one they'd squished beneath the statue of the smiling fat man. "A great, *great* many battles."

The warriors were just staring at him, or staring at the skulls. Each one of those was worth more banknotes than they'd be paid in their whole lives.

"And now I'm on my way back to Vadal City with these and the *rest* of my cargo."

The risaldar looked up from the skull by his foot, mouth agape. "There's more?"

Jagdish walked to the back of his wagon. The entire crowd followed him. He unlatched the tail gate, let it fall open, and then threw aside the concealing cloth.

The bottom of the wagon was *full* of demon bones.

"There'd be more but we killed these in rough country with no real roads, and I only had access to so many donkeys to pack them out. We killed an even bigger one too, though we had to drop an entire mansion on him to do it. Couldn't carry that fellow out though. The bones simply weighed too much."

"Oceans!" The risaldar practically staggered to the wagon, and then had to hold onto the wood to keep from falling over. Then he realized where they were and looked fearfully back over his shoulder. "We're right on the border! If Sarnobat knew about this treasure they'd send their entire army after it! Nayak, send for the other paltans. Tell them we need to be reinforced now. Move! Now, damn it, now!"

As one of the men sprinted to get help, Jagdish laughed. "I crossed all of Sarnobat with this *by myself.* But on that note, I could use an escort back to Vadal City so that I can deliver this to the great house personally."

"Of course, Risaldar Jagdish! Anything you need."

Jagdish looked down at his flimsy sash. "A proper uniform would be nice, if you've got one to spare."

The soldiers were staring at Jagdish now like Keta's fanatics looked at Thera. Word of this would spread to every barracks and every drinking hall, and knowing soldiers, by next week it would've been twenty demon skulls instead of three and Jagdish would've sword fought half of Sarnobat to get here.

This was how legends were born.

Chapter 24

◆◆◆◆◆◆◆

Word had spread, even more quickly than Jagdish had expected. By the time they got to his home province, there was a small army guarding his one-wagon caravan. Of course, they weren't his to command. Not even close. In fact it was obvious the officers didn't know what to do with him. He was outside of their command structure. On one hand they'd surely gotten word that he'd last been seen riding with a terrible criminal, but on the other hand he had brought them a fortune worth of magic. So they were polite, guarded his demon wagon, and waited for word to come down from their superiors as to what to do with him.

However, each night they made camp, more soldiers had approached Jagdish to hear tales of his adventures. And Jagdish had been happy to tell them. Not just because all Vadal warriors loved to spin a tale, but also because Jagdish knew his best chance for survival was for it to become too politically unpopular for Harta to kill him. Nobody liked executing heroes.

So Jagdish had talked and talked. Only he'd started at the beginning, at that fateful party where he had been among the men who had dueled Ashok Vadal, and he told nothing but the truth. Always with the truth, because an honorable man had no use for liars... And besides, other Vadal warriors had been there. Despite the first caste's official version of events, and apparently the Capitol had even made a play out of it—performances of which had been banned in Vadal—Jagdish figured the basic truth would have filtered down to the rank and file by now. Yes, Ashok had secretly been born a non-person, but he was still the greatest combatant possibly in the entire history of the world, so there should be no dishonor in losing to such a foe. It had been mighty Angruvadal that had killed the Thakoor he had been sworn to protect, not Ashok. Bidaya had committed suicide as far as he was concerned. That was the risk one took when they tried to pick up an ancestor blade. That might not be a popular opinion with the first caste, but it was what it was, and the warriors all knew it.

Jagdish told them of how as warden he'd sparred against the Black Heart daily, even though his listeners thought him either mad or fearless or both to do so. He had to hold back tears as he talked about the slaughter of his men at Cold Stream, and then control his anger over how he'd been treated by their command afterward. Then he spoke of finding out that one of his prisoners was a tracker of magic, and his decision to free Gutch in order to pursue the Black Heart.

Truth and honor were wonderful things, but Jagdish liked to leave the next part a little fuzzy in the telling, so he'd kind of skipped over the bits where he'd taught a gang of religious fanatic rebels how to be better soldiers. Besides, what his audience really wanted to hear about was fighting wizards and demons.

Regardless, Jagdish was honest about the involvement of Ashok Vadal. Hated now though he may be, Ashok had still managed to kill a squad of demons mostly by himself, and done it without the aid of mighty Angruvadal... *Oh, you have not heard? Angruvadal is gone, my friends.* Then he'd had to break that terrible news to his people because they'd not known of the destruction of their ancestor blade. Most of them had been hoping that somehow their sword would return to them again someday. That part was always heartbreaking.

Jagdish's story had it all, heroism, adventure, tragedy, and triumph. After several days of this he had become very good at telling his story. There was a rhythm to it, catching the audience, and bringing them along through the ups and downs. He was starting to understand why Keta had enjoyed preaching so much.

Whenever they crossed into another garrison's territory some of his guard would drop off to return home, but those were immediately replaced by others. Surely some ambitious phontho or local wizards must have contemplated trying to seize Jagdish's treasure for themselves, but since riders had already gone ahead to alert their Thakoor, such greedy ambitions would only end badly for them. So instead each province had contributed more soldiers to accompany Jagdish's caravan to demonstrate their devotion instead.

Which meant that each night Jagdish had a new audience.

Some of them believed him. Some did not. But ultimately only one man's opinion would really matter.

Sadly, it appeared Harta Vadal did not care about legends.

When they were one day out of Vadal City several members of the Personal Guard joined them on the road. Since the Personal Guard answered only to the Thakoor, all of the provincial garrisons were obligated to obey their commands, and those commands were exceedingly clear. They took command of the column. Jagdish was unceremoniously taken into custody. They confiscated his sword, which was a bad sign. But they did not tie his hands, which was a good sign. Some of them stayed with the wagon, but the rest would escort Jagdish. He was put upon a fast horse and they rode for the city.

Even though the Personal Guard was his old unit, he was acquainted with none of the men he was riding with. Jagdish tried not to show how nervous he was as he asked them questions. Were they going to the great house? What did Harta intend to do with him? Yet they were uncommunicative and refused to answer.

Their lack of response, and his lack of a sword was making him very worried.

"If I'm to be executed, can we at least stop and see my wife and child first, so that I may say goodbye? She's been staying with her family while I've been away. It's not very far off our path. I've not seen them for a long time. I'd like to at least hold my son once before I die. Give me at least that. Half a ton of demon has got to at least be worth that small mercy."

The Personal Guard were all seasoned warriors. Most of them had been assigned wives and had children of their own who they often went for months without seeing because of their duties. He could tell his request struck their hearts, but orders were orders, so they'd not stopped riding.

Only they rode past the fork that would take them to the great house and an audience with the Thakoor himself. Jagdish knew the city well, so he quickly figured out where they were heading instead, and a cold lump of dread had formed in his stomach.

They went to Cold Stream Prison.

They rode past the spot where he and Gutch had defeated the wizard Lome, and through the gates where Jagdish had single-handedly tried to hold back a prison break. Inside the damage had been repaired, the bloodstained walls painted over. New warriors had been obligated to serve as guards. They did not know him.

It felt odd to be in a place so familiar, but in such a painfully different position.

"I take it you've not brought me here to give me my old job back," Jagdish asked, already knowing the answer.

The ranking member of the Personal Guard was a warrior named Girish. "I'm afraid not."

"Execution then?"

"Not yet. Holding for now. I truly am sorry."

Jagdish nodded. "It's fine. Fate's a stonehearted bitch though, isn't she?"

"Indeed she is, Risaldar. Indeed she is." Girish said that with resignation rather than cruelty.

Jagdish knew the process well, having overseen it many times. He'd be stripped and searched for processing next.

"One last request, Girish, from a former member of the Personal Guard to one current." He reached into his recently acquired uniform and pulled out his most prized possession in the world, the pocket watch he'd won in a bet in this very courtyard. "Would you see this gets to my wife? I'd like my son to have it."

"I will do so. You have my word."

As Jagdish was locked in a tiny, dark cell, in the prison he'd once been the warden of, all he could do was laugh and say, "Well, this is ironic."

Chapter 25

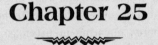

Thera felt as if she was floundering in the ocean again, being bashed against rocks by forces beyond her control. She despised the feeling.

Ashok had intercepted her in the tunnel to warn her about the plague that was destroying the Cove. Keta and the people inside didn't realize just how dire their situation was, but Ashok did. He'd seen it before and knew that though the Protectors didn't know how it spread, it was extremely contagious, and usually fatal. What Keta thought was the end of the sickness was just the beginning. Things were only going to get worse.

There had been no other choice. She'd taken her people right up to the gates of the promised land only to make them turn back. Now she had eight hundred people counting on her to come up with a way out, as they hid from Lord Protector Devedas, consuming their dwindling supplies, while many more faithful were inside, dying of some mysterious jungle disease.

This was worse than being Sikasso's prisoner. In the House of Assassins she had been responsible for herself and that was it. She had never asked to be in charge of all these other lives. And she just kept collecting more of them! It was the stupid bolt from heaven that had picked her for this, ruined her life, destroyed her family, and forced her into this awful situation. Why would the gods want her to go through all of this and drag others down with her? The gods were cruel, petty, uncaring monsters.

Only cursing the gods was as pointless as yelling at the sky.

They'd returned to the valley and made camp for the night. Word of the sickness had spread, and fear had spread with it. Some of her people were ready to riot. Others were tempted to flee. The only thing scarier than the Protectors was a plague. At least they might escape the Protectors. If it wasn't for the fearsomeness of the Sons, she suspected she might have had a rebellion within her rebellion.

She'd gathered those she considered the brightest of her followers and tried to come up with a plan, but their conflicting opinions had offered her no easy way out. She'd not even had Ashok there because he had insisted on staying away from the group for a time. He'd told her that disease could not linger in the blood of one who had been a Protector, but it could still cling to their skin, so he'd rejoin her once he'd burned his clothing and washed his body.

While the rest bickered, she realized just how much she'd come to count on Ashok's blunt counsel. It wasn't missed until he wasn't there to offer it. They all knew it was only a matter of time before

Devedas found them. It was either push on looking for another place to hide—an unlikely find for a group this numerous—or risk a terrible disease in the place that was otherwise perfect.

No decision had been made that evening. Thera's sleep had been spent wrestling with nightmares of people crying bloody tears as they pleaded for her to aid them.

At dawn the first day of their seemingly hopeless quarantine, Thera went off by herself, found a downed tree, and practiced throwing her knives. Her damaged hands made sure she was still awful at it. It was said that Vane had the best arms and the keenest eyes in Lok, so no one could throw a spike, knife, or chakram better. By her family's standards she had become downright shameful, but she found the repetitive motion and walking back and forth to pick up the blades helped her think. She'd done the same thing in her husband's gardens, while plotting how to murder him and get away with it.

A few years ago Thera knew she would have just run off by herself and left them to their fate. That was no longer an option.

Whether by accident or design, the gods had picked her. They'd reached down from the sky and stabbed her in the skull with their will. Since then the Voice occasionally popped up to speak some cryptic words that later came true. The battle in the graveyard of demons had shown her it was capable of a great deal more. You'd think with most of the Forgotten's faithful about to perish from a disease, and the rest stuck waiting for the Protectors to find them, the fickle gods would tell her *something*. But oh, no.

Not those spiteful bastards. The Voice only seemed to like to manifest at the most inconvenient times. If the Lord Protector rode into the valley below at the head of an army, then she bet the Voice would be sure to speak up loud and clear so he'd know right where to find her.

When the Voice came upon her, it shoved her out of her own head. Occasionally she still suffered from seizures caused by the bolt. When those events occurred, she was vulnerable, helpless, and useless. It was Keta who had stayed by her side and kept her alive during those episodes. He'd been a loyal friend for several years, but now he was probably going to keep getting sicker and sicker until he wept blood and died and there wasn't a damned thing she could do about it.

Anger filled her, both at the gods, and at life in general. Keta was the one who was good at this religion business. She hated it. She'd wanted nothing to do with Ratul's revolution. Keta had taken the words of the Voice and used them to give the casteless courage. The gods might not know it, but they needed Keta far more than they needed her. These fools needed a real leader, a visionary, not some poor woman whose fondest wish was to be left alone. Sure, the gods had stepped in to save her, but not the man who actually believed in them and wanted the job.

And with her mind focused on a problem other than the throwing, she sunk her knife perfectly into the wood with a solid *thunk*. Just like the old days.

There had to be a way to fix this.

Thunk.

Of course the gods had stepped in to save her. She was the Forgotten's vessel. Part of him lived inside

her head. The gods might not give a damn about their
followers, but they took action when they needed to
defend themselves. To protect her from the demons,
the Voice had briefly given her magic the likes of which
even the House of Assassins had never seen before.

Thunk.

Ashok said the Law knew of no cure, but Sikasso
had believed that magic could fix any physical problem,
even regrow severed limbs. You just had to know the
right pattern. The wizards had tried to teach her how
to use magic, but she'd been terrible at it. Except in
the graveyard, during that moment of crisis, the Voice
had shown her exactly what to do to save herself.
The magical pattern had appeared before her with a
clarity the wizards could only dream of.

Thunk.

They had plenty of demon parts to make magic, a
veritable fortune of the stuff. The wizards had showed
her that magic was just an incredibly fine type of
matter that could be used to manipulate other matter
into new forms. Flesh and bone included. If the gods
would show her a pattern again, she could cure this
disease, cleanse the Cove, and save them all.

Thunk.

However, the gods had only taken that drastic action
when her death seemed certain. And even then, they'd
not saved her clean. Oh no, she'd paid a price. They'd
given her a molten spear sufficient to kill a god, but
using it had crippled her hands in the process.

Clang.

That knife bounced sideways off the log.

Regardless, Thera knew exactly what she had to do.

❖   ❖   ❖

"This is madness," Ashok said.

"I don't think so," Thera responded with false bravado as the two of them walked up the now dry tunnel. "The Voice performs miracles but only when it's convenient for the Voice. So I'll force it to act."

"By contracting a deadly plague?"

"Yes. Then the gods will either show me the magical pattern to cure it, or they'll lose their mortal vessel."

"Holding yourself hostage is madness," he muttered.

"How many times have you risked your life because you thought it was necessary to keep a vow?"

"A great many . . . But always because my duty required it. You have made no vow to these people. They are beggars who imposed their will upon you. What if these supposed gods laugh at your attempt to coerce them?"

"Then I guess I'll get sick and die with the rest of the fools dumb enough to fight the Law." This was hard enough without having the one person she thought she could always count on doubting her sanity too. Regardless, she lifted her flickering torch high and marched on.

"What if the gods do not know a cure either?" Ashok asked.

"Then they're terrible at their jobs," Thera snapped.

"I would not find that surprising in the least."

"Look, Ashok, I can't just leave Keta and those people to die!"

"Why not?"

Sometimes Ashok made her clench her teeth. How dare he ask her questions that she didn't really have answers for herself? "Why did you go out of your way to save those two casteless children in Jharlang?"

"That..." Ashok trailed off. "I do not know."

"At the time you cared for no one. You made that perfectly clear. It wasn't the legal thing, nor the smart thing, but you still acted because you felt that it was the *right* thing. You almost got us all killed. Your hasty actions got me captured by wizards. But even then we both know you'd probably still do it again anyway. This is like that." Thera knew that Ashok was always truthful with her, so she put the burden on him. "If you were in my situation, right now, what would you do?"

To his credit, her protector mulled it over. "I would not have thought of this strategy."

"But if you had?"

"It is foolhardy, but if you make the assumption that the Forgotten will cooperate, then it may work," he admitted. "You would risk one life to save a multitude."

"At least we're past the part where you have to add the caveat that criminal lives aren't worth anything."

He shrugged. "However, I am not you. I am expendable. You are not. I am supposed to keep you safe. This is the opposite. I should not let you do this. You are my obligation."

"They're all my obligation now," she insisted. Not because the Law said so, or the gods, but because they had come to her looking for help, and she hadn't turned them away. She could have. But she didn't. That made her responsible for them. She didn't even like most of them, but she would do whatever it took to help them.

Ashok was obviously displeased with her decision, but he did not debate it further.

✦   ✦   ✦

Keta's guards became very excited when they discovered that their prophet had returned. They rushed to the entrance when they saw the torch-light approach and began to babble all at once. It seemed that Ashok's grim pronouncement to Keta had leaked, and the knowledge of their impending doom had left them shaken. There had been much wailing and crying about how the gods had forsaken them and they were all going to perish, so on and so forth. Except the presence of the Voice now changed everything.

It took all of Ashok's will to resist the urge to smite the hand off the first guard who touched Thera on the arm to guide her out of the tunnel. It was unknown what caused the Blood Eye or how it spread, but he had seen what it did to people. It destroyed one from the inside out, crumbling away, bit by bit. That hand could have belonged to the foulest assassin and it would have been no more dangerous.

They were rushed up out of the pit and across the rim of the crater to where a large building had been carved from the solid rock. The walls were bare of decoration, though there was the faintest hint they might have been painted before being worn away by wind and weather. The deep window wells might have once held glass, but now they were closed by hanging blankets. Ashok did not know what this place had once been, but it was easily the size of a small city's government house. It must have been rather impressive once. Now it served as a hospital.

Inside there was a multitude of sickly, coughing, wheezing, bleeding people, lying on piles of straw. The air smelled of rot and death. Flies buzzed. Volunteers knelt by the sick, trying to comfort them, wiping their faces with damp rags stained pink.

Ashok was immune to disease, and in that moment, he was very thankful for that fact. But the presence of his obligation in this plague-ridden place filled him with unease. Even Ashok's hardened heart ached at the sight of children lying there, too weak to move, with flies crawling on their faces and drinking the moisture from their open eyes, but despite his pity he wanted nothing more than to whisk Thera away and set fire to the place to protect the rest of Lok from this scourge.

Thera hesitated, the fear and revulsion plain upon her face. Because the Law so thoroughly addressed matters of cleanliness and sanitation, outbreaks such as this were relatively rare, but everyone knew just how dangerous they could be. There was no more ignominious way to go into the great nothing than rotting away in your own decaying filth.

When they had first met, Thera had portrayed herself as a mercenary creature who cared only for her own well-being and to the oceans with everyone else. Ashok understood now that had been an act—so convincing that she had even believed it herself—but those times were over. She was putting herself in great peril to help others. It was as selfless an act as any he'd ever seen. As her protector, he found it vexing.

Thera gathered up her courage and walked into the hospital.

Keta was there, moving between the mats, offering his people sips of water ladled from a bucket he carried. He looked up as they entered. For a moment the exhausted Keeper was dumbfounded, but then a giant smile split his face. "Thera! I knew you would come!"

All the suffering people looked her way, though for many it was a struggle just to turn their heads. Those who could rise, did. Most did not. But there was hope on their faces, the ones who were still coherent at least.

"I'm here," Thera said. "How can I help?"

Chapter 26

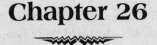

Though he was not very good at such things, Ashok spent the next few days tending to the sick and afflicted. Even though the resilience granted unto him by the Heart of the Mountain should have made him ideal for such duties, sadly, it came as a shock to no one that the man known far and wide as the Black Heart was much better at harming than healing. However, as long as Thera served in the hospital then he would not stray far from his obligation's side. Since Ashok could not abide sloth he might as well make himself useful.

This duty should not have been so difficult. He was born casteless, but the memories of those squalid times had been stripped from him. He'd been raised instead as a member of the highest caste, except those years had been spent in the austere environment of the Hall of Protectors, rather than the pampered palaces of Lok's highborn. Ashok was very familiar with suffering and pain. He should have been better at dealing with the agony of others, yet he was not.

He did not know how to offer comfort. He followed Keta's example, providing food when they were hungry, changing wrappings once they became filthy and blood crusted, and giving water when they were thirsty, but each time they looked up at Ashok with simple, pleading eyes, to ask him if they were getting better, he was unable to lie to them, so he remained silent.

Each time felt like a betrayal. He did not understand why, but it did. Keta had told these people about him, building him up to be some kind of mighty hero sent by the gods to aid them.

Ashok did not feel much the hero.

Thera was much better at such things, but he could see that she was becoming attached—hugging and calming every sick child, speaking at length with every adult about their hopes and fears and dreams—but since the gods had not given into her demands yet, she suffered greatly each time one of them died.

So he offered his services in other ways. Ashok was good at digging graves. He'd learned that on a beach in Gujara what seemed an eternity ago—though really it had not been that long at all—only there would be no graves dug for those who died of the Blood Eye. Some diseases liked to linger in the soil. The Law was clear on this matter for good reason, and even rebels would not argue with something as sensible as the command to burn contagious bodies to ash.

So each day Ashok gathered wood from the surrounding mountains, made a pyre, and carried the fresh bodies to it. Man, woman, and child, the bodies all seemed far too light and empty. He would wait until dark so that the cloud of rising smoke wouldn't attract the eyes of the Protectors who were searching for them. Then Ashok would burn them and tend the fires while wondering what he would do if Thera herself ended up in the pyre.

One sundown he was joined at the corpse pile by a man named Javed.

Ashok had seen him a few times around the Cove. Javed was of the worker caste—a merchant of some kind—and something of a hero to these people, having saved Keta and the fanatics they'd met on the road to Haradas from a wizard assassin who had hunted them in the snow. Keta had spoken highly of Javed, praising his work ethic, intelligence, and faith. Ashok had no use for the last one, but the first two were valuable traits. Javed was also one of the healthier men left in the Cove, so he had taken on a great deal of the Keeper's responsibilities in managing the place.

"Good evening, honored guest." Javed gave him a low and respectful bow. "Please accept my humble offering of veneration."

"You're a northerner?" Ashok asked, since the greeting would have been the most appropriate one to a newcomer of extremely high status in Vadal lands.

"I was not so fortunate, sir," Javed said as he raised his head. "I'm from Zarger, caravan born. I just traveled the bounteous north extensively in my time as a rice trader."

"I see." The nomadic caravan people were probably the only group in Lok who got around more than the Protectors. "There is no need to give me deference. I'm merely another criminal."

"Ah, of course. Old habits die hard. As the Keeper

has declared, this is a new society without castes, your only status is what you build for yourself, and we are all equals below the gods. Forgive me. I am Javed."

The former merchant was taller than most men, but not nearly as physically imposing as Ashok. He must have obtained some status in his life, because despite currently wearing the filthy clothes of a field hand Javed still carried himself like a man of importance.

"I am Ashok," he said because it was polite, rather than because there was any doubt to his identity. "Keta has spoken highly of you."

Javed waved away that compliment. "I am merely happy to serve."

"I was told this place would've fallen apart without you this spring. According to Keta, you are the man who kept the crops growing while many of the laborers had become too ill to tend them."

"The Keeper is too kind. All I did was take over the management of the terraces. It is simply because my old position required a great deal of organizational skill, which is something this place lacked... I mean no offense to the faithful by saying that. They are brave and strong."

"Yet not always wise. It is fine. I always appreciate hearing the truth."

"As one should. I have come to love Keta as a brother, but sometimes I worry that if there is a problem he can't immediately solve he'd prefer to leave it to the gods to handle. Myself, I prefer to do the best I can and then hope the gods make up the difference."

Even though it was only them and several corpses in the area, such illegal religious talk out in the open still made Ashok uncomfortable. "What can I do for you, Merchant?"

"Nothing, General. It was I who came to offer my services to you. Do you need any help here?"

It was a grisly business, avoided by most. The dead's loved ones weren't even present because they were too sick to walk from the hospital to the burn pit..., or they'd already gone in it. Ashok would not turn down the assistance. It took a lot of fuel to render a body down to ash. "Grab an axe."

It took a while to gather that much wood, especially since it was quite the hike from the rim of the crater to the slopes where trees grew above. If the Cove had been functioning properly they would have whole teams of men out cutting logs to prepare for the next winter, but the plague was ruining everything.

The two of them searched out fallen trees and dried branches. Ashok carried the heavy things. Javed, the light. The merchant was by no means a weak man—he was far stronger than most of the fanatics—but nearly everyone was frail when compared to Ashok.

"This should be enough for tonight," he told Javed as he dropped an armful of tree limbs onto the pile. The impact caused a great cloud of buzzing flies to leap off the bodies. Such was the indignity of death. "Hopefully this duty will not be required tomorrow."

"I pray that's true." Javed piled up the last of the kindling, and then wiped the sweat from his brow. "Gods willing."

It took Ashok several tries to get the leaves smoldering with his fire starter. He had brought no oil to help it along, but a few minutes later the branches had caught. It quickly spread to the clothing. Even the Black Heart had to look away as the bodies caught. He would tend this as long as necessary to make sure the job was done, but he would take no pleasure from it.

The burn pit had been placed on a terrace some distance from where most of the fanatics had settled, but in the distance Ashok could see a great number of faces turning their way as the fire grew and the light caught their eyes... But then the people went about their affairs. They all knew what the light meant, but death had become so common here that they were barely fazed by it.

As the two men walked away from the blaze so as to not be caught in the oily smoke, Ashok told Javed, "You are fortunate to have not fallen ill as well."

"Some of us have been lucky so far. My father was warrior caste—well, supposedly he was. I never met the man. My mother said he was a caravan guard. I must have inherited my robust constitution from him."

"My casteless father cremated bodies." It had been a while since Ashok had thought of that, but right now the parallels were grimly amusing. His next father had been a fabrication, but he'd spent most of his life believing that the man had perished in a fire, and the man who had been like his father in the Protector Order had taught him how to make the corpse piles grow. Ashok did not believe in such concepts as destiny, but it appeared he was never meant to escape the horrible smell of burning flesh.

"If I may ask, General. What do you intend to do about the extermination of the casteless?"

"So you have heard..."

"The prophet told Keta, Keta told his trusted men. Most of them can't keep a secret like I can, so I give it a day at most before this entire settlement knows about what's going on out there."

"One can either die serving the Law or die resisting it. Either way the Law will go on."

"But the Sons of the Black Sword defeated ten times their number with hardly a loss and captured two cities."

"An exaggeration, and the reality was only made possible by surprise, fortunate timing, and a gang of idiots sacrificing themselves because of their pride. Even if these people were not wasting away, they are nothing compared to the combined might of the warriors of Akershan and the forces of the Capitol. I do not have the answer. Whatever the prophet orders me to do, it will be done."

"Ah, Keta told me that your devotion was to her rather than the rebellion...I do not fault you for this. She is a chosen of the gods and we are but dregs who follow her about. But what if she catches the plague? What will you do then?"

Ashok scowled at the fire. "Maybe it is as you said, Merchant. I will do my best and you can hope your gods make up the difference."

Chapter 27

Thera wept in private.

While working in the hospital she forced a constant smile upon her face. False cheer was better than nothing. She held the swollen hands of dying children and told them they were going to be fine, even while their eyes filled with blood and their lungs stopped working. A hard woman by nature, she swallowed her pride, tried to give comfort, and showed no pain. They really truly believed that as their prophet she would have the power to heal them. She'd thought so too maybe, at first. But the Forgotten had remained silent.

She did this all day and all night, covered in sweat, and flies, and dried blood, and vomit. When the Voice had told her and Keta to leave the Cove to go find Ashok, this had been a hopeful place, bright and vibrant, everything that Ratul had hoped for. Now it was dying, a sickness in its bones.

Keta had found her a quiet place to sleep, away from the hacking coughs. The buildings the Ancients had carved from the sides of the crater were massive things, with a multitude of rooms, all of them empty, their original purposes a mystery. The growing rebellion had made its home here since Ratul had discovered the place and they still hadn't mapped the whole thing. She could have had her own palace—albeit an empty one—but instead she had asked for a space in the hospital. Even with as many sick as they had, there were still plenty of rooms.

Thera went to her quarters only to sleep and to rage at the gods.

The bed was made of an old blanket upon a pile of straw, and Thera sat on it, staring at her hands. A little girl had died while holding onto those hands not ten minutes ago, her tiny fingers a memory on the scar tissue of her palms . . . One second they had been talking, the next she was gone, blank red eyes looking off into the endless nothing. The little girl hadn't even been scared, just tired of being in pain, and she'd told Thera she was happy the prophet had finally come to take her pain away. Then she'd just . . . died.

That one had almost broken her. Thera couldn't keep up her mask. So she'd stood up, told Keta she needed a moment to rest, and then she'd retreated to her quarters.

"Why won't you help them?" Thera asked the thing in her head, bitterly.

Even though the Voice had been with her since she was a child, she rarely tried to talk to it. It was an unwelcome companion. If she could get rid of it, she would. If Sikasso had kept his word she would have gladly given it to the House of Assassins to be rid of the thing. It used her, got her in trouble, and never, ever gave anything back.

She hated the Voice. Tonight she let her hate be heard.

"I've asked you for nothing. Now I'm begging you for this. Show me how to cure this plague."

The silence was deafening.

"You taught me how to make magic in the graveyard of demons, but that wasn't to save me, it was to save yourself." She grabbed a fistful of her dirty shirt and tugged at it. "Look at this filth. Surely, I've caught the disease by now too. Good! I'll probably die, and then you'll be homeless. Just like all the casteless camped outside because they were stupid enough to listen to your promises."

Thera stood up and shouted at the ceiling. The bolt had come from the heavens so it made sense gods lived in the sky.

"You selfish bastards! I thought I was selfish. I tried to care about nobody, but it's only because I had to be, to protect *you*! You've cost me my house, my father, everyone who has ever listened to your promises has died, and yet you do *nothing*! You told them to rebel, and they obeyed. Now you've abandoned them! They'll die, your rebellion will die, the Law will live forever, and you'll remain forgotten as you deserve!"

She waited. *Nothing*.

Thera let out a scream of rage and frustration, clenched her damaged fists, and stormed from the room and down the hall.

"If you will not do it for me, then do it for them. If the useless Voice will not act, then I will. We are not the *same*! I'll keep comforting them until my lungs stop working and my eyes fill with blood, and with my dying breath I will curse you for the fraud you are!"

As she made her way down the winding stairs, Thera dried her eyes and tried to compose herself. Though she'd lost all hope, she couldn't let the people see that. It would kill them. They needed her to be strong. As she got close to the hospital she heard the coughing and smelled the corruption, and her heart broke all over again.

She stopped there on the stairs, unable to go forward. All this was too much. All those people counting on her outside, their lives were in her hands. They'd followed her, and when they were caught it would be her fault. Plague on one side, Protectors on the other.

But a child of Vane never backed down from anything. So Thera forced her legs to work, and she continued down toward the hospital.

Apparently, it had been listening to her demands though. Normally, the Voice didn't really speak to her, it spoke through her. This time was different than before. An odd sensation came over her, almost as if the invader that lived inside her skull was borrowing her brain. Thera's vision became blurred. Her head began to ache.

Searching.

The Voice found what it was looking for, and then it offered her a choice. She didn't know how she knew, but the knowledge was clear as day. The answer was available, but granting it might harm her physically, and afterward the Voice would be unavailable until she was fully recovered. Such ancient knowledge was not given easily. Somehow, she understood the old patterns were encoded, and the Forgotten would only grant her so many keys to decipher them. It could either help her with this problem now, or she could save this blessing for something more important later. The offer came with a warning. Choose wisely. She could not have both.

That choice was not difficult at all. Her decision was immediate.

The door was unlocked. That was when the pattern appeared before her eyes, glowing lines crisp, every particle moving into the exact place, just as it had in the Graveyard of Demons. Only this time the pattern wasn't designed to kill, but rather to save.

The light vanished, as quick as it had come, leaving her stunned and dizzy. Thera slipped and tumbled down the rest of the stairs, sprawling face-first onto the stone floor. She scraped her elbows and split her lip.

Keta saw her fall, dropped his water bucket, and rushed to her side to help. "Thera!" He took hold of her arm, gentle and firm, surely thinking another seizure had come upon her. The water from his bucket sloshed past her legs. "Are you all right?"

She was in a lot of pain, but there was no time for that. She had to act while the pattern was still stark in her memory. "There's a pack with some demon parts in my quarters. Get it. *Now!*"

To his credit, Keta did not waste time arguing. He sprang to his feet and ran up the stairs.

Others tried to help Thera. They got her standing, but she was so dizzy it took everything she had to stay upright. Her head was pounding. The place where the bolt had struck her felt like it was on fire. They must have thought the sickness had come upon her as the faithful began to wail and cry to their gods.

Pushing the helping hands away, Thera stumbled over to the nearest bed. A little boy was staring at her with bloodshot eyes, afraid, not for himself, but for the lady who his parents had sworn had been sent by the gods to save them. She knelt—more like fell—next to him. "Don't worry. It'll be fine," she assured him, but the words were really for her, as she struggled to remember the exact nature of the vision.

Keta returned, running as fast as he could. "I've got it!" He opened the pack for her.

Thera reached inside and grabbed a fragment of demon bone. She was no wizard. She'd barely been able to feel the magic before, and that was before most of the feeling had been burned from her fingers. But desperate, she took hold of that scrap, and called upon the rudimentary skills learned within the House of Assassins. Then she called upon the gods she hated—*please let this work*—as she laid her other hand against the cheek of the dying boy.

Chapter 28

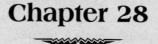

Late that night Inquisition Witch Hunter, fifteen-year senior, Javed snuck up the mountainside to the spot where he had left his supply of demon bone cached. Avoiding the tired, coughing sentries was child's play, especially since he was the one who had assigned them their stations. It was one of the many duties Keta had delegated to him over the last few months, so Javed made sure only the dumbest of the casteless patrolled this particular slope.

His clothing and beard stunk of smoke and sweat. He had spent his day ingratiating himself to delusional fanatics, and his evening stacking twigs with the most dangerous man in the world. That at least, had been rather educational... Enough so that he felt it was for the best to send a report to the Grand Inquisitor.

Javed was not a licensed wizard, but witch hunters were given a special dispensation to learn a few magical patterns which could aid in their duties. The Order of Inquisition had taught him the tiger form for when he needed to move great distances quickly or track someone across the wilderness, the ability to step *outside* of regular space for when he needed to enter places unseen, and the pattern for sending information from one piece of demon bone to another for times like this. Because Javed was a very intelligent and ambitious individual, he had picked up a few more. Unofficially and off the books, usually learned from criminals and unlicensed wizards, but his superiors did not need to know about those. It was rumored Grand Inquisitor Omand had done much the same sort of thing during his time in the field, and it was said that he might have known as many as *ten* patterns, which was an astounding number, especially for someone who had not devoted his whole life to deciphering the magical arts. Omand had a whole Order to run and a coup to plan!

Javed ran uphill with a surefooted swiftness that did not match his current humble appearance. It had been nerve-wracking to test his mask before Ashok Vadal, but thankfully any fear that might have slipped through had probably been seen as that of a normal religious fanatic, anxious about meeting his idol for the first time. Javed was a professional liar. He knew his acting had been flawless. Protectors might be terrors in battle, but they were as simplistic as the masses when it came to the subtle arts of manipulation.

It was difficult to pick out the landmarks in the dark. It would have been impossible without a lantern if Canda hadn't been bright and the sky cloudless. But when Javed found a particular misshapen pine tree, that told him it was time to go down the ridge a bit, where he found the pair of boulders that he'd buried his cache beneath. He would have loved to hide this closer to the room he claimed as a dwelling, but that was risky with so many fanatics around, especially their curious children who made a game out of exploring the ruins. A minute of digging freed the cloth-wrapped bundle filled with small demon bones, vials of liquids, and bags of mysterious powders. Each of those had a purpose, none of which he wanted to explain to a snooping fanatic.

He picked out a demon knuckle. The next digit of that particular finger would be waiting at the communications station of the Inquisitor's Dome, hung on the wall next to dozens of others. Each of those representing some witch hunter on a secret mission... Though Javed was certain no others were nearly as important as his. This pattern could be used to send information from any bone to any other, but it took far less effort and energy when they came from the same demon, and even less when the bones had been adjacent. It took a moment to prepare his mind for the pattern, and then another to prepare his report. Brevity was important. The longer the message the more valuable demon would be used up.

"Ashok Vadal and the prophet have arrived at the hideout with approximately eight hundred additional rebels. I can confirm that Ashok no longer bears Angruvadal. The prophet is attempting to treat the plague. Everyone believes she will save them, but I've seen no powers from her yet. I believe she is insane and hoping for a miracle. Despite this Ashok remains devoted to his obligation. Neither of them seem inclined to make war against the Law at this time. As expected, the sickness has taken the fight out of the rebels. Please advise how to proceed."

Once the message was imprinted on the bone, Javed focused until he could feel the magic burning like a red-hot ember in his clenched fist, and then sent the words off on the wind. Once done, he settled down to wait for a response. He doubted it would take very long.

It had been a while since his last report. Demon was too valuable to waste on frivolous things, and the Cove was too isolated for any traditional methods of Inquisition communication. If there was no response tonight, he would continue obeying his last set of instructions until directed otherwise.

The forest was quiet, and manual labor really was tiring, so Javed took a nap and tried to dream about all of these fanatics being put to the sword by his masked brothers. It wasn't that Javed particularly hated these people, for hate was a strong word. They simply existed as obstacles in his continual rise through the ranks. He was not in this for the Law. Javed cared about as much for the Law as he did the dictates of Keta's false gods. The Law merely gave him an excuse to do something he enjoyed. He had befriended Keta because that was his job, and when the time came he would stab him in the back with an equivalent amount of emotion.

Ironically, Javed himself was a criminal, for he was complicit in the Grand Inquisitor's scheme to overthrow the judges, which was far worse than anything these rebels hoped to do. Yet Javed had eagerly pledged himself to Omand's dark councils. With great risk came great opportunity, and once Omand—or some handpicked puppet—ruled in the Capitol, Javed would have status beyond imagining.

Not that he really cared about such things but trying to attain the impossible kept him motivated.

The sting in his palm brought him back to reality. The bone was buzzing with a furious energy, indicating it had received a message. From the vibrations, sound rather than images. Javed looked around, and then listened intently to make sure he was not being spied upon, before he activated the last bit of magic in the bone and set the words free.

Surprisingly, the voice belonged to Grand Inquisitor Omand himself, not one of his many underlings. It was the middle of the night. Did the man ever sleep?

"It is time to end the plague. Make sure all credit goes to the false prophet. You have done well. I wanted the rebels to stay put, and not squander so many assets needlessly. It is hard to rebel when you are too sick to walk. Now that Ashok is present to lead them, they can become a proper threat again. Even without the sword we should be able to wring some use from his name. The Great Extermination is only beginning. The casteless will need someone to rally around. Become vital to him, Javed, as you have to the Keeper of Names. I will provide an incentive for Ashok to fight. Akershan will drown in blood before the summer is over."

Message complete, the bone crumbled to dust. Javed blew it away, and then wiped the residue on his pants. He stretched, yawned, and went to remove the bag of metallic poison he'd left stewing like a tea bag in the pipe that provided most of the Cove's water supply for the last few months. Inquisition alchemists had been using this particular mixture for centuries. A large dose killed quickly, and since the symptoms were usually mistaken for a rare northern disease, the Inquisition remained blameless. A little of the stuff would kill slowly, to keep a population weak and manageable, but once they were no longer being dosed the effects would subside within a few weeks. Most of the afflicted would recover, though many would continue to have health problems for the rest of their lives. That was fine. At least he'd kept them here so Omand could use them effectively, instead of sallying forth to get themselves killed fighting against the extermination order.

Hours later, with poisons gathered and reburied, Javed returned to his temporary home. Though it wasn't even sunrise he was surprised to find everyone not only awake, but truly joyous for the first time in months. It was a celebration. They were dancing and singing, laughing and praising their gods.

A woman ran past Javed. He'd not seen anyone willingly expend that much energy in a while. "What's happening?"

"Master Javed, where have you been?"

"I had to repair a fence on one of the terraces so the cows wouldn't get out. Please, sister, what's going on?"

"You missed the miracle!"

Javed wanted to toss the jabbering woman over the side of the cliff. "What miracle?"

"The prophet has healed the sick."

That was impossible. It would take weeks for the toxins to leave their systems and weeks more for them to even begin to recover their strength. "Who was healed?"

"Every last one!"

Chapter 29

≈≈≈≈≈≈

It was a good feeling to finally see his years of effort bearing fruit. There were rumors of war as old tensions flared between Harban and Makao. A desperate Vadal was probably going to invade one of its neighbors in the north soon. In the south, the rebellion had actually captured cities. *Whole cities!* They had not held them for long but the very idea of even briefly losing territory to criminals was unimaginable to the Law-abiding citizens of the Capitol.

The extermination trials had stalled temporarily because of the rebellion's astounding success in those troubled regions, but the important thing had already been accomplished, with thousands of terrified non-people fleeing across the borders. Word was spreading to every house, and casteless quarters across all of Lok were panicking. Even the lowest of the low, with seemingly nothing to live for, still desired life. There had been costly riots and violent reprisals. The Chamber of Argument had grown increasingly acrimonious as Artya had continued fighting to restart the trials. The judges from the western houses were too proud to admit to just how much their agricultural production depended on casteless labor, but shortages were already causing economic upheavals and that problem would only get worse. If all went well tonight he would have the votes to start a new, expanded phase of the Great Extermination very soon.

Few could see it yet, but the Law was teetering on the edge of a very dangerous precipice.

Grand Inquisitor Omand was having a wonderful time.

And best of all, Ashok Vadal lived. Though his expression had been hidden behind his mask at the time, Javed's message had brought a smile to Omand's face. He had been worried that he had wrung all the usefulness from the Black Heart's reputation that he could. The Inquisition was still secretly paying the surviving members of the House of Assassins to commit atrocities in Ashok's name, but they lacked the impact of the real thing. Nobody could unnerve the first caste quite the same way as Ashok Vadal.

Though he had a multitude of spies Omand would often go out and about the city by himself to get a feel for how the people really felt. Firsthand observation was always more valuable than secondhand reports. Though he was one of the most powerful men in the world, all he had to do was leave his mask behind, change into appropriate clothing with the badge of some other office, and nobody ever noticed him. The Grand Inquisitor was infamous, but very few people knew what he actually looked like, and even for those, Omand was an expert at changing his appearance, accent, and mannerisms. His time as a witch hunter enabled him to blend into any environment until he was just another piece of scenery. These jaunts also enabled him to get away from the dome, and the eyes of his subordinates, so that he could indulge his other proclivities in private.

Omand delighted in hurting people in various ways. It was one of the few things that gave him actual joy. Luckily inflicting pain upon others was a valuable skill for an Inquisitor to have, so he had risen quickly through the ranks, until he had discovered the great game, and the endless competition that was politics. Those two things were what Omand lived for. Politics and pain. Everything else was mundane and gray.

It was during one of his secret nightly outings that he had first noticed a change in the mood of the city, which was already drearier than normal since the destruction of Shabdkosh and the debut of Artya's play about the Black Heart's rebellion. It was in a secret brothel, which catered to those of high status—but illegal tastes—that Omand had realized that the Capitol was truly afraid. Normally a dull, listless, vapid people, addicted to their aristocratic comforts, the first caste was unused to real fear. It was an unfamiliar feeling to the truly powerful.

Wars and rebellions were nothing new to these people, but those things were always distant, and happened to other, lesser people. Decisions were made and their inferiors would live or die. However, a bitter former Protector with a magical super weapon, at the head of an army of bloodthirsty non-people, daring to threaten *them*? Now that was absolute madness, and Shabdkosh had brought that madness far too close to home. Ashok's name was now heard in every government building, spoken of in hushed tones at dinners, and it even intruded into the politest of conversations at parties. It was remarkable how much his grim celebrity had captured the imagination of the Capitol.

There was graffiti in the alleys now, always some variation of Ashok as a nearly demonic figure, spilling first-caste blood. Most of it drawn by workers or warriors who chafed at being assigned to a city filled with their demanding betters, but some of it was painted by the youth of the first caste, who took perverse pleasure in the discomfort of their parents. For the first time in most of their lives, the highest caste had discovered a threat that might actually be able to reach out and touch them. This had unnerved the simpler creatures among them.

There was another piece of graffiti visible now, just outside his carriage window. Omand caught just the briefest glimpse of it upon the back corner of the Order of Agriculture and Irrigation building. It was a terrible image, very crudely done, but they had given Ashok fangs, making his face almost a caricature of the Law, and his black sword was cleaving the head off a figure who was probably supposed to be the Chief Judge.

Such a petty display of lawlessness, in the very home of the Law? *Remarkable.*

"Taraba, make a note," Omand told his assistant. "Find a few of our Inquisitors who are good painters. Or better, who will admit to defacing public buildings in their youth, so that it may look more natural, and have them create more of these fearsome Black-Heart images around the Capitol."

"I shall do so." The two of them were riding in the Grand Inquisitor's carriage on their way to important business. "But just to clarify, you want our men to deface government buildings?"

"It's for a good cause. But make sure they are subtle." It went without saying that such a discovery would be embarrassing for the Order, so he would have to disavow their obligation, declare them imposters, and have them executed like common street trash. "It would not do for them to get caught."

"Of course, sir." Taraba did not actually write any of that down. The young man had a most impressive memory, and obviously would never document his Order conspiring to violate the very Law they were obligated to uphold. "If I may be so bold as to offer a suggestion?"

"I would love to hear it, Taraba."

"In addition we should have our artists put up some images of Lord Protector Devedas pursuing the fiend Ashok. Make Devedas look heroic, a beacon of hope if you will. If you intend to install him as your puppet king to replace the judges, it makes sense to get the people thinking of him in a fittingly appropriate manner. If we make them evocative enough, the images should catch on and then the hooligans will do our work for us."

"Hmmm..." Omand pondered on that. "The dichotomy of the dark being chased away by the light, the frightening man with the black heart versus the handsome man with the silver armor, straightforward good against evil makes for compelling imagery. I like it. Very good, Taraba. See to it."

"I shall, sir. Thank you."

It was an excellent idea. Taraba was a loyal man, also a clever one, but not too clever that he might become disloyal. Unlike Omand, or even someone like Devedas, Taraba had a perfectly acceptable amount of ambition. Omand figured that once everything settled down, the new government had been installed, and Omand had taken up some *advisory position* to the new king, Taraba would make a good Grand Inquisitor. He was still too young and inexperienced for the obligation, but Omand intended to keep running everything himself anyway, so it wouldn't really matter.

They had reached their destination. The carriage came to a stop and the door was opened by an Inquisitor who had been waiting for them. Several more Inquisitors were positioned on the mansion's stairs, wearing steel armor, their helms modeled to look like the leering face of the Law. The mansion's doors had already been smashed in with hammers.

"I see that you started without me," the Grand Inquisitor said as he climbed down from the carriage.

"Apologies, sir," stammered one of his men. "I was told we were to secure the property and—"

"It's fine." Nothing was going to ruin Omand's good mood tonight. Besides, he was too old for kicking in doors. He had young, expendable Inquisitors for that sort of thing. "Is everyone in the household accounted for?"

"Yes. No one resisted. We are searching the place for religious contraband now."

"Very good." Omand knew there would be no such evidence here, which was why he had arranged for one of his men to plant some. He glanced across the street and saw that the commotion had gathered a crowd of curious onlookers, many of them wearing clothing indicative of wealth and privilege. They were curious. Once they saw the golden mask of the Grand Inquisitor himself at the scene, they became nervous. It was rare that the Inquisition performed such an overt show of force, especially in a wealthy district, and even rarer to have the head of that nefarious Order present. This was a special occasion indeed.

Even though his men had already cleared the building, Omand kept a tiny piece of black steel in his hand so he could call upon its magic at a moment's notice. He had not been the most successful witch hunter in the history of his order by being complacent.

This was not the first time he had been inside this very impressive mansion. He had attended events here, both as himself, and in disguise as a less important man. Parulkar Akershan threw some of the most noteworthy parties in the Capitol, which was an impressive feat, and also a terrible burden upon his financially struggling house. Sadly, all his efforts, all the favors earned and alliances struck, would be for nothing, because Parulkar had ended up in opposition to Omand, and nobody played the great game better than Omand.

The servants, slaves, guards, and even grandchildren of Parulkar Akershan were all waiting along the back wall of the great room, frightened and being guarded by Inquisitors, but the judge himself was reclining on his couch, looking amused and annoyed that there were intruders in his living room. When he saw Omand enter, Parulkar nodded in greeting. "Ah, Omand, I am glad to see you. There seems to have been some confusion with your underlings. Now that you are here we can get this misunderstanding sorted out. Please, have a seat."

Omand stopped in front of the couch but did not sit down. "Inquisitor Satya, I will question Judge Parulkar personally. You will take every other member of his household to the dome for interrogation."

As the Inquisitors began to roughly herd everyone from the room, the children started to cry. The warriors begged for mercy. Nobody wanted to go to the dome.

Parulkar became enraged at the brazen display, as any important, Law-abiding man would. "How dare you? We've done nothing wrong!"

"We shall see." Omand kept his voice smooth. "Parulkar Akershan, you have been accused of transgressions against the Law."

"I am no criminal. I will not be treated as one." Only the warriors obligated to protect him were currently being loaded into a wagon, and everyone else in the room worked for Omand, so that declaration had no teeth.

"Leave us so we may speak privately," Omand told his Inquisitors. All of them did so, except for Taraba, who walked around the couch to stand directly behind Parulkar. A good assistant always knew without being told where his master would best need him.

When the others were gone, Parulkar snarled. "You are playing a very dangerous game, Vokkan snake. I am not some lowly arbiter who will piss myself at the sight of a mask."

"No. You are not." Omand kicked a cushion over in front of the couch, and then sat cross-legged before the judge. There was no need for foolishness like trying to loom over his opponent. There was no need to put on any airs. Then Omand took off his golden mask and rested it upon his knee. This was the first time he'd shown Parulkar his face, on purpose at least, and the judge would be trying to figure out what hidden meaning such a display meant.

In truth, Omand was merely craving his pipe. "Do you mind if I smoke?"

"Feel free. Do so knowing that every minute of my time, or my family's time, which you waste will be removed from your life a hundredfold."

"Please, leave the threats to me. I am the professional." Omand took out his pipe and tobacco tin from one of the pockets inside his robe. One nice thing about the Capitol was the almost total lack of humidity kept his tobacco from clumping. He gently put a bit in his pipe, used his ebony tamper on it, put in a bit more, and then lit it with a match that appeared in his hand as if by magic. Parulkar waited, fuming, while Omand went through his ritual.

The old judge had been around for a long time. Everybody in the Capitol was guilty of something, but Parulkar was sharp enough never to be caught. He was one of the few people Omand had no leverage against. He could not be blackmailed nor bought. Despite the general moral weakness inherent in the first caste, Parulkar was one of the old breed, a man of strong opinions and unbending nature. It was men like this who had created the Law to begin with, and every now and then that strong blood showed through.

Omand actually respected Parulkar for his obstinate ways, but he was on the wrong side of the game and was thus a liability. Fortune had given Omand a way to write off that liability. He would have been a fool not to take it. Plus, on a personal level, he found this sort of interaction rewarding. There were a multitude of ways to inflict pain on others.

"What are you playing at, Omand? You will regret this harassment. I have many powerful friends."

"Not as many as you believe," Omand said as he enjoyed the taste of fine Vadal tobacco. "Tell me, is your grandson a tax collector?"

"I have twenty grandsons. I don't know what post each of them has wound up with. Only half of them are worth a damn."

"His name is Pankaj."

"The dumbest of the litter." Parulkar rolled his eyes. "I've not seen him in years. What embarrassing thing has that fop done now?"

The lad did have a history of bad decisions, but from the Inquisition's dramatic entrance, Parulkar should have realized they were not here for a minor offense. Omand drew upon the pipe and took his time answering. "This one was a rather serious transgression."

The judge snorted. "The boy has a grandiose opinion of himself, so that's not surprising. How much is it going to cost me to fix his mistakes this time?"

Omand exhaled a pungent cloud. "Everything."

Parulkar chuckled, but then he realized that Omand was not joking. "What did he do?"

"You have heard about the fall of the city of Chakma to the rebels?"

"Yes," Parulkar answered suspiciously. "Did Pankaj allow himself to be taken hostage? Do I need to pay a ransom?"

"Oh no. He's dead."

Parulkar gawked at him. Usually the first caste

tended to dance around bad news, not deliver it so bluntly. "A tragedy. How?"

"He was executed by Lord Protector Devedas for treason, because Pankaj helped Ashok Vadal overthrow the city."

"What? Impossible!"

"Oh, it is very much possible. And there is no doubt as to his guilt, since after opening the gates to a gang of criminals, your grandson then declared himself the king of Chakma, and flaunted the Law concerning the worship of illegal gods in front of several hundred witnesses."

All the blood drained from Parulkar's face. He looked like he might be ill, and it certainly wasn't from the shocking loss of a loved one.

Omand waited for the judge to collect himself.

"Pankaj has always been an idiot, Grand Inquisitor." Earlier it had just been his first name, as if they were equals, but oh, *now* it was his title. "But I had no idea he was insane. He was barely a member of the family at all. We only tolerated him because his father was such an honorable, Law-abiding man, and we vainly hoped he would grow out of his foolish ways as he aged. Since he did not, I say good riddance to the louse."

Omand nodded. "Ah, the difficulties of family... I have no children myself, though I like to think of myself as a father to all my Inquisitors. But you can see the problem we face here today, can't you, Judge Parulkar? This is not some quarrelsome son getting into untidy duels, or an embarrassing daughter who got pregnant before her marriage was arranged." His voice grew low and dangerous. "Pankaj was a *religious fanatic.* That is not just something that happens. That is not a thing that wayward children simply blunder into. Terrible beliefs must be *taught.* They must be handed down in secret. And now it is the duty of the Inquisition to discover where this cancer spread from so that we may cut it off the bone."

Parulkar swallowed hard. "I can assure you it was not learned from me, nor my family. We are honorable servants of the Law."

"Perhaps...and perhaps not. The Inquisition assumes nothing. Your entire household will be interrogated. The guilty will roast upon the dome. Those who are not themselves fanatics, but who suspected others of that behavior yet remained silent, will be stripped of status and sold as slaves. They will serve five years per criminal they failed to inform upon."

"You can't do that to my people! I am a respected man."

"Respected men do not overthrow cities and rule them as god-kings. You are now suspected of fostering rebellion. Your replacement has already been arranged. Your position and obligation will be temporarily given to your cousin, Faril Akershan, who will represent your house until the Inquisition clears you of this wrongdoing."

Parulkar's eyes narrowed. The disgust was plain on his face. "Faril, the loyal dog who eats scraps from the Grand Inquisitor's hands. I should have known. I did not understand why Faril would volunteer some of our lands to your bizarre crusade against the fish-eaters, but I saw no reason to intervene. I see now that my silence was insufficient. You only accept fawning adoration."

"Truthfully, I find fawning adoration tiresome." Omand leaned back on the cushion and chewed on the stem of his pipe thoughtfully. "Regardless, for the time being your life belongs to the Inquisition. None of your friends will step into this particular bog. The whole affair is rather embarrassing, even by Capitol standards."

"You do not care about foolish Pankaj. You are just using him to remove me. Why? How have I wronged you?"

Parulkar was a steadfast ally of the Chief Judge, and often sided with Harta Vadal in the Chamber. Those two were really the only other men in the Capitol with the clout and wherewithal to form a coalition sufficient to stop his plans, but Omand just smiled and said nothing.

The judge was a sharp one though. "I recognize that you hold the advantage here, legally and politically, Grand Inquisitor, but a man with nothing to lose can be very dangerous. If I see no other way out, I might be desperate enough to see how many of my old friends would still come to my aid and call for a vote of competence against you. It would be interesting to see how many judges believe you are abusing the power of your order."

"That would be inconvenient," Omand agreed. He had already counted the votes and knew he was probably safe, but it would still look bad. "But tell me, what kind of alternative way out do you envision for yourself? Other than being stabbed while trying to escape custody by Inquisitor Taraba here."

The judge looked back over his shoulder, to where Taraba was standing, masked and silent, one hand resting on the hilt of his sword. Inquisitors did not put as much effort into individual combat as Protectors, but Taraba was still very good with a blade. His face couldn't be seen, but he stood with a confidence that said his target would not have a chance.

"You wouldn't dare strike down a judge."

"On the contrary." Omand laughed. "Nothing would amuse me more. Usually such a high-status death would be hard to explain, but you had a remarkably overachieving criminal spring from your line, so I believe I could make my report a plausible one."

Inquisitor Taraba gave the judge a polite nod, as if to say it was nothing personal.

Parulkar turned back to Omand with involuntary tears forming in his eyes. The tears were real, telling the Grand Inquisitor that he had won a complete victory. "Please, leave me my dignity. Spare my family from slavery. I will declare that with Great House Akershan in crisis, my Thakoor needs me at home more than I am needed here. I will name Faril as my successor and then I will immediately leave the Capitol."

"Forever," Omand added.

Parulkar had been here so long that he probably couldn't even remember what his homeland looked like, but he gave Omand a curt nod. "Of course. Forever. As far as you are concerned MaDharvo might as well be on the other side of the world."

"It practically is. But this is good. A man should return to die in the house he was born. It keeps the heritage strong. I think our caste is often too quick to forget where we come from." If everything went according to plan Omand didn't intend to die at all. However, if he had to remain mortal he wouldn't mind expiring in Vokkan. Its cutthroat politics and vicious infighting had made him the man he was today. "Very well, Judge. I accept this reasonable offer."

"Thank you, Grand Inquisitor."

Omand gathered up his mask and stood. "When you are all settled in MaDharvo, send word, and I will have your household released from the dome so that they may go and join you."

The judge almost balked at that cruelty, but he should have known that Omand would keep some insurance. He dipped his head in submission. "I shall leave this very night."

"Good." Omand then made a big show of looking around their opulent surroundings. "Unfortunately, it seems you have no one left to help you pack. You will have to travel light. Come, Taraba, we are done here."

"I feel that went rather well," Omand said as his personal carriage took them out of the city and across the desert toward the Inquisitor's Dome. "Don't you?"

The only other passenger was young Taraba. "I would agree. You capitalized on an opportunity and deftly used it to remove an enemy."

"Indeed. When the stakes are this high, one cannot be hesitant. However, with Parulkar banished and Harta Vadal distracted, I feel as if I am running out of potent adversaries. Most of the judges are easily manipulated. It is becoming almost too easy to get what I want. This worries me. I would hate to become complacent in my old age."

"There is still the Chief Judge himself to deal with, sir."

"Yes, a capable man, and a staunch traditionalist. As

long as he directs the affairs of the Chamber, things will not be allowed to spiral too far out of control. As he often repeats in his speeches, Lok has faced great turmoil before and every time adherence to the Law brings us back to prosperity. If I were allowed to give speeches in the Chamber, I would tell them that too many of the judges will vote to keep things the same only because change frightens and confuses them. It is hard to look forward. It is easy to look back. If a man walks backward, eventually he will fall off a cliff." Omand sighed. "It is difficult at times, to be a man of vision. Speaking of which, is there any new word about Asura's Mirror?"

"No, sir. Historian Vikram and his family have disappeared."

"That man is as much a Historian as I am. Vikram was a cunning raider some conniving Historians decided to make their guard dog."

"Several witnesses have seen Vikram heading west into Harban. As directed, I've made his capture our number-one priority."

With an active rebellion in the south and murderous Ashok still on the loose, people might question why the Inquisitors' most wanted man was a lowly Historian, but luckily the judges who nominally oversaw his Order rarely paid attention to such dirty business. "He will be found. And the others we seek?"

"It has been confirmed that Protector Karno and Devedas' woman, Rada, stayed with Vikram for a time, but then went their own way."

"Did we ever find out how they knew each other?"

"Vikram was friends with Rada's father. She probably sought shelter there."

Omand did not like coincidences. Having two people he was hunting turn out to have a connection was no mere accident. "Perhaps. And Protector Karno?"

"We've had no further contact since Apura."

By *contact*, Taraba meant that Karno Uttara had killed two valuable witch hunters and many Zarger warriors before they'd managed to kill him, or at least that was what Khoja's message had said... Though the senior witch hunter had protected himself by adding that he had been pursuing their primary target at the time, had not himself seen Karno's body thrown into Red Lake, and was going off the Zargers' word, so could therefore not personally confirm the Protector's death. By the time the Inquisitors had eluded Vadal pursuit and snuck back across the border, he must have floated away.

"And Rada?"

"Khoja is observing the librarian from a distance. She is still Harta Vadal's guest."

"More like Harta's hostage," Omand mused. That situation could be useful for him though. If any harm was to come to the lovely young lady, then Devedas the Fearsome would take that as a personal insult and seek revenge. He doubted very much that Harta would survive such an encounter. The heart was a strange and unpredictable thing, but even ambitious men like Devedas had exploitable weaknesses. Devedas already hated Harta because he suspected his involvement in Ashok's fraud, but couldn't prove it. Assassinating Rada while she was in Harta's care would implicate Great House Vadal, and surely push Devedas over the edge. That would be an interesting way to get rid of that particular annoyance. Omand would file that option away for later.

Something about this situation was troubling Omand though. "I doubt that Vikram would have entrusted his obligation to anyone else, but it also worries me that someone so clever would let himself be recognized in Harban. I wonder if he is using himself as a decoy to draw us away from the real prize."

"You think he gave Asura's Mirror to Protector Karno?"

"Possibly. Dispatch someone who can change into a fish to check the bottom of the lake to see if it sank with his corpse. Or he might have given it to someone else we do not even know about yet. Or perhaps the librarian." He had originally wanted her in his possession so that he could have leverage against the Lord Protector. Omand had originally assumed she was just some woman Devedas had fallen for, because even the ambitious were stupid when it came to love. But with her repeatedly escaping his hunters, it seemed there was more to the librarian than he initially assumed. After all, Devedas must have seen something in her worth forming an attachment. Perhaps Vikram had seen the same thing? "I should have Khoja find out if she has it."

"That will be very dangerous for him, sir. Harta Vadal has surrounded himself with bodyguards and wizards since the death of his mother. Even a member of the House of Assassins would have a hard time getting in there unseen. If our man is taken alive and exposed as an Inquisitor..."

"A valid point. I will ponder on it for now. Since it is doubtful she even has it, then it is not worth going to war with Harta Vadal yet. But if she does..."

Taraba nodded. It was obvious that he was confused and wanted to ask why the Asura's Mirror was so important to their mission, but he refrained. If the Grand Inquisitor wanted you to know something, he would command you to know it. The lad understood much of Omand's plans, but not all. Even the most loyal and trustworthy of his allies could never be told what was truly at stake. Taraba was his right hand, but even he could not know what had been revealed to Omand by the demonic prisoner who swam in the tank beneath their dome. It was one thing to plot the destruction and rebuilding of the very fabric of their society, but Omand doubted even his most steadfast associates would follow him on his mission to enslave their ancient gods.

Omand's quest sounded mad, even to himself at times, but he could not deny what he had seen, and in the darkest forgotten corners of Lok he had laid his eyes upon strange things that no other man alive had ever seen. Was the mirror absolutely necessary to success? Probably not. However, when a man was seeking to become immortal, he used every weapon at his disposal.

The Grand Inquisitor inclined his head to look out the window across the darkened desert, deep in thought. Whatever the ancient beings were, gods as the simpletons thought of them, or simply wizards with abilities beyond anything the world had seen for thousands of years, the ancients had accessed power beyond his wildest dreams, greater than black steel or demon bone...and Omand alone had been shown how to seize it.

Rather than answer his assistant's unasked question, Omand began to pontificate aloud. "It is understandable that people fear destruction. Upheaval leads to death, starvation, disease, so on and so forth. But in the grand scheme of things, destruction is necessary. Old forests must burn so new trees can grow, then we cut those trees down to build houses, then we raze those houses to erect mansions. Every time man builds, first we must destroy. The demons destroyed the old world, and we made a new one ruled by kings. Then we destroyed that world to make the Law. Destruction is a bloody mess, but a necessary one. You must destroy one world before you can create a new one. Creation and destruction . . . One cannot exist without the other. Do you understand, Taraba?"

"I think so, sir."

"Good." Omand reached beneath his seat and pulled out the wrapped package that had been delivered to him earlier. He handed the bundle across to Taraba. "This arrived from Akershan a few days ago."

Taraba lifted it and discovered there was a solid heft to the package. "What is it?"

"It is a catalyst for change. Open it."

Taraba untied the knots, pulled back the cloth, and then examined the thing inside. It was made of oiled steel, carved wood, strips of brass, and danger. "It's some manner of compact Fortress device."

Taraba might not have been very familiar with such things, but he was careful to keep the dangerous metal end pointed away from his body as he picked it up by the wooden handle. "Most curious."

"It is of a type we've not seen before. It was seized by Devedas right after a rebel used it to kill one of his Protectors. It seems that our current criminal infestation has a surprising number of these stockpiled. Most are larger, and mechanically simpler, but this one could be concealed beneath a robe, and from what we've been able to ascertain, has a very reliable method of ignition. The others you need to hold a match to them. This one produces its own sparks when you activate it."

"It's so small, can it possibly be as powerful as the usual ones?" Taraba asked hesitantly.

"Still powerful enough to open a Protector's skull and spray his brains across the grasslands."

Taraba carefully turned the device in his hands so as to not accidentally blow a hole in his master's carriage. "Damn those Fortress cowards hiding on their island. If it weren't for that narrow strip of ocean, we'd have been rid of them long ago."

Omand smiled. He would've said the same thing himself when he was young and hotheaded. Now, he often suspected that it was the ocean which protected them from the Fortress, not the other way around. "Regardless of their barbaric ways, their weapons are deadly, especially in quantity. They make casteless rebels the equal of warriors who've trained their entire lives. The Law has stopped the proliferation of such things, but everyone knows to be afraid of them."

A moment ago, Omand had spoken about the beauty inherent in destruction . . . By that standard, this device was a work of art.

"I have a very important assignment for you, Taraba."

Chapter 30

Even though Rada knew she was little more than a political bargaining chip, she much preferred staying in Vadal City to hiding at a goat farm. As the personal guest of Harta Vadal, she was not allowed to leave the grounds of the great house and she was always being watched by guards. However, it was the most lavish and comfortable of prisons. Harta had an excellent personal chef, and best of all, Great House Vadal had an extremely large library, possessing dozens of unique works the likes of which she'd never seen before.

There were several Vadal histories that had no contemporary in the Capitol Library. There were no copies of any of those there, and she was certain of that, because she'd inventoried and cataloged those sections herself. Perhaps upon her return to the Capitol she could arrange for a delegation from the Archivist's Order to travel to Vadal to make copies. When she'd suggested this to Harta, he had seemed completely ambivalent, which would be good enough to secure the agreement...But who was she kidding? As soon as the Grand Inquisitor found a few judges to sign a warrant, she'd be labeled a traitor, and Harta would hand her over to be roasted to death upon the dome.

Nobody in the Capitol Library would ever even know these rare volumes existed in Harta Vadal's personal library if that happened. Well, and also...she'd be dead, which was, frankly, a bit more frightening than having an incomplete collection.

Despite being her captor, Harta was not a brute. In fact he was a rather articulate, intelligent, and even charming man, when he felt like it. He usually invited her to dine with him, and often had her join him for his evening stroll around the manicured gardens of the great house, where they would engage in pleasant conversations.

It sounded almost romantic to describe it that way, but there was nothing romantic about Harta Vadal. If Harta loved anything other than politics, she'd not yet seen evidence of it.

Rada had no mind for politics, because politics meant dealing with people, and Rada couldn't really stand being around *people*, but she had read a great many books on various political subjects, and listened dutifully as her father had tried to teach her about the politics of his obligation, in the hopes that she would someday be given his obligation as head of the Archivist's Order. Thus she knew enough about the topic to understand that Harta was purely a political animal. He lived for politics the same way she had lived for books.

The nightly dinners and garden walks afterward tended to be Harta and five to seven invited guests, all of high status, but of varying offices, selected based upon their knowledge, importance, and whether or not Harta saw any value to them at the time. The events were really more like business meetings, as the Thakoor picked their brains and coldly tried to puzzle out how various issues could be twisted for his benefit.

At first she had been invited to dinner because the topic had been *what is the Inquisition really up to?* She had told Harta everything she felt she could— without endangering any of the secrets entrusted to her by Devedas or Vikram of course—including the Inquisition's attempt to silence her about the true identity of the casteless as the descendants of Ramrowan and his priests, though Harta had grown bored at the ancient history lesson and told her that he had no time for such esoteric trivia. Afterward he had laughed and declared her to be "a useless academic, knowing everything, while simultaneously understanding nothing."

However, Harta must have found some of her opinions enlightening, or perhaps amusing, because he had continued to request her presence at dinner thereafter. Rada was fine with this because living the luxurious life of a Thakoor's advisor was better than acting like the prisoner she really was.

So she had passed the last month politely giving her opinion on various issues whenever asked, and otherwise keeping quiet. On many topics she did not have enough experience to have formulated her own beliefs but being well read and having an almost perfect memory she could always recite what others had written about them. Harta seemed to find this useful at times. All Rada could do was hope that when

Omand inevitably sent someone through proper legal channels to retrieve her, Harta might have grown fond enough of her—like a homeless kitten—to intervene on her behalf once again.

However, Rada was astute enough to notice that whenever a particularly sensitive topic arose, where the learned men of Great House Vadal needed to discuss something which might put them at odds with Grand Inquisitor Omand, Rada was not sent for. Which meant that Harta did not want her to know anything that the Inquisitors could interrogate out of her. A very bad sign indeed.

Harta had not asked for her company tonight, so the topic must have been one not needing an Archivist's perspective. She was fine with that too, because that was one more night she didn't have to socialize and listen to the incessant chatter of first casters sucking up to their Thakoor. So she'd gotten a plate of fruits, nuts, and cheeses from the house slaves, picked a few books from the library, and retired to her nicely furnished guest quarters to read in peace.

This life wouldn't be too bad, if it hadn't been for the threat of looming doom. If she was lucky she might just be able to hide out in Vadal, reading books, until Devedas took care of all those criminals and came to get her.

There was a firm knock on her door.

Rada answered and found a warrior of the Personal Guard waiting. There were a multitude of the men wearing the gray and bronze about the house, but she knew this one personally.

"Hello, Luthra."

"Senior Archivist." He was in his dress uniform,

rather than his armor, but that couldn't fool her. Luthra was a killer, she'd seen that in Apura when he'd dealt with the witch hunter. But killers were her life now. Ever since she'd gotten entangled with the conspiracy against the casteless, she'd befriended many killers. She even planned to marry one. Oddly enough she had associated with more killers than librarians in recent months!

The bodyguards had been very polite to her on the journey here, and she'd almost started to think of a couple of them as friends since her arrival. Luthra among them, though right now he was all business.

"The Thakoor has requested your presence in his dining room."

"Oh, he's changed his mind then? Let me grab my sash." The servants hadn't been able to find her any proper clothing with Capitol Library's insignia on it, but they'd at least been able to find her something in the right colors. Even far from home, Rada felt that she should represent her order.

"Of course." Luthra waited patiently in the doorway for her to get dressed.

She went around the corner. Rada really wanted to make sure the Asura's Mirror was still properly hidden. She'd squished her satchel far behind one of the wardrobes in the hopes the slaves wouldn't see it when they dusted. She hated just leaving a priceless black-steel artifact unsupervised, but Harta had declared her a guest, and "guests" didn't get searched—that would be impolite—so the privacy of her belongings had been respected so far. On the bright side if what Vikram had told her was true, whoever was dumb enough to touch it might leave some fingers behind.

If Harta found out she possessed such a treasure, he'd be sure to claim the mirror for himself. Hospitality be damned, black steel was worth a fortune. Of course, it was still there, right where she had left it. Facedown obviously. She'd not dared look into it since the first night with Vikram, when she'd discovered that it wasn't just a mirror but also a window to...*something*.

As she dressed she called out, "Have you heard anything else from Apura?"

"About your Protector friend? I'm afraid there's nothing new."

Harta's callousness aside, on the road north Rada had pestered the Personal Guard about the fate of Karno until they'd relented and sent a message to the men who had chased the Zarger back across the border. There had been signs of a battle, and a bunch of pulverized corpses, but none of them had been a gigantic bearded man. She fervently hoped Karno was alive, but it was also possible the witch hunters had captured him or carried off his body. She knew that Luthra had told the garrison commander to send word if they found any trace of poor Karno.

Rada checked her reflection in the mirror to make sure her makeup was still good. She normally didn't care about such things, in fact she rather hated smearing itchy greasy pigments on her face. Her sister, Daksha, had taught her how to do this, but it had taken Devedas to teach her that she could actually be considered beautiful. She was trying hard to look her best now because Harta seemed like the kind of man who would be less inclined to throw away something pretty, as opposed to something plain.

Satisfied, she walked back into the main room. That

was when she noticed that Luthra did not appear to be his normal jovial self. Of the house guards she'd dealt with the most, Girish was the dour one. Luthra was usually upbeat and rather talkative. However, tonight he looked distracted and perhaps a bit nauseous, as if someone had just delivered some dire news. Her immediate fearful thought was that Inquisitors were here, but that was illogical. Friendly or not, he probably wouldn't be that upset if they'd finally come to take her away. That would be *her* problem.

"What's wrong, Luthra?"

"There was a dark rumor going around, but it looks like it's been confirmed by a few sources." He spoke like a beloved relative had died. "Angruvadal is gone."

She had to search her mind for a moment to recall who that was, but it wasn't a person at all. "Your house's ancestor blade?"

"Yes. It was destroyed."

Rada didn't have much firsthand experience with warfare, but everybody knew how amazing and important those rare weapons were to each of the Great Houses. It was said that a bearer could single-handedly defeat an army, and though she assumed that the historical accounts of such feats had become exaggerated, in warrior terms they were still a big deal.

"I'm very sorry. Did the criminal Ashok break it?" That sounded like the sort of horrible thing such a monster would do. The sooner noble Devedas took care of him, the better.

Luthra still seemed to be in shock. "It was lost in battle against Somsak raiders, in some Thao mountain town nobody's ever heard of, back at the beginning of winter. We're just getting details of this now."

This was dark news for Great House Vadal indeed. A black-steel blade was incredibly important, not just for what it was capable of, but for what it stood for. Houses had fallen as a direct result of losing their ancestor blade. No wonder the poor warrior was grieving. The equivalent loss to her would be if someone burned a section of the Capitol Library down. She shuddered at the thought.

However, on a purely selfish note, this revelation warned Rada that she'd best tread extra carefully tonight. Harta had been relatively cordial thus far, but he was a powerful man who literally held his fate in her hands, and he was sure to be in a very sour mood now.

Luthra escorted her to Harta's personal dining chambers. As the head of an Order, her father's estate had been large, even by first-caste standards, but it paled in comparison to the magnificence of this place. Great House Vadal was the wealthiest of all the houses, and their Thakoor's home was designed to demonstrate that so that all visitors would understand their place. Even though Harta usually spent three-quarters of the year living in the Capitol he still maintained an inordinately large number of servants here, and from the way they were bustling about carrying off empty dishes, dinner had already been finished. Rada was a late addition. It was a good thing she'd already nibbled on a plate of cheese.

Luthra entered the room ahead of her and announced, "As requested, Senior Archivist Radamantha Nems dar Harban."

Tonight's dinner topic must have been something relating to the military, because several of Harta's guests were of the warrior caste. Books had taught her what

all the various ranks and medals on their uniforms
represented, but you didn't need to be a scholar to tell
that these men were of high status. Anybody would've
been able to tell that just from the sheer *weight* of
awards they wore. Rada found it funny that the caste
which was devoted to such grim duties liked to decorate
themselves with more colorful ribbons than Daksha's
vapid party friends.

"Join us, Librarian." Harta had a wineglass in one
hand, and he gestured for her to sit with his other.
"I have need of you."

In addition to the important military men, the
chief house wizard was present, as were a couple of
arbiters, all of them reclining on cushions around a
low table. It was a warm day by Vadal standards, so
slaves were there to fan them. Luthra took up position
with the other guards who were always present—for
Harta was rather paranoid about assassins—and Rada
moved over by the cushions.

Though Rada didn't care for social things, the
Capitol Library had a great number of very important
patrons, so she'd been taught how to always give the
proper amount of respect for their respective status.
How much respect did Harta rate? There were only
twelve Great House Thakoors in the world, and he
was the only person keeping her from getting handed
off to the Inquisition, so all of it.

She bowed, as was the northern style. "How may
I assist you, noble Thakoor?"

"You all need to see this. She's read more books
than damnable Ashok has killed men, and she has
a memory like a parlor trick. She can remember all
of them."

That was an exaggeration, but she wasn't about to correct him. Harta looked a bit flushed, and she doubted this was his first glass of wine tonight. "I am happy to serve."

"Go ahead, Phontho. Ask her your question. If anyone will know such trivia off the top of their head, it is Rada."

One of the military men nodded, then turned toward her. "In the history of Lok, how many houses have survived the loss of their ancestor blades?"

That question told her everything she needed to know about the nature of their conversation thus far. "That's an easy question. The answer is none of them. There are twelve, or were, twelve remaining ancestor blades spread among twelve Great Houses."

Harta snorted. The officers shared a stricken look as the Thakoor drank the rest of his wine.

"So we're doomed," muttered one of the arbiters under his breath.

"I'll have none of that foolish talk here," Harta snapped. The arbiter bowed his head. Harta shook his in disgust, then held up his empty glass so a servant could rush over and fill it. "Let us be honest. Our ancestor blade has already been lost to us for the last twenty years. This simply seals it. My mother kept us on top without it, and I will continue to do so. It was only the naïvely hopeful that thought Angruvadal would ever return to us from the wicked hands of that fish-eating fraud. Now Radamantha, you gave the true yet simplistic answer, now give us the real answer."

"Well..." She thought about not just the facts, but the facts that Harta would want to hear. Luckily, she had read a book on this very topic once. "There are twelve swords and twelve Great Houses in recent years, but there used to be many more black-steel weapons in circulation. They have been lost over time for various reasons—"

"Like being used by dishonorable scum for dishonorable ends." The officer who said that looked like he wanted to spit on the floor but refrained. Which was good, because Harta would probably have him killed for defacing his rug.

"Among other reasons, yes. The swords seem to have some manner of code, roughly in accordance to the Law, but their interpretation remains a mystery to mankind. When they are sufficiently displeased, they self-destruct in a most violent manner, and the owners seldom understand why. It has not always been one weapon per house, but historically speaking they've been wielded in a wide variety of ways. A house could have multiple, or none at all. Even vassal houses had them at times. If a house lost its sword, that didn't mean that the house immediately ceased to exist. Oftentimes houses continued for generations without a blade before falling—" She caught herself. That would not be what they'd want to hear. "Or merging with another. Duels have been fought against outsiders, who claimed a house's sword and returned it to their own. This is always a possibility because swords require their bearers to accept all honorable challengers to try and claim it."

"So I suppose we could just throw our army one at a time into some black-steel meat grinder until the sword decides it likes one of us better," said Harta. "Brilliant!"

"Or in a few notable cases, a stronger house without

an ancestor blade has conquered a weaker neighbor who still had one, claimed it as the spoils of war, and made it their own."

"Really?" one of the officers leaned forward. "Such as?"

"Well, one of the remaining handful for example. According to *Parsa's Complete Compendium of Black-Steel Relics*"—which had been a rather dry and exhaustive read, yet there had never been any mention of Asura's Mirror in there either, so perhaps it hadn't been as complete a compendium as the author had supposed—"in the year 657 Great House Harban's only sword was broken, but in a 668 war they defeated Great House Lahkshan in a battle in which their bearer was mortally wounded. Forty days after he succumbed to his injuries that sword chose a new bearer from among the warriors of Harban, and they've held it ever since. There have been others before that as well."

"How many?" Harta demanded.

"Four, possibly five." Rada did not add that was out of hundreds, and all of the more recent examples ended with the newly swordless house eventually being gobbled up and turned into a vassal, like Somsak or Vane.

"Four or five . . . And surely none of them nearly as great as Vadal," Harta told his dinner party.

The phonthos began to nod.

"We all know the sword was mostly symbolic. When was the last time my father personally went to war? There are so few ancestor blades left the great houses never actually use them for anything important because we're all too frightened we'll break them. They're fickle things. Choosing an evil bearer and then getting offended and breaking when it gets used for evil? Angruvadal deserved to shatter."

It was obvious it made the warriors uncomfortable to hear their Thakoor talk so dismissively about the sword, but they weren't about to publicly defend the honor of the thing that had taken the life of Harta's mother.

One of them must have been feeling a little brave though. "My Thakoor, it is true the sword was mostly symbolic, yet it was a powerful motivator to the men."

"Don't lecture me about symbols, Phontho. I create them every time I give a speech. My words in the Capitol have done more to strengthen this house than anything Angruvadal has done over the last two decades while it was in the hands of villainous Ashok. We may not have an ancestor blade, but we have something that matters far more in these modern times. *Money.* I can still pay for the biggest army and the most wizards. To the oceans with mighty Angruvadal. Who needs petulant black steel when you have banknotes instead?"

From what Rada knew about warrior culture that should have been considered low and dishonorable talk, but apparently to get to such lofty ranks you needed to be more politician than warrior, so they merely nodded along at their Thakoor's drunken boasts.

"That said, I understand having a black sword is important to your caste. Mine too. Just the threat of using one bolsters my work in the Capitol. Even if we never use the damn thing, just the knowledge of its existence grants us prestige. My heart breaks, not for Angruvadal, but for what Angruvadal's loss means to our house. We are far better off with a sword than without." Harta lingered on that thought.

Finally, one of them asked, "What do you propose, Thakoor?"

"Vadal is inferior to no one. We will not stand idle while lesser houses gloat over their treasures. We are Vadal. We take what we want. You heard the librarian. It has been done before. We are far stronger than any of our neighbors. Let us claim one of their ancestor blades."

Rada's mouth fell open. Had she just caused *a war*?

The warriors seemed simultaneously excited and nervous about the idea. "You speak of no mere raid but a full invasion, sir. The Capitol would never approve—"

"I will handle the Capitol, Phontho. There's always pretext for war when you have enough judges as friends. Now we must decide who to invade. All of them have valuable territory Vadal can make a historical claim to. Your assignment is to pick the house we can defeat at the lowest cost. Show me the target and I will invent their crime against us."

"Sir, usually in unrestricted house war the bearer wouldn't be present. Not just because of the risk, as you've already said, but also because if one side sends an ancestor blade to the fight, then the other side will respond with theirs."

"Your point?"

"With no bearer of our own to counter, our opponent *will* send theirs. Instead of a contest between warriors, it becomes a magic-fueled bloodbath."

"Good. The sooner they send him to the front, the sooner we can kill him and take his sword. Your obligation is to figure out how to accomplish this in the most efficient manner possible. If they do not send their bearer out to play, you will simply have to seize their territory until they have no choice but to send their ancestor blade against you. Vadal does not *bide its time*. Vadal does not merely survive. We *conquer*. We take what we want, and I want a new sword. You will give me the report about the best way to do this in three days. You are dismissed, Warriors."

The members of the militant caste obediently did as they were told. Rada noted that they'd been despondent when she'd arrived, but now there was a fire in their eyes, and a quickness to their step. These may have been old men now, but they'd been raised to fight and were still eager for glory. It was in their blood.

"They will recommend Sarnobat," the house wizard said after the warriors were gone.

"Of course they will." Harta set aside his wine and wiped his lips with a napkin. "I am fine with this. Vokkan is the bigger long-term threat to Vadal's security, but their army is strong. We could beat them, but only at great cost. Thao is safe from our warriors' wrath. Though they have the smallest army of our neighbors, their terrain is easy to defend. Whereas Sarnobat's army is smaller than ours, the trade roads make resupply easy for us, and their raids have been a perpetual annoyance which our commanders would love to decisively punish once and for all. Warriors tend to think with their emotions like that, but in this case emotions and logistics are on the same side. The solution is so obvious there isn't really a decision to be made, but I will still let them feel like it was their choice. It's good for their pride."

It was interesting, Rada thought, that though Harta

had appeared to have drunk a bit too much wine while the warriors were here, as he explained the issues of invasion, he did not sound even the least bit tipsy. It had been an act for the warriors' benefit. That emotional caste would expect some manner of reaction over the confirmation of the loss of their sword, and heavy drinking to console yourself was an acceptable warrior tradition.

But Harta was of the first. He only cared about results. "With this recent and unexpected shipment of black steel, every one of our wizards will be well supplied and ready to strike when the Sarnobat ancestor blade takes the field."

"That is most generous of you, Thakoor. We will be ready."

"Excellent. My greatest concern is should we over-commit our forces against the wolf in the east, will the house of the monkey see that as an opportunity to claim some of our territory to the west? However, Vokkan ambitions are a problem I can stop from the Capitol. Their merchants need Vadal markets far more than we need their goods. Their workers will not stand for a prolonged conflict. The fools have allowed the worker caste far too much clout in that house. I will use this as leverage."

"You are wise, Thakoor," declared the arbiter.

"The librarian isn't the only one who studies things. I will meet with the bankers and arrange to apply pressure on Vokkan. Now, begone. It is time for my evening walk." The rest of them stood. Including Rada, who was still reeling from the idea that she might have inadvertently caused a house war. She already held herself responsible for allowing a genocide!

"Not you, Rada. You shall accompany me around the gardens."

She stopped and tried her best to not look nauseous.

As they walked from the dining chambers down a hall filled with magnificent paintings of scenes of Vadal glory, with two of the Personal Guard ranging ahead and two more behind, Harta gave her his arm and a cold smile. "Thank you for your help tonight."

She didn't feel particularly helpful. "I appreciate your hospitality and your protection, Thakoor, so I'm happy to assist however you require, but I'm an Archivist, not a strategist. I wasn't trying to encourage bloodshed! If that is how you took my information—"

"Oh, poor naïve Rada. We're both of high birth, but you've been so sheltered in your library that you don't truly understand the ways of our caste." It was difficult to tell with him, but Harta seemed genuinely amused. "First off, never denigrate your ability as an advisor. Your perspective is a peculiar, academic one, but such an odd view is sometimes valuable. Second, don't worry. You caused no bloodshed... Well, not this time. The casteless extermination order is clearly on your head, but they're not real people so their deaths shouldn't trouble your conscience. In this case I've been looking for an excuse to justify a house war against Sarnobat for ages."

It was like the great weight resting upon her shoulders was taken away, but the one in her stomach, the nauseous, sick, about to be involved in a house war weight remained. "Then why bring me into it?"

"My informants tell me that behind closed doors the warrior caste worries I may be too ambitious and will thus spend their lives frivolously. Warriors have a very narrow view of conflict and can't see the big picture like we can. To be fair, it's because they're the ones doing the bleeding. It helped my grieving leaders to hear the idea of a sword-stealing expedition come from an outside source, where I, like them, merely reacted with all too human passion when offered a spark of hope. They will tell their men that they saw fire in my eyes and steel in my voice, and when a man thinks his Thakoor truly cares, he'll fight harder."

"Do you? Truly care, I mean." She honestly couldn't tell.

Harta laughed. "Of course I do. I would do anything for my house. But the histrionics and emotions that the warrior caste eat up have no place in the first. We must always be logical, rational, calculating, manipulating. Our obligation requires it. These are all things your father should have taught you."

"I think he tried." Rada did not add however that her father was basically a decent, kindhearted man, nothing at all like Harta, who she thought would happily drown a sack of kittens in a bathtub if it made Vadal a few banknotes.

"That is a father's duty. I have six children myself. I have seen to it that every one of them has had the finest tutors. The brightest of them will be my heir, most will be obligated to various Orders to secure the favor of the Capitol—and to then use their new authority in ways which benefit Vadal—and my dumber children will be married off to other houses to cement alliances."

Such callousness was alien to Rada. She truly loved her obligation. The idea of using her position at the library to benefit Harban—a place she barely knew— was not only illegal, it was incomprehensible. She did however understand the part about marrying off the less-capable children though. It was a good thing Daksha was so pretty.

"My father is a good man, Thakoor. I am sure he will be greatly pleased that you have treated me with such hospitality and will be sure to remember this favor. He loves his children very much."

"I see mine rarely, but when I do, I do not totally dislike them."

Harta rarely spoke about his personal life. She could see why. "That sounds nice," she lied.

"The first caste has no room for frivolity, Rada, everything, and I mean *everything* we do must be for the betterment of our obligation. This persistent management is what keeps Lok strong and prosperous. It is why we are the most important caste. All this beauty..." He gestured at the expensive artwork which covered the walls. "It's not for our enjoyment. It's to establish to our inferiors how important we are, how much better we are than them, so that they will continue to allow us to manage their lives."

And here she was thinking that art was to be enjoyed by looking at it. "What about when people do not wish to be managed?"

"Chaos," Harta said simply. "Which is why we must convince them obedience is necessary. The Law is necessary, thus we, its administrators, are necessary. Every decision we make must be based upon whether it fosters loyalty from the lesser people, or rebellion. The primary responsibility of the first caste is to see to the eternal perpetuation of the first caste."

"I thought it was to serve the Law?"

"Same difference."

They walked down the stairs and outside into the magnificent gardens. Colorful birds were nesting for the night in the trees. Insects buzzed, chirped, and clicked. Vadal was blessed with a temperate climate. Everything grew here. Having grown up in the Capitol, where water had to be shipped in via aqueduct, this much green still seemed alien to her. Sure, the Capitol had gardens, magnificent ones in fact, but she also knew that they only existed through great cost and labor. She'd seen the expense reports filed in the library. In lush Vadal, growing things seemed comparatively effortless as far as she could tell.

Since it was just the two of them—well, and all the guards, but they were a polite distance away and didn't really count—Rada decided this was her chance to see if she could find out what Harta planned to do with her.

"May I ask if you have heard anything else from the Inquisition, Thakoor?"

"I have not actually. There has been no communication, no warrant, nothing. Which is rather interesting in and of itself. Omand put forth a great deal of effort to capture you, but it seems he was only interested in doing so quietly and unofficially. I wonder why?"

"I don't know." Another lie. But she didn't dare tell this man about the true nature of her relationship with Devedas. As far as Harta was concerned, she wanted him to believe the Protectors were interested in her because she was witness to a crime, and not the beloved of the Lord Protector, whose life could be used to coerce that illustrious man. "It must be because they forced me to lie on that report."

"Of course. But then I wonder, why not simply

murder you? That would ensure your silence. Omand
has no shortage of disposable killers who would never
be traced back to his Order."

She could never tell with Harta just how much he
actually knew about anything. He must have suspected
there was more to her story than she was letting on,
but for whatever reason he seemed content to wait,
rather than just having the secrets beaten out of her.

Rada knew that with her complete inability to
understand the inner workings of people, she was a
lousy example of her caste, but her father had tried
to teach her a few things, and one of those was that
information was power. And here she was with a man
who had his fingers in everything, so she might as
well take advantage of it.

"I am baffled, Thakoor. What do *you* think Omand
is plotting?"

"Now that is the question . . ." Harta stopped to
pluck a purple flower from a vine. He smelled it,
found it not to his liking, and dropped it on the grass.
"The Grand Inquisitor is currently one of the most
powerful men in the Capitol."

"I heard he used to be a witch hunter, and that
he knows a lot of magic."

"Yes, he's supposed to be supremely skilled at
such things, perhaps the best in the world. He's also
a man of vile tastes. Last time he was a guest here
one of my servants disappeared. But I don't speak of
magical power or murderous inclinations. I speak of
real power. He has spent years building a network of
contacts the likes of which Lok has never seen before.
As a collector of secrets and blackmail, a great number of the judges are either afraid of him or wish to

curry his favor. His Order has become strong, with its hooks into everything, yet it remains subtle, so as to not draw too much ire. Omand has amassed a great deal of power, but to what end he intends to use it for, I don't yet know."

Colorful lanterns were hung everywhere, but there was still a lot of shadow in the garden. Rada didn't quite know her way around yet so she couldn't tell where they were heading. She'd never been in this secluded part before. The guards in the lead seemed to have some location in mind though.

"With Omand being such a force, I am faced with a decision. Vex him, or ally with him?"

Rada felt a sudden pang of fear. Would there be a masked Inquisitor waiting for them? Was he about to hand her over?

"You need to learn to hide your feelings better, Rada. Lucky for you, I have no interests in allying with a spider. My mother had to deal with his plots and made me swear an oath for the good of our house that I would never trust that man. Though I don't yet know Omand's ultimate goal, I very much doubt it will be to Vadal's benefit. Thus, he will remain my opponent."

That was a relief.

"However, sometimes it is useful to trade with an opponent. Perhaps Omand simply hasn't thought of something suitably beneficial to offer me in exchange for you yet..." Harta chuckled at her discomfort. "I can see what you're doing, Rada. You're trying to play the part of an advisor, trying to make yourself useful to me, so that when the time comes and I am offered a temptation sufficient to trade you, that

I won't be able to because I've come to see you as so indispensable."

"That's not at all—"

"Spare me, Librarian. You've read some history books about political machinations. I'm the man people like you write those books about. Your efforts amuse me. If you wish to truly become an indispensable advisor, then you'd best start acting like one. An opportunity presents itself now. Let's see how you do."

They reached a clear area of manicured grass. A fountain bubbled in the center. Curiously, there were a few other guards already waiting there. Standing between them was a man in dirty, tattered clothing, with shackles on his wrists, and a sack covering his head.

"What's this?"

"The next thorny issue I must deal with. How best to rid myself of this criminal without causing too much consternation among the lesser castes. Half of Vadal thinks of him as a hero, the other half thinks he is a villain. His name is Jagdish."

Rada had overheard guards and servants carrying on about this man. Truly, he was the talk of the house. Some heard that he was a foe of Ashok Vadal, others a friend, sometimes, inexplicably, both. Yet all agreed that he was a killer of demons and wizards and had ridden into Vadal with a caravan full of treasure. Rada hadn't known what to think because his wild exploits sounded like something out of an adventure tale.

"Right now I need to decide the most politically expedient way to kill him."

Chapter 31

~~~~~~~~~~

"You know, lads, the bag over my head is completely unnecessary. I can tell right where we are." Even blind Jagdish had felt the turns of the carriage and the thump of its wheels. He knew Vadal City too well, so he could tell they'd gone to the great house, but not through the main entrance where they'd be seen by many witnesses, but to the quieter back way in. They'd marched him through that gate, and now that Jagdish could hear the fountain, smell the flowers, and feel the soft grass beneath his bare feet, it was obvious they were in the gardens. "I used to serve here, remember?"

"Silence," one of the guards warned him.

Jagdish didn't know any of these men. The Personal Guard had been totally gutted and everyone replaced after Bidaya's embarrassing demise. He'd only gotten the name of one of them...Girish it was, and Jagdish hadn't heard his voice yet. But if Harta was about to pronounce judgment, he needed to know. "Is Risaldar

Girish on duty tonight? I'd like to know if he kept his word and delivered something to my wife for m—"

A guard punched him in the stomach.

The man could hit too. Made sense. The Personal Guard weren't just for looking pretty. You had to have proven yourself professional *and* hard as nails to get this obligation. Jagdish's abdominal muscles hadn't been ready for such an impact, and it left him gasping.

His body was already bruised and aching from the several beatings he'd caught in recent weeks. Surprisingly, none from the prisoners though. Even though he was their former warden many of Cold Stream's captives had been there during the wizard's attack. He'd killed a mighty lot of them during the prison break, but that had been nothing personal. The survivors treated Jagdish like a hero for avenging their lost brothers and cellmates. The prisoners had been terrorized by those wizards that night. They knew what was what.

Rather the beatings had come from the new guards of the Cold Stream garrison. After Cold Stream's disgrace every man who had served under Jagdish had been shipped off to other units, and replaced with new, unlucky bastards. Since there was almost no chance to earn glory guarding a prison and many opportunities to lose it, the new guards were bitter about their post. They'd taken that bitterness out on the target who was easiest to blame. The current warden had ordered his men not to kill Jagdish, but despite that he had managed to *fall down the stairs* a few times now. How very clumsy of him.

Most of the new replacements were fine, decent sorts, but a few of the warriors had cruelty in their hearts. Giving such men authority over others was a terrible leadership decision which would only create more problems for the troubled garrison. If Jagdish had been their commander he would've broken them of such unlawful foolishness, but he wasn't the risaldar now was he? No. He was just another prisoner.

Regardless, Jagdish would remember the cruel guards' faces, and if by some miracle he was ever restored to his caste he would track those particular men down and demonstrate to them what a real duel looked like. It was amazing the difference when your opponent was actually allowed to fight.

Come to think of it, that made two units in a row that had needed complete restaffing after Jagdish had served in them. No wonder he'd gained a reputation for bad luck. Hopefully the Sons of the Black Sword were still in one piece, but considering he'd not seen them in several months and they were at war with the whole Law-abiding world, that was doubtful. Which was unfortunate, as they were brave men, probably the best Jagdish had ever known.

It had been a difficult time for him in prison, not just because of the swift and merciless violence which had been routinely visited upon him, but mostly because of his own ignorance about what was going on outside the walls. He still thought of the Sons as his men and it was troubling not knowing what was happening without him there to guide them. Ashok was an incredible combatant, a force of nature really, but his inability to empathize with his soldiers made him a bad officer. Not on purpose mind you, for despite his dark and well-earned reputation Jagdish knew that Ashok was a good man, albeit a damaged one. Except you had to have been a regular soldier to understand a regular soldier, which was a difficult task when you were the nigh unkillable, superhuman, limb-threshing embodiment of the Law. He worried all the Sons would die simply trying to keep up with their general.

Yet far more worrisome than the fate of his men was the knowledge that he was only a few miles from his wife, and he didn't know what was happening to her. Had Pakpa even heard that he was still alive? Or did she grieve him as if he were already dead? Not knowing was almost enough to break a man's spirit. Well, perhaps a lesser man, but not Unbreakable Jagdish. He kept telling himself that as long as he had something to fight for, he would never ever give up.

Though . . . finding out how Pakpa was doing was the real reason he'd wanted to ask Girish about the delivery of the pocket watch.

Being put in the gardens meant that he was either going to meet secretly with Harta himself or someone else of great importance. Jagdish would have a chance to plead his case and ask for mercy. All he'd ever wanted was to be a good soldier and a good leader. It was by cruel twists of fate that he'd ended up sucked into the whirlwind that was Ashok Vadal.

One would think that a meeting in an idyllic garden would be a good indicator of leniency, but that assumption would be incorrect. Jagdish knew from personal experience that Bidaya had often used the garden as a discrete place for an execution she didn't want in the public eye. Dump a few buckets of water on the grass to dilute the blood, have the house slaves toss the corpse into some casteless's pigpens, and nobody was ever the wiser. It made sense that Harta would adopt this family tradition from his mother.

He heard new voices approaching. It was a man and a woman having what sounded like a polite conversation. There were more footsteps accompanying them as well, those were wearing boots, and from the creak of weights hanging from leather belts, they had swords... Oh sure, *now* the Personal Guard was allowed swords in the house. He'd had to duel Ashok Vadal with a *knife*!

"Kneel."

Jagdish was roughly shoved down and the bag was ripped from his head. Even though the gardens were lit only by flickering lantern light he'd been wearing the hood so long he had to squint as his eyes adjusted. Still, just from the self-assured haughtiness of the shadow standing before him he knew it was Harta, Thakoor of Great House Vadal, and ultimate decider of Jagdish's fate.

Jagdish bowed deeply, head near to the grass, and held it for a respectfully long time.

Even though Jagdish had been stationed here he had never really spent much time around Harta. Bidaya had been Jagdish's master. In those days Harta rarely came home, and had spent most of his time in the Capitol, where his gifts best served Vadal. It was said Harta was so good at giving speeches he could convince a southerner to buy snow. In the few times they had met, Jagdish had found Harta to be unctuous around his mother, while insufferably conceited toward everyone else... But that was normal among the first caste he had observed. Bidaya had been an insufferable hag to work for, but she had been exceedingly sharp. Hopefully, Harta had inherited her wisdom, but not her cruelty.

"Rise." Vadal's most eloquent man merely sounded annoyed. "So you are the warrior who rode with Ashok."

There was no use in lying about it. "Yes, sir. In order to get revenge against the wizards who attacked our house and killed my men, yes I did." Jagdish did not look down as he spoke. Dirty, battered, hungry, it didn't matter, he looked his Thakoor in the eyes. Let him see Jagdish spoke truth. He had lived with pride, he would die with pride.

"You make no excuses for this?"

"I cannot. I figured I could find them, but I knew I couldn't beat them on my own. I needed help. We tracked them for hundreds of miles, then slaughtered them in their home. When the deed was done, I gathered all the treasure I could carry and brought it here to present to you, my lord. I'm no wizard, but I believe it was rather a lot."

Harta surprised him by actually laughing out loud. "It certainly was!" He looked to the guards who were flanking them, and they took their leader's mirth as a sign that it was okay for them to find it amusing as well. "I'm amazed at the audacity of this man."

Jagdish could see now there was a woman present too. The rather comely young lady wasn't smiling. In fact she looked worried for him. Jagdish had seen that expression before. It was how the tenderhearted looked upon a condemned man as he was being marched to the gallows, which meant that Harta had probably already told her what he had in store for Jagdish tonight.

He didn't want to die. He wanted to fight for his house, lead a command, love his wife, and raise his son.

"Thakoor Harta, I apologize for any trouble my quest has caused you, but it was something which I was compelled to do. I knew the Black Heart was a criminal, but I needed a criminal to beat a criminal, in a land where I could not legally go."

"You admit to breaking the Law?"

"I do, part of it at least, but I only did so to uphold the rest."

"That's was not your decision to make, Warrior. Everyone has their place."

"My place was taken from me, along with my dignity, and my name. I was trying to earn them back."

It was plain the way Harta's mirth abruptly ceased that it had never been real at all. "Let me see if I understand . . . You freely associated with the greatest criminal in the world, the man responsible for destroying our house's sword, who tarnished my family name, who *killed my mother,* and yet somehow you thought you could just stroll back into Vadal and buy my forgiveness with a wagon full of bones?"

"No, sir. I buy nothing. The demons are yours by right. I seized treasure for you because I am a warrior of Great House Vadal. That's what we do on raids."

"I should slit your throat right now."

"That is your decision to make, Thakoor. My life is yours to spend."

"You won't beg for mercy?"

Oh, it was sorely tempting. *Sorely tempting indeed.* "Warriors are not supposed to *beg.*"

"Such dignity, even in rags. Good. It annoys me when I find cowards among your caste. All your people should be as eager to die for this house as you clearly are. In fact, a large number of your caste have adopted the belief that you are some kind of avenging champion, righting wrongs, and collecting heads. That's the only reason you've not already been executed."

So Jagdish's grand entrance plan had worked... Not as well as he'd hoped, but he wasn't dead yet. *Take that, Gutch.*

"You see, Jagdish, I stuck you in that prison in the hopes that the people would forget about you once they found some new shiny thing to distract them. Instead, your imprisonment seems to have had the opposite effect. My informants tell me they're singing songs about you in every warriors' tavern in the city. The man they remember for dueling fearsome Ashok *every day,* then ran off and turned into a demon hunter. The stories are so outlandish they're scarcely believable to a skeptical man, but the gullible are eating it up. The warriors' morale has been low since Ashok's betrayal, but in you they have found something to love. Warriors are simple. They like to have their heroes, don't they?"

"Yes, sir. We do."

"However, I can hardly have them making a hero out of someone best known for his disobedience. That sets a dangerous precedent. They're wondering where you've disappeared to, and some of them have even begun muttering that your absence is my fault. The malcontents are saying that I am *unjust* to punish such a hero. I can't by definition be unjust, because I'm the one who decides what the Law means in this land. Justice is whatever I say it is. Do you understand why such rot is an issue?"

"Yes, sir. Officers are taught allowing dissension leads to contempt for authority. Contempt for authority destroys the effectiveness of a unit." In that particular respect, being Thakoor was just like being a risaldar, only on a far grander scale.

"I was warned you are a clever one. My time is valuable, Jagdish, so I will be frank. I want to kill you. A public execution would send the message that criminals are not tolerated in Vadal, but would further depress my warriors, and the timing for that is very inconvenient. On the other hand, a private killing makes it appear to my caste that I am unconfident, or maybe even afraid of drawing the wrath of the Black Heart."

"You could let me live," Jagdish suggested.

"Yet on a personal level, it would please me to see you die," Harta said, ever so earnestly. "I really want to kill Ashok Vadal, but he's not here. You are. You're the next best thing. Would killing you upset him, do you think?"

Jagdish was trying to be truthful, but that question was making it extremely hard. He swallowed. "I don't rightly know, sir."

"Because if given an opportunity to hurt Ashok Vadal, even a tiny fraction as much as he has hurt this house, I would be a fool not to do so . . ." He turned toward the woman. "Don't you think so, Rada?"

She seemed to shrink back. The young lady was also dressed in the finery that declared her to be a member of the first caste, but it was apparent she was uncomfortable with all of this life-or-death business. "I . . . I don't . . ."

"Spit it out, Librarian. I've not got all night. Show me that you are worthy of your caste. It is time to make the difficult decisions."

She appeared to be a mousy thing, but there was some steel in her after all, as she drew herself up to her full, not very impressive bearing, and declared, "If this man won't ask for mercy for himself, then I will do it for him."

"Mercy? Ha! Mercy is not *good enough!*"

Harta surprised Jagdish then, by kicking him in the chest. On his knees with his hands bound there wasn't a damned thing he could do about it, not that he would have defended himself against his Thakoor anyway, because then every member of the guard present would've stuck a sword in him a heartbeat later. Dust rose from Jagdish's filthy clothing as Harta's sandal hit. The Thakoor didn't have warrior muscle by any means, but he was a robust man, and there had been a lot of emotion behind that kick, so it still really hurt. Jagdish flopped over onto the grass, grimacing, ribs throbbing.

"Mercy is an abstract concept, Rada. The First must deal only in concrete reality. Every decision is a calculation that either benefits or harms our obligation." He kicked Jagdish again, in his already sore stomach this time. "You want to prove yourself an advisor? Then advise. What should I do with this man?"

Somehow Jagdish's fate had wound up in the hands of some woman he'd never met before. Harta's desires were plain and ended with Jagdish's blood watering the garden. If she was seeking Harta's approval then the easiest thing in the world would simply be to agree with him and offer a suggestion for a public or private death.

Shockingly, the woman did not back down. "You spoke earlier of your warriors' perception of your ambitions. You do not wish to be seen as selfish by them, especially as you send them off to war. You can mock my plea, but Chief Judge Samudra Vadal once wrote that mercy is the cheapest investment we can make in the lesser castes, as it costs us nothing, but returns us loyalty tenfold."

"Quoting one of my own ancestors at me...sly. Only this investment is not cheap. It requires the sacrifice of my pride. And that is *very* valuable. I am Thakoor. What will people say when they see that I have failed to punish an ally of the Black Heart? They will say I am weak. They will say I'm afraid." Harta placed his foot on Jagdish's head and put his weight down, crushing his face into the grass. It hurt. It felt as if his neck might break, but Jagdish clenched his teeth together and made no sound. Harta extended one hand toward a guard. "Give me your sword."

The guard drew his blade, flipped it around, and extended it hilt first toward his Thakoor. Harta took it, then placed the tip against Jagdish's back. The tiniest bit of pressure was enough to raise blood from the skin.

Jagdish prepared to go into the endless nothing.

"Wait! There's a way you can take all the credit and none of the blame."

"Hmmm..." Harta paused in his murder. "Go on, Rada."

"If showing mercy to this criminal will encourage more crime, just erase his crime."

"What?"

"It benefits your warriors to have a living hero before they go to war. You've got a perfectly good one right here. All you need to do is tell the people that you're the one who made him a hero. Jagdish did not disobey if he was following your orders to track down those wizards the whole time."

"You want me to claim that I dispatched this fool on a secret mission?" This time Harta's laugh sounded genuine, because the Thakoor wasn't taken by surprise very often. "How would that explain his association with the Black Heart?"

"It's as Jagdish said himself, he used one criminal to get close to other criminals. It's like in *The Tale of Jaswinder* when the Chief Judge ordered Jaswinder to pretend to be a bandit in order to infiltrate the lair of the Bandit King."

"I do not know that history."

"It's actually a romance."

I am going to die, Jagdish thought.

"But the strategy is sound," Rada hurried. "*You* sent Jagdish on this mission. He may have failed to capture the Black Heart, but he still killed a hundred illegal wizards and a dozen demons along the way!"

With the Thakoor's sandal crushing his head, Jagdish wasn't about to correct her wild exaggeration of enemy numbers. Then Harta lifted his foot, and Jagdish gasped as most of the pain left his skull.

"An interesting ploy, Rada. Because if it was I who sent Jagdish on this quest, then I must share in his glory. The master always receives credit for his servant's labors."

"All will say it took incredible wisdom for a ruler to recognize such hidden talents," Rada agreed. "Spare this man's life and you will be mentioned in all the same songs as he is. As for the first caste, they will not think of you as soft, but rather shrewd, because even while your house was reeling you sent your fiercest warrior to track down Angruvadal. When Jagdish discovered Angruvadal was lost, rather than despair, instead he brought home other magic to replace it. You are a man of action, Thakoor. They can hardly fault you for not catching Ashok when all the might of the Capitol and even mighty Devedas and the Protectors haven't been able to catch him either."

Jagdish rolled over enough to see his Thakoor's expression. Harta still held the sword and was mulling over what to do with it.

"And here I was, testing you to see if your naïve academic proclivities could be overcome, and if you would be pragmatic enough to suggest how I should best kill this man . . . and instead you offered me another possibility, which though personally annoying, actually does benefit my house. I was too close to this particular issue to see such a simple, yet elegant, solution." Harta handed the sword back to the guard. "*That* is what advisors are for. Perhaps you can make yourself useful after all. Well done, Rada."

"Thank you, Thakoor." She sounded extremely relieved.

"Pick him up," Harta ordered. The guards immediately grabbed Jagdish by the arms and hauled him to his feet. "I have made my decision. Do you understand what just happened here, Warrior?"

"I think so, sir."

"Do you understand what our story is going forward?"

"I do. Yes."

"Do you have a problem with this?"

The choice between sharing the glory with an

unrighteous fop or bleeding to death on the lawn, was an easy one. "No, sir. It was you who sent me on that mission. It was your idea all along. You're very wise."

"Correct. If I find out you ever say otherwise, then I will be forced to revisit my decision. Now, if I can't be seen punishing you, then I must be seen rewarding you." Harta looked at the guard who was standing by Rada. "Luthra, what do warriors usually do when one of you does something suitably heroic?"

"An increase in rank and status, as well as corresponding awards for valor, Thakoor."

"What is the most prestigious of those awards your people can ever get?"

"The highest award for gallantry in battle is the Param Vir Chakra." Luthra answered without hesitation, because no symbol was more respected among their caste than the Wheel of ultimate bravery.

"Did my mother ever grant any of those?"

"No, sir. It's been a long time since the last recipient. Not since the siege of Sudorat has one of those been awarded."

Harta turned back to Jagdish. "Then I'll see to it that Jagdish is given one of those. A fitting trophy for a demon hunter."

Jagdish could only stare at Harta and blink. Getting stepped on had made his head swim less than those words. All of the Personal Guard were stunned as well. Even though the award was so ancient it dated back to before the Age of Law, before there had even been a warrior caste, the Wheel had been awarded only a couple hundred times, and most of those posthumously. Every warrior in Vadal had been raised on the stories of those mighty few.

"I'm unworthy."

"I don't care. I merely need the warriors to think you are. That requires status . . . And rank, I suppose. Thus, I promote you to the rank of phontho with a single star."

Jagdish was speechless. Phonthos were granted between one and five stars, but even the first tier of that mighty rank led *ten* paltans. Even with minimal staff, unreinforced, that was at least five *hundred* warriors. *Oceans!* He wasn't just skipping several ranks, with his lowly birth it would've taken him a hundred years of perfect effort to achieve such a station. He was only a risaldar, the lowest form of officer! As a phontho he'd have *ten* risaldars under his command.

"I will inform the Vadal High Command about this promotion. They can throw a parade or whatever it is you warriors do before they dispatch you to the eastern border, as far from my sight as possible." Harta looked over Jagdish with barely concealed disgust. "Clean him up."

Then the most powerful man in Vadal simply walked away.

Jagdish's knees were quivering. His hands were shaking so badly that the chains were audibly rattling. Apparently, he wasn't the only one who had been absolutely terrified and trying to hide it because once the Thakoor was out of sight, the woman, Rada, stumbled off to the side and loudly threw up in the bushes.

"Sorry about slugging you in the gut earlier," said the guard next to Jagdish as he unlocked the shackles. "But, brother, I've got to say that was the most intense promotion ceremony I've ever been to!"

Chapter 32

~~~~~~~~~~

Hair and beard trimmed, bathed, wearing a new sword, and in an opulent uniform with phontho's badges hastily sewn on each sleeve, Jagdish walked out of Great House Vadal feeling like a new man. There was a star on his turban and joy in his heart.

Several members of the Personal Guard were waiting for him at the back entrance. They stood at attention and barked his name and rank. It wasn't just because of his newly given status, he knew soldiers well enough to tell these salutes showed real respect. These men were sworn to secrecy about the things they saw within these walls, but despite their knowing how Jagdish had just earned his dubious reward, they still seemed proud that a former member of their unit had made it big. Harta's lies aside, Jagdish was probably the only regular person they'd ever met who'd fought demons *and* wizards *and* lived.

"Thank you," Jagdish told the men. "Please, go about your duties."

The guard dispersed, except for the warrior Luthra, who greeted Jagdish with a formal bow. "Good evening, Phontho. Due to the, uh … suddenness of events, there's no guest room prepared for you here at the great house. We can provide you quarters at our barracks in the meantime."

Jagdish couldn't help but grin. Luthra was much younger than he was, but he looked to be a sharp one. "No need to mince words, Havildar. I've been in your boots. You're trying to spare the master of the house the indignity of seeing a scrub like me beneath his roof. No offense is given. I'm so happy to be alive right now that I'd gladly sleep in the dirtiest swine pen in the casteless quarter and I'd still wake up refreshed."

"Sorry. I'm not used to being able to speak freely with a man of such advanced rank as yourself." Luthra's speech made it obvious he too had earned this obligation through proper soldiering and not being a high-status man's son. "You're welcome to bunk with us inside the walls until the High Command sends you east, or if you've got somewhere else to go in the city, I can loan you a carriage and a driver."

He was so excited to see Pakpa that he would've run to her father's house, even in these new, far too stiff, boots. "Just a horse would be wonderful."

"Consider it done." Luthra signaled for one of his men to run to the stables. "I was told that you were asking about the whereabouts of Risaldar Girish earlier."

"He delivered me to Cold Stream. Seemed like a good man."

"The best of us," Luthra agreed. "He's off on a gate inspection but he's due back later tonight. I can't wait to see his face when I tell him he missed all the excitement."

"I asked him to deliver a personal memento of mine to my wife and wanted to see if it had been done... but now I guess I get to just go see her myself!"

"If Girish the Steadfast said he'd deliver it, then I'm sure it was. Permission to speak freely, sir?"

"Being asked that will take me some getting used to. Of course, Havildar."

"What the Thakoor was saying about the warriors' morale, he's not wrong. You've been away, but the mood's been sour in Vadal City since the business with the Black Heart. It's hard to be betrayed by something you've looked up to your whole life. When word gets out about Angruvadal for sure being gone they'll be heartbroken. There's not a young warrior in Vadal who didn't at some point dream about being chosen to bear that sword."

"Me as well," Jagdish said softly. In fact, he'd been on his way to duel for the black sword when he'd gotten into all this mess.

"Then you know it'll be good for them to have something else to believe in. To be able to look up and say, see that one? He was just like us once."

Jagdish was still dizzy with the new responsibilities that had been placed upon him, but Luthra was sincere. His caste truly needed him right now. "I will do my best."

"I hope so!" Luthra laughed. "When I was young, I wanted to be a Protector when I grew up. Every warrior my age will admit they were inspired by Ashok Vadal, if they're honest at least. We do need heroes. That was a kick to the sack. But I'll tell you,

I've served our Thakoor for long enough to know his moods. I thought for sure you were a dead man."

"As for that, who was the woman whose wise counsel saved my life?"

"Radamantha Nems dar Harban of the Capitol Library."

"Really?" Jagdish never figured he'd owe his life, status, and fortune to a *librarian*.

"Really. And beyond that I'm not allowed to say how we ended up with her as our guest, even to someone of your newly exalted status."

"Please give her my thanks." The guard who had run to the stables was returning, leading one of the mares they kept saddled for emergency messengers. Not just that, tell Lady Radamantha if she ever needs any favors, anything at all, from the world's most fortunate warrior, Jagdish is at her disposal. I owe her my life. Now I'm off to see my family."

Dignity of his new office be damned, Jagdish was so excited to go home that he rushed to the horse and leapt into the saddle. The poor animal reared in surprised. "Farewell, lads."

"Good luck, Phontho."

Jagdish kept it to a trot until he was out the gate, and then he coaxed his horse into a run.

Triumphant, Jagdish rode through the streets of Vadal City. It would have taken another rain of demons to wipe the grin from his face.

He was forced to slow down as he passed by the looming mansions of the first caste and the big government buildings. Off-duty soldiers saw him, then quickly got out of his way when they saw the insignia of an important man. After he went by surely they talked, for most of the phonthos were known to them, and who was this man so young to wear such a distinguished rank? Even a warrior born from the highest bloodline had gray in his hair before reaching that kind of status.

Jagdish couldn't help but shout at the warriors who were hurrying to salute him, "*I am Jagdish and I have returned!*"

They gaped at him, but they heard, and they understood.

Let them talk. Let the whole city know. Let everyone speak his name, for Jagdish had returned home with honor. He'd waded through swamps while wrestling a train of mules to do it. The heaviest weight he'd been dragging that whole time hadn't been demon bone, but the shame of his damaged name. With that weight gone he felt like he could fly. He was no longer Unlucky Jagdish or Jagdish the Failure or even Prisoner Jagdish. He was the Phontho Jagdish, hunter of demons and killer of wizards.

He would go to the east where he would serve his house, train his men, and lead by example. There would be raids back and forth, as there always was, and Jagdish would be so devoted to fulfilling his duty that success would be inevitable. Harta hated him, and he would be exiled to the border for now, but Thakoors didn't live forever. Someday Jagdish would return to this city and one of these massive estates he was riding past would become his. He and Pakpa would live here, and it would be his children reaping the benefits of having high-status blood. Only unlike most of the fops he'd known, he'd raise his children right, to be proper warriors, not soft and coddled, and they'd have to train hard like everyone else so they could grow up to be leaders deserving of respect.

As he crossed through the warriors' district, all the warriors were saying his name. With a thrill it went through the crowds. Even the workers on the streets knew who he was. If Harta said these men needed a figurehead, then Jagdish would do that job! He'd do it with pride, but not too much pride, because Jagdish knew a leader's biggest job was to serve. He'd give these men pride because pride made the march easier, it made the armor lighter, and it made the sword arm strong. Pride kept you alive. Pride had kept *him* alive.

Ahead he spied a familiar wagon. It was the rig that had just transported him from Cold Stream to the great house gardens. It was stopped at one of the more popular warriors' halls in the city. He'd once sat in that very tavern and drank until the alcohol had given him enough courage to duel Ashok. It must have been the end of their shift and the guards had stopped to cash in some of their beer rations before returning to their barracks.

It said a lot about his mood that Jagdish didn't dismount, go inside, and use his newfound phontho powers to have the men who'd abused him mercilessly whipped for their Law breaking. But no, as Harta had shown mercy to him, he would be merciful to them. And as satisfying as it would have been to go in there and challenge them to a duel, Pakpa was waiting. Though perhaps tomorrow he would pay a visit to the warden and educate that officer about the idiocy of having men who rejoiced in cruelty be left in charge of captives.

He rode past his old house, though there was

nothing for him there now. Pakpa had gone to live with her family in the workers' district. The place had probably been assigned to a different officer, more than likely some other young risaldar who'd just had his marriage arranged. Only whoever that stranger was couldn't possibly be as lucky with wedlock as Jagdish had been! It was a tiny home, but it was where he and Pakpa had shared a bed, so it would always be special to him. He would miss this tiny house, but come to think of it, a phontho's stipend was ten times that of a risaldar, so he'd build his bride a new mansion in the east, like she deserved!

The worker's district was still loud and bustling, even at night, though it was nothing like the mud- and soot-encrusted chaos that was Neeramphorn, where he'd spent days hiding in the shadows and sleeping beneath steam vents. Vadal City was bright and clean, with the factory walls covered in flowering vines and decorated with colorful banners advertising their various products and services.

"I am Jagdish and I have returned!" he shouted at the batch of tired warriors who were marching out of the district at the end of their patrol. They gawked at him, confused as to why the man in the fancy uniform was yelling triumphantly.

But the rest of the people here when they heard his name, they *recognized* it. Realization dawned on their faces. This was the hero who'd crossed through several rival houses to make their house rich with demon parts. Gutch had tried to tell him once that most workers couldn't afford pride. That made them harder to build up than a warrior, but that meant they were also harder to tear down. They just got by, good or bad, no matter what, plodding along. But Gutch was wrong! If only Gutch could see the look on his peers' faces, he would see real pride right now, Vadal pride. His name brought them hope!

Workers bowed. Their women waved and blew him kisses. Children ran after his horse. Funny, it turned out that workers needed something to believe in too, and his heart rejoiced. Jagdish had succeeded beyond his wildest dreams, and now all the people of Vadal would celebrate with him.

A moment later the estate of Pakpa's father came into view. It wasn't really a house, so much as a giant bakery that they'd added apartments onto for the family living quarters. People were still coming and going, delivering sacks and carrying off baskets. Jagdish came to a stop, got off his horse, and hitched it to a post. He knew many of Pakpa's relatives from the wedding party, but he didn't recognize any of these. The workers looked at him curiously. They might not know warrior ranks, but it was obvious from the ornamentation of his uniform that Jagdish was a very important man.

"Is Pakpa here?" They obviously didn't know of who he spoke. "Never mind. Move aside, for I am Jagdish and I have come to take my wife away from all of this." So excited he could barely think straight, he pushed his way into the bakery. "Pakpa!"

Despite the hour most of the bakers were still there, steadily going about their duties, cleaning vats, sweeping floors, and feeding wood into enormous stoves. It was all very industrious. This place supplied various warrior barracks around the city, and for that Jagdish was very thankful because his marriage had been arranged to secure a contract between the castes. He owed his happiness to bread.

"Pakpa!" He didn't see her, but that made sense. She was a new mother, so she probably wouldn't be toiling in front of a hot fire. "Pakpa?" He grabbed a passing child by the sleeve, who seemed rather surprised to see a warrior here. "Have you seen Pakpa?"

The boy shook his head in the negative, frightened.

"Are you sure? She's the daughter of the head baker."

"The boss ain't got no girl here I know of, sir warrior."

Confused, Jagdish let go of him. The child was probably just an idiot. He went back to his search. "Pakpa!"

Another baker intercepted him, this one a short, thick man, who was dusted in flour up to his elbows. "Jagdish? Is that you?"

"Aye. It's me." He'd met this one at the wedding, one of his wife's multitude of cousins, though he'd forgotten his name.

"Sorry. I didn't recognize you in such finery."

"I've returned for Pakpa."

The baker's eyes widened as a pained look came over his face. "You don't know?"

He froze. "What? Where is she?"

"I . . . I'm sorry, Jagdish. Pakpa's dead."

His world came crashing down.

The baker kept talking . . . something about a difficult childbirth and them calling for the surgeon but how no one arrived in time. Only Jagdish was having a very hard time understanding the words. The room began to spin. He had to grab onto a table edge as his knees went weak. Flour got all over his new coat.

He nearly fell. The baker reached for him, but Jagdish shoved him away. "No."

He couldn't breathe in here. There was too much dust or something. He was choking.

Jagdish made it out the door. He tried to gasp for air, but it was like there was nothing there. This wasn't thick moist Vadal air anymore, it was like the high, sharp air of the mountains that cut your face. Heart hammering, he stumbled down the boardwalk until he couldn't walk, so he sat on the edge and tried to comprehend the incomprehensible.

The bakers came outside after him, a bunch of them now. Like before, the workers were saying his name, only this time it wasn't with awe, but rather pity.

Pakpa . . . No . . . It can't be.

They were all babbling, but it might as well have been in some gibberish tongue for how little it made sense. Someone was touching him on the shoulder, and he realized it was Pakpa's mother. She was weeping. She'd had months to get over her shock and grieve for her daughter. This was a fresh sad cry for him.

"This is a mistake. You must be wrong," he told them.

Only the truth was plain on their faces.

She was gone. And he hadn't been here. She was gone because he hadn't been here. If he'd been here, then surely he would've been able to do *something*.

His presence had reawakened her family's grief, and the bakers began to wail and carry on. Sick and angry, he shouted, "No!" Jagdish struck the boardwalk with his fist. It caused the nearest workers to flinch away in fear. "No! No! No!" He kept punching the wood until Pakpa's mother forgot her place and grabbed his arm before he broke his fingers.

She babbled something in his ear, meant to be soothing, but Jagdish couldn't understand her over the sobbing.

There was the sound of hoofbeats as another rider approached. "Make way! Coming through!"

Dazed, he wondered why he could understand a warrior's words, but not those of the workers. It must be a matter of tone. Or perhaps he had just trained himself to always listen to his comrades no matter how dire the situation was . . . Jagdish looked over to see a grizzled warrior in the uniform of the Personal Guard parting the crowd. His horse had obviously been pushed hard. This man had been desperate enough to move through the streets at a speed dangerous to bystanders.

When the new arrival saw Jagdish sitting there without dignity, he swore. "Oceans! I'm too late."

"Girish?" Jagdish asked, confused as to what the man he'd asked to deliver his pocket watch was doing here.

The senior warrior dismounted. "When Luthra told me you'd been released I tried to catch up to warn you."

"You knew about Pakpa? Why . . . Why didn't you tell me?"

"I thought you were going to be executed soon. I didn't want to torment a condemned man with news he could do nothing about." Girish approached with hands spread apologetically. "I am truly sorry."

This made Jagdish furious, but if their roles had been reversed, he knew he probably would've done the exact same thing. It was a good thing for Girish and Jagdish both that he kept his head even when the world was falling apart all around him.

"I should have been here, Girish. I wasn't here. She can't be gone. This is a bad dream. I'll wake up soon. I was going to take her away and build her an estate in the east. I can do that for her now, so we can raise a proud family." The change had been so sudden. Moments ago he had been atop the world, and then he'd been cast into the oceans to sink beneath the waves of hell. Then a terrible realization struck him—Pakpa had been in childbirth—and he turned to Pakpa's mother, frightened. "What happened to my son?"

"That's what I've been trying to tell you, Jagdish," she said. "You've got no son."

He'd not just lost the woman he'd loved, but the son he'd never even had the chance to love. He'd not thought he could feel any worse, but suddenly he was crushed with a despair beyond imagination. It was as if a hail of arrows had just pierced his chest and all he could breathe was fire through the holes in his lungs. Jagdish had never felt so alone.

"You've got a daughter."

Chapter 33

The Keeper of Names should have been happy. It seemed the gods were well pleased with their chosen people. The prophet had returned and brought the Forgotten's warrior with her. She'd miraculously cured them of the miserable lingering illness. The dying had stopped. The people had rejoiced. Their population had surged as the multitude of faithful Thera had brought with her moved in. They had plenty of land, with rich soil already irrigated and fields free of rocks. Javed had organized the newcomers by their skills, and now the terraces were flourishing. They were promised a bounteous harvest.

It had been a winter of murder and a spring of plague, but the faithful had survived to see another season.

He should've been giving thanks to the gods. Only rather than joy, Keta was engulfed in a deep melancholy he couldn't shake. Though he knew his feelings were profoundly illogical, such understanding changed nothing. He felt what he felt, even if it wasn't the gods' will he do so.

The Voice had commanded him to go and find Ashok, because it prophesized that Ashok alone could lead their armies against the Capitol. Keta had crossed the continent and risked his life to get to the former Protector only to find their chosen in prison. Once free, Ashok had lived up to his dark reputation as the most dangerous man in Lok. At first, he had repeatedly threatened to kill poor unassuming Keta. Yet Keta had remained steadfast, knowing that—no matter how unlikely it was that the Law's ultimate killer was supposed to turn into the rebellion's champion—the gods would not lead them astray. It had eventually worked out. They had even become friends, of a sort.

That made the discovery that Thera had fallen in love with Ashok even more painful.

The revelation should not have stung. Rather he should have been happy for both of them. Thera was the best woman he had ever known, a prize that any rational man—who could look past her obstinate ways—would want as a wife. It was no surprise that a man accustomed to the highest status would pair off with the most important woman in the world.

Of course Thera had chosen Ashok instead of someone like Keta. How could she not?

Even though castes weren't supposed to matter here, and despite he and Ashok both legally being the lowest of the low, Ashok still acted as if he was the highest of the high. It wasn't pride either. If it had been, Keta would have a reason to hate him. In fact, it was the opposite, with Ashok despising himself because of the fraud of his birth. Despite that,

Ashok remained instinctively noble, aloof, sometimes even cruel—but never with intent toward cruelty. He was confident yet did not brag, Ashok simply told the truth as he saw it. Swordless, he still carried himself with the dignity of a bearer. Lawless, everything he did retained the moral conviction of a judge.

They had both come from nothing, only Ashok's memories had been erased by wizards to hide the scandal of Angruvadal choosing a little casteless blood scrubber to wield it. Keta remembered all of his life. The squalor, the hunger, the regular tragedies and daily indignities. He remembered well the constant gnawing fear that was the life of non-person and had the whip scars on his back to prove it.

Legally they were less valuable than livestock, so of course casteless didn't *marry*. Despite the Law they still paired off and loved each other and made children just like the real people. Sometimes these casteless even managed to stick together in the semblance of what whole men would think of as families. He had recorded hundreds of examples of this into the great book since becoming the Keeper of Names. As for him however, Keta had been with several casteless women, he might even have left one of them with a baby for all he knew—assuming any of them had survived the uprising in Uttara—but he'd never really *known* them. Their names, and how they felt in the dark, that was about it. The relationships had been brief, lustful encounters, and then they'd been sent off to other masters and never seen again.

Now he was a *free man*, and an important one at that. Yet, on the road with Thera, once of the warrior caste, he'd often felt like an imposter. Though he tried to put it aside, sometimes Keta still reflexively returned to the submissive meekness that every non-person learned to adopt around their betters in order to survive, and he hated himself for it.

When they'd first met, he'd found Thera to be abrasive and self-centered. She should have been thankful for the gifts she'd been given but was instead angry at the very gods for picking her. Then he'd come to understand that she was a product of her past, just as he was. There was far more to her than she let people see, and over time he'd come to respect her determination. On their long journey, respect had turned to love. Except Thera was the prophet and he was her priest, so he'd said nothing. He didn't even know if such feelings were appropriate or not. The gods certainly hadn't said anything about it. Would they approve? Unsure, he'd hesitated.

The Keeper of Names was always confident and certain. Keta was not. They were the same person, but two very different things. The Keeper of Names was the high priest of the returned Forgotten, who taught all who would listen with a passion that swayed even the hardest heart. Keta the man was small, balding, and not particularly noteworthy. After being kidnapped by wizards, the Keeper of Names demanded their prophet be retrieved because she was the Voice of the gods who could guide them with the wisdom of the gods. Keta had simply wanted Thera back.

Perhaps, in a small way, he'd assumed if they were together, eventually Thera would grow to feel about him the way he felt about her. That had been the lazy decision of a coward. Even when she'd cured his sickness by her touch, in that moment when he had loved her more than ever, and she had shone like the heavenly messengers Ratul had talked about, he had still hesitated to tell her the truth...

Not that it would have done any good. He'd not known that Ashok had already bedded her then. Keta only would have embarrassed himself.

Of course Thera had chosen Ashok. He was the sort of man who made the people wish to be ruled by kings.

So be it. He would continue to serve her because the Forgotten willed it.

Enough self-pity. Keta had a religion to manage.

"Good morning, Keeper," Javed said as Keta walked into the large room that served as their church. There was very little furniture in the Cove, so most of his preaching was done with the faithful sitting on the stone floor.

Many of the various trinkets and artifacts the people had brought with them had been placed here for worship. Some of these were new, while others had been kept hidden from the Inquisitors and been handed down in secret through the ages. Like the little statues of men with elephant heads, or beautiful women with extra arms, or the smiling fat man, and even one with a man—probably casteless since he was so skinny and dressed only in a loincloth—with his hands nailed onto some sort of Inquisition torture device. The old symbols were all so different in style that at times Keta suspected they had no relation to each other at all, and he still had no idea which of these, if any, was the physical representation of the Voice.

"Javed." He greeted the man who had become his right hand over the last few months. A great many of them owed their lives to the former rice merchant, not just for saving them from the fat wizard who'd hunted them for sport during the winter, but also for the incredible work he'd done since. "All is well I hope?"

"It is. The newcomers are still working hard. Some of those formerly of the warrior caste were a little haughty about doing manual labor, but all it took was a word from Ashok and they've put their shoulder to the wheel."

Keta smiled. It was good sometimes for the warriors to be reminded that the only caste that existed in the Cove was freemen, equal below the gods. "The people seem happy."

"Morale is high. That's mostly your doing, Keeper."

"My actions are mostly symbolic," Keta said dismissively.

"You've helped orphans find new parents to take them in. You've performed ceremonies and blessed the crops. Your preaching is especially valuable. Almost everyone stops what they are doing to hear your words. Even the once mute slaves the Voice freed from the Lost House are waking up and occasionally speaking a bit now and then. All of this is because of your ministering to the Cove."

Keta accepted the compliment. Very few knew how much exhausting effort he had put into making this settlement work. "As have you, my friend. Is there anything else that requires my attention today?"

"One of the Sons of the Black Sword has pronounced his undying love for another of the faithful and the two wish to be officially married before the gods."

"Huh..." Keta smiled. "That is unexpected news. Which ones?"

"Ongud, that round-faced Akershani clerk, and Kalki, the potter from the swamp people."

"Even in the most trying of circumstances, life goes on." Keta had married people before, but those had been rushed affairs during desperate times. In the Law-abiding world it was arbiters who approved marriages arranged by house and caste. They had none of that here, but strangely enough it was one of the very first things the faithful had begged their Keeper of Names to do for them. He didn't even know if it was really part of his intended duties or not, but it made the people happy to feel the gods had blessed their union. "The Sons are beloved figures. This will be a celebration. Would you take care of scheduling that for me?"

"Of course, Keeper. There is one other pressing matter though. We're going to need to send someone out to purchase certain supplies soon."

Keta frowned. They had been sealed off for months, but every time they drained the lake it risked discovery. "Ashok is certain the Protectors are still searching the region."

"I defer to your wisdom, Keeper. It is dangerous, but we need a great many things that we simply lack the resources to make here ourselves. Tools, tack. The Sons have weapons in need of repair. Of the new arrivals we've got a smith, but no anvil, and we have a brewer with no—"

"Wait . . . We have a brewer? Of beer?"

"Yes, as well as other spirits that are popular in Akershan, but—"

"I didn't know we had a brewer!" Keta was truly happy for the first time in days. Of course they had alcohol in the Cove, because if there was a plant that could be fermented, the casteless knew how to make a drink out of it. However, traveling across Lok pretending to be a man of status had spoiled Keta to such luxuries as drink that didn't taste of dirty feet. "Take from the banknotes Thera liberated from the wizards and use whatever's necessary to get that man any equipment he needs."

"As you wish," Javed said. "I've already made a list. It'll take at least two of the wagons and five or six men, but there's always merchant caravans moving across the Dharvan Bench this time of year, so they should be able to find what we need without showing their faces in any of the nearby cities."

"Good idea." He didn't know what he would do without Javed. Keta himself was very skilled at organizing and record keeping—his meticulous running of a storehouse was the reason he'd been one of the rare casteless allowed to learn how to read, write, and do math—but with most of his attention being consumed seeing to the spiritual needs of their people, it was good to have someone else competent to manage the day to day things.

In fact, now that there were so many people in need of ministering Keta could barely keep up, he had been thinking that the time had come to expand their fledgling order. Their priesthood didn't really have an organization—if a real hierarchy existed the Voice had not seen fit to reveal it yet—but Keta intended to offer Javed some sort of priestly title to make his status official. Surely the gods knew the man was worthy of it.

"I will prepare an expedition then. Don't worry. I'll choose someone clever to be in charge, with at least one or two of them worker caste so they can purchase things without being suspicious."

"Excellent. If there's nothing else pressing, I need to prepare tonight's sermon." Coming up with an entire religion worth of doctrine was rather a lot of work.

Ratul had only told Keta a few of the old stories in the time they'd had together, and what the faithful had handed down in secret through the ages was often conflicting or downright odd. With hundreds of new faithful, he'd spent a great many hours updating the names and family lines in the genealogy, but there was nothing in Ratul's old demon-hide-bound book that answered Keta's deepest questions.

"Will it be about life after death again?" Javed asked.

"That's the topic which gives them the most hope. The ancients obviously believed it, but the Voice has said very little about the specifics. Our bodies are just meat, but while the Law says the spark dies with it, I say the spark lives on. Where does the life go? Some of the faithful think we go to a paradise to dwell with the gods in luxury, others think that life goes into a baby, and you live another life, over and over, until you get it all right."

"Absurd." Javed snorted.

"Javed!" It was a rare display of disrespect from his assistant. "Followers of the Forgotten can't insult other faithful's beliefs! This leads to division!"

"Forgive me, Keeper. As I told you, many in the caravans believed in the old ways, but my mother never spoke of such things as being born over and over. That makes no sense. Babies are very dumb. For this to be true, babies would be clever. I mean no disrespect to our brothers and sisters who believe such tripe, but I find the idea silly."

Keta would never be so quick to dismiss any of the faithful's traditions. A few years ago he hadn't even heard of Ramrowan, and yet he had inherited his priesthood's highest office. "We won't know for sure until the Voice tells us. In the meantime, regardless of which theory is right, telling the people that they've been lied to about the great nothing after death, when there is actually a great *something*, is an incredible motivator."

"Of course, Keeper."

Keta stopped by the statues when he saw that one of his people had placed a new token next to the old ones. It was a little metal hook to symbolize when the gods had brought Ashok back to life. "A powerful idea indeed."

"Truly the Forgotten is merciful," Javed agreed. "Have you tried asking about the specifics?"

"Ah..." Keta shrugged. In truth, he had been avoiding Thera lately. "The gods speak when they want to be heard. You can't rush them."

"Do you mean the Voice, or the prophet who contains it?"

Keta didn't rightly know, but he doubted he'd have much luck pushing either. Receiving the ancient healing knowledge had left her weak and exhausted for days, but Thera appeared rested now. After so much turmoil, she even seemed *content*. Keta didn't want to ruin that for her. Let her be happy...as she shared her bed with another.

That thought made Keta scowl at the hook. "The prophet will do what she wants, as she always does."

"Of course." Javed tilted his head toward the chapel's entrance. "We have a visitor."

The tall, lean shadow darkening their doorway was unmistakably that of Ashok Vadal, a rare sight in the church, for Ashok was probably the least faithful person in the Cove. It was odd. Keta was devout in all his doings but too timid to act because he was worried the gods wouldn't approve, while Ashok paid the gods no heed at all, and they granted him power over death itself.

"Ah, Ashok. What brings you to the church this fine morning?"

"We must speak of your defenses." Ashok walked in, saw the line of statues, and scowled. Though he was unquestionably dedicated to Thera, it was obvious that the sight of so many illegal artifacts still caused a reflexive revulsion in the former Protector.

"What about our defenses?"

"They are inadequate." Ashok resisted the urge to stomp on the trinkets and turned back to Keta. "It is only a matter of time until the Law finds this place."

"The gods have kept us hidden from their eyes so far."

"A vast country, a sparse population, and luck have done that more than your gods. The lake covers your entrance, but we have no roof to hide beneath. There are wizards who can turn into hawks to ride high on the mountain winds."

"I thought Inquisitors shape-shifting into birds, snakes, and cats was a story mothers told their children to make them afraid of the Capitol," Javed said.

Ashok shook his head. "The power is real. I'm surprised one of them hasn't flown over this crater yet. There is no way to conceal all of our activity forever, so we must decide what to do when they find us."

"Everyone here is willing to fight, plus we have your fearsome Sons of the Black Sword now," Keta said.

"The Sons are good," Ashok allowed.

"One might even say miraculously good," Keta suggested.

"Jagdish taught them well, and they fight with

remarkable skill and dedication, but they are few in number. When the Capitol discovers this place they will send an overwhelming force to crush us. I have some ideas to improve our defenses, but I believe they will still be insufficient to resist an actual siege."

"The gods led us here for a reason."

"Ratul led you here because it was convenient."

Ashok's lack of respect for his old master annoyed Keta. "Have you asked the Voice? You're with her every night after all." Keta didn't know why he added that last part in a snide tone. It just slipped out. He immediately regretted it.

Javed must have caught the jealousy in Keta's voice, and gave the Keeper a curious look, but Ashok didn't seem to notice at all.

"I have not asked Thera. I do not put as much stock into the enigmatic riddles the Voice dispenses as you do. I have come because you once proclaimed there was a prophecy that when the time came the gods would provide us with weapons that could defeat even the forces of the Law. I believe that time will be upon us soon. Was that an idle boast, or do you actually have a plan?"

He knew Ashok intended no offense, but that didn't change the sting. It was as if he was saying Keta had done nothing here, and this marvelous society outside the Law had just sprung into existence all by itself.

"The gods don't make idle boasts, Ashok. You should know that by now. They've already begun providing weapons to ensure our freedom, and I'm sure there will be more to come. Let's go right now. I'll show you."

He had never spoken of this secret to anyone else, but it was time. Keta walked out of the church.

Curious, Ashok followed. As did Javed. Good. Let them all see that he had not spent his time idle. He had been hard at work long before any of them had ever become involved in the gods' great work.

"Javed, would you kindly get a few men with shovels? And Ashok, you will want your war leaders to see this."

They set out upon the single road that wound down the crater. To their right were the buildings carved by the ancients, imposing and mysterious, while toward their left was the pit. To step off here would mean a steep drop to the next terrace down, or if you got enough of a running start, perhaps all the way to the hot lake at the bottom.

Keta didn't know much about construction, but enough to know that this place was truly remarkable. If it wasn't for the dam and reservoir above them, and the drainage tunnels to divert the overflow, most of the crater would be filled with water. It was truly a miracle the valves still worked. He had seen the legendary architecture of Vadal City. The buildings in the Cove, even though rather plain and square in comparison to the ornate carved facades of the Vadal, were every bit as big, and probably far sturdier. The same road circled the interior all the way down, thirteen levels, and somehow maintained a nearly continuous gentle grade. The road's surface was made of layer upon layer of gravel and tar. Both materials had probably come from the interior of the crater, since there were dig pits along the interior, and an oil seep that had turned the lowest terrace into a marshy bog.

The Cove was truly a blessed place, with seemingly endless resources. The ancient dam fed them clean water, the slopes had plenty of trees to cut, and they could even get oil for their lanterns below. Even during the bitter winter, the lake at the bottom remained steaming hot. Warm air rose up the pit and kept the place temperate. Even with the new arrivals the place wasn't even close to crowded. The casteless still liked to sleep piled up in the same room because it was what they were used to, but they could spread out and live like the first caste, everyone in their own quarters if they felt like it. There were hundreds of rooms, and still more being discovered all the time.

The thing they'd not found yet was another way out. There was the main drainage tunnel, and that was all. Perhaps someone like Ashok could scale the rocks above, or a wizard could fly out, but for the rest, if the Cove was besieged, there would be no escape. Ratul, recognizing that weakness, had prepared a way for the faithful to defend themselves. Keta had found the instructions the previous Keeper had left behind, but had not tried to use them yet. Ratul had been very specific that they should not reveal these tools too early, because then the rebellion would squander them piecemeal, like they had in the past.

By the time he reached their destination, they had drawn a bit of a crowd. Javed had gathered a few freemen and their tools. Ashok had found one of his havildars—the polite young man from Kharsawan thankfully, instead of the tattoo-faced maniac Somsak—and several of the faithful had seen them walking, become curious, and tagged along.

There was a patch of flat dirt at the end of the top level. If they had been in a regular city, it would've been thought of as an empty lot. Nothing grew here but weeds. Keta counted off a careful twenty paces toward the center, prayed to the gods that Ratul's note had been accurate, and ordered, "Dig here."

The laborers had no idea what was going on, but they did as he directed. Ashok watched, mildly amused. "What manner of treasure did your gods leave us that it needed to be planted in the soil?"

"Perhaps it is a potato," Javed said.

Ashok actually laughed.

"The gods didn't *plant* it," Keta said defensively. "Keeper Ratul did."

Ashok's laughter died. That had got his attention.

The hole got deeper and deeper until the diggers were waist deep. When one of the casteless grew weary in the sun, the warrior Eklavya jumped into the hole and took over for him. And when the other did too, Javed took his shovel. Time passed, but the two of them were strong, and eager to see what was down there.

"It looks like they are digging a grave," Ashok suggested.

A grave for the Law maybe, Keta thought, and then wondered how he could work that symbolism into his next sermon.

Four feet down one of the shovels hit something solid. Eklavya scraped at it, then declared, "It's wood."

Javed thumped it with his shovel and was rewarded with a hollow *thunk*. "I think it's a crate."

"No," Keta corrected. "It's a trapdoor. You'll need to clear it all off so we can open it." He turned to one of the faithful women who had been watching. "Shalini, would you fetch us a rope?"

Ashok looked down the row of buildings that had been carved from the rock, and then noted how this one rectangular area was suspiciously empty. "Ratul buried a house."

"Only a small one. Ratul was a very busy man. He said it had probably been a root cellar. He buried it only after he filled it with potent weapons delivered by the gods themselves. It has been sealed to protect them from the elements."

Ashok jumped down into the hole. "Give me that," he said as he took Eklavya's shovel and went to work. Their general moved with such inhuman energy that the other men simply had to get out of the way. A few minutes of Ashok's frenzied labor was equivalent to what a regular man could do in half an hour. Once the hatch was mostly uncovered, Ashok pried up one edge with the shovel blade, leveraged it up enough to get his fingers in, and then wrenched it free. It still had hundreds of pounds of dirt on it, but Ashok didn't seem to notice.

Keta walked to the edge and looked down. It was very dark inside, but he could make out a stone floor below.

Ashok didn't wait for the rope. He simply stepped into the dark. It was a good eight-foot drop, but he landed softly. Keta could see their general turning in a slow circle as he took in the contents, then he moved out of sight. There was the sound of heavy wood being dragged across stone. A moment later, Ashok swore, "Saltwater."

"What is it?" Keta called.

"Get down here, Keeper. Now."

Shalini had come back with a rope. Eklavya secured it, and Javed tried to help Keta down. He brushed his assistant's hand away. Keta was not by nature an athletic man, but he could scale a rope just fine.

The air was choked with fresh dust, and the motes swam through the beam of sunlight.

"It's very dark in here," Keta muttered as his sandals hit the floor. "We need a lantern."

"No fire!" Ashok snapped. Then he thought better of it, raised his head toward the light and bellowed, "Eklavya, allow no lanterns, no torches, or sparks, anywhere near here."

"Yes, sir."

Ashok grabbed Keta by the sleeve. "Try not to move in a way that makes static."

Keta was not sure what that meant, so he held perfectly still. The air felt very cool and dry, probably why Ratul had picked this particular hole. As his eyes adjusted, he realized that the room looked much like every other one the ancients had carved, but it was much bigger than expected. There were wooden casks stacked along one wall, and rectangular crates and square boxes against the other. Ashok had pulled the lid off of one of the big ones.

Inside the crate were Fortress rods, the long type, side by side, packed in what appeared to be grease. He'd seen these things before, even used one himself once to try it out. It had punched him in the shoulder hard enough to leave a bruise and had made his ears ring for a day, and his target, a melon, had exploded rather spectacularly. The rebellion had acquired nearly twenty of the frightening devices over the years from the crazed alchemists of Fortress. Their strange island was just off the Ice Coast of Akershan. But those twenty weapons were spread all over the great house, and they'd probably lost half of them when Chakma was retaken. There were six in this one box alone.

Then Keta realized there were many more of that same size crate. He counted ten.

They must have been thinking of the same question, because Ashok pulled the lid off the next crate with his bare hands. It should have taken a pry bar because of the nails, but Ashok didn't care. Inside were six more of the devastating fiery-arms. Then Ashok tried one more crate and found the same number inside.

That meant . . . *Sixty rods! Oceans!* Ratul really had been busy.

Then Keta turned toward the wall with all the casks, and realized those must be filled with the deadly, black Fortress powder, which burned with a fire so intense and rapid that it obliterated anything nearby. No wonder Ashok had shouted his warning about fire. The last time Ashok had dealt with the stuff it had blown a mansion to pieces and left him buried in the rubble for days.

Keta and Thera had been taught how to make Fortress powder years ago by a cagey old rebel who had claimed to have learned it from an actual Fortress alchemist hiding somewhere in Lok. It wasn't that complicated, really, dehydrated stale piss, sulfur, and charcoal in the right proportions, but they'd only ever made a few jugs of the stuff. The quantity stored here was simply insane in comparison.

Ashok broke open one of the smaller boxes with his heel. Then he reached inside and pulled out a fistful of something. Keta squinted to see, so Ashok stuck his hand into the light. They were balls of gray lead. Ashok gave Keta a pained look as he let them drop from his fingers. They hit the stone, and rolled away, one by one. Disgusted, Ashok wiped the gray residue they left on his hand onto his pants.

"There is nothing more illegal than this," Ashok whispered. "I've never heard of so many of these things in one place at a single time. This is a profound evil."

"The Law says our very existence is evil, Ashok! Mine, yours, Thera's, all these good people counting on us. And that existence will end if we can't defend ourselves. These things are no different in principle than a crossbow, just stronger and louder, and they're far less dangerous than your beloved Angruvadal was. The important thing isn't what they can do, but what the warriors think they can do! Once they know we have these, even the Capitol will be afraid to come against us!"

"I do not like this," Ashok muttered.

"Don't let your heart be bothered. A weapon is only as evil as the man who bears it." Keta couldn't find his voice to proclaim his own desires, but the Keeper of Names did not hesitate to speak with fire and passion in defense of the faithful. "Let us vow to use these for good, only for self-defense, only to save innocent lives."

Ashok seemed unconvinced, but he had no choice. He was a slave to his vows. Keta was the real free-man here.

"I've sworn to protect the prophet, and by extension, her people, but *this* . . ." he gestured at the rods. "This fills me with unease. This changes everything."

"Why? Because with them our casteless rabble actually stands a fighting chance against the mighty forces of the Law?"

Ashok thought about it for a long, painful moment. "Exactly."

"I told you the gods would provide."

Chapter 34

～～～～

Vadal City was a loud, busy place. One of the biggest and most crowded cities in all of Lok was not enjoyable for a man who preferred quiet contemplation. He had grown tired of the constant chatter and hum weeks ago.

It was probably one of the richest cities too, with vast markets that rivaled even the Capitol's legendary bazaars. It was said you could buy anything in the markets of Vadal City if you knew where to look. There were thousands of people coming through here every day, buying, selling, haggling, and thieving.

Nobody noticed just another leprous beggar.

Covered in dirty rags from head to toe, the beggar sat in the shade of a brick wall. On the other side of the wall was a smith who specialized in repairing the tools of the worker caste. The constant hammering was making it more difficult for him to eavesdrop on the conversations on the fourth floor of the building across the street, but since this position enabled him to see the only exits, it was still the best place to wait.

The beggar had set a tin cup in front of him. It was empty. Vadal City was wealthy, but they had no charity for a beggar who just sat there. In this colorful place, even their lepers had to be entertaining if they expected scraps. The ones who sang songs, or danced for people's amusement, their cups got coins, and occasionally a whole note even. He had never learned to dance, plus he didn't dare stand up, because then people would notice how alarmingly large he was. His deep voice was surprisingly good for certain songs, hardy, western marching songs mostly, but he did not wish to draw that much attention to himself.

The snake charmers made good money it seemed. They played flutes *and* the people were always excited at the opportunity to see a cobra bite someone. Even the beggars who crawled along on moldering stumps telling sob-inducing stories designed to elicit pity got something dropped in their cups. He got nothing, because he just sat there, trying not to be noticed. He made a terrible beggar. It was a good thing he had been obligated to a different career in his youth.

Across the street was a textile shop. The apartments above it were rented out to merchants and travelers, and sometimes Inquisition witch hunters pretending to be merchants, which was what brought him here today. The topmost floor had windows which granted a view of the walls and towers of the magnificent great house, less than a quarter mile away.

It was a good staging area if your primary mission was to spy upon the keep itself, especially since from the top floor you could sneak out onto the roof tops at night to peer down into the grounds. The tiger man and some of his lackies had been staying there for the last month. Which meant the beggar had been here slightly less time than that, because it had taken him a few days to track them down.

Lying in garbage in soiled rags that hid all but his eyes, for weeks on end, didn't leave much time for other activity, but this beggar was a man of single-minded determination. Whenever the watch came by and prodded him with their spear shafts to check if he was still alive, he would move enough to let them know they didn't need to call for the corpse collectors quite yet. When he was sure the Inquisitors on the fourth floor were sleeping, he would get up and find something to eat. Since he couldn't just obligate some lesser status person to give him nourishment on demand as he was used to, eating usually meant picking things out of the trash that would make a fish-eater vomit. On the bright side, he was immune to illness. Though eating garbage still made his stomach ache. Discomfort was part of the job. He had done worse.

Even though it was a few hours after sundown the market remained busy. The Capitol markets stayed open all night because it was so damnably hot there that the people became almost nocturnal, sleeping through the worst of the unforgiving sun. Vadal had wonderful weather year round. These people had no excuse for conducting business at inappropriate times. They were addicted to trade. In the far west—where he was from—people kept sensible hours, rising with the sun and not staying up too late, so they would be able to labor in the fields again the next day. In Uttara even the warriors and the first caste kept farmers' hours.

But not Vadal City. There was no time for sleep.

Only trading and music. These people never seemed to stop with the singing. So it was difficult to weed out the hundreds of other excited voices to focus in on the magical conversation that was happening on the fourth floor. Luckily the witch hunter had left the window open.

It was barely a whisper, audible only because of the Heart of the Mountain. He could tell that the words were being delivered by magic, an *extremely* expensive method of communication. Thus this message must be an important one. Once he recognized the magical voice as belonging to Grand Inquisitor Omand himself, his suspicions were confirmed.

"Khoja, we have found Vikram Akershan. He does not appear to have the mirror. Nor was it at the bottom of Red Lake. I must assume that he has given it to the librarian. I am aware of the risk, but you must strike as soon as possible. See if she has the mirror. That is the most important thing. Take her, alive preferably, and bring her back to the dome for safekeeping. If you are unable to do so, make her death look like the fault of the Vadal. It is vital that you are not caught. It is better to die quietly than be discovered as one of us. If taken alive, you will be disavowed. I know you will succeed though, because you were one of my best students. Good luck."

That was all the beggar needed to hear. As he stood up and stretched, his back cracked. After a month of shambling about hunched over, it was the first time he'd shown anyone in the market his full, rather impressive, height. Several people noticed him, because they were not used to shaggy lepers a full head taller than most.

Rather than walk across the street, he turned and went into the smith's shop. A bell rang as he opened the door. "Excuse me," he said to the waiting customers, as he cut in line. Because of his stink and the filth upon his rags, the workers quickly tried to get out of his way.

"Begone, untouchable!" the smith shouted, as he did every time he'd seen the beggar around his place of business. But then the expression on the man's face changed when he saw the sudden difference in the beggar's demeanor. Like most smiths, he was well muscled, but it was plain just from the sheer presence of the man that this beggar could snap him like a twig. This was no mangy stray as believed, but a deadly wolf. It was amazing the difference just standing straight did. Good posture was very important.

"I need to borrow a hammer." He didn't speak like a humble, down-on-his-luck dreg of society, but rather a man of status.

"What?"

"A hammer. All of my weapons and armor were on a pack horse. I believe it was eaten by a magical tiger. It's a long story. I would show you the token of my office to make this official, but it was on the same horse. Hurry up. I need to go kill someone. Give me a hammer. *Now.*"

His words and demeanor frightened the other customers, and the bell rang again as some workers fled out the door, probably to get the guard. The smith was rather confused by all this, but he didn't argue with the suddenly frightening giant in rags. Instead, he went back into his forge, and called out. "What kind of hammer?"

"The biggest one you have."

The smith returned a moment later. "How about this one?"

He took it from the smith's hands and hefted it. It was about a two-pound head, on a handle of about eight inches of stout hickory. It wasn't a proper war hammer, but it would have to do. "Acceptable." Then he noticed that the smith had retreated back behind his counter. There was a great number of powders and concoctions for the searing and staining of metals on the shelf behind him. He pointed with the hammer. "Is that red powder the kind that makes smoke that burns your eyes out?"

"Yes. It's for the etching of zinc or steel. The green is for copper."

He stuck the hammer through his belt, and then grabbed both bottles from the shelf.

"Be careful! If those two mix together they'll make a caustic cloud that'll rip our lungs apart."

"Excellent. This will be all."

"How're you gonna pay for those?"

"I'm not."

"Who are you?" the smith stammered.

"Protector of the Law, nineteen-year senior, Karno Uttara." The bell rang as he left.

Karno walked across the street and into the textile shop, which—once again—upset the clean and non-stinking customers.

"You can't come in here, leper!" the shopkeeper shouted. "I'll call the watch!"

"Send for the corpse collectors as well," Karno said as he made his way between the shelves of colorful fabrics. "They will be needed."

He walked up the stairs, each heavy footfall slow and methodical. There was no need to rush. Khoja would need time to gather all his Inquisitors in the city. It would be very difficult to get into the well-guarded great house, and if they made it out with Rada alive, they would still need to exfiltrate the city. They would not attack until the darkest, sleepiest part of the night, when the Personal Guard would be sleepy and vulnerable.

There were two rooms on the top floor, both rented by Inquisitors pretending to be something else. Karno had watched their comings and goings. Even without their masks they were easy for him to spot. Predators recognized other predators . . . Unless of course one of them was wrapped in rags and lying in a gutter, but most people were not as dedicated to their work as Blunt Karno.

The witch hunter must have been eager to get started, because he had already dispatched one messenger. Karno heard the slap of sandals rushing down, so he put the jars of poison off to the side, squeezed his bulk into the corner beneath the stairs of the second floor and waited.

The Inquisitor was a young man that Karno had seen many times over the last few weeks. He had never left anything in the beggar's cup. As he rushed past, Karno stepped out, wrapped one massive arm around his neck, and hoisted him from the ground. He didn't even need to use the Heart of the Mountain for that. Karno was simply that strong. To his credit, the Inquisitor was tough, so rather than panic, he kicked Karno in the leg—a move which was basically useless against a man of his density—while pulling his hidden knife. Karno simply caught that wrist and squeezed the bones together. The knife fell and stuck into the floor. A moment later the Inquisitor was out of air and thrashing.

"How many remain upstairs?" Karno relaxed his bicep enough to let his victim get a breath. "Tell me and I'll let you live."

"Two," he lied.

Karno knew there was double that, possibly more. It was a good effort on the Inquisitor's part, trying to get him killed like that. He could respect it, but he snapped the man's neck anyway because he had a job to do. Devedas had asked him to protect Rada. That obligation didn't end simply because he'd been bitten by a tiger, stabbed six times, and then been left for dead facedown in a lake.

He dumped the body quietly, gathered his jars, and then proceeded to the top floor. There was a small landing with two doors. He'd watched the windows, so he knew Khoja slept in the last room, and that was where he had just received the message from the Grand Inquisitor. Pausing to sharpen his hearing, Karno found that there was movement in both rooms, and from the sounds of steel clanking and leather creaking, Khoja had already passed on Omand's orders. They were arming up, preparing for their raid.

He unscrewed the lids of both jars. Even holding his breath, the vapors that came out made his eyes water. He tried the first door. It was unlocked. He opened it to reveal there were two Inquisitors inside, dressing in dark clothing and buckling on sword belts. Before either could react, he hurled the jars across the room. They spun, dumping their glittering contents through the air. Then Karno closed that door to let them sort it out.

The angry shouts turned to screaming, and then coughing. As they desperately flung themselves at the door to open it. Karno just placed his bulk against it to hold it closed. Karno was immovable. He pulled the smith's hammer from his belt and waited for the rest to react to the noise.

It didn't take long.

The other door flew open and an Inquisitor ran out. She was dressed as a slave of the great house, a common enough sight in the market, so that told him what their plan to snatch Rada had been. She produced a pair of knives from seemingly out of nowhere and came at him, jabbing and slashing. The Inquisitor was very good.

Karno was better.

Keeping most of his weight against the door so the others couldn't escape, he intercepted one blade with the hammer's handle. Then knocked the other aside with his palm, and then the first again by catching her forearm with his elbow. She kicked him in the thigh. He took it. She slashed for his neck. He smashed the hammer into her arm. A good impact, but only enough to bruise flesh, not break bones. She cried out and retreated.

Another Inquisitor rushed into the hall carrying a curved sword. It was relatively short, but still had more reach than his little worker's hammer. The thumping to his back had weakened. Either they were dying, or one of them had run off to try and climb out the window. So Karno stepped away as the sword zipped through the air to rebound off the wood.

The door flew open, temporarily blocking the swordsman. An Inquisitor spilled out, clawing at his eyes and wheezing. Karno shoved him, sending him flipping over the railing where he bounced headfirst off the stairs below.

A horrible, tear-inducing cloud rolled into the hall. Hopefully the place would air out before the watch arrived. He didn't want to harm any Law-abiding people. But these scheming Inquisitors? *To the oceans with them.*

The swordsman pushed past the door. Karno kicked it into him, putting him off balance. Then he pushed forward. The curved blade came up in a disemboweling arc, but Karno knew all the tricks. He'd spent decades learning how to apply brute power and blunt force against the best swordsmen in the world. This was child's play for a man who'd learned from Ratul and trained with the likes of Ashok or Devedas. He kept driving forward, not giving the swordsman room to work.

The woman darted past both of them. He swung for her head, but she dived forward, rolled, and came right back up. One of her knives zipped through his rags, but missed his skin. Only now he had an enemy on both sides. Oh, she was very good indeed.

The three of them shifted back and forth. The smaller Inquisitors lunged at their bigger target, but then danced back before he could strike them. The poorly constructed landing shook beneath their feet. The poor things actually thought they had him. He had no time for this foolishness, so Karno called upon the Heart of the Mountain to grant him speed.

They did not see that coming.

The edge of the sword was meant for his head, but he caught it with the hammer, hooked it sharply downward, and then brought the chunk of iron back into the Inquisitor's face. Teeth flew. Blood sprayed the walls. He turned, as the woman's knife missed his back, spinning into her, and the hammer clipped her shoulder hard enough to break her collarbone. She stumbled. He kicked her *through* the railing. She bounced off the far wall, missed the stairs, and plummeted the four stories into the middle of the textile shop.

The swordsman swung desperately. Karno stepped inside, blocked it, arm to arm. He latched onto the sleeve with his free hand and twisted, grinding joints, leveraging the man down. When the back of his skull was exposed, Karno hit him with the hammer, a solid whack, right to the base of the neck. The impact planted the Inquisitor hard enough to break the floorboards beneath.

The Protector looked up to see Khoja standing in the final room, staring at him, furious. Karno's rags had slipped during the fight, allowing the witch hunter to see his face. "I was told you were dead."

"They were mistaken, Witch Hunter Khoja..." He nodded in greeting. "Rada is in my protection. I will not let you harm her."

"I didn't want to. I had a very good plan to sneak her out alive, but you ruined it. If she dies now, it's on your head."

The last Inquisitor he had gassed stumbled onto the landing in a red haze. Karno brained him with the hammer. But that momentary distraction had been all that the experienced Khoja had needed. Because when Karno looked back, the man was gone, replaced with a tiger.

And it leapt out the window.

Karno ran over, only to see that the sleek form was bounding swiftly away, leaping across the darkened rooftops of Vadal City, heading straight for the walls of the great house. The Protector climbed out the window and gave chase.

Chapter 35

Rada was sitting in her room reading a book, as was her after-dinner custom, when all the shouting started.

That was most unusual. The great house was usually rather peaceful after dark. Harta had no patience for frivolity. Even the soldiers, whom she imagined were as raucous as all young men tended to be, remained extremely polite and professional when their Thakoor was in residence. The house slaves were not given to outbursts either. So what was all that racket?

She carefully marked her page with a bookmark so she wouldn't lose her place then walked to the door to see what was going on out there. One of the Personal Guard was rushing up the hall. Surprisingly, his sword was in hand. It was rare to see steel drawn here. The last time had been when Harta had been about to execute that poor fellow Jagdish, and it had been months since she had saved his life.

"What's going on?"

"An intruder's been seen on the grounds. Stay in your quarters and lock the doors!"

Rada quickly closed the door and threw the bolt.

The warrior had seemed genuinely afraid. Even as paranoid as Harta was about assassins, there hadn't been an alarm raised the entire time she'd been here. Below her balcony she heard more men running through the gardens. It had to be something serious to cause this much consternation.

Then Rada realized that she could hear them so precisely because she'd left the balcony door open. The night breeze in Vadal lands was as refreshing and fragrant as all the books about the place had claimed, so she liked to leave it open. She was on the second floor, but Harta was worried about wizard assassins, and what was climbing an ivy-covered wall to a wizard?

The silk curtains were drifting in the air. She brushed them aside, closed the balcony door, and locked it as well. That ought to do it.

She turned around and bumped into the black-clad man who had been standing behind the curtain.

Startled, she jumped back, but before she could even let out a shriek he struck her in the face.

Rada had never been hit before. Not like that. The floor rushed up to meet her. The room was spinning. She could taste her own blood.

Worst of all, she realized that he had broken her glasses. They were lying there, in pieces. And then he kicked her in the stomach hard enough to send her sliding across the floor.

There was no air. She couldn't breathe. Then her muscles unclenched enough to gasp for air. The man crouched next to her, smashed one hand against her

mouth and ground her head against the rug. She tried
to struggle but he was insanely strong.

"Stop it, silly girl," he hissed. "Make a sound and
you die."

She could feel the hot indent of his knuckles on
her cheek.

"Where is the mirror? Do you have the mirror?
Tell me. Now!"

It was the witch hunter who had tried to take her
in Apura. "What mirror? I—"

He hit her. Then he hit her again. And again. In
the face. In the chest. He put his knee on her pelvis
and let his weight rest upon it. He jabbed one thumb
under her jaw, into the bundle of nerves there, and
pushed. She screamed, but it was uselessly muffled
because his other hand was clamped over her mouth.

It was the worst pain she'd ever felt. He could
have killed her, easily. But he didn't. He didn't want
her to die. He wanted her to suffer. "Where is the
mirror, Librarian? Tell me, or I'll beat you to death
and then search for it myself. My orders are to take
you alive if possible, but that's secondary to reclaim-
ing the mirror." He took his hand away so she could
answer, but then before she could, backhanded her
across the eyes. "Where?"

She was crying. She didn't even mean to. The tears
were just falling out. One eye was swollen shut. Her
ears were ringing. "In the satchel. Hidden behind
the wardrobe."

The brutal witch hunter stood up, dragged the piece
of furniture out of the way, and retrieved her bag. He
opened the flap, looked inside, and seeming satisfied,
closed it. He threw the strap over one shoulder and

went back for her. "Here's how this is going to go, Librarian. My master wants you alive, but he wants this mirror more. I regret this unsubtle method, but your friend forced the issue. You're coming with me. Cooperate, stay quiet, and you get to live. Cry for help, and I'll kill you." He grabbed her by the arm and roughly yanked her to her feet. "Let's go."

Rather than go to the hall, he tugged her toward the balcony and undid the latch she'd uselessly fixed. Once outside, he paused there, in the dark, scanning across the garden. There were lanterns moving about, but none near enough to see them. She didn't know what he intended to do. She was in a dress. She could hardly climb—

He wrapped one extremely firm arm around her waist. "Make a sound and I'll slit your throat." And then he vaulted over the edge with her.

They hit the grass and rolled. The Inquisitor seemed fine. Rada was so shaken she could barely stand, but he dragged her back up again. They went around the corner of a sculpted hedge. "Don't scream when you see what I've done here."

She didn't know what he was talking about, but then she tripped over something, and landed in a puddle that was hot and slick. With a shock she realized that she was on top of a mangled body. Before she could reflexively cry out, his hand was over her mouth again. It was one of the Personal Guard, and though it was hard to tell in the shadows, it looked like he had been ripped apart by a wild animal . . . By a *tiger*.

"That's right, Rada," he whispered in her ear. "You're just slowing me down. Inconvenience me too much and I will change form. Whenever I want to, I can just jump over the wall to escape, but the last thing I would do before that is eat your pretty face. Come on."

As he pulled her out of the blood puddle, her hand landed on something, hard and metallic. She nicked herself on the sharp edge before realizing what it was.

Rada palmed the warrior's knife. She kept the blade up along her forearm so it wouldn't be seen.

The witch hunter shoved her along ahead of him, as he kept looking back over his shoulder. Harta's wizards would be on the prowl and he knew it. The guards were still shouting but their noise seemed to be getting farther away. The gardens were extensive and confusing in the dark, but the witch hunter seemed to know where he was going. She assumed they were heading for the back gate.

If he got her out into the city, they would disappear. And then she would be taken to the dome. They'd either kill her for knowing too much, or they'd use her as a hostage to try and force Devedas to their will, but she knew such a man would never bend to evil men, no matter how much he loved her. So she was dead either way.

Rada was no warrior. She'd seen bloodshed, several times now, but it wasn't her way. She was first caste. They had people for that. She was terrified, in pain, and desperate, but she had nothing to lose. It made the choice to fight easy.

She waited until they got closer to the back gate. There were bound to be guards there. They were in the deep shadows, but the smell told her they were getting close to the stables. The witch hunter paused, listening. There were voices ahead. She didn't know what his plan was, but she doubted they were getting out without him murdering more members of the Personal Guard, and she'd become quite fond of a few of them.

"He's here..." the witch hunter murmured, though she didn't know who he was worried about.

The horses inside the stables whinnied and stamped nervously. Maybe they smelled the blood on her clothes, or maybe the witch hunter still had some tiger scent lingering on him—she didn't know how such things worked—but they were afraid. Not as afraid as she was, obviously. But hopefully afraid enough their noise would attract a guard.

Sure enough, she saw a lantern approaching. She caught a brief glimpse of the blue-gray and bronze uniform of House Vadal as the light swung back and forth. The guard was heading their way. The witch hunter slowly reached for the sword on his hip. The Personal Guard were loyal to their master, but a few of them had gone out of their way to be kind to her, even keeping her company during her stressful stay. She would not have any more of their deaths on her hands. Not if she could help it.

Once all his attention seemed to be upon the approaching guard, Rada turned the knife around in her hand. The handle was still sticky with its owner's blood. She'd read many textbooks on anatomy, but strangely enough that didn't translate to real life confidence as to where to stick a man.

He was still holding onto her other arm, so he was close. Too close to miss.

Rada drove the knife into his back.

The Witch Hunter reacted immediately, far faster than she'd expected. He still had her arm, so he twisted it hard, then he drove it back into the socket. She had no choice, it was drop or break the bone. She went to her knees, and he side-kicked her in the ribs. Rada crashed hard against the wooden stable. Her head rebounded off a board, leaving her dazed.

The satchel containing the mirror had fallen on the ground. Grimacing, the witch hunter reached back and found the handle still sticking out of him. As he plucked the knife from his body, he let out a wheezing hiss at the pain. "Library bitch!" Then he grabbed hold of something attached to his belt. The air seemed to shimmer with something far darker than the night, like a perfectly black cloud, and then a tiger stepped out.

It padded toward her. Rada was still stunned from the impact. All she could understand was *teeth*. Razor-sharp *teeth*.

Terrified, Rada tried to get to her feet, but the tiger pounced. Effortlessly knocking her back down and pinning her beneath. She could feel his hot breath on her neck.

Right before the jaws closed around her throat, the tiger was *gone*.

Someone had leapt from the top of the stable and tackled the beast. The two forms went rolling across the grass into the moonlight. It was a flash of furious movement, one orange, black, and white, the other in ragged, dirty clothing. The human being came up on top. For one brief moment Rada saw a hammer rise, and then *pow!* It came down on the tiger. The man hit it like that several times, beating it like the drum in a Capitol pageant, whaling on it as the tiger twisted and thrashed.

But the tiger got his hind legs up onto the man's chest, sunk the claws in deep, and then hurled him away.

The tattered man hit the wall next to her. The horses inside were screaming in panic at the presence of the great cat. With a shock, Rada realized who it was.

"Karno?"

The tiger was injured. Its head seemed misshapen. One of its front legs was hanging, limp. Rather than try to finish her, he lunged for the satchel to snatch up the strap in his jaws.

"The mirror!" Rada cried out.

Karno flung his weapon. It spun through the air and clipped the tiger on the side of his head. The tiger lurched to the side. The satchel came open, and the mirror rolled out. It flopped over, the terrifying, reflective side up, right between the two foes.

The tiger was stumbling, dizzy, but Karno was having a hard time getting up as well. Both of them were hurting. There was a lot of blood leaking from the toe-claw holes on his chest. It had slashed him wide open. She couldn't lose him, get him back, and then lose him again.

Only the tiger form had been broken. There was that black flash again, and the animal was gone, leaving only the witch hunter. Except now there was a jagged bone sticking out of his forearm and the side of his head was covered in his own blood. "Damn you, Librarian." It was obvious he wanted nothing more than to end her, but he hadn't been lying earlier. The mirror came first. "This isn't over," he said as he limped toward the treasure.

The witch hunter reached down to grab the mirror. Rada's head was pounding too much to stop him. Karno seemed to be meditating or something. However Protector magic worked, Karno's was occupied with keeping him from bleeding to death.

Except then the oddest thing happened. When the

witch hunter went to scoop up the device, his fingers went *through* it. Just for a moment, as if it wasn't a mirror at all, but rather a *hole*. To where, she didn't know, and never wanted to find out.

The witch hunter tugged. Only whatever lived in the mirror, whatever odd thing it was that she'd seen floating in the vastness of space when she'd first tested the device in Vikram's basement, *did not let go*. It pulled *back*. Suddenly the witch hunter fell forward, his arm disappearing up to his elbow into the mirror. "What is this?" He pulled hard, trying to free himself.

It was terrifying, watching a piece of black steel devouring a man, but also strangely fascinating, and Rada couldn't look away.

The quiet murderer may have been hard as nails, but he let out a bloodcurdling shriek as the mirror swallowed him up to his armpit. "Let go of me!"

Karno had finished concentrating on whatever he'd been thinking about, because he got up, took hold of one of the boards of the stable fence, and wrenched it off. He went over to the trapped witch hunter, and then bashed him over the head with it. The board snapped in half, but so did the witch hunter's skull.

The body rolled off the Asura's Mirror. The mirror looked exactly the same as before.

"Where'd his arm go?" Karno asked.

"I don't know."

She should have been frozen with terror, but remarkably her muscles still worked. Evil or not, that thing had been entrusted to her. It might have just eaten a man's limb, but it was still her obligation. She had promised Vikram to keep it from the Inquisitors, so she grabbed her satchel, and used the leather to protect her hands as she maneuvered the mirror inside safely. Despite what she'd just seen, the Asura's Mirror didn't do anything odd to her. Once it was secure, she stumbled to Karno's side.

"I thought you were dead! Are you all right?"

He looked down at the weeping lacerations across his torso. Somehow, the blood had slowed to a mere trickle. "I'll be fine. You look awful."

She'd assumed as much. Her face felt like it was on fire. She could barely see, barely hear past the pounding headache, and couldn't stand without wobbling. She didn't know how warriors dealt with this sort of abusive nonsense all the time.

"Don't move!" someone snapped at them.

She recognized the voice. "Luthra?" Rada turned and saw that he was the guard with the lantern. His sword was in his other hand and pointed directly at Karno. Luthra took in the dead witch hunter, and Rada, but he didn't lower the weapon. Karno looked like he was in great pain, having just had his chest clawed to ribbons, but she knew the Protector would still easily defeat a regular soldier.

"Luthra is a friend, Karno."

"Rada, what's going on? Are you all right?" the guard demanded.

"This wizard beat me, but I'm fine." That was a lie. She very much wanted nothing more than to lie on the ground and sob but fighting to the death certainly caused a cascade of conflicting emotions.

"We saw the tiger scale the walls and sounded the alarm. So the assassin was here for you, not Lord Harta. And this"—he looked up . . . and up—"must be the Protector Karno you talked so much about."

"He is," she assured him. "He saved my life. Again. You'll find the dead man is the Inquisitor we faced in Apura the night we first met."

"Let's get you to the surgeon," Luthra said.

"Hold, Warrior," Karno said as he put his big arm over Rada's shoulder. She wasn't sure if he was helping hold her up, or if she was helping prop him up. It could go either way. "The Inquisition will not rest now. Her only chance is to vanish. Your Thakoor thinks he can use her to bargain with, but it's no longer safe for her here. Rada needs to be in Protector custody. Give her to me."

"My Thakoor doesn't give a fish about the Protectors, certainly not here!" Luthra looked back and forth between them. He had always seemed to her a kind man, but also a smart and loyal one. His obligation was to protect his house. He should have ordered her back to her room and had his men deal with Karno. Except Luthra didn't shout for reinforcements. Instead he looked back toward the gate, and then toward the great house, obviously torn. "Oceans."

"Please, Luthra." Her face was beginning to swell so much it was hard to talk. "Either they'll murder me, or eventually Harta will sell me to the Inquisition. You know your master will as soon as they name the right price. Have mercy, please."

She and Luthra both knew that though Harta wasn't exactly an evil man, he wasn't a good one either. The Thakoor constantly talked about how the first caste needed to make the difficult decisions, spending lives like notes. Rada knew she was just another asset, to be used, and then liquidated when inconvenient.

"I'm obligated to serve my house and the Law.

This is one or the other! Protectors are the Law, but between the Law and Vadal, my heart belongs to Vadal... Only I don't see how it benefits Vadal to have another innocent woman die on the dome. Oceans!" Luthra took pity on her and sheathed his sword. "I'm an idiot."

"Oh, thank you, Luthra, thank you."

"Luckily, for all of us, I never saw either of you. Most of us are congregating around the Thakoor's quarters. There are only regular warriors manning the gate while my unit searches the grounds. I'll call them over here when I find this body. That's your chance to sneak out. Get her out of here, Protector."

"A wise choice, Warrior," Karno said.

The two of them started walking away. "Where will we go?" she whispered.

"I'll think of something," Karno answered.

"Wait," Luthra called after them. "I know someone who would give you shelter. There's a man of very high status who owes Rada his life."

There was only one person he could be talking about. Luthra had passed on his message of sincere gratitude to her, but she'd not thought about it much since. She'd simply been trying to do the right thing. "You can't mean..."

"Yes. His estate is on the eastern border, but he's in this region recruiting warriors for his new garrison."

"This man would even hide her from your Thakoor?"

"He said he'd do anything for her and meant it. That particular favor I think he would do just out of spite."

"He is a man of honor?" Karno asked, suspicious, because those were few and far between.

"Very much so, Protector. His name is Jagdish."

Chapter 36

It was a clear dawn, but something in the air told Devedas that the weather was about to change. He thought about it as he sat next to the campfire, drinking his morning tea. Perhaps it was the sharp edge to the wind, or the way it caused waves to move across the endless fields of grass below, but there was definitely an energy, a tension, to the air. In the far south where Devedas had grown up, one needed to pay close attention to the weather, because if you were caught out in a storm in Devakula, you were usually never seen again.

It had been a fruitless season. While they'd searched for Ashok, the grass had grown tall and turned to gold. Spring had turned to summer, and in these lands that was a time of wind, lightning, and fires. He and his Protectors were camped on a rise at the edge of the western Akershan hills. To one side were steep mountains, still capped in snow, and to the other, were plains as far as the eye could see, only interrupted by the tents of the warrior caste, who had been obligated to be Devedas' hounds.

The hounds had lost the trail, but Ashok was close. Devedas knew that the same way he knew the weather was about to turn evil.

By the time they had left Chakma, wind, rain, and migrating herds had obliterated any trace of Ashok's passing. Without an indicator of where to go, they had begun a systematic search of the most likely region. They were checking every gully, ravine, cave, or hill, and questioning every shepherd, farmer, slave, and casteless they came across.

It was a terrible waste of ten Protectors. The Order wasn't very big to begin with. While they searched uselessly here, surely criminals elsewhere flourished. Or worse, criminals who should have been caught by them were being dealt with by the Inquisition instead, which made his order look ineffectual in comparison.

Unable to sleep, Devedas had risen early, so he had seen the tired warrior on a haggard horse ride into the camp long before dawn. Wherever the man had come from, he had been riding hard because his animal was lathered in sweat. He had ridden right to the phontho's tent to give his report. One did not wake a high-status man lightly, so it must have been important.

Since Devedas was above yet outside their official chain of command, he had not bothered to walk over to see what was going on. It would either concern him, or it would not. Whatever the news, he would deal with it after he broke his fast.

The Protector who had been on watch had been more curious than his commander, however. With Ashok's gang making a habit of ambushing warriors at night, Devedas had made sure that there was always at least one Protector with his augmented senses watching over the camp in addition to guards placed by the regular warriors. This shift belonged to six-year senior, Usman Thao.

"There's been a messenger, Lord Devedas."

"I saw. What was that about, Usman?"

"Word from the Capitol. The casteless extermination begins anew."

Devedas closed his eyes and swore. What in the salty hell were the judges thinking? There was no time for such foolishness. All they would accomplish was driving more desperate fools to join the rebels. When he opened his eyes again, Usman was still standing there, looking pained. He was a lanky young man, and obviously not wanting to give his commander news that was sure to upset him.

"There's more."

"Sorry, sir. Yes. They've expanded the scope of their killings and added three more regions, including the one we're in now. Our escort has been recalled and reassigned to help the culling. We're losing all our warriors."

Devedas' initial reaction was a flash of anger. Finding Ashok was far more important than massacring helpless fish-eaters. He didn't need them for the fight, but he needed scouts. He needed numbers to watch the plains and keeps their ears open. This was an insult. He was the *Lord Protector*. In this situation there were only a few people who had the authority to take away warriors he had already obligated. "Was this the Grand Inquisitor's doing?"

"No, sir. It's by orders of the highest Akershani judge in the Capitol, a man named Faril."

Omand may not have put his stamp on it himself, but since it was one of his lackeys he might as well have. Even when they were nominally on the same side, it was as if the Grand Inquisitor couldn't help himself. The nefarious mask was compelled to sabotage others. In his search for power Devedas had allied himself with the Grand Inquisitor, a decision which he had come to regret, but there was no turning back now. Frustrated, he wanted nothing more than to punch something, but it wouldn't do to show such emotion in front of his men.

"Oceans. Do these fools not realize they're only going to make things worse here?" But even as Devedas said it, he already knew the answer. Omand did nothing without weighing all the risks and rewards first. He had a reason. It was more than likely a selfish and evil one, but the reason would be there.

Usman continued his report. "They're going to break camp and then ride to the next town to put the casteless there to the sword . . . Or at least the ones stupid enough to stay put who didn't flee across the border weeks ago. I can't imagine there's too many left anywhere in the north of this house."

"You'd be surprised. A Protector has no home except where the Law tells us to be that day, so we forget most are not like us. They are creatures of habit, even the non-people. Leaving a home is hard when it's the only thing you've ever known, even when it's just a casteless shack where you sleep next to your pigs to stay warm. I imagine there will still be a great number of them available to kill pointlessly."

Yet that reminded him of a prediction he had made when they'd first arrived in these lands and seen the butchering of the casteless firsthand. His former brother wouldn't be able to abide such a crime, and let's be honest, whether the Law approved or not, this was a terrible crime. Devedas might not like the Great Extermination, but Ashok would *despise* it.

They were both children of the Law, but Devedas was also the son of a disgraced bearer and a conquered house, and that drive to regain what had been taken had shaped him into the man he was. Ashok had only the Law, and now that he had been stripped of it, would be compelled to create his own new Law. For without Law, Ashok was empty. He would not allow this crime, of that Devedas was certain, because they had been brothers once, closer than blood. Ashok was perhaps the finest killer who had ever lived, but he never delighted in bloodshed. He did what needed doing, and never more. The sheer excess of the Great Extermination would offend him to his core.

The slaughter had drawn Ashok out of hiding last time. It would surely do so again.

"This isn't right, sir," Usman said. "A Capitol judge may outrank you, but he's far away, and you're here. If you tell the warriors we still need them, they may balk at disobeying their house, but most of them would rather have the honor of hunting the Black Heart than the indignity of chopping up helpless untouchables. By the time word gets back to the Capitol, surely we'll have found the rebel's hiding place."

"No. Let them go."

Usman seemed uncertain. "I know you think he's near, but there's still a lot of mountains to search. Without our scouts, how will we find Ashok?"

"Don't worry." Devedas threw the last of his tea into the fire, and watched it hiss into steam. "He will find us."

Chapter 37

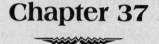

In a life filled with turmoil, the last few months in the Cove had been a rare season of peace. It had actually been...happy.

Such an unfamiliar feeling made Thera nervous.

She sat on the flat roof of what had once been their hospital, watching the warm glow of the sun rise over the eastern rim. This particular building was mostly empty now, avoided by most of the faithful because of the great many deaths that had occurred within its walls, but she'd never bothered to pick different quarters. She'd seen no need. Besides, the superstitious religious fanatics thinking the place was haunted gave her a little more privacy.

Living in a giant bowl surrounded by mountains meant the sun appeared late and set early. An extra hour of shadow was a small price to pay for food, warmth, and security. Since summer had come, she found sleeping beneath the stars more comfortable than sleeping inside a featureless stone square.

Ashok lay on the blanket next to her, still fast asleep. The man had a remarkable ability to go several days without stopping, and then sleep whenever the opportunity presented itself for as long as possible. She found it was better to let him rest while he could.

Thera watched Ashok's chest rise and fall with rhythmic breath. He was covered in scars, dozens of them. Punctures, lacerations, and burns, but whatever strange healing power the Protectors had had made all of those fade until they were little more than lighter traces on his deeply tanned skin. However, the biggest and most unfaded was the grisly mark where a molten shard of Angruvadal had been buried in his heart. He'd been cut so many times it was like reading a map, and every road had been a fight. Ashok's body was a testament to just how durable a body could be.

He'd received many of those trying to rescue her. This man had *died* trying to rescue her. Thera was too old and jaded to harbor a silly girl's ideas about romance, but say what you will, there was something about having a man willing to kill and die for you.

What had begun as a reluctant obligation, had turned into an unlikely partnership, and now . . . she didn't really know what to call it. For years she'd had to be suspicious and hard. It was the only way to survive. She could never relax, never relent. It was all strife, as people—or gods—tried to use her. The bolt had taken her health. Her arranged marriage had taken her pride. Wizards had taken her freedom. And demons had taken her hands.

Now, for the first time in a long time, the only thing anyone was taking from her was what she was willing to give. Ashok would never betray or abuse her. It was difficult for someone like her to admit, but she thought she might actually *love* him. Perhaps some of that silly girl lived in her still after all?

Life was good. So she feared it would not last.

She was a woman, but a warrior caste one. Thinking about emotions was complex and messy. Thinking about conflict was straightforward, and strangely enough, soothing. So Thera turned her attention to the far side of the crater where one newly formed unit of her newly formed army was already up and training.

Sixty men were practicing maneuvers on one of the terraces. She watched, fascinated, as lines of figures marched back and forth. From here they didn't look so different from when she'd grown up in Vane, seeing her father's troops practice. Only most of these weren't from a warrior bloodline and raised on stories about their valorous ancestors, they were casteless. And the poles in their hands weren't spears, but rather the incredibly deadly Fortress weapons.

Though they had trained with them according to the instructions Ratul had left behind for Keta, they had only been able to actually fire their devices a few dozen times. Since the rods were so loud, Ashok was worried about the echoes catching the keen ear of any Protectors who might be nearby. So they had waited until the summer storms had begun to move through the mountains, and then they joined in during the thunder. Even those brief displays had been rather impressive, and though most of them missed, a volley of lead balls was still sufficient to obliterate their targets.

The rest of the time the *gunners*, as Ratul had called them, practiced moving, pretending to load and fire their devices, per the commands of their newly obligated commander, Gupta, who had once been a miner in Jharlang. Ashok had picked the worker for that duty, because in his words, *Gupta has no respect for traditional ways so will not mind violating them, as well as a great desire to cause destruction.* It had seemed odd to her that Ashok would choose a worker for a warrior's rank, but Ashok didn't really see the Fortress rods as proper weapons anyway. They were simply machines that performed a task. Who better to manage machines than a worker?

Regardless, Gupta seemed remarkably well suited for the assignment, and the workers and casteless beneath him seemed eager to put their marvelous devices to the test.

Gupta hadn't been their only promotion. Since their number of able-bodied men had grown into an actual, respectable force, they needed leadership and supervision. Ashok had given the infantry to Eklavya, Shekar their skirmishers, then named three new risaldars. Besides the already-mentioned Gupta, Toramana was given the archers, most of whom were his loyal Wild Men anyway, and Ongud would command their cavalry. Some of them lacked in experience, and Ashok worried that he might have promoted them beyond their capabilities, but each was still the best choice possible.

Thera mostly considered herself a figurehead, but she'd grown up in the house of Andaman Vane, genius tactician and legendary war leader. She knew what real warriors looked like. She'd come to know each of those fanatically dedicated men and approved of Ashok's picks. When the Law came for them, they would do. If the Cove was besieged, they could hold out for a very long time. Even if the tunnel was dry, it was a choke point that could be easily blocked. Their greatest danger was from above. Sikasso was more than likely dead, but she'd seen what his people could do. A handful of wizards could fly in one night and effectively decapitate the entire rebellion.

It was odd, that even in a peaceful, contemplative moment, her thoughts turned toward their inevitable destruction at the hands of the Law.

There was some commotion on the rim. Someone was running and waving their arms. It was too far away to hear, but she had the impression they were shouting.

Ashok stirred awake next to her. "The spotters have seen someone camped in the valley below."

She marveled how even while asleep, he was more alert than a longtime criminal. "Someday you will have to tell me how you can hear so well."

"You know I cannot." Ashok sat up and squinted toward the rising sun. "They're saying it's our expedition Keta sent to purchase supplies, returned. They're going to drain the tunnel to let them in." He reached over and began gathering up his clothing.

"What are you doing?"

"I'll be there when they arrive to make sure it really is our people coming back, and not assassins."

"It'll take hours for the lake to go down. No one is pestering either of us yet. It's a beautiful morning. There's no need to rush off. Slow down and appreciate life, Ashok. There will surely be another crisis for you to worry about soon enough. Stay. Enjoy the morning with me."

"I already enjoyed the evening with you."

Even a woman who spoke on behalf of the gods could blush. "That you did. It's just that..."

"What?" he asked, genuinely concerned.

Thera tried to find the right words. "A feeling is all."

"The Voice?"

"No, nothing like that. It's been quiet. There's something else though. I had a dream last night, nothing prophetic mind you. The gods haven't had anything to say since they showed me the pattern to stop the plague, this was just an uneasy dream. I can't even really remember what happened in it, but it left me with a feeling that all this? It's about to change."

"How?"

"I don't know." Though obtuse to the subtle ways most amorous couples communicated, Ashok was a straightforward sort, so she'd found the best thing to do was just be direct with him. "And that scares me."

"Then I will stay as long as I can."

She leaned into him. Human affection was an unfamiliar thing for Ashok, and it still didn't come naturally to him, yet he put his arm around her and kissed the top of her head. He didn't even seem to notice the scar there that had changed her life.

Funny. Thera rarely thought of the bolt from heaven as *changing* her life. She usually thought of it as *ruining* her life. But today, briefly, it hardly seemed ruined at all.

"I don't want things to change, Ashok. I'd spend the rest of my life here with you if I could."

The man who'd had nothing except his oath to live for, surprised her then by saying, "I would like that too."

Perhaps there was some romance in Ashok Vadal after all.

❖   ❖   ❖

The news from the outside world was dire.

Half the men Javed had dispatched had returned, ashen faced and shaken. The three who made it back had been born of the worker caste. The other three had been casteless. They had not been so lucky. Despite the different stations of their birth, they had all been united, brothers in the faith, dedicated to Keta's vision. The paltan of warriors who had come upon them on the plains had not cared when the workers claimed these casteless were their property, and their labor necessary for the survival of their settlement. The orders were clear. The Law had spoken. And the casteless had been dragged from the supply wagons and hacked to pieces, as their worker friends had watched, helpless.

Keta listened to the horrifying tale unfold. He was sick to his stomach. It had been he who had ordered their mission. It had been Javed's idea, but Keta was the one ultimately responsible for sending those freemen to their doom... But that wasn't all. Oh no, the situation was much worse than that.

"The extermination's not just a few places like before. As far as these warriors knew, it was all over the northern half of Akershan. They're killing *all* the casteless. We saw smoke plumes across the plains, 'twas gray homes burning."

All of the rebellion's leaders had gathered in the chapel to hear the report. They were sitting in a circle and exchanged nervous glances as the tale continued.

"When the warriors attacked the casteless in the spring, it was in small groups. Not no more. Now the warriors go about in great big groups, hundreds of men from place to place, because they're scared of the Sons of the Black Sword coming after them. And before, most of the warriors were happy to let the casteless who ran off get away. If they crossed into the next province, it weren't those warriors' problem no more. Now, they kill all the casteless, and look beneath every basket and bushel for them hiding. And any who try to get away, they run them down. We saw them crushing women and children beneath their horses' hooves with our own eyes!"

Many of them looked to Thera for guidance, but the prophet just sat there, stone-faced. Keta knew that expression all too well. That was what Thera looked like when she furious and trying to hide it beneath a mask of forced calm.

"This cannot stand," Toramana shouted. "When I delivered those hostages I made our demands clear. We would leave them be if they left the casteless be." The chief of the Wild Men banged his palm against the floor for emphasis. "They have not. Now we must keep our word and go back to war!"

Keta glanced around. Everyone who was of the warrior caste was nodding along at the swamp man's rage. He knew anger led to rash decisions. His own careless anger had once gotten everyone he'd ever known in Uttara executed for rebellion. "We mustn't act without thinking. Sending out all our forces will tell the warriors exactly where we are."

"If not now, then when? If not for this, then for what?" Toramana asked.

"The rebellion must be smart. If we throw our lives away uselessly, then the dream of freedom for all of Lok dies with us." Keta put his palms together as a sign of respect to the swamp man. "I'm not saying not to respond. I agree with you, wise chief. I think we must. The question is *how* should we respond?"

Nobody had a good answer for that.

"I may have an idea," Ongud suggested. Keta liked that particular one. More jolly than savage, he was still devout and passionate in his faith, even by the standards of the Sons. "There's a huge casteless quarter in Garo. That's the next closest city. Do you know if it's been struck yet?"

"Not yet it hasn't. Some of the merchants we traded with had just come from there, said it was quiet." The poor exhausted worker shook his head. "The warriors we ran into were working their way west, town by town, methodical like. They'll get there eventually though."

"We might be able to get there in time to save those people." Ongud turned toward Ashok, who was sitting at Thera's right hand. "General, I know these lands, or at least all their logistical challenges. The Akara River Valley was reclaimed by the Akershan less than thirty years ago. The Garo used to belong to Great House Dev, and they were happy there. Like my people in Khedekar, they're still resentful about being taken over. The Garo are required to keep their warrior caste small, less than five hundred men."

"Your point, Risaldar?"

"Five hundred warriors is still more than enough to dispose of a few thousand casteless. The fact they haven't yet is telling. Vassal House Garo is on poor land. It's got three seasons, snow, fire, and flood. It's a hard place to make a living. They need their caste-less labor to survive. Killing their casteless would be like slitting their own throat."

"I know a thing or two about vassal houses rebelling," Thera said. "Do you think the Garo will fight their masters over this?"

"They're not my people. I can't say for sure," the young man said. "But they're proud, and if the Akershani warriors who come to ruin their livelihoods were distracted contending against the Sons of the Black Sword, rebellion might become an irresistible opportunity for them. Worst case, we fight them. Most likely, they stand aside and watch us fight their masters. But if the gods bless us, they will rise up against our foes as well."

Keta had been told Ongud's dream was to be some manner of horse soldier, which was a proud status among his people, but he'd been made a supply clerk because it had been seen as an insult to someone suspected of holding religious thoughts. The foolish Akershani should have made this man a tactician, because his mind was sharper than his sword.

Ashok scowled as he mulled it over, but he offered no rebuttal against Ongud's proposal. That probably meant it was illegal, but strategically sound.

The people of Kharsawan were supposed to be cautious by nature, so of course it was Eklavya who voiced the concern they all felt. "That's not the worst scenario. That would be we go forth to fight and are crushed by a far bigger force. Then they follow our trail back here and destroy this place."

"If I may," Javed interjected. Keta's trusted man was sitting by his side. "This sounds like a good plan, but I'm a simple merchant by training, so I do not know. Sending our army out of the Cove is a momentous thing, which once done, can't be taken back. Perhaps we should ask the gods, and see if the Voice will guide us?"

All eyes turned to Thera.

Keta felt bad for her right then. He knew she hated the pressure. At times like this he used to be the one to comfort her, to tell her she was the right one, and to assure her that the gods wouldn't have singled her out for their greatest blessing otherwise. But it was Ashok at her side now, not him. He could only pray that the gods would not allow him to lead her astray.

Thera took a deep breath. "I've not spoken of this. I'd hoped it wouldn't matter. Before the Voice showed me how to heal the sick, it offered me a choice. It's help then, or it's help later. You all know what I chose."

Keta hadn't known about any of that. "Since many of us here are only alive because of you, I'd say you chose wisely."

"Thank you, Keta. Normally the Voice speaks only when the Voice finds it convenient. It's not just something I can command. At the time, I didn't know what I would be choosing between. But now, I'm pretty sure it was this. If I'd not been given that pattern then, the Voice would tell us what to do now. We're on our own. For how long, I don't know."

"That's most inconvenient," Javed mused.

"Do you question your prophet?" Toramana bellowed.

"Of course not, my mighty friend. I meant no such thing," Javed assured him. "I believe the gods speak through her or I wouldn't have crossed the entire world to be here. I'm just saddened to not have the chance to hear their counsel firsthand, like you have."

Toramana seemed to accept that explanation and calmed down. Keta had to remind himself that Javed had been off mending fences during the miracle and had never seen the Voice manifest for himself. He could hardly blame the man for being disappointed.

Keta studied every face in the circle. He saw commitment, but also, fear, for if they did the righteous thing, it put all their lives at risk. One didn't need the gift of prophecy to know how they would fare against the entire might of the warrior caste if there was corrosive fear eating away their hearts. It was his duty on behalf of the gods to help make them brave.

The Keeper of Names raised his voice, proud, unwavering, and declared, "We call this blessed place the Creator's Cove, because the gods who made the world wanted their faithful to have a safe place in it. But before the Age of Kings it had another name. Ratul learned of it in the oldest of books. This place was once known as the Hall of the Marutas."

"What're those?" Shekar of the Somsak asked.

"The Marutas were ancient storm gods, masters of lightning and thunder. Violent and aggressive, when they went into battle against their foes, they made a roar like lions . . . Their time is gone, but ours is now. Today, let this not be the Cove, but the Hall. The Forgotten has given us thunder. Now, let us roar like lions."

Nearly every man in the circle gave Keta a determined nod. Ashok displayed no emotion.

"Very well. If the gods have left this decision to us, then let us make it. If anyone thinks we shouldn't try to defend the casteless, speak now." Thera waited for a response. She even glanced toward Ashok, but he remained there, unmoved.

Keta realized that Ashok was the only man who could sway her from the decision she had already made. In that moment, it wasn't about the fate of the casteless, or the rebellion they had built, it was about one woman's happiness. Would she do the right thing?

"That's it then." Their prophet sighed, knowing her selfish happiness was over. "Ride, Sons of the Black Sword. You know what to do."

Thera found Ashok in their quarters, gathering up his armor. Of course, he heard her coming, and stopped when she entered, his back turned, helmet in his hands.

"I'm sorry, Ashok."

"Feel no guilt for your command. This confrontation was inevitable. I will leave Murugan here to see to your safety."

"You don't have to go. I can just say that the Voice said you needed to stay here, with me, to protect this place."

"That would be a lie." Ashok dropped the helmet onto the blankets and straw that had been their bed and turned to face her, candid as always. "It would dishonor us both."

"It wouldn't be the first time I've had to choose between honor and survival. That's the story of my life. Surely by now Devedas knows you've declared the casteless are under your protection. He's out there. He'll be ready for you, and he won't be alone. Protectors will be following the slaughter like a pack of vultures, waiting for you to show your face."

"That's what I would do."

"You're going anyway."

"Devedas has vowed to kill me. I do not wish to harm him, but I will do what is necessary."

"What's necessary is you coming back to me in one piece."

"Then I will have to kill my brother." Ashok went to her and put one hand, surprisingly gentle, against her cheek to wipe away a tear she'd not even realized was there. "The Law was all I ever knew. It was the very substance of my being. When it was taken from me, I was left without reason or purpose. I yearned for death."

She put her ruined hand over his. "And now?"

"What was meant as punishment turned out to be a reward. They made you my obligation. You became my reason to live."

A woman made of stone had let herself be vulnerable long enough for a black-hearted killer to learn what it meant to be kind.

Then their time together was over.

Chapter 38

~~~~~~~

Their journey south took nearly a week. By the time the Sons of the Black Sword reached Garo, they found there was a massive army waiting for them there.

No . . . Ashok thought as he used the enhanced vision granted to him by the Heart of the Mountain to survey the long valley below. *Two armies.*

The larger force flying the yellow lines on the green field of Great House Akershan was camped to the south of the small, walled city. The other flag was an unfamiliar purple with a diagonal white stripe, and they had massed on a bluff just outside the walls. The two did not mingle.

"What do you see, General?" Risaldar Ongud asked him.

The two of them had ridden ahead to scout. Ongud because he had traveled through here before, and Ashok because of his superior senses. Ashok told him.

"The purple banner is Garo. The white symbolizes the cold, unforgiving river that cut this valley in two, and the purple is because this whole valley blooms with a certain wildflower for a week or so every spring. It's actually very lovely."

Ongud had postponed his wedding for this, so Ashok would allow the man some wistfulness. "The Garo appear to have four paltans on the field."

"That's about half their force. The rest will be holding the walls. As a vassal house, that small force is all they're allowed. I've served with some of these people. That fact does not please them."

"The Akershani have..." Ashok scowled as he tried to pick out separate paltan's flags. He gave up after twenty. "Over a thousand warriors."

"Oceans, that's a lot... The casteless quarter is right there outside the city walls. Why haven't they just killed them already? There's not a damned thing they could do to stop them. The Garo might not like it, but if they fought, they'd only end up getting crushed themselves." But the bright young officer quickly realized the answer. "That army is waiting for us."

"Correct." Ashok assumed the holding action was Devedas' doing. The Akershani warriors probably just wanted to get their grisly business over with and go back to their homes to drink and forget the things they'd had to do. "That entire casteless quarter is their hostage."

"We can't just abandon them... But we can't fight five to one. Well, three to one, if the Garo don't join in."

Legally, the vassals would be obligated to fight alongside their masters, so Ashok found Ongud's predictions optimistic. Ashok put his fingers to his lips and gave a sharp whistle. Horse flicked one white ear in annoyance.

A moment later the rest of his officers rode down toward them. The main body of their force remained concealed in the trees above. There would be no way for their force to approach the valley floor without being seen. To intervene here would require a stand-up fight on ground chosen by the enemy, which was the very last thing they wanted.

Ashok found himself wishing Jagdish was here. He suspected his old friend would have been excited at the glorious possibilities, as he moved his forces about like pieces on a game board. Despite his archaic title of general Ashok had no head for large-unit tactics and he knew it. He'd participated in a multitude of battles, many far larger than this, but never as a leader. Protectors were roving forces of destruction. Mere warrior commanders did not direct Protectors in battle. They simply roamed about, causing ruin as they saw fit.

In this arena, he knew he lacked wisdom. That was what these men were for.

Shekar had been with Ashok the longest. He would lead their fifty skirmishers consisting of lightly armored, fast-moving horsemen. He was Somsak, who were raiders by blood and tradition, and no one fought with more savagery than they did. Hopefully his men would follow that example. Shekar took one look at the orderly farmland below, a grimace crossing his tattooed face, because farmers were nothing more than waiting victims to a Somsak, and then he spit on the ground.

The miner Gupta had joined the Sons in Jharlang as well. The squat, ugly little man had never lived by the warrior's code, but he understood how to lead others in dangerous situations, blind and dirty, where the slightest imprecision meant being crushed or trapped until you suffocated. Having not lived by the sword, Gupta was not bound by traditions or biases and had embraced the Fortress machines. Sixty gunners, consisting of workers and the smartest of the casteless, would follow his commands.

Prideful Toramana was tiny Gupta's opposite. Once a leader of his own tribe, most of their fifty archers had been his loyal Wild Men. Having survived wizards and demons all of his life, that confidence was well earned. As was their way, all the swampers had painted their faces with ash to mimic skulls. That frightening visage would be the last thing many Akershani saw today.

Calm, orderly, meticulous, and professional, Eklavya would have been a perfect example of Kharsawan's warrior caste if it hadn't been for his illegal religious beliefs. One hundred and ten men, most of them workers or casteless, would march into battle as his spearmen. War was new to them, but not to Eklavya, so hopefully they would heed their risaldar's voice and not break.

Last was Ongud, who had long dreamed of being cavalry like his father and grandfathers. The innocuous young man didn't look fearsome, but Ashok suspected he had the keenest mind of any of his officers, having spent the days of his low status obligation studying the histories of battles and reading the works of Lok's greatest war leaders. Thirty horsemen, most of them warrior caste, would follow Ongud's charge.

Ashok watched as his five officers studied their soon-to-be battlefield. The decisions they made in the next few minutes would decide the fate of the rebellion forever. Their numbers were rather lopsided by proper warrior-caste standards, with a great many combatants who could ride somewhere to fight on foot, but very few who could actually fight from horseback. Traditionally a risaldar would lead about fifty men, but Eklavya had over three times as many spearmen as Ongud had who were properly trained in mounted bow and lance. It took mere weeks to teach someone to stand in a line and thrust a spear in a passable manner, while it took a lifetime to create a horse archer.

"We will make a corpse pile so big the gods will see it," Toramana proclaimed.

"The Keeper says that there is life after death," Eklavya said. "This seems to be as good a place as any to find out if he's right."

"A good place to die?" Shekar snorted. "A better place to kill. Let the nonbelievers do the dying today."

"I like that, Somsak," Gupta told the raider who'd once terrorized his village. "If we send enough of them over it'll get too crowded and their ghosts will have to come back tell us what's on the other side."

They all had a laugh at that.

"You are good men, for a bunch of criminal fanatics," Ashok told them truthfully.

As his men debated how to proceed—not one of them suggested retreat—Ashok noted a group of ten riders depart from the Garo camp, moving exceedingly quickly. They were flying no banner, but they had the look of warriors on a mission. They set out upon the dirt path that would bring them directly to where he and his officers were. The Sons had passed workers in the fields, but none of them had rushed ahead to warn the Garo as far as he'd been able to tell. Someone on those walls must have been armed with a spyglass and been continually scanning the surrounding hills to have spotted them so quickly. Ashok pointed out the riders.

"Scouts?" Ongud asked, squinting.

"I don't think so," Ashok muttered. "Stay here. I will go down to speak with them."

If their intent was battle, it would be one against ten, but nobody argued with their general. Ashok nudged Horse and started down the trail.

The Akara Valley was a rugged place, steep on both sides, then flattening out along the river. The vegetation on the slopes was mostly thick brush, with wide patches of purple-hued grass, while the bottoms were farmed. Ongud said that the river often overflowed its banks, terrorizing the Garo with floods, and demon incursions were common. They were only twenty miles from the sea after all. Even the farmhouses hundreds of yards from the river were on stilts or built on artificial piles of rocks to keep them above the flood plain. Ashok hated floods. It was just evil water trespassing on land. This was truly a cursed place.

The ten riders were on powerful Akershani steeds, and they made excellent time up the winding trail. Horse was so aggressive he naturally wanted to charge them, to demonstrate who was the strongest, but Ashok wouldn't let him. Instead they stopped in a field where he would be easy to spot, and Horse angrily ate grass while they waited.

Eight of the riders halted. Two of their number slowed to a walk but continued their approach. Their armor appeared to be of excellent quality. One wore a wolf's skull over his helm, and the other, older man wore a purple sash that marked him as someone of rank and status. They were armed with the forward-curving swords of the southern style, designed for chopping. That style was very familiar to Ashok, mostly because he had sparred against one like it many times in the hands of Devedas.

Ashok had also donned his Protector armor. What had once been silver was now stained black. The Sons had told him he made an imposing figure, and it must have been true, because the two emissaries seemed nervous. Ashok reached up and removed his helmet so they could see his face.

They stopped, twenty paces between them.

"Welcome to Garo lands, newcomer," said the one with the sash. He was about sixty, but still possessed a strong voice, a commander's voice. "I am Ranjan Garo, phontho of this garrison."

Such an important man didn't ride out to collect taxes or stamp traveling papers.

"I am Ashok Vadal, criminal." He gave a polite bow.

"As suspected." Then he turned to the rider next to him. "Your guess was correct, my son."

"The Akershan have certainly been waiting for him." That one took off the wolf helm, revealing a face that was vaguely familiar. "Well met again, Ashok Vadal."

"Do I know you?"

"It's no surprise you don't recognize me. The last time we met my face was black and blue from the beating I received from Akershani pig dogs, and I was covered in mud and blood from where they left me on the plains to die with an arrow in my back."

"Ah..." Last he'd heard Thera had left the wounded man behind because he'd not wanted to continue on with their gang of refugees. "It is the warrior who did not like massacring casteless."

"It wasn't an obligation any honorable man would aspire to."

"Honorable men do not often get much of a say, even when theirs are the vilest orders," Ashok said. "That is the Law."

The young warrior looked pointedly up the hillside to where Ashok's army was hidden. Somehow their position had been given away. The Garo's scouts were better than expected.

"You seem to have a bit of an issue with following the Law yourself, Ashok Vadal."

"I do not claim to be honorable. Not anymore at least."

"You've already met my youngest son, Rane Garo," the phontho said. "It was because of the nature of that meeting that we are speaking politely now, rather than me having my men hound you from our valley."

"You could try." They obviously knew he had brought a significant force, but that didn't mean they knew how strong the Sons were. Ashok glanced down at the waiting armies. Neither force was mobilizing. The Garo knew the Sons were here, but they had not yet passed that intelligence on to their masters. That was telling. "However, I think this polite method benefits us both."

"What brings you to Garo lands, Black Heart?"

The name was not meant to give offense. Everyone in Lok had heard of the fearsome Ashok Vadal by now. It was simply another title, no more, no less. "I have declared the casteless to be under my protection. I was informed the warriors are killing them again."

"This is true. Our cattle go unfed and peat undug as our non-people hide terrified in their shacks, awaiting their doom."

"And we can't even protect our own property. This nonsense supposedly comes all the way from the Capitol," Rane snapped. "This valley turns into a frozen bog seven months of the year. It's a fight just to survive. We can't hardly do that with half our laborers dead. House Dev never would've agreed to such wasteful stupidity."

"Enough." The phontho held up one gloved hand. "We do not need to speak of our house's internal problems with outsiders. Return to the bodyguard and wait. I will be along in a moment."

"Apologies, Father." Chastised, Rane put his wolf helmet back on. Surprisingly, he gave Ashok a respectful salute, and then rode away.

The father watched him go, before speaking again. "Like many of our young warriors, he's hotheaded and impetuous. If not for you, he would've died in a ditch, and he knows it. My greatest regret is allowing our Thakoor to draft some of my men to aid in this asinine extermination. It has brought us nothing but mourning, as several of our defiant youth were killed for disobeying those shameful orders. We hold no hate in our hearts for the non-people here. Because you saved his life, my son begged me to talk with you rather than simply attack. My superiors would not like this."

The tone told Ashok much. "Does your Thakoor know that we speak now?"

"Heh. You'll learn there are two kinds of vassals, Black Heart. Those who retain their pride, and those who are happy to lick the boots of their conquerors. Our Thakoor will know only two things today, this conversation never happened, and the taste of Akershani shoe leather. Your saving the life of my son gave me the excuse I needed to come out here and warn you away, but honestly, my people gain nothing by fighting you."

Such talk was treasonous. Legally, this was not for the vassal house to decide. No wonder he had sent the only other witness away. "What do you propose then?"

"No one can fault a warrior for falling back inside his fortifications, to protect his city from a deadly invader. Especially when his more powerful masters are already on the field with a far superior force. You two will fight. I will watch. You are not my friend, but you are also not my enemy. Come not against the walls of Garo, and it will remain that way."

"I've no desire to raise my sword against anyone other than those who would harm the people I've vowed to protect."

"Then we have an understanding, Black Heart. Do what you must, then leave this place. Against Akershan, you may win, or you may lose. Either way their warriors will be too busy to murder all the casteless I need kept alive to fill my storehouse. There is no benefit in sending my men to die on behalf of a house who despises us, fighting for the cause of starving ourselves quicker. Whether it is the corpses of rebels or occupiers floating down the river at the end of the day, Garo will be content."

"Acceptable," Ashok agreed. Though the phontho's ignoring the Law still galled him, he was coming to understand the pragmatic necessity of such low behavior. "Surely someone will find out that the two of us spoke here beforehand."

"I will say that I simply rode out here to warn away a trespasser."

"Trespass will be the least of my crimes today, Garo."

"I will say I tried, yet sadly the criminal did not listen." He shrugged. "Be warned though, there are Protectors nearby, waiting."

"I figured there would be. How many?"

"I do not know. But among them is Devedas."

Ashok had suspected his former brother would be here, but the news still saddened him. One of them would more than likely die today. "I know him well."

"I only know him by reputation. But when I was Rane's age, I served his father, who was the greatest war leader the south lands have ever known, a man of pure determination, who had no equal on the battlefield, with or without his ancestor blade. When that sword broke, it didn't just break him, it broke our people. I was there when, unable to accept his failure, he cast himself into the sea. The fall is worse the higher you are. If the son is even half the man his father was . . ."

"He is more." Devedas' father had given up. Devedas was not capable of *giving up*.

"Then good luck to you, Black Heart. You will need it. Try not to destroy too much of our property in the process. Oh, about that, the fields of oil grass—that's the plant with the purple sheen—should it catch, it burns fierce hot and spreads faster than a man can run this time of year. My people have a saying in this valley, only a fool marches through the oil grass when there's lightning in the sky . . . Unfortunately for the occupiers they are not my people, so they've not heard this saying."

"Noted."

The phontho rode back to his bodyguard. Ashok returned to his army.

Chapter 39

~~~~~~~~~~

From a barn loft on the side of the valley, Devedas and a few of his Protectors watched as the rebel force moved into the open.

"A few hundred is a good showing for criminals," said Broker Harban. "Should we go help?"

"Let the warriors handle it," Devedas muttered. "We're here for Ashok. Nothing else matters."

The rebels seemed better organized than expected. In the rare time you caught them in a group, fanatics fought like rabble. Nothing more than a gang. These lines were orderly. That should not have surprised him. Ashok had that sort of influence on people. By presence alone he made everyone else work harder to be better.

A horn sounded. Their enemy spotted, the Akershani army sprang into action. Hundreds of men ran to saddle their horses, and hundreds more took up their spears.

"They should have spotted them much sooner,"

Jamari Vadal muttered. "They should have already had flankers in position."

"Indeed," said Devedas. "Except I suspect the masters delegated that responsibility to the locals. This is their home ground after all." Curiously, the Garo army was moving too, but not toward the riverbank to where it made sense to engage and hold the invaders, but rather toward their own gate. "They're retreating behind their walls."

"Never trust a vassal house," Jamari snarled. "Cowards."

Devedas knew that assessment was wrong. These lands had once belonged to his family. The Garo had earned a bad reputation in polite circles. They loved drunkenness and promiscuity. They were conniving and prone to violence... But in all the times he had heard his father speak of the Garo, he had never once questioned their courage. In fact, quite the opposite. They were reckless and always eager to fight. Or at least they had been for Great House Dev.

"No, Jamari. A careless master is rewarded with disobedient servants. That's the lesson here."

Devedas would not have been a weak master. It was curious to think that this place should have belonged to him. It was a poor land, but it was a paradise compared to the unforgiving frozen wasteland where he'd been born. Those banners flying over the walls? They should have been his family sign. That army? Should have been answering to his commands.

Well... All of Lok would obey him soon enough. The only thing standing in his way was Ashok.

With ten Protectors at his disposal this humble barn had briefly turned into the strongest fortification in

Lok. They had an excellent vantage point to see the armies were in motion. There was quite the distance between them still, and they would both be looking for advantageous ground. It might be hours before they actually engaged. The Protectors were tense. They'd waited a long time for this opportunity, and it was difficult knowing their great nemesis was this close.

"Patience, lads. Ashok's the only target we care about today. Without him, these criminals are dust. Don't worry. It won't be long now. He's never been content to wait in the back. Battle is in his blood. Whether it was the wizards who built him, the sword who made him that way, or maybe he's just the most combative casteless ever born, Ashok won't be able to resist its call. Once we see him, we strike."

The barn was quiet except for the constant creaking caused by the growing wind. The sky was gray for a summer day, but dark clouds were gathering over the mountains. There was a distant flash of lightning.

As the rebels got closer, Devedas called upon the Heart to sharpen his vision. It was still difficult to tell at such a great distance, but they seemed remarkably confident. They weren't moving like men condemned to be slaughtered by the professional warriors who outnumbered them. They actually thought they had a chance. Religious fanaticism caused delusions like unto the strongest drug.

The criminals had no uniform. Some of them wore bits and pieces of armor. The majority of them were armed with spears. Then Devedas noted that most of those still on horseback seemed better armed and equipped. Their colors were faded, but he saw colors that had to be from Kharsawan, Thao, and even

Akershan. It appeared the rebels had collected some real warriors after all.

Where are you, Ashok?

He would be easy enough to pick out once battle was joined. Wherever the carnage was greatest, that would be their former brother's doing.

They may have had some warriors but apparently none of them were experienced tacticians, because the position the rebels were taking made no sense. They were moving toward the low ground. They had the fierce river with tall, steep banks on their right flank, wide open fields ahead of them—where the superior Akershani cavalry could maneuver and rain down arrows on them with impunity—and their entire left flank was unprotected hillside. Already, Devedas saw that the Akershani phontho had dispatched a paltan of heavy cavalry and two of infantry to claim that high ground. They were unopposed. Once the main body made contact in the front, those three units would be able to charge downhill directly into the rebels' vulnerable side or sweep around into the rear. Pinned between that and the water, it wouldn't take long for untrained casteless to break and run. Then the cavalry could ride down the survivors at their leisure.

"They're going to shove them right into the river," Jamari said.

Devedas drummed his fingers against the wooden door frame he was leaning against. It made no sense. Ashok was smarter than that. Had living without the Law driven him completely mad? Did he want this rebellion to fail? Was this some elaborate attempt at a glorious suicide?

Or far worse, what if Devedas had gotten it all

wrong and Ashok hadn't been drawn out at all? What if he'd remained in hiding, and the Protectors were wasting their time on these foolish criminals while the real prize was hundreds of miles away?

The phontho who had lost at Dhakhantar had been a doddering senile fool. The one in charge today appeared to know his business. His infantry was marching across the farmland, taking their time, conserving their energy. He had twice as many spearmen as the entire rebel force combined.

The Akershani cavalry was arguably the best in Lok. Second best if you were debating that point with someone from Zarger. They were ranging ahead of their spearmen, readying their bows. Devedas had seen them in action before. They would ride back and forth, harassing the enemy with a constant rain of arrows, while being too fast to get hit back easily. And then once they saw an opportunity, or their infantry created an opportunity for them, they would exploit it. One good charge would gut the enemy.

What are you doing, Ashok?

Much of the afternoon passed as the enemy took their time maneuvering into position. The Sons were ready. The Keeper of Names—who had insisted on accompanying them for some baffling reason—was moving up and down their lines, chanting, and pronouncing blessings upon the faithful. Ashok had found that annoying, but the men had seemed to like it, so he had allowed Keta his rituals.

Most of the men were afraid, but not all. The true Sons, the ones who had already been tested and found worthy, were confident, or at least they acted that way for the others. After all, they had fought a demon and won. What were mortal foes compared to the spawn of the sea?

So they'd taken up their position, and then waited, eating their rations, sharpening their swords, some of them even napping. There were dark clouds over the mountains to the north, indicating there would be harsh summer rains later, but for now it remained a warm and windy day. Those who were wearing armor sweated beneath it. Horses' tails flicked to keep away the biting flies. The warriors understood that the worst part was the wait, but they were used to it. For the workers and casteless, the painful anxiety was a new discovery.

Though unorthodox, Ashok had found no terrible flaw in their plan. They would let the enemy think they were some mere gang of criminals... Until it was too late.

As the Akershani moved toward them, Ashok's army made ready.

The time had come.

"Lord Protector, there's something amiss," Usman Thao said. "Note how the rebel troops are divided."

They were spreading out to defend the indefensible. That wasn't odd enough? "What is it, Usman?"

"The rebels in their middle. Their formation is different. The first rank kneels. The second half stands behind them."

Maybe they thought to present more spears toward the enemy? Though surely the Akershani wouldn't be stupid enough to let their cavalry charge yet. They'd seed terror by planting arrows in flesh first, let that fear grow, then reap the harvest.

Except Usman was right. Something felt wrong about the enemy center. The rebels' equipment was a haphazard collection of battlefield pickups. They had no standardized load out. Even those he'd been thinking of as spearmen were armed with a variety of spears, pole arms, long pikes, and their second rank had axes and hammers…But the odd group in the middle, their weapons were all of uniform length, which was a bit too short.

Those aren't spears.

That realization came far too late.

Ashok watched as the cavalry approached, galloping across the Garos' fields. He could feel the vibration of hooves. The ground was firm, throwing up dust rather than mud.

Gupta stood just behind his line of nervous gunners. "Not yet. Not yet! If one of you touches off early I swear by the Forgotten's eyes that I will drown you in that river myself, so help me gods! We fight as one. We strike as one. *As one!*"

"As one!" many of the gunners shouted back.

"What? I couldn't hear you!"

"*As one!*"

"You're damned right. You heard the Keeper's words. He blessed us to be like the lords of thunder and lightning! Let's show these Capitol-loving scum the gods have returned!"

Ashok watched those casteless carefully. They were terrified. And rightfully so. In a moment arrows would rain down on them. Most of them were strangers to that sort of thing. It led to shaking hands, tearing eyes, and loosened bladders. Warriors had their whole lives to learn to control those natural things. These freemen had recently been thrust into it. Luckily their new risaldar seemed rather good at distracting them from their fear.

"You are capable with the motivational words, Gupta," Ashok said as he rode by.

"By the will of the gods I've survived three cave-ins during my life, General. Keeping men from giving up hope when they're buried alive was a lot harder than this. Everything is easier when you can still see the sunshine." Then he raised his voice to a ragged bellow so his gunners could hear once more. "*We will show them the power of the storm gods!*"

One paltan of enemy cavalry was speeding ahead of the others. That risaldar had claimed the honor of drawing first blood. These were the early stages, the testing of defenses and resolve, and the prebattle posturing that warriors loved so much. The warrior caste was flamboyant that way. Akershani horse bows generated enough force to kill a man in excess of a hundred and fifty yards. It was really difficult to actually hit anything at such an extreme range, but a line two bodies deep made a big target. Something told Ashok this lead risaldar would want to be sure. There was no glory in wasting arrows, only in killing. They would close to within sixty or seventy before striking, then wheel away to circle back and do it again.

Ashok had seen what Ratul's weapons had been capable of during practice. "Give the order to fire when they are one hundred yards away."

"That's pretty far, General."

He only said that because Gupta did not grasp just how far a speeding arrow could fly. Warriors spent years building the specific muscles necessary to consistently draw powerful bows... Which was another reason the Fortress rods seemed like cheating, since malnourished casteless could easily match such a feat just by yanking on a piece of metal with their fingers.

"Wait for one hundred yards, Risaldar."

"Not yet! Not yet!" Gupta roared at his increasingly worried men. "Hold, you good-for-nothing bastards!"

Two hundred yards.

Ashok looked toward the riverside. Toramana was ready. Then he looked toward his left. So was Ongud. Shekar's raiders had moved to the hillside flank to cause trouble. Eklavya's infantry were positioned on both sides of their gunners, ready to rush forward to protect them.

One hundred and seventy.

The cavalry was getting uncomfortably close. Fifty men intended to launch arrows their way. If they did, some of his men would probably die. Such was war. And it was only the beginning of what would be a long day.

"Guns up! Guns up!"

The two lines of casteless shouldered their illegal weapons. Gupta had taken Ratul's commands and drilled them into his freemen, over and over and over, until the actions had become instinctive.

One fifty.

"Ready!"

Sixty men pulled back the devices atop their weapons. Sixty mechanisms locked into place with a series of metallic *clicks*. They were more like spring-loaded clamps which held flints, but the sound made Ashok think of bear traps being set. He had inspected the illegal weapons. Their construction was surprisingly uniform, and though it pained him to say it, almost graceful.

One twenty.

"Aim!"

The devices were pointed in the general direction of the riders. Previously the gunners had only fired upon targets like gourds and logs. These were bigger, but much faster. If you missed a gourd, your friends laughed at you. If you missed a warrior, he'd split your skull.

One hundred.

"Fire!"

Akershan felt the wrath of the storm gods.

The noise was a continuous, deafening roar across the line. The impact of steel plates against shoulders made the skinnier gunners stumble back. Horse reared up, angry and kicking because of the frightful sound, but Ashok was too fascinated watching the carnage to pay his mount any mind.

Some of the gunners had flinched, punching holes in the dirt only a few feet ahead of them. Others had wobbled and hurled their projectiles high into the air. However, most of the balls cut a path through the tall grass. Those which hit flesh did so with incredible force, tearing ghastly chunks off bodies. War-horses tumbled, their momentum carrying them end over end. Men were flung from the saddles. Then the scene was obscured as a thick white smoke rolled across the front line.

As the stinking smoke cleared, Ashok could see that the sheer shock of the display had broken the cavalry paltan's spirits. Only a fraction of the riders had been hit, but the sudden fire and noise had unnerved the rest, and they spun about and ran without launching a single arrow. Every Law-abiding citizen had been taught their whole life to fear Fortress magic. If Devedas was watching, that horrific display surely shocked him to his core, because by the Capitol's best estimates there weren't supposed to be this many Fortress rods in all of Lok, let alone in one place.

The men started to cheer.

"Reload!" Gupta shouted. "Now, damn it! *Reload!*"

The gunners went through the actions Gupta had forced them to do hundreds of times before. It was a good thing Ratul had even drawn them pictures. Ashok didn't understand the complicated process, nor did he care to learn. Powder went down the tube. Then a patch of fabric and one of the lead balls were driven home with a wooden dowel. It was a mystery how or where his old sword master had gotten these things, but they were unlike the rare Fortress rods he had encountered during his time as a Protector. Those had required a wick to ignite and had seemed far clumsier. The last thing the gunners did was pour some powder in a brass funnel on top. These made their own sparks through a mechanism that seemed as confusing to Ashok as the guts of Jagdish's little pocket clock.

If he'd had a little clock of his own to check, he would bet that most of Gupta's men had their weapons ready again long before a single minute had passed. He didn't know if that was good or not, but Gupta seemed rather unsatisfied as he went down the line yelling at his slowest and clumsiest men as they fumbled about.

The other enemy cavalry paltans had turned around when they'd seen their lead unit decimated and were moving back behind the perceived safety granted by their spearmen. That would limit the harassing arrows for a while. Wounded horses cried. No matter how many times Ashok had heard that noise, he still hated it. Their first volley hadn't even been that effective, but Ashok could see how a normal man would find such a display unnerving.

"Forward."

His risaldars heard his command and repeated it. Then the little army that the Akershani had expected to sit pinned next to the river to be destroyed at their convenience began advancing instead. All except Shekar and his skirmishers, who Ashok had left to guard their hillside flank.

To the credit of the enemy leader—whoever he was—there was no panic at the sight of so many Fortress weapons. Flags were waved, orders were relayed, and then the Akershani infantry began to march. The unit which moved to take the center consisted of their heaviest armored, carrying round shields and swords. They lacked the reach of the spearmen, but their phontho must have hoped the Fortress magic would bounce off so much metal. To their sides were hundreds of spearmen. Behind those, waiting for their chance to strike, were groups of horse archers. It made for a rather impressive sight.

"They appear to be fine specimens of the warrior caste. May I break them, sir?" Gupta asked hopefully.

"As you wish, Risaldar." Ashok looked around. This little farm seemed like as good a place as any to make their stand. The enemy would have to cross an open field and climb a small wooden fence to reach them. "*Halt!*" The order was relayed.

"Gunners. Aim for the ones with the spears on the right," Gupta shouted. Those were farther, but without the shields they made for a softer target. They were still quite some distance away so they didn't really know how much wood and metal the soft lead balls would go through. They'd launched these things clear across the Cove from terrace to terrace just so Gupta could see where they hit and figure out the trajectory. Ashok didn't need to tell the former miner how to do his work. "Remember, boys, it's just like tossing a ball. Lead's got a curve like a rainbow. We'll hold the front blade a few feet over their heads and lob them in. *Ready!*" Gupta surveyed his men and seemed to approve "*Aim!*"

Ashok waved his hand to signal for Ongud to prepare his cavalry. Depending on how much damage the Fortress rods did, they might be able to take advantage of it to ride out and do a bit of harassment of their own.

"*Fire!*"

The thunder rolled down the line. Smoke and fire belched forth. And nearly two hundred yards away a handful of men dropped, creating a few neat holes in the Akershan line. Other warriors immediately rushed forward to fill the gaps.

"Reload! Reload!"

"That's it?" Ashok demanded. *Such a racket for so little return.* "The swamp men's arrows could do better."

"They're rather far still, General! We'll do better with the next one, I promise."

"Keep it up then. When they get close enough to

charge, you gunners fall back behind the infantry." It would do no good for most of his casteless to get chopped to bits.

"Yes, sir!"

Speaking of the swamp men, Ashok saw that Toramana was spreading his archers out, hiding them behind trees, haystacks, fences, and rocks. These people had spent their lives surviving hit-and-run battles against wizards and the occasional demon. Ashok wasn't going to even try to make lunatics who painted their faces to look like skulls stand in the open launching neat volleys. They were hunters. Let them do what they did best.

Ashok kneed Horse and went toward the cavalry. His mount was glad to get away from the noise and smoke. He stood in the stirrups to better see the field. There was one thing that troubled him more than the entire army arrayed against them, but he saw no Protectors yet.

Gupta kept his word, because this volley did far better than the last. More balls smashed into bodies, tore holes through flesh, and broke bones. Probably ten warriors were swept from the Akershan line that time.

Back in the Cove, they had dug some of the projectiles out of the dirt to see what happened to them. They were usually found several inches deep, even in packed clay. When the balls were shoved down the barrels of the Fortress weapons, they were perfectly round and smooth, but when they hit they were moving with velocity sufficient to smash the lead flat, and spread it into various wicked, cutting shapes. It would cause ghastly wounds against any living thing. Warriors were brave, but it would be difficult for even the most stalwart of them to see the man at his side get a piece cut out of him by an enemy so very far away.

Sure enough, the spearmen on that side faltered. Their march stopped for a moment. The paltan behind them crowded against their backs, while the heavy infantry kept moving on without them.

"Gupta, switch to the middle now. Our cavalry will move against the crippled spears. Remember, watch for the situation we spoke of earlier!" He waited for the gunner risaldar to signal that he'd heard the command, and then Ashok rode toward Ongud and shouted, "Is the cavalry ready?"

"Ready, General!"

"Go harry their wounded side." They'd already covered this before, but Ashok wanted to make sure his instructions had been heeded, so when he pulled alongside Ongud he said, "When I go out there, whatever happens to me, you keep doing your job. I want to be seen. Do *not* come after me. When you see the silver armor, get out of the way."

Ongud jerked his head in a nervous semblance of an understanding nod. The young warrior was so excited he could barely contain himself. "Yes, General!"

"Then go."

"For the Forgotten!" Ongud roared.

Their cavalry rushed forward, speeding toward the injured wing of the enemy formation.

Another volley erupted, this time slamming into the Akershani center. Over a dozen men were hit that time. Their shields did *nothing*. Wood turned to splinters and the living bodies behind them turned into meat for the buzzards.

It turned out that as the distance closed, their

gunners became *far* more accurate, and far more deadly. The heavy-infantry risaldar must have realized that as well, because he screamed for them to charge, trying to get out of the open. Normally they'd have kept up a steady march, trying to conserve their energy so they wouldn't be sucking wind when they got into contact distance, but a leisurely march through the hayfields today meant certain death.

Ongud's cavalry rushed up to within screaming distance of the bewildered spearmen before launching their arrows. Bodies were pierced. They rode parallel to the enemy, dropping men the whole way, until the enemy cavalry set out after them. The young risaldar had been waiting for that, and he signaled for the Sons to veer back toward the safety of their lines. The arrows meant for them landed uselessly in the field.

Jagdish would be proud, Ashok thought.

"Ashok! Ashok!" It was Keta who was screaming his name, trying to get his attention. The Keeper was pointing at the hillside above them. "Up there! They're coming!"

He saw. With the Sons' fearsome cavalry out of the way, the Akershani warriors who had been sent to flank them had begun running downhill. It was not nearly the surprise that Keta thought it was. He had left Shekar to deal with them.

Sure enough, when he checked the Somsak were already on it. Sharpening his vision enabled him to pick out Shekar and his men riding along the bottom of the hill. Through the power of the Heart of the Mountain he was even able to make out the savage grin upon Shekar's face. He was enjoying this far too much. The tattooed risaldar licked his fingers and held them up to check the direction of the wind one last time, and then signaled his men to set the oil brush aflame. Several men ran along the bottom of the hill, dragging lit torches through the weeds.

The vicious raider had even waited until the flankers were halfway down the slope before lighting their funeral pyre. The Garo phontho had spoken true, for the dark plant immediately caught. The brush was only knee high at most, but the bright orange flame that erupted from the stuff was tall as a man, and hungry as any fire Ashok had ever seen. Within a few seconds the entire bottom of the slope was aflame, and it began to climb, spreading rapidly uphill.

The Akershani saw the wall of fire coming at them, realized it was fueled by the same stuff they were standing in, turned, and ran for their lives. Except now they were struggling uphill. Fire didn't care about up or down. It only wanted to consume. The black smoke washed over them, stealing their precious air. Their horsemen would probably make it. Most of their footmen would not.

Gunners' thunder brought Ashok back to the front. This would probably be the last volley that Gupta's line would get off before the enemy reached them, but that closeness made them particularly deadly. Skulls ruptured. Limbs were severed. Wounded men fell screaming, only to be tripped over by the men behind them. Most of the heavy-infantry paltan and many of the lighter troops behind them were struck by the incredibly lethal projectiles.

And then Toramana's arrows began to fall.

They were not launched in a great flock like the gunners' lead, but with singular precision. Each of the

Wild Men had survived in an unforgiving place, where a missed arrow meant a hungry belly. A lumbering warrior was a much easier target than a running deer.

The simple wooden fence turned into a deadly barricade as the warriors slowed to climb over it, only to be pierced by arrows. Their armor stopped many, but not all. Hands were pinned to wooden beams. Men screamed as they lay bleeding and helpless in the tall grass.

As his gunners retreated, Eklavya's infantry rushed forward, spears lowered. The two forces collided at the fence and the main battle was joined. The Akershani heavy infantry were superior to a mob of mostly casteless, but their numbers had been devastated by the Fortress weapons.

He looked back to the valley's edge and marveled at just how dangerous the oil brush was, because it had already claimed the bottom third of the slope. The regular grass had caught as well, but it was nothing compared to the fury of the angry weed. The enemy flankers were still running, desperate to escape. Some of their clothing had caught on fire, others had tripped and fallen over the roots, and been burned before they could get away.

Ongud's cavalry was playing a deadly game, avoiding the superior numbers of enemy horsemen, while still antagonizing their main body. Luckily the enemy horsemen were scared to get in front of the gunners.

Shekar's paltan—their assignment to burn the hill complete—had mounted up and gone to join their companions. The raiders had one other—very illegal— surprise. They had taken clay pots, drilled a hole in the lids to set a wick, filled them with Ratul's stored

Fortress powder, and then sealed the pots with wax. The powder bombs had been their prophet's suggestion. The idea wasn't from the gods, but rather because Thera was fascinated by the stuff.

The raiders broke into small teams, each one riding to a different spot behind their line before dismounting. Thera's bombs would be fickle enough as it was, trying to light them on fire and hurl them accurately from horseback would be suicidal. Shekar took the honor of lobbing the first one. He held out the pot for one of his torch men to light the wick, then he hurled it as hard as he could over the heads of their spearmen, out into the enemy ranks.

The detonation was rather impressive. Men were tossed on their backs as dirt and blood rained down on them. Smoke covered the field, further confusing the Akershani. Except more kept coming. Despite the terrible casualties inflicted by the Fortress weapons, the Sons were still drastically outnumbered. Every one of Eklavya's men were fighting like savages—casteless, worker, or warrior, it mattered not. They had no reserve. There was nowhere to retreat. It was win or die. Even Keta had joined in, dragging their fallen wounded away from the fray.

All of his forces were occupied. There were no commands left to give.

It was odd. One should not be *proud* of criminals. Yet it was what it was.

The time had come to draw Devedas to him. Ashok surveyed the battlefield one last time, picked his ground, and then charged into a paltan of enemy warriors by himself.

Chapter 40

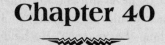

From Devedas' vantage point in the barn, he could see that the fight was not at all the easy thing the Akershani had been expecting. They had an actual battle on their hands. It appeared there weren't that many trained warriors among the rebels, but even the unskilled fought with heart and ferocity. And those damnable Fortress things! He had gaped in awe at their sheer destructive power. They'd shattered the hardest men like glass and left the field drenched in blood. Akershan's elite had never stood a chance. Devedas had been taught to hate the things and seeing Protector Abhishek killed had made him despise them even more, but for the first time in his life he truly understood why the Law banned them. In a world where every man had his mandated place, those in charge could never let the weak have a tool which enabled them to so effortlessly match the strong.

It was very difficult to watch so many flagrant violations of the Law and not get involved. His Protectors were eager for the fight. They obeyed his command to hold, but for many of them it was obviously a very difficult order to hear. They hated criminals. They were born for combat. Law-abiding men were dying. And yet their Lord Protector had told them to wait.

Where are you, Ashok?

One side of the valley was engulfed in flames. The sky had turned black and was raining ash. The rebels with the Fortress rods had not used them for a few minutes, but there were still small explosions going off all over the battlefield as the rebels tossed flaming Fortress devices into the Akershani lines. Each detonation spread wounds and chaos. Then Devedas realized why the rods had been silent. The rebels armed with them were moving up the now ashen hill, probably trying to get elevation so that they could fire down upon the warriors again.

"The Akershan are losing their will, sir," Jamari warned him. "Some of them are already fleeing. If we don't act soon, the criminals might actually win this."

That seemed inconceivable. Various rebellions had won small victories over the years, this one in particular had even claimed a few towns—albeit briefly—but the idea of an actual army of this size losing to criminals was preposterous. Or at least it would sound that way to the sheltered high-status men of the Capitol. The judges didn't understand suffering, fatigue, or pain. Their feeble minds could never imagine that postbattle feeling, beyond weary, soaked in blood, muscles aching from swinging a sword, as you counted off how many of your friends were still alive. No. The judges were soft and useless. Which was why they needed to go.

And also why he was the one to replace them, otherwise Omand would just swap one oblivious bureaucrat for another, and Lok would be no better off.

"If the warriors lose, then they lose. That's on their heads. Ashok is more important. The moment after we take Ashok's life then you are free to kill all the criminals you want."

They didn't like it, but they would obey.

"Look!" Protector Ranvir pointed.

Devedas watched as a lone rider in black armor upon a magnificent white stallion traversed the field. The horse leapt effortlessly over a farmer's fence, charging heedless of the danger right into a crowd of soldiers who were climbing over an irrigation ditch. The man in black laid about him with his sword, smiting heads and arms from bodies.

He squinted, for even the Heart had its limits for picking out fine details at such a distance. Everything in his life came down to this one moment. He had to be certain, for to reveal themselves too early would allow Ashok to escape. From here it could be Protector armor but painted to hide the shine. *Could it be?* But then his question was answered when the man in black caught a spear that had been flung at his horse, spun it about, threw it back, and impaled two warriors with it.

"That's him."

"You're certain, master?" Jamari asked.

The man in black paused, looked directly at the tall barn ... and lifted one gauntlet in greeting ... Of course he did. Because Devedas had picked the exact same lookout position that Ashok would have if their situations had been reversed.

Hello, brother.

"Converge on the man in black."

Ten Protectors of the Law leapt from where they'd been waiting. There was an incredible amount of magical energy drawn from the Heart of the Mountain as all of them called upon it at once to grant them swiftness of limb. Devedas stepped from the loft, dropped twenty feet to the packed dirt below, and began sprinting across the farm.

Vaulting over fences and low stone walls, the Protectors quickly reached the fields. They were in a loose group as they sprinted toward Ashok. There was no need to issue orders. These Protectors knew what to do. The farthest two on each end of their line began veering off. They would surround the entire paltan that Ashok was hacking his way through, and then all of them would work their way inward until the Black Heart had no way out.

Except it appeared Ashok wasn't even trying to escape. On the contrary, he leapt from his mount so that he could kill warriors more efficiently. The white stallion—now splattered red—kicked a warrior's helmet flat, and then trampled another man beneath his hooves as he ran away.

They rushed past the obviously apprehensive phontho and his command staff. A cheer went up as the warriors saw ten suits of gleaming silver armor cutting through the tall yellow grass. *The Protectors have joined the battle. Victory is assured.*

Let the warriors take heart, but their lives were not his concern. Devedas had more pressing matters to deal with first.

As they reached the edge of the fight, Devedas

slowed a bit and waited for his Protectors to spread out and encircle the target. Whichever way Ashok darted, there would be someone there to intercept him. The warriors who saw the men in silver were quick to get out of their way.

The rebel in black armor was twisting and turning between the spears, dropping warriors left and right. Nobody other than Ashok moved with such precision and killing grace. There was no ancestor blade in his hands, but even with regular steel he was an artist. Being surrounded only meant that he could kill in multiple directions as the poor doomed warriors tried to keep up with an inhuman force of will. He was using the techniques taught to them by sword master Ratul, but refined, to be even more pragmatic. There had never been any beauty to Ashok's style, only efficiency. In the time it took Devedas to push through the crowd, three more warriors had been crippled and two had been sent into the great nothing.

Devedas' certainty was absolute. This was the criminal the whole world had been searching for.

"*Ashok Vadal!*"

The black helm turned toward Devedas for just an instant, before he had to dodge around a spear thrust. In response Ashok clipped the back of his attacker's leg, severing tendons, and sending the warrior to the ground.

The other warriors had instinctively flinched back when they heard Devedas roar their opponent's name. No matter how much courage a warrior possessed, that name gave pause. The pile of dead and dying along the banks of the irrigation ditch gave even more.

The pause granted them a small moment of quiet

among the chaos. So the man in black reached up, unhooked the chain mask from his helmet and let it hang, exposing a familiar face. "Hello, Devedas."

The Lord Protector looked across the warriors. The highest rank he could see was a mere havildar. Their risaldar was facedown with a hole in his back. "Withdraw."

"But Protector—"

"*Leave us!*"

This was Protector business. The warriors picked up their wounded and carried them away. Devedas waited until they were gone before turning back to Ashok.

They'd been brothers once. They'd saved each other's lives more times than he could count. Through hardships unimaginable to lesser men, through wars, campaigns, raids...fire, blood, and carnage, they had stood together. Devedas had loved this man, but now the Law, honor, and ambition all required Devedas to slay him.

"We chased you across half the world, but it's over now." Devedas spread his hands, indicating that Ashok should look around.

He did so, surely noting that whichever way he turned, there was a man in silver armor, waiting. The nearest rebels were close enough that the noise of battle could be heard, but Ashok was all by himself. There was no one to help him. Despite certain doom his hard features displayed no emotion.

The Protectors were armed with a wide variety of weapons, whatever they were personally most skilled with, swords, hammers, axes, various pole arms, all were ready in their hands. Slowly, they approached, until Ashok was standing in the middle of a ring.

"It appears you brought a sizable piece of the Order with you."

"I thought I would need them. When we set out I believed you still had Angruvadal."

"Understandable then." With that sword, it would have taken ten. Without it, he had no chance at all against so many. Ashok bowed. "Brothers."

Every Protector here had looked up to Ashok before the revelation of his true identity. Some of them might lie to themselves and deny it, but of course they had. For Ashok Vadal had been the best of them, everything that a Protector should aspire to be, the righteous living embodiment of the Law.

Many of them returned his polite greeting. Others remained in angry silence. A Protector could devastate a normal man, as all the blood pooling in the bottom of this ditch testified, but all here had all touched the Heart of the Mountain. Even the proudest among them knew that Ashok was good enough to defeat any one of them, maybe two, or even three as he had in Neeramphorn. Against ten? This would be an execution.

Albeit a costly one.

"You know I'll get some of you. I do not wish for any of you to die."

"Did you say the same to Ishaan before you stabbed him in the heart?" snapped Broker Harban from the opposite side of the circle.

"I did," Ashok answered. "And I am sorry that he didn't give up when he had the chance. He was a good man. As you are all good men. It would sadden me to kill you."

"Then just end it here, Ashok," Devedas pleaded.

"It was your sword that made you honor bound to always do your best. Angruvadal is gone. There's no need to shed any more Protector blood. Bare your neck and let us end this crime."

Only Ashok shook his head. "I can't. I have another obligation now."

"To who?" Devedas angrily gestured toward the battle. "To these scum? To a bunch of Law breakers who spit on everything you've ever stood for?"

"Every man has his place."

"You're not even a whole man!" shouted Kushal.

"By birth, no. For that fraud I was as deceived as the rest of you. I never intended to betray the Order. The choice to align myself with these criminals was made for me...I have come to terms with it. This is my place now. As the Law is yours to protect, then those who would be free of its yoke are mine."

That had been Devedas' greatest fear, for never in the world had there been a man of more singular will than Ashok Vadal. And now he had found something else to believe in.

"I am truly sorry it must end this way, Ashok." Devedas was somber.

"Me too." Ashok reached up and put his mask back on. "Let us begin."

Though the battle still raged, hundreds of men screamed in agony or rage, as metal clanged against metal, bowstrings thrummed, and bombs exploded... inside the circle it seemed almost calm.

The calm did not last.

Chapter 41

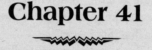

Ashok had known this reckoning would come and had long dreaded the day. Now that it was here, surprisingly enough, he found himself at peace with it. Though the Law had made him an enemy to the Order, he bore no hatred for these men. The Protectors had once been his family. It was with great sadness that he would cross blades with them. Yet he would fight without reluctance for Ashok truly wished to live. For that to happen, Protectors would have to die.

So be it.

Fifth-year senior Kushal came at him first. Hailing from the same Great House, but far younger, the experienced Ashok's treason must have struck Kushal especially hard. Ashok's very existence offended all who obeyed the Law, but it was a terrible mockery against Great House Vadal. The man entrusted with their sacred ancestor blade had lost it and brought shame to all who bore their name.

Unlike many of the Protectors here, Kushal had

never had the opportunity to spar against Ashok. Surely, he had been given warnings about Ashok's skill, but if so, had not truly comprehended them.

So it was Kushal who stole the honor of striking first. Ashok killed him for it.

He'd seen the sword thrust coming and shifted to the side just enough for it to glance off his breastplate. His instantaneous response had been a draw cut up across Kushal's throat, so hard and fast that chain broke and leather split. The edge was exactly aligned with the angle of the blow. It was a perfect cut.

The other Protectors stood there in silence as their young brother stumbled away clawing at his throat. Ashok had cut him to the spine. All the precious blood that had been in his brain was dumped down the front of his armor while the fresh pumped into the sky. Not even the Heart of the Mountain could save a man from such a wound. Kushal dropped his sword. It stuck, point down in the dirt. Then he fell on his face as his blood drained into the ditch.

Anger and pride had killed Kushal more than Ashok had. One could not strike so clumsily at one of the greatest swordsmen in history and expect to live.

The others would not make such a foolish mistake.

They would come at him, two or three at a time, but never so many that they would get in each other's way like the warriors he'd been fighting before. They would sting him, cut him, bludgeon him, wear him down, and then the moment he slipped—and slip he would for even the Black Heart was human—they would deliver a crippling blow. Since it could only aid one thing at a time, the moment he received a wound sufficient to kill a normal man he would have to turn the Heart of the Mountain's power toward staying conscious instead of granting speed and strength to his limbs. Then the Protectors would finish him off.

He glanced toward the hillside ... He needed more time. So Ashok grabbed Kushal's sword, pulled it from the ground, and spun it once to fling the clinging dirt from the tip. The Vadal blade felt good in his off hand. They would be coming at him from all sides, so he would use the western two-sword style. He could strike more effectively in one direction with only a single blade, but that would do him no good if he was getting stabbed in the back at the same time.

The Protectors didn't speak. There was no need for Devedas to tell them what to do. Kushal's twitching corpse was sufficient reminder to respect their opponent. They were professionals. They simply acted.

It was another Vadal man who led the attack. Jamari flicked his sword at Ashok's eyes, but he whirled away, then dove over the mace Broker Harban aimed at his knees. Ashok rolled across the ground, wrist, elbow, shoulder, as Ranvir slammed his glaive into the dirt where he'd just been. He leapt back up just in time to be struck in the chest by a chakram that had been hurled by Tanhaji Kharsawan. The razor-sharp disk bounced off the steel, revealing a silver streak beneath the paint.

Ashok used his second blade to parry a thrust at his back, and his primary to shove aside a descending pole arm. By the time the glaive hit the ground, he kicked Ranvir's leg out from under him, but before he could stab that Protector, Broker shoulder checked Ashok back. He stumbled but kept his feet. Broker was the second biggest man in the Order, so that impact had been like getting hit by a running ox.

Instinct told him that he needed to break through and run. There was no surviving this fight. Instead he stood his ground. Ashok would not abandon this ditch. It was his ditch now.

The Protectors circled. As predicted, they came at him three at a time.

Ajinkya attempted to deliver a mighty overhand blow with his battle axe. Ashok intercepted the handle with his main blade. It still hit hard enough to slide his boots through the grass. He slashed Ajinkya across the belly with Kushal's sword, but failed to penetrate the armor. Broker swung his mace at Ashok's helm, and all he could do was duck, driving himself forward into Ajinkya, who tripped and fell.

Ashok went rolling over him, landed on his knees, and then stabbed blindly backward. Ajinkya cried out as the sword slipped past his shoulder plate. Ashok twisted the blade out and then dove to the side as Ranvir's glaive trimmed the grass he'd been kneeling on. From the prone, he struck, and struck again, lightning quick. But Ranvir's greave stopped one, and then Jamari's sword intercepted the other. He almost managed to get back up when Broker's heavy mace clipped the back of his helm, wrenching his neck hard. Then Jamari kicked him in the chest. His ribs felt it even through the steel, but the momentum of the blow helped him upright.

They kept at him, but Ashok feinted, causing his opponents to flinch. It was enough of a break in their frantic pace that Devedas ordered, "Hold."

Even with the Heart, Ashok's arms burned. His neck ached and his ears rung. So he was glad that Devedas signaled for Rathod to help the wounded

Ajinkya out of the way. Ashok had gotten in a lucky hit that time. The puncture wound he'd inflicted had severed the main artery across the top of the chest, but a Protector could live through such.

"I can still fight!" Ajinkya shouted, even as his companion dragged him through the grass by the strap on the back of his armor.

"I would prefer to spend as few Protector lives as possible today," Devedas snapped. "Stand back and wait for the Heart to heal you." He waited until Ajinkya wasn't going to be stepped on. "Continue."

It was a blur of movement, as each of them used the power of the Heart to attack faster than a normal man could even dream of. In the blink of an eye, dozens of blows were exchanged. Ashok moved back and forth along the bank, jumping across the ditch when he needed to, trying to stay ahead of his former brothers. He had fought five demons once. This was worse.

The Protectors took turns trying to kill him, but there was no real pattern to the deadly dance now. They were too smart to become predictable.

Glaive, sword, and spear, Ashok was cut. Mace and hammer he was bludgeoned. Like him, the older Protectors had been taught by Master Ratul, and he recognized most of the techniques they tried against him, and he defeated each in rapid succession. What the younger lacked in skill, they made up for in strength and enthusiasm.

Body drenched in sweat, breath becoming ragged, Ashok fought on. For each assault he turned aside, there were two more aimed at him before he could punish the first. It took everything he had to survive. The sword he had been using, chipped from countless

impacts that day, snapped as he struck Usman Thao
across the helmet with all his might. The Protector
dropped, his bell rung, but Broker immediately took
advantage of that opening and smashed his mace into
Ashok's side, lifting him off the ground.

Gasping, wheezing, Ashok tossed the Vadal blade
to his strong hand and barely managed to turn aside
Broker's next strike. Except Rathod brought his sword
down on Ashok's shoulder. The plate stopped the
cut, but the impact drove Ashok to his knees. Jamari
promptly snap-kicked him in the face.

Spitting blood on the inside of his facemask, Ashok
spun his sword overhead, driving the Protectors back
as he regained his feet.

Dazed Usman was crawling away. Ajinkya was standing, but focused on stopping the bleeding. And poor
Kushal was gone. That was three out. Seven remained.
Ashok knew he would run out of blood pressure before
they ran out of Protectors.

Then...a whisper.

In his mind he saw what was coming next. In his
chest, he felt a black-steel fire.

Angruvadal.

Ashok heeded the warning, and reached back,
unseeing, to catch the haft of the speeding pole arm
in his palm. The shock of the hit traveled up the
bones of his arm, but it was better than letting the
heavy blade break his pelvis. There was no way he
should have known that was coming.

Hello, old friend.

Still latched onto the glaive, Ashok stepped into
that swing, collided with the Protector, and smoothly
rolled him over his hip.

Ranvir landed hard on his back. Ashok struck downward.

This time Lord Protector Devedas himself parried the killing blow.

Now, here was the true opponent. His equal had joined the fray.

Devedas launched into a flurry of attacks. His southern sword was heavier, which in the hands of a lesser man would have made it slower, but in the hands of Devedas, it was swift as the blizzard winds which had made him. Ashok outfought the storm.

The onslaught went on and on. For a moment the other Protectors were frozen, amazed, as the two best swordsmen in the world collided. Their wonder did not last long before they jumped back in.

Jamari's sword struck him in the back. Ashok lurched forward. The curved blade of Devedas sliced a groove across his plate. Broker's mace crashed into his upraised arm. Ashok cut him with the other. As he stumbled away, Angruvadal warned him again, and Ashok barely had time to pull back before another chakram flew past his throat.

All the Protectors were right on top of him. The ring of steel was closing in.

Ashok fought and fought, crashing into Protectors, rebounding, and then striking in another direction. He gave them the fight of their lives. He injured many but each time was injured himself in turn. His real heart was pounding. His limbs aching. Bleeding from a dozen cuts and swelling from a multitude of bruises, the pain was becoming too much. He needed to use the Heart of the Mountain to control his injuries, but to slow even a bit meant death.

Angruvadal told him that Tanhaji was spinning another chakram around his gauntlet, just waiting for the right moment. Rathod was coming up his blind side to try and stab him. He saw a way out, and without hesitation, took it. When Tanhaji threw, Ashok caught it with his gauntlet, and spun with the momentum, releasing the heavy metal disk a foot from Rathod's face. The whistling steel was driven through the front of Rathod's helm and embedded itself in the Protector's skull.

Rathod dropped, but Jamari and Devedas used Ashok's overextension to strike as one. A Vadal straight blade pierced deep into his side, as the curved sword of Dev smashed into his head. Ashok's helmet went flying. The world twisted. Somehow Ashok shoved them both back, before falling to his knees.

His skull was cracked. He couldn't see out one eye. It felt like his liver had been pierced. Ashok had no choice but to call upon the Heart to stop the bleeding or he would have immediately blacked out. The instant the Heart changed focus his arms and legs felt like molten lead. His useless muscles burned. The skin beneath his armor was spreading black and blue. Blood and snot were running from his nose and down his chin.

The Protectors knew it was over. Ashok was crippled. Everyone stopped to catch their breath.

"How are you even still alive?" Devedas asked in wonder. "You should only have the skill of one man now, not forty generations of bearer, except you still fought like you had Angruvadal with you."

"I do." The wizard Sikasso had called Ashok a hybrid, but not of man and demon, but of man and black steel. Ashok didn't know if this was true or just another of the assassin's lies, but there was no doubt now that some part of Angruvadal survived with him. He put one shaking hand over his heart. "In here."

"I don't understand."

"Neither do I, brother. Neither do I."

He was severely injured, but Ashok turned the Heart away from his hurt for just a moment in order to sharpen his hearing. Only one ear was working. The other was filled with blood. The battle still raged. Men were dying. *His* men were dying. But a great many of the Akershani warriors were quiet, eyes upon this scene, knowing that they were watching a historic moment, so they could one day tell their children and grandchildren about how they were there when the infamous criminal Ashok Vadal had finally been put down like a man-eating tiger that had been terrorizing a village.

But that wasn't what Ashok was listening for... It took him a moment—and even that was enough to make him swoon from the blood loss—to pick out the sounds he was looking for.

The word. *Ready.* And then a long series of metallic *clicks.*

Devedas knelt in front of him. "I want you to know that was most impressive. You truly were the best of us... Well, second best." Devedas smiled, but it was forced and sad, yet for a moment it was almost as if they were just two old friends at the end of a very long journey.

Ashok laughed. "It was a good battle."

Aim.

"Truly. You are a legend. It took *ten* Protectors to defeat you!"

"Forgive me, Devedas . . . but I'm not defeated yet."

Ashok toppled backward into the ditch.

As the Sons of the Black Sword made their battle plans he had told Gupta what to watch for, to wait until the Protectors were totally focused upon him, and the gunner risaldar had done as commanded. From their new position up the ashen hill, they had a clear view of Ashok's defeat. The Protectors were all near, standing close around Ashok to hear his last words.

Fire.

Sixty lead balls flew through the tight-packed group of Protectors.

Chapter 42

Flesh and bone were no match for the storm gods' wrath. The dense projectiles ripped jagged holes through plate to smash into the flesh beneath. Keta had spoken of a roar like lions, but from where Ashok was hugging the bloody ground, it sounded more like a swarm of angry hornets buzzing past, only these hornets hit like the spiked end of a war hammer.

A body fell on top of him, gushing hot blood. It was Jamari, who had been struck several times. The Protector cried out as Ashok rolled him aside. To his credit, Jamari tried to draw his dagger to keep fighting, but Ashok plucked it from his weak grasp, and left him in the ditch as he climbed out to survey the damage.

Only a couple of the Protectors were still standing, though they too had been hit. The rest had been struck down. A few were obviously dead, with multiple ghastly wounds inflicted upon their bodies. Others were groaning, calling upon the Heart, trying to stop the bleeding. Tanhaji was looking in disbelief at the jagged bone sticking out of his leg. Broker Harban had been shot through the helm, and as he ripped it off, revealed that one eye socket had been completely obliterated.

Devedas was among those still upright, but he had one hand pressed against his ribs. When he took his bloody hand away, the hole began to leak profusely. He'd been pierced through the lung. When Devedas realized the sorry state his men were in a look of pure anguish came over his face. "What have you done?"

"What I had to," Ashok said as he picked up the sword Jamari Vadal had dropped.

The Akershani warriors had been watching the spectacle, expecting to witness the end of Ashok. Instead they had seen the mightiest group of Law enforcers any of them had ever seen assembled, instantly and brutally cut down by nothing more than a casteless mob. They'd already taken heavy losses. Powder bombs were exploding in their midst. Their friends had been ripped apart by terrible magic too fast to see. The damnable rebels refused to budge. And after all that, the Protectors, the unstoppable force of the all-seeing Law, who they had expected to help them . . . *gone*.

That was the end for them. Warriors began to scatter. The direction didn't even matter. Just as long as it was away from the gunners. Some officers tried to rally their troops, but that simply drew the arrows of Toramana's hunters. Word spread quickly. Warriors who hadn't even seen the carnage were told about slaughtered Protectors and became afraid. Risaldars called for retreat.

Ashok and Devedas both had been in so many

battles they could read the situation well. The phontho's wishes no longer mattered. He had lost control of his army. Fear and disorder had claimed them. The rebels were now in control. Once their leader realized that, the horn would blow, signaling their retreat.

Despite the punctured lung, Devedas started toward him.

"Wait, Devedas. Think. My army is still in one piece. The battle is already lost. Get your wounded out of here. Enough Protectors have died today."

Furious, Devedas glanced down at his men, and hesitated as he realized that at least half of them could be saved. "You know we can't just abandon this place to criminals!"

"I'm not trying to capture this land. I'm trying to defend its people from you."

"They're not real people. They don't *matter*!"

"*They do to me!*" Ashok bellowed.

Devedas took another step, then hesitated. "I can't return to the Capitol saying I let the Black Heart win! I've got to return triumphant or not at all."

They were so few in number as it was, losing so many at once would be a terrible blow to their already disgraced Order. Yet it still saddened Ashok that he seemed to care more about the fate of the men who had just been trying to kill him, than the man who commanded them. He had expected better of his old friend. Ashok had been calm before, but a cold rage began to build. Much of that anger was directed inward, at himself, at the knowledge of what he was and had been, for he knew he had been just as devoted to the Law, and just as willing to let his people die in pursuit of its defense.

"Then I will make you an offer, Devedas. As I give your men mercy, I will also grant you your wish. I'll allow them to leave the field. Those who can walk can carry those who can't. The Heart will save who it wants, and they can live to defend the Law another day. But you and I... We stay and we finish this."

"A duel then."

They were both hurt. Neither would be able to use the Heart for anything beyond sustaining their lives. Ashok would not accept Angruvadal's help. That would not be honorable. It would be a test of skill and character.

"You order your Protectors off the field and I will do the same for my army. You have my word."

"What good is the word of a criminal?"

"It is all I can offer. Accept it, or all of you can go beneath the hooves of my cavalry."

Devedas recognized he was trapped. All his men could do was lie there and try not to die. "Just the two of us, just like before."

"We're not children anymore."

"I don't think either of us ever really were, Ashok. I accept your offer."

The wounded had been gathered. The battlefield cleared.

"What will they do with all the dead, do you think?" Devedas asked.

"The Garo will probably throw them all in the river and let them be carried out to sea," Ashok answered. It seemed practical, but very disrespectful. "The ocean's rather near."

Devedas snorted. "No wonder these people were

always whining to my father about their demon troubles."

The two of them sat on the farmer's wooden fence, watching the storm roll in. The winds had picked up, causing ripples through the grass. At least the grass that hadn't been trampled by boots. Parts of the hillside still burned. The coming rain would probably put it out.

They had both taken off their armor. Devedas at first, because he'd needed to stitch shut the gaping hole through his chest so the Heart could do its work. Then Ashok had removed his as well, to keep things fair. The pieces were piled next to each other on the ground, lamellar plates, chain, and leather, one set silver, one set black, both filthy.

Keta had called Ashok a lunatic for holding this duel. He'd argued they had nothing to gain. They had the upper hand. The Sons could have easily finished off all the powerful servants of the Law, and maybe such a loss would even be enough to finally convince the Capitol to leave them be. Only Ashok had known that was nothing but a dream. The Capitol would never ever stop, especially not now. The Law required absolute obedience. It could not tolerate even the tiniest deviation, for to do so would be to set a standard that would cause their entire edifice to crumble.

The Keeper of Names had been right about one thing though. Ashok had nothing to gain by dueling Devedas, and everything to lose ... Except that didn't matter. This wasn't about logic or any grand strategy. Ashok didn't know what it was really, except necessary.

It had been hours since they'd soaked the Garos'

fields in blood. The Protectors had gone east with the defeated Akershani. The Sons had headed back up into the mountains. At first Devedas had been furious with him. Eventually anger had subsided into resignation. What was done was done. They both recognized the inevitability of this moment. Emotions would only make them easier to beat. So they had sat together and waited to heal.

Now it was only the two of them and the dead.

Devedas took a long drink from the wine skin that the Sons had left for them. "Ah. That's much finer than the stuff we had last time we drank together." He tossed the skin to Ashok, who caught it, and then took a drink himself.

Perhaps he was very thirsty, or just needed to wash the taste of Fortress smoke from his mouth, but it really was good. Shekar had probably stolen it from a Garo farmhouse. "When was that?"

"Gujara...When I delivered the message summoning you back to the Capitol, and found you digging a grave for some random casteless."

That seemed like a very long time ago. "I think that was when this all really began."

Devedas chuckled. "Hardly. This travesty began when a little casteless boy picked up a priceless ancestor blade and for some baffling reason it didn't immediately slice his hands off for the insult."

"Overall, that is true. I meant that it was upon that beach, jungle on one side and hell on the other, when the first cracks appeared in my then perfect obedience." He passed the wineskin back.

"You've never been given to introspection. That's damned near poetic by your standards." Devedas took another drink. "They took a casteless brat, wiped the slate clean, and made you into the ideal servant of the Law. It stuck for twenty years. That's impressive. Those Vadal wizards do good work."

"I suppose we were both created by the circumstances of our past."

Devedas was quiet for a long time. "I suppose." Then he shook his head, as if such thoughts left him bitter. "I came from everything and received nothing. You had nothing and received everything."

"When we spoke in my prison cell, you were going to punish all of the conspirators who made me. How did that work out?"

The Lord Protector shrugged. "Politics got in the way."

Not unexpected, but unfortunate. "Harta Vadal deserves to die for his part in this."

"I know. And to think of how bitter I was when I believed Mindarin was summoning you back to give you my current office. I was so very jealous. Little did I realize he was calling you back to ruin your life in a vain attempt to assuage his guilt. Besides, most of being Lord Protector is getting pushed about as a piece in the games of worthless know-nothing judges."

"No one should be untouchable, not even judges," Ashok muttered. "An important man can break the Law with impunity, but a low-status man who just wants to be left in peace is hounded to the ends of the world. A Law applied unevenly is no Law at all."

"Agreed," Devedas said. "That's why after I'm done here, I intend to fix it."

"How?"

Staring into the distance, Devedas pondered on it.

A decision was made. "You've always been the one person I could confide in, so I might as well tell you this secret as well. There's no other witnesses here. In a little while I'll either kill you, so you can't talk, or you'll kill me, so it won't matter... I'm going to be king."

"That's absurd."

Except Devedas wasn't joking. "No, really. I discovered a plot to overthrow the judges and crown a single leader for all of Lok, so things would be like it was back during the Age of Kings. Rather than try to stop them, I decided to join them."

Ashok couldn't believe his ears. All he could do was gawk in astonishment at Devedas. He never in a million years would have imagined hearing such treasonous words from his old friend. "What?"

"Their ideas were not without merit. Our current system is dying. The bigger it gets, the more corrupt it gets. The Capitol only exists to make the Capitol richer and the great houses can't sustain that forever. There're too many pigs feeding at the trough and new piglets born every day. There's too much rot. It's all crumbling. Eventually it will fail. Better to do it now, while the good parts can be saved. If there will be a king, it might as well be me. At least I'll do it right."

"You have always been consumed with ambition, but that is madness."

"Why? By what measure is it madness, Ashok?"

He had started to reflexively snap *because it is illegal*, but what did that matter now? He had laid waste to the Law today, breaking it as he saw fit in pursuit of his new goals. The buzzards gathering above demonstrated how much love he still had for the Law.

So Ashok had no answer, for he was no better than Devedas was.

"So you are a criminal. Just like me." Ashok wasn't even angry, just disappointed.

"I'm the Lord Protector and you're a rebel. That makes us very different kinds of criminals."

If only Devedas knew that it had been the highest levels of the Capitol which had put him on this path, but that was one way they were different. Ashok kept his oaths.

"Don't give me that sanctimonious look. The Law is corrupt. We both know it. The judges only care about their own comfort. I'm trying to correct it, to fix its deficiencies, to put someone with sense and honor in charge for the betterment of every house. Your people are the ones trying to destroy it."

"They don't want to destroy it. They just want to be left alone."

"The Law will never allow that . . . Maybe you shouldn't be so quick to judge me, brother. Perhaps a wise king would spare these criminals, where the unbending Law would not."

"Would you?" Ashok asked. "Would good King Devedas actually spare these people?"

Devedas mulled it over. "Should I lie, and say yes, in the hopes that you simply let me win? Your life in exchange for all of theirs? Look around. After today, how could I—or any ruler—allow this rebellion? If they can succeed here, then they can do it anywhere, and Lok will shatter into a hundred quarrelling nations. No, I'll not lie to you, because you're not stupid enough to believe in fairy tales."

The two of them passed the skin back and forth

in silence while they waited for the Heart to heal their wounds enough to finish the fight. The wind continued to pick up. The clouds were coming in. The sky was growing darker.

Devedas broke the silence.

"I must know one thing though, Ashok. The last time we met, you longed for death. I could see it in your eyes. The only reason you lived was because Angruvadal demanded it... Oh how I curse myself now for not dueling you when I might have claimed it."

"Why didn't you then?"

"Maybe it was because I suspected despite the truth, despite who you really were, the sword would still like you better, as it did the first time." Devedas ran his finger down the scar that split his face. "This is my constant reminder of my failure. It's always with me. In that prison cell, doubt led to fear and hesitation. I lost my chance. Afterward, I vowed I would never let another opportunity so great pass me by."

"So you're claiming it's my fault you are conspiring to take over the Capitol?"

"In a way, yes."

Ashok didn't want that to be true, but it probably was. If he was still alive at the next new year, he would follow the traditions of the swamp men, and build a little sin doll to write upon it, *inspired a good man to do evil*, to throw into the great bonfire.

Ashok sighed. "What is this thing you must know, Devedas?"

"Why do you fight so hard now? Surely you don't believe all this nonsense about old gods. What happened to the Ashok who simply wanted to sulk off and die?"

"It's complicated."

"Simplify it for me then."

"A woman."

"Really?" Devedas laughed hard. "That's not complicated. It's the opposite of complicated! Ashok Vadal has fallen in *love*? I didn't know that was even possible. Unbelievable!"

"Why? Is the broken toy of wizards not allowed happiness?"

"Don't be embarrassed. I mean no offense. Not for that at least. We're going to fight to the death in a minute anyway, so there's plenty of offense taken, but not for that. I am happy for you, truly. She must be quite the woman to have captured unstoppable Ashok."

"She is," Ashok said truthfully. "I cannot say either of us is *captured*, but we have come to an arrangement I find pleasing."

"Since we are sharing secrets, I too have found the one who will be mine. You would like Rada, though she's not at all what I expected my wife would be."

Protectors were supposed to be married to their obligation. They weren't allowed relationships beyond the services of pleasure women while they were in the Order for good reason. It was only after their obligation was complete that they could go on with a normal life. It was yet another crime, but what was taking an illegal wife compared to overthrowing the entire government?

"How is she not what was expected? Is she ugly?"

"Not at all. She's very pretty, but she's also very smart. However, it's a bookish sort of smart, if that makes sense. More than that, she's earnest." A genuine smile split Devedas' face, and for just a moment Ashok saw the good man he'd once known, free of

the jealousy and ambition which had corrupted him.
If Devedas won the duel, this woman, whoever she
was, might someday make him a good man again.
"Do you understand?"

Probably better than you do ... Only that went
unsaid. Ashok merely nodded.

"Rada came to me in distress. I've known a great
many women, but she was the first who was actually
interesting. I was rather surprised actually, yet the
heart wants what the heart wants."

"I'm sure if I don't kill you, she will make a fine
queen."

"She will. I've got Karno watching over her to keep
her safe from my fellow plotters."

"Surely Blunt Karno is not part of your conspiracy."

"Oh, of course not! He's probably the only man
I've ever met more honest than you."

"Then this Rada is in good hands. Also, I am glad
Karno was with your lady, instead of here today."

"So you wouldn't feel the guilt for causing Karno's
death as well?"

"He probably would have ripped my head from
my shoulders before we got that far. The man fights."

"That he does. To old friends." Devedas took one
last drink, savoring it, because he knew it might be
their last together, and then handed over the nearly
empty skin.

"To old friends." Ashok finished it. "It seems we
are out of wine."

"It was good while it lasted ... Are you ready?"

Everything hurt. His muscles were stiff. There
were still small fractures in his bones. His head ached
from nearly having his neck snapped. But the severe

laceration in his side had sealed enough to move without making it worse. It was a shame to use so much of the Heart's precious magic on two unworthy criminals. "I am ready."

Devedas took a deep breath and held it to test the integrity of his lung. He exhaled. "So am I."

They hopped off the fence and took up their swords. Ashok had kept Jamari's sword because in size and shape it was very similar to what Angruvadal had been. All traditional Vadal blades were based upon Angruvadal, three foot long and straight.

Devedas tested his own sword, spinning it deftly about. That was not for show. He was stretching out the tendons of his wrist. Forward-curving southern blades had been based on their ancestor as well, the one which had been shattered by Devedas' father.

Across the grass, they walked away from each other, stopping when there was ten paces between them. Ashok cracked his damaged neck. The clothing they had been wearing beneath their armor was basically bloodstained rags now. They looked more like a pair of vagabonds than the finest swordsmen in the world.

"Is there anything else that needs to be said?" Ashok asked.

"I don't think so," Devedas answered. "You?"

"I apologize for everything." And he very much meant it. "I want you to know that I do not hate you, Devedas."

"I wanted to hate you, Ashok." Devedas gave him a melancholy nod of acknowledgement. "I tried. I failed."

The wind blew through the grass. There was a rumble of thunder, and a few cold raindrops began to fall upon them.

"Offense has been taken," Devedas stated.

"Offense has been given," Ashok responded.

The duel began, not in a sudden burst of movement, but in absolute stillness.

It had been two decades and hundreds of fights since the last time they had clashed. Both of them were far deadlier now than when they'd come down from the mountain. They were more experienced, but neither was overconfident because of that. In battle, just because something had worked once didn't mean it would work again.

One thing had not changed from their first clash. Ashok would accept no help. The shard of Angruvadal buried in his chest was silent. Live or die, he would do this himself.

Swords already in hand, there would be no quick draw this time. The two opponents studied each other, waiting. They were both beings of pure focus.

Devedas moved first.

The lunge was quick, the cut quicker. Ashok had been ready though and parried as he sidestepped. The responding thrust for Devedas' midsection was turned aside.

That had been a test.

They circled, aware and calm. There were no words, no sneers or taunts. Devedas often fought with fury as opposed to Ashok's cold pragmatism, but in this particular duel his opponent would not give in to his base nature. Passion granted energy and ferocity, but once that was spent, victory would go to the one who made no errors.

Ashok feinted, trying to trick Devedas into guarding high. He didn't fall for it. Again, now low. Instead Devedas broke contact and resumed circling.

The first to make a mistake would die. They both knew it.

Lightning flashed across the sky. Devedas attacked. Ashok dodged and countered. They traded blows ten times before the sound of thunder reached them.

They parted and circled. It was all about timing and distance. Neither of them were foolish enough to fall into predictable pattern. Rhythm was for fools and dancers. Rhythm could be predicted and interrupted. Such were the teachings of Ratul. They both had memorized all those lessons. Devedas had killed the old master with his sword, and Ashok had taken Ratul's place as the greatest traitor in the history of the Order. Yet, his lessons remained valid.

Devedas struck a mighty overhand blow. His blade was a bit slower, but also heavier and more durable. Rather than try and block, Ashok leapt back. Devedas missed, but it wasn't a close enough miss to leave him in a bad position for a counterattack.

Despite the many wounds he'd taken from the Protectors, Ashok allowed no place in his mind for pain. There would be no weakness shown, no tightness of tendon, twitch of muscle, or grinding of bone for Devedas to take advantage of.

Ashok feinted left, and then sent an underhand thrust at Devedas' body. The Protector turned and sucked in his stomach, barely dodging the steel. Ashok winced as Devedas' response sliced across the top of his arm.

They parted once more. This time Ashok's sleeve was red with fresh blood.

Devedas saw the injury, but he took no joy in it. There was no smirk. No pride. He knew Ashok could take a hundred cuts that size and still have the strength to end him with one good strike.

They struck simultaneously. Blades flashing back and forth. Bodies moving with perfect speed and balance, without thought, because thought took too long. Thought got in the way. They simply acted.

With the Heart of the Mountain controlling their wounds, their real hearts were pounding from the exertion. The sky had grown cold, but they were both sweating. Lungs burned as they fought on.

All it took was the smallest slip on wet grass, but Devedas stumbled, just a tiny bit. And Ashok was on him. Lunging in at a bad angle, his push cut still caught Devedas across the chest, slicing him to the collarbone.

Only rather than fall away, Devedas stabbed in response, the curved blade going in at a harsh angle into the meat of Ashok's leg.

They broke and parted, but the circling was slower than before.

Ashok couldn't help but wince as he put his weight down on his injured leg. Blood was staining his pants, but it had not hit the artery. Devedas reached up and crammed a bunch of his silk shirt into the weeping cut on his torso to staunch the bleeding. Both wounds would cause them to slow down. Neither would be immediately fatal.

These facts were recognized. With a mutual nod, they continued.

They clashed. An ugly hit that time, edge upon edge, as steel chipped. Devedas forced their blades down, then slammed his fist into Ashok's skull, but Ashok had already driven the knife-edge of his hand into the wound upon Devedas' chest. The Protector grimaced as Ashok twisted his fingers, widening the wound. Their blades came apart, and Ashok was cracked across the jaw by the pommel of Devedas' sword.

As he flung the droplets of blood from his fingertips, Ashok realized they were somehow over two hundred feet from where they'd started from, and the sky had grown dark and angry with storm clouds. Where did the time go when you were trying to kill your best friend?

It began to rain hard.

They went at it again, brutally, savagely. Their limbs were growing weary. Ashok's leg could no longer hold his weight strong enough to dart back and forth. Ashok was taller, but Devedas weighed a bit more. They collided, both of them blocking the other's sword hand with their off hand. Ashok snapped his head down, smashing Devedas' nose flat with his forehead. Except the Protector kicked him in his wounded leg. Ashok's knee buckled and he dropped.

He still managed to catch Devedas' descending blade, but not the boot that flew up to kick him in the chest.

Ashok crashed into—and through—a wooden fence. He landed on the hardpacked gravel of the road to Garo.

Devedas leapt through the fence after him, but Ashok had already sprung back up. It was swords, fists, and knees, as they collided. Ashok wasn't quite quick enough, and the heavy tip of the southern blade sliced across his chest.

They stumbled apart. Ashok's shirt was hanging open. His body slick with blood. Devedas paused, granting him enough time to feel the wound and see that he'd been cut to the sternum, right above the pattern of scars inflicted upon him by molten Angruvadal and Sikasso's hook. Devedas straightened out his broken nose so he wouldn't have to breathe entirely through his mouth.

The already laboring Heart of the Mountain slowed their bleeds to a trickle, so that they could continue. They'd slice each other to bits if the Heart let them. As the two of them paused there in the road, in the rain, heads appeared atop the city wall. They had observers. The brothers would give them a good show.

"Ready?" Ashok asked.

Devedas spit out a glob of blood and wiped his lip with the back of his hand. "Ready."

The rain was pounding hard, soaking them to the bone. Ashok went low, slashing for Devedas' legs. The southerner leapt back, and responded high, swinging for Ashok's head. They spun back and forth in the road, narrowly avoiding steel. Blades crossed again, edges chipped, and Devedas shoved him back. His boots slid through the puddles, before he was able to wrench his sword free to smash Devedas with the hilt of the Vadal blade.

Reeling, with cheek gashed open, Devedas broke free, and swung hard, trying to disembowel him. Except Ashok dove beneath it and rolled through the water, slashing. Devedas roared as the blade opened his calf. The Protector tried to hit Ashok before he could get up, but Ashok caught the descending sword with his handguard and twisted it aside. The southern blade hit the road. The tip was planted deep.

Devedas tugged, but the blade was stuck in the

hardened tar. From the ground, Ashok kicked with all his might. His heel crushed Devedas' fingers against the hilt. The sword popped free and went flipping out into the grass. It landed with a clunk, ten feet away.

The Protector watched it go. Then he turned back to see the tip of Ashok's stolen sword pointed at his guts. Ashok kept it aimed there as he slowly got back to his feet.

Devedas was still ready to fight, but the advantage now belonged to Ashok. There wasn't much an unarmed man could do—no matter how skilled—against an equally skilled man armed with three feet of sharpened steel in hand.

"You have me."

He did. With his leg seizing up and his body growing cold from the blood loss, Ashok should've finished it. But instead he nodded his head toward where the sword had landed. "We must be certain. I will wait."

Devedas nodded respectfully. Then knowing that he wasn't going to just be struck down from behind by a dishonorable enemy, limped over to his sword, and tried to pick it up. His damaged fingers wouldn't close around the handle, so instead he retrieved it with his left hand, then spun it once to clear the mud. "If our situation was reversed, do you think I would've granted you that courtesy?"

Ashok met him at the edge of the grass. "I believe you would."

"You alone always thought the best of me, Ashok."

Their battle had taken them to the bank of the mighty Akara River. Far below them, the water sped by, fast, cold, and frothy white. Ashok looked upon it with great distrust. It would have been terribly ironic if after all that a demon popped out and ate them both. The ocean wasn't that far away and surely the creatures of hell had smelled the blood.

There were no demons to be seen however, just the occasional dead Akershani soldier floating briskly by.

They closed the distance.

One would think that having to switch sword hands would be a great disadvantage, but Ashok had fought Devedas enough times to know that it wouldn't make that much difference. He was proficient with either hand and like Ashok, had also trained in the western twin-weapon style. The curved sword shot back and forth, but Ashok intercepted it, flat on flat, and sent Devedas stumbling back.

The slope was steep. The ground was loose and rapidly turning to clinging mud. The sudden strain on the muscles of his wounded leg were almost too much. The Heart of the Mountain could barely keep up.

The damaged swords crossed again, high. Ashok threw his knee into Devedas' side, but the Protector surprised him by rolling into it, sweeping Ashok from his feet, and hurling him down the hill.

Landing on his back, he slid through the mud. Before he could lift his blade, Devedas stomped his boot down upon the sword, trapping it against the ground. Devedas was over him, but rather than attack Ashok's body, his target was Jamari's sword. Devedas roared as he called upon the Heart to give him strength for one brief moment. The heavy southern blade sped downward in a mighty chop. Metal rang against metal.

And then Ashok was sliding free, because all he was holding onto was a hilt and about a foot of sword since the rest of it had just been snapped off. Ashok rolled to get out of range, and then fought his way back to his feet, keeping the ruined remains of the Vadal blade between them.

The end was a useless flat. The whole thing was bent. It was still better than nothing, but Devedas would easily outrange him now. "You've got a bad habit of breaking swords, brother."

He had allowed Devedas to retrieve his weapon. He had been wrong in assuming that if their situations were reversed his opponent would have done the same. There was no courtesy given.

Devedas attacked.

Ashok tried to dodge the cut, but he wasn't fast enough. Steel parted the flesh of his shoulder. He countered, but Devedas was easily able to dodge the dagger-length weapon. When Devedas came at him again, it left another cut across his thigh, shallow, but burning.

This couldn't last. He'd be cut to pieces at this rate. It was time to change the terms. Doing so was dangerous, but he had no other choice.

He interrupted Devedas' next swing by hurling the broken sword at his face and then diving for his waist. The Protector knocked the weapon aside, and unfortunately still had time to turn his sword into Ashok on the way in. It put a long cut down his back and into his hip, but then Ashok was on him.

They crashed to the ground and slid through the mud. Ashok started striking with his fists. Devedas tried to turn his curved blade into Ashok's side, but he managed to get his elbow down to block it. It cut deep into his arm, but better that than his guts.

Devedas was on his back, Ashok tried to get higher to keep him down, and strike at his vulnerable eyes or throat. Devedas had no choice but to let go of his sword.

Rolling down the hill, Ashok kept hitting him. Devedas hit him back. Ratul had been a master of every weapon, but also of bare hands. Every one of his students could kill with any weapon or none at all. Devedas got ahold of the last rags of Ashok's shirt, yanked them across his neck, and attempted a choke. But Ashok managed to hook his hand around Devedas' broken fingers, and with a mighty twist, ground them into the damaged joints. Devedas lost control of the choke, but he didn't let go.

They thrashed through the mud, punching, and kicking. Both of them were trying, but the slippery mess made it difficult to latch onto a limb long enough to twist and break it. There would be no submission here. It was to the death.

Devedas punched him in his already damaged ear. Head spinning, Ashok dropped an elbow into Devedas' face. The two of them hit the Akara and were instantly covered in water. They were in the rocky shallows, fighting in only a foot of treacherous, freezing hell.

Somehow Devedas ended up on top, and he'd found a rock. It smashed into Ashok's forehead. Blood went everywhere. Ashok couldn't see. He couldn't hear. He would not quit.

His thumb found Devedas' eye. He stabbed hard. Devedas finally gave some indication of feeling pain, and bellowed incoherently. The rock came down to brain him again, but Ashok knocked it aside with his forearm, and then he punched Devedas square in the throat. His old friend flinched back, struggling to breathe.

Ashok found his own rock, twice as big as his fist, and cracked Devedas in the side of the skull with it.

It had been a devastating hit. Falling back onto land, Devedas flopped face-first into the mud. Everything hurting, Ashok crawled up after him. Stunned, Devedas rolled over. Ashok grabbed him by the throat. There was blood dripping from the river stone as he raised it overhead to deliver a killing blow.

It was over.

Dazed, incoherent, all Devedas could do was stare up at him, and then at the raised rock.

It had to be done. Devedas would never stop hunting him. For him to live—for Thera to live—Devedas had to die. Not so long ago, the instant Ashok had found out that his brother was plotting to overthrow the Law, he would have ended him without hesitation. It had taken becoming a criminal to learn what compassion was.

"You've become weak," Devedas croaked. "Ratul would be ashamed."

"Yield."

Devedas closed his eyes and sank deeper into the mud. "I can't stop. You have to die. All of you have to die."

The bloody rock was shaking in his trembling hand. "Leave us be! That's all I ask."

"There could never be peace for you, Ashok sword breaker. If not me, then it'd be someone else coming for you." Devedas opened his eyes again, revealing that one was entirely filled with blood. The other held tears. "I'm sorry."

And then Devedas ran the small knife he'd had hidden in his belt across Ashok's neck.

It was a terribly sharp little thing, opening vein and artery both. He let go of Devedas to shove his hand beneath his ear to try and stop the bleeding, but blood came squirting between his fingers.

"You're the greatest man I've ever known, Ashok. I will try to rule in a way that would make you proud."

His vision was swimming. His body was cold as the Akara. The Heart of the Mountain was already overwhelmed, and even the powerful artifact couldn't keep up with all the blood being stolen from his brain. He sank down, until he was face to scarred face, looking down at his brother.

"I'll have a golden statue of you erected in the Capitol, twenty...no, fifty feet tall, so I can show the people what true devotion looks like."

Angruvadal had agreed not to help him for the duel. It changed its mind.

The black-steel shard turned to molten liquid.

"Shh...rest now."

Ashok hit Devedas in the head with the rock.

The Protector hadn't been prepared for that sudden burst of strength. Ashok hit him again. And again.

That old familiar instinct came upon him, as Angruvadal warned him of danger. This time it wasn't a suggestion, but a command.

Stop.

Ashok hit him again. Devedas head flopped to the side.

Enough.

Angruvadal was warning him to stop, but furious Ashok roared as he lifted the rock high overhead and

prepared to bring it down with both hands to destroy
Devedas' skull and spread his brains through the mud.

A jolt of incredible agony radiated out from the
shard in his chest. This had to be what a heart attack
felt like. Ashok screamed as lightning traveled down
every vein and artery. The rock fell from his nerveless
fingers to plop back into the mud.

This one is still necessary.

Ashok rolled off his unconscious brother to lie there
in the mud next to him, helpless as they both used
the Heart of the Mountain to stay alive.

The molten fire of Angruvadal gradually cooled.
The whispers stopped.

A long time passed as they lay there beneath the
rain. With one hand pressed to his throat, Ashok
slowly turned his head so that he could see Devedas,
with skull broken and face so swollen he was barely
recognizable. It took a few more minutes before his
throat was solid enough to risk speaking. Devedas still
couldn't move, but he could hear.

"Angruvadal has spared your life twice. There will
not be a third chance."

"So be it," Devedas whispered.

Slipping in the mud, so weak he could barely stand,
Ashok got up, only to discover that there were a great
many watchers standing in the dark above them. It
was the warriors of vassal house Garo, and most of
them were holding bows with arrows already nocked.

Among the observers was the phontho, Ranjan
Garo. Next to him was his son, Rane, who looked
ashamed as his father lifted one hand to signal for
his men to draw back their bows. Twenty arrows were
aimed at Ashok.

"We had an agreement," Ashok said.

"Yet you are still here," the phontho replied.

"I am leaving."

"Yes. Only I will decide how."

"Please, Father. Don't do this."

"Silence, Rane... Are you still alive, Lord Protector Devedas?"

Devedas coughed. "I live."

The phontho stroked his long beard. "I knew your father. He was a great leader. He taught me that whenever possible, a Thakoor should have a wizard among his court, to spy upon those who would conduct illicit business in his lands. Thus I was told of your conversation with the Black Heart. If you were to become king, would you free the once loyal subjects of Dev from the tyranny of their new masters, Akershan?"

It was a dark and illegal bargain. Ashok already knew what the proud and pragmatic answer of Devedas would be. And of course if he didn't, they'd both end up dead in the river, and Ranjan would just lie and say they'd killed each other during their duel.

"You served my father well. As king, I would free this house," Devedas croaked. "You have my vow."

The negotiations had gone so smoothly that his archers' arms hadn't even had a chance to get tired. "Then the Garo will bend their knee to a son of Dev once more."

"This is dishonest, Father!" Rane shouted.

"Survival is the most honest thing of all, my son," the phontho said with great solemnity as he signaled for his archers. "Kill the Black Heart."

Ashok was barely alive as it was. His throat had

just been cut. Too weak to evade, there was no way he could survive being pierced by so many arrows.

Bowstrings thrummed.

Except he didn't die. As Angruvadal still needed Devedas for some mysterious reason, so too must it have required Ashok to live. For when he opened his eyes, the arrows were stopped a few inches away, as if frozen in air turned to ice. Only the intervention was not without cost, as the sudden, violent twisting of reality snapped and released a concussive wave of force.

Ashok was hurled violently into the rapids.

Chapter 43

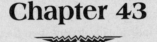

Interviewing and testing soldiers had made it a long and tiresome day for Jagdish. Normally a phontho would be appointed to an existing garrison, but his promotion had been so sudden the warrior caste of Great House Vadal had no place ready for him. Honestly, they didn't really know what to do with him. But with rumors of house war in the air a military buildup had begun. They had given him a budget, but no men to pay with it. So Jagdish had decided to get out ahead of the looming war by putting together his own garrison while he waited for the high command to get off its ass.

Besides, he'd needed something to do other than sit in his vast house, lonely and bitter, listening to a baby cry.

He'd been traveling across Vadal for the last weeks, stopping at every warrior's district to find men who were currently unobligated to a command. The unfortunate part about that was warriors who were unobligated usually held that ignoble status for a reason. It was hard to put together a glorious unit made out of drunks, fools, and discipline problems. Yet he knew from personal experience, that just because a warrior was currently unloved by his superiors, that didn't make him a bad warrior. Sometimes they were just unlucky.

Jagdish did not accept any warrior desperate for an assignment. He had gone through too much and worked too hard to foul this up now. He took the time to speak with each one individually, to question their motives and their commitment, and several times to spar, ride, or foot race, against the cocky ones himself. Most phonthos were too old for that sort of thing, but Jagdish preferred the hands-on approach. He'd gathered many that way, but still had a hundred more to go.

Exhausted, he made his way up the stairs. His lodging for the night was the top floor of an inn that would have been far too expensive to stay at when he was a mere risaldar. It turned out luxury was rather meaningless when you had no one to share it with.

There was a giant man waiting for him in the shadows at the top of the stairs. He was wearing a big straw farmer's hat that hid his features, but it was clear this was no farmer, unless he farmed anvils. The stranger was about as big as Gutch, but while Gutch was fat strong, this one appeared to be just plain strong, and though dressed like a worker, he stood like a warrior. Comfortable, confident, but ready to move.

"Good evening, Phontho Jagdish."

Jagdish looked up. If this man was looking for an obligation, Jagdish was ready to hire him on the spot, just for the sheer intimidation value he could bring to the unit. Oceans, even if he was an imbecile he could just use him to load boulders in a trebuchet and still come out ahead. But no . . . Jagdish had a system. He needed to interview him to make sure he wasn't some manner of dreg or lunatic. "If you're here about the new garrison, I've not got my scribe nor my obligation papers with me. Come back first thing in the morning, Warrior."

"I'm not warrior caste."

He snorted. "Well, that's a shame. Just look at the size of you."

"I'm Karno Uttara," the big one said quietly. "Protector of the Law."

Jagdish sighed. He'd been through this before, though that Protector had shown up in his fancy armor and flashed their frightening golden symbol in Jagdish's face to begin that interrogation. "Protectors dress like field hands now, do they?"

"I would show you the token of my office if I had it with me."

"Sure, you would." But in the off chance he needed to be respectful to such an illustrious servant of the Law, he added, "If you are who you claim, you know Harta Vadal has explained my actions, and I already told you people I don't know where Ashok went after Bahdjangal."

"This is about a different matter. May we speak somewhere privately?"

He reached the top-floor landing. "Whatever for?"

That was when he noticed that a woman had been standing behind the giant the whole time. She stepped into the light and unwound her head scarf so he could see her face. "We need your help, noble Jagdish."

He almost didn't recognize her, with bruises healing all over her face. "Librarian?" It was so unexpected that it took him a moment to remember the name of the woman who had saved his life. "Radamantha?"

"Just Rada is fine. Sorry to bother you but—"

"No, no, come in." Jagdish hurried to his room and unlocked the door. From the look of her, someone had attacked a lady of the first caste. He was bound not just by Law, but by honor and decency to offer her all his hospitality. "Are you all right?"

"Well, not really."

The Protector snorted.

"It's complicated," the librarian said.

Jagdish shut the door behind them. Rada was from a Capitol Order, which meant that the big man probably was a real Protector. "What's going on? Please have a seat." He gestured toward the cushions.

Karno remained standing, and oddly enough, watched the windows. But Rada sat down. The ungraceful way she moved suggested that she was exhausted and had been on her feet for a while.

"What happened?"

"It's a long story."

"Which she should not tell," Karno interjected.

Rada looked around the luxurious room. "You seem to be doing a lot better since the last time we met."

In truth, Jagdish paid no attention to such things. His life was a bittersweet parody of what he'd worked for. There was duty to focus on, and in the hours he wasn't fulfilling that duty his life was empty, cold, and gray. He had a daughter he couldn't even look at without thinking of her lost mother and falling into a deep melancholy. His child was being looked after by servants at his estate. It was irrational to harbor bitterness toward a baby, but every time he held her, he couldn't help but think about how her birth had deprived him of the love of his life, and that unwarranted bitterness made him feel guilt and shame. It was not little Pari's fault Jagdish had not been there when his family had needed him.

"I am doing well."

"And your family?"

Enough pleasantries. "What do you need my help with, Rada?"

"Before I ask for any favor, Luthra told me you had given your oath to repay my kindness for helping you with Harta. Is this accurate?"

"Of course. Anything. I am a man of my word."

"I need somewhere to hide."

"From who?"

"Well . . ." She hesitated awkwardly. "Your Thakoor, all of Great House Vadal's warriors, and the entire Order of Inquisition."

"Oh . . ." Jagdish blinked. "Is that all?"

Chapter 44

Since Gutch was a man of vast wealth now—and he'd gained said wealth by robbing the most murderous wizards in the world—he hardly went anywhere without his cadre of bodyguards. Of course none of them were half the warrior his good friend Jagdish had been, but they were loyal, or at least he was paying them enough they should be. One could never really tell about such things.

He actually enjoyed the quiet walk across the city of Guntur himself. It turned out that men important enough to rate bodyguards were seldom alone. In fact, over the last few months Gutch's rapidly expanding household had collected not just bodyguards, but also a personal secretary, four slaves, a chef, a food taster to make sure nobody tried to poison him, he'd had affairs with two different mistresses, was working on a possible third, and he'd even purchased some racing horses, as well as a couple of supposedly well-trained war dogs to watch out for assassins, though mostly those beasts just sat around, eating huge quantities of his food and leaving even bigger piles of dung upon his expensive rugs.

So it turned out that the life of a rich man was seldom a lonely one. Yet for this particular meeting, Gutch had decided to come alone. As far as his household was concerned, his money had been earned through proper legal channels . . . not illegal magic smuggling. That sort of distasteful business was frowned upon by all right-thinking sorts, and also Inquisitors who in his experience were all very angry all the time.

He had sold enough demon in the underground markets of Kharsawan to stimulate the entire economy. It wasn't like he needed more money, but Gutch had to admit that the message he'd received had made him rather curious.

Very few people knew that he had been an associate of Ashok Vadal. Most of those were off being fanatical rebellious criminal types, and not inclined to blackmail someone they considered an associate. Or they were murderous magical assassins, and if Sikasso's bunch found him . . . well, that lot would be far more inclined to saw his head off in revenge than to try and extort banknotes from him.

So it was curiosity mostly that had brought Gutch to this factory on the outskirts of the worker district late that night. The note had not mentioned blackmail specifically—only an unspecified *opportunity*—but for what reason other than blackmail would someone tell him that they knew his real name, that he had ridden with the Sons of the Black Sword, that he still had time to serve for a prison sentence in Great House Vadal, and that they wished to have a clandestine meeting to discuss such things?

Now normally, that sort of message meant it was time to run, but the other downside of being a man of wealth and status was that he had accumulated a lot of stuff and simply didn't want to leave it all behind. He still had sacks full of banknotes ready in case he needed to flee in case of emergency, but Gutch was enjoying his newfound luxury, and frankly didn't really want to start over again somewhere else. So he'd brought some bribery money, and also his decorative *walking stick*—which actually had a steel rod for a core—just in case he needed to bludgeon someone to death.

The factory was small, but still open even at this late hour. Workers were coming and going. Curious, if the blackmailer intended for this meeting to remain a secret. The sign said that their business was *toolmaking*.

A well-dressed woman met him at the entrance. She was probably around forty years old, but still rather easy on the eyes for a woman of such advanced age, and rather well kept up, in fine silks, makeup, and fashionably styled hair. Gutch reflexively smiled. Even with multiple mistresses half this woman's age, Gutch was by nature a charmer.

Apparently, so was she. "I was told to expect a man of magnificent height and proud girth, so this must be Gutch, forge master smith of Vadal City."

"Forge Master Gutch is an artisan of some fame." He looked around to make sure no one else was close enough to hear them over the banging and rattling coming from inside the factory. "I would never dare claim such honors. I am merely Vinod, a humble merchant, who recently moved to these Kharsawan lands to purchase a vineyard."

She laughed as if all that was a very funny joke. Then she beckoned him to come through the doorway. As she did so, he noticed for the first time the precious jewel on her sash denoting her office. She was a *banker*... the highest possible status of the worker caste. Everybody needed notes. Capitol bankers were the ones who printed them and loaned them out to the great houses, making hers a very important office indeed. Bankers had more money than most judges—a fact which certainly pissed off the first caste—surely one of them wouldn't need to blackmail the likes of him.

Also, she had magic on her person. A great deal of it too. Gutch had always had a gift for sensing such things. This was real, irreplaceable black steel too, not the more common but inferior demon.

"I am intrigued," Gutch said aloud.

"I knew you would be. That's why I left you that cryptic message. Now come along, time is short. Hurry, hurry."

Curious, Gutch followed her into the factory, where a crew of eight men were sitting at workbenches, using hand files to shape small metal parts. That old familiar stink—metal, fire, and oil—struck his nostrils and brought joy to his heart. That was the smell of creation.

"You are an interesting man, Gutch. I keep my eye on interesting people. However, you didn't come to my attention for a very long time because you weren't part of the prediction. I knew others had a part to play, each one vital, like the little parts in these machines. You, being an anomaly, weren't interesting to me until you fell in with the warrior Jagdish."

He had absolutely no idea what the attractive banker was blathering on about. "You know Jagdish?"

"We have never met, but I still follow the progress of all the interesting people. Jagdish is a mighty phontho now."

"Really?" Gutch laughed. It was amazing the man was still alive! "That madman pulled it off then. Good for him!"

"Oh yes. He has a very important part to play in what's coming, a very important part indeed. As do you, I belatedly realized. As does everyone who has come into contact with Ashok Vadal in fact."

"Well, me and the Black Heart aren't exactly chums... More temporary business associates of convenience."

"No matter. Ashok is a vortex of instability. He is the avalanche. He is the flood, the tornado, and the wildfire. Which is why you must help him once more."

"Whoa, whoa, hold on now. I've experienced plenty of fiery floods and whatnot already. I'm a man of leisure and prosperity now, and I'd prefer to keep it that way."

"You say that, but you don't mean it." She just shook her head and grinned. "Ah, silly Gutch. You'd grow bored just lying about, and deep down you know it. There's work for you to do. Every part of the great machine needs to fit together in order to function."

He thought she might be touched in the head. "What machine are you talking about?"

"The greatest one of all. I am but an engineer. My duty is to make things work, because if our plan doesn't, then one of our competitors' plans will. To the fanatics, I have to appeal to their faith. To the warriors, their pride. But for you, a man of business, I can be direct. How would you like to become the wealthiest man in Lok?"

He laughed. "Who wouldn't?"

"A great many people actually. As I was trying to explain, every piece has unique motivations, and I must know them so I can coax them into place. You are the consummate example of the worker caste, seeking perfection in his craft, and of course, a corresponding reward. So I can just pay you."

"Wait . . . You're serious?"

They'd been walking through the workshop the whole time and had reached the back wall. Without explanation, she reached up and pulled down hard on one protruding brick. There was a creak of hinges as a secret door opened. It had been rather well concealed, even to his experienced eye. The odd banker shoved it back, revealing a hidden storage room.

Gutch gasped when he saw the contents. "Saltwater, woman!"

There were racks and racks of Fortress rods, wood and steel, dozens of the deadly things. With a shock, he looked back at the workbenches, and realized that the pieces they were filing to fit were parts for the weapons. They were building them *here*. In Lok. On the mainland.

"There's a great upheaval coming, Gutch, the likes of which the world hasn't seen since the days of Ramrowan. You were a smuggler, which means you know the underworld and its trade. You understand how to move illicit goods from one place to another. But more importantly you were a forge master. Most people don't realize what that means, but I do. You're a maker, a builder, but more importantly, you're a leader who can teach others to build things. I have plans, simplified for ease of manufacture. I have banknotes to speed things along. Now I require someone who can expand this operation."

His mind was still reeling at the sheer, brazen, out-of-her-bleeding-mind, audacious illegality of the whole thing. It took him a moment to catch up with the madwoman's words. "Expand? Where?"

"Everywhere, Gutch. I've already started, but there is still so much work to do."

"Who in the oceans are you?"

"A good question. You may call me Mother Dawn."

Chapter 45

The warrior Bharatas rode Khurdan all the way across Akershan to the great house in MaDharvo. He was thin and malnourished. His injuries had not become infected, but they were healing slowly, and he still suffered from a near-constant headache.

At least the pain and hunger helped distract him from the grief, because it was easy for his thoughts to turn back to how his parents and sisters had all been killed during the occupation of Chakma, put to the sword for not bowing to a religious fanatic. Their fate left him sad, but also proud, because he came from a stubborn line.

Bharatas had nowhere else to go. His defeated paltan had ceased to exist. The phontho he had been obligated to bodyguard had been taken as a hostage, and then killed himself in shame after being released. So south he had rode.

The entire long journey he couldn't understand why he wasn't seeing large numbers of troops moving north to annihilate the rebels once and for all, but the plains seemed empty. It should have been obvious by now that things were not going well in the northern provinces. Surely someone else must have delivered the report to their Thakoor by now. Their bearer should have been dispatched to defeat Ashok Vadal at least.

As a warrior without obligation, he hoped to come across a unit that he could offer his services to. He had been defeated and his unit disgraced, but he was still a superb horseman, and better with a sword than almost anyone in his house. Warriors from the southern barracks would need someone to guide them in the north, and no one knew the land between Chakma and the Dharvan Bench better than he did.

It wasn't until he reached the outskirts of the MaDharvo that he found out why the army wasn't marching. The guards at the checkpoint were glad to share the grim rumor that their bearer had been accidentally kicked in the head by his horse...a very ignominious fate in a land of riders. Supposedly, he had been lying unconscious in his chambers, wasting away all summer.

The Thakoor couldn't just have the man suffocated or starved, because their ancestor blade might take offense at such a dishonorable end for its bearer and shatter itself. So the house slaves were keeping him alive. Rather than mobilize to fight the rebels, the phonthos and every high-status warrior of the southern garrisons were waiting for their bearer to perish. If they were off campaigning against rebels they wouldn't be around to try and pick up the sword. Glory in battle was one thing, but there was no glory higher, or status greater, than becoming a bearer.

As he was told this news, a terrible black fury descended upon Bharatas. His family had been butchered by fanatics. The northern garrisons had been decimated by poison, ambush, and Fortress weapons, yet were still being expected to massacre all their casteless. All while these warriors, his supposed brothers, were sitting here fat and comfortable, waiting around for a man in a coma to slowly perish, just for the one in a thousand chance his sword might pick one of them to wield it.

His rage made the pain in his skull grow even worse. That throbbing curse was a constant reminder that Ashok Vadal had defeated him and left him to die on the plains. Ashok Vadal was the reason his unit had been destroyed, and the reason his family had been butchered by criminals. And Ashok Vadal was still alive because Bharatas' house was diseased with greed and cowardice.

A man in a coma could live for years. The northern provinces did not have *years*.

He didn't even have a family left to bring shame to, so his decision was an easy one to make. He lied his way into the great house's walls, saying that he had an important message from his phontho for the Thakoor's ears only. No one here knew of his old master's suicide, and Bharatas still had his traveling papers and password, so they let him in.

Once inside the walls, Bharatas took Khurdan to the stables. Even the city folk of MaDharvo hadn't forgotten the old ways, so their steeds came first. He was fine with dying, but he wanted to make sure his loyal companion would be cared for after he was executed. As a warhorse she was certain to go to a

new home. She was far more valuable than he was...
All Bharatas had left to live for was revenge and his
horse, so once he was certain Khurdan would be fine,
he entered the great house.

It wouldn't do for a messenger to go before the
Thakoor smelling of weeks of travel, so he was taken
to the baths. As soon as the servants took their eyes
off him, Bharatas snuck out. In a quiet corridor he
grabbed a house slave, and by knife point, demanded
to be guided to the bearer's chambers.

There were two warriors posted on the bedroom
door. It wouldn't have mattered if there were a hundred, he still would have went for it. He shoved the
slave girl into the guards and attacked in a berserk
rage. With surprise and fury on his side, he quickly
dropped both guards, but it made a lot of noise. There
wouldn't be much time before a horde of warriors
descended on this place.

Once inside the bearer's bedroom, with strength
born of desperation he shoved a heavy wardrobe in
front of the door to buy some time.

The bearer must have been a proud warrior once,
but he had shrunk to nothing since his injury. It was
more skeleton than man lying in the bed before him,
but his chest was still rising and falling, and upon
it rested the sheathed form of Akerselem. Bharatas
had never seen the famous sword in person before,
but every warrior in their house knew of its legend.

It was said that a dishonorable death would cause
an ancestor blade to shatter, but it could not be
honorable for a warrior to rot, helpless like this.
Bharatas was terrified that the constant pain in his
head was making him do something stupid, but he

couldn't turn back now. Seizing an ancestor blade in an honorable duel was one thing. There was nothing honorable about this. It was like putting down a horse with a broken leg.

The guards began smashing the door open.

It was said that when a warrior took up an unclaimed ancestor blade, it measured their worth. If the sword found them lacking, it would cause the warrior to cut themselves. The more displeased the sword was, the more damage it inflicted. It wasn't unusual for dozens of warriors to die or dismember themselves before an ancestor blade chose its next bearer.

He reached for the sword, and then hesitated. "Mighty Akerselem, I am Bharatas, son of Arun. I know I'm not worthy to be your bearer. I have been defeated in battle. I have not kept my obligations. The man I was supposed to protect cut his own throat because of my failure. I expect you to kill me for daring to pick you up, and that is all I deserve. Please do not break, for you are wasted here guarding this husk of a man. I attempt to draw you in order to force my brothers to act. Your people in the north are in danger. A rogue bearer named Ashok Vadal has brought blood and terror to our lands, and only you can defeat him."

Splinters flew as a war hammer knocked a hole through the door. Warriors shouted for him to stop.

"If you do not slay me here and now, then I vow that I will use you to kill Ashok Vadal."

Bharatas seized Akerselem.

It found him worthy.

Chapter 46

The Chief Judge was still a powerful orator when he put his mind to it.

"This trial for the so-called Great Extermination has proven a failure. Every good thing Arbiter Artya assured this chamber would happen has not happened. Instead it has been a curse upon our people. Respect for the Law has not increased. It has declined. The rebellion was not destroyed. It has grown. Thousands of disobedient casteless were killed, but their foolish ways have spread to millions in the lands of every other house, including those which had no issues with their non-people before. Casteless, usually dull minded and manageable, have turned into desperate, wild beasts once they believed they were cornered. For even the most docile of animals will struggle once they realize they've been led into the slaughterhouse."

The chamber was quiet for once. No one dared interrupt or jeer. He rarely spoke, and because of that rarity, his words were powerful. Tonight, the Chief Judge had called them to account.

"The earlier studies saying the casteless would be easily culled in a single season have proven overly optimistic. This endeavor has cost us greatly, in notes, and in lives. Some here have argued that we are now committed to this Great Extermination, that we must finish what we have started. I would respond that when a man has departed on a journey, when he realizes that he has climbed up the wrong hill, he turns back, and rights his course. He does not continue blundering in the wrong direction to the incorrect destination out of stubbornness.

"Do not let pride chain you to your previous mistakes. Do not let your disgust of the unclean animals who live beneath our society blind you. Search your hearts and you will see that I am right. Voting to return to the correct path does not make you weak. It does not make you a *casteless lover* as some here have vilely insinuated. As many of you know I have a beautiful garden in this city. I do not like weeds, but when I find one I do not burn the entire garden down! No. I have my servants carefully remove the bad plants to protect the fruit and flowers. I do not like moles and pests, but when they nibble at my cabbage I do not have my servants dig up everything and salt the ground. I let loose a cat. And anyone who insinuated the master of that garden was a lover of weeds and vermin would be immediately dismissed by all right-thinking men as a hyperbolic imbecile."

Angry looks were exchanged across the Chamber of Argument. The Chief Judge was dancing on the edge of giving outright offense, but no one spoke, because there was no good rebuttal.

"There is a vote scheduled tomorrow. Will we stop this foolishness, recognize that we have taken a wrong turn, and gone up the wrong hill? Or will we press on, to some unknown destination? The non-people have been content to remain beneath our notice for centuries, and we have been content to ignore them. It was a mistake to meddle in traditions. Thus tomorrow, my vote will be to turn Lok back toward sanity, and to end this foolish extermination."

He banged the end of his staff against the floor, signifying that he was done speaking. The Law said the Chief Judge automatically had the honor of holding the staff—and controlling the proceedings—simply by virtue of being present. His point had been made. He didn't deign to take questions or have debate. His lofty status meant he was above such things. He simply passed the staff back to the judge who had been scheduled to preside over this session and walked away.

The Chief Judge left the chamber through the main entrance, surrounded by his usual cadre of bodyguards and servants. There was a crowd waiting outside, some who adored him, and some who despised him. Though tradition declared there was no requirement for him to listen to rebuttals inside the chamber, the rules were not so clear on the street, and men began to shout questions at him about his speech.

"How can you say spare the casteless now? After Chakma! After Shabdkosh, or Sutpo Bridge?"

Normally he would not bother replying because the angry people with the questions didn't have the status to matter. However, because of his abrupt departure from the chamber his servants hadn't had a chance to bring his carriage around yet. Since he was stuck here for a moment the Chief Judge began to respond to some of his rhetorical challengers.

"I did not say forgive the guilty. Criminals must be tracked down and destroyed, especially Black-Hearted Ashok. Except the only things most non-people are guilty of is being slothful and dim-witted—"

"Death to the Law!"

The Chief Judge turned to see who had said something so shockingly, profoundly illegal. There weren't very many casteless in the Capitol, and they were usually never seen, but somebody still had to clean out the sewers or cart off dead bodies, so there were some number in the city. He couldn't remember ever actually seeing one out in public before though.

"The Forgotten will be remembered!" the casteless shouted as he ran up the steps, shoving his way past surprised arbiters. His clothing was nothing more than a dirty old blanket and some rags, but out from beneath the blanket appeared an object of gleaming metal and wood. As the casteless pointed it up the stairs, one of his warriors immediately leapt in front of the Chief Judge.

There was a sharp bark and a flash of fire.

The Chief Judge stumbled back, pressing his hand to the sudden sting in his neck. His bodyguard fell, and rolled wetly down the steps, a hole torn clean through the top of his chest.

The casteless threw his loud weapon on the ground, and then ran away through the cloud of gray smoke that had suddenly appeared. Once they got over their surprise, several warriors gave chase.

Servants caught the Chief Judge before he could fall. When he took his hand away, blood squirted from the hole in his neck. Servants tore their garments off and pressed them against the gash to no avail. Others ran to get a surgeon. The bodyguards who had seen combat already knew it was a mortal wound, and they could do nothing but hold their master as he died.

The highest-status man in the world bled out on the steps of the Chamber of Argument, in the heart of the Capitol, in front of dozens of witnesses. The Fortress rod that had taken his life lay there on the stone, a mute testament that the subhuman casteless were not so docile after all.

Several minutes after the assassination, Grand Inquisitor Omand arrived at the scene. He was told that the murderer had somehow eluded his pursuers, but not to worry, because the warriors would not rest until they rounded up every non-person in the Capitol for torture and questioning. Omand studied the still-warm bodies. The Chief Judge had gone into the great nothing beyond life, eyes wide open, but totally unaware of just how important his sacrifice had been.

Then Omand walked over to the discarded weapon. Everyone else there had been afraid to touch the thing, but Omand picked it up and turned it over in his hands, muttering to himself behind his mask, a half-remembered line from a forbidden tome, translated from one of the ancestor tongues. The young witch hunter had only given the illegal book a cursory glance before throwing it in a bonfire, and couldn't recall exactly how it went, yet the elegance of one line had lingered with him for decades.

"I am become death . . . The destroyer of worlds."

The next day the vote to expand the Great Extermination to every province in Lok was unanimous.

Chapter 47

〰〰〰〰

"We've got another one over here!"

Bodies had been washing up on shore all morning. The mainlanders must have had a great battle across the water, because there sure were a lot of floaters. And it was battle for sure that had done them in, not plague or famine, because the bodies all clearly bore the marks of the weapons that had killed them. The waters were so cold they weren't even rotted yet.

The demons had eaten well, for sure! It was rare they got any floaters like this here, because the demons were usually quick to pull down the free meat. Demons sure loved human meat. Only this battle must have been big enough that even the demons had been sated. Most of the bodies were missing chunks from where the demons had nibbled, but many were still in good enough shape to have some salvageable clothing.

They worked fast, keeping the carrion birds off and watching out for demon sign as they tried to strip the bodies of any valuables. Whoever had thrown these in the river, they'd already taken all their valuable metal, for there was no coins or armor, just the occasional button, buckle, or pin, but there was a great deal of cloth, which was exceedingly precious here. Even the bloodiest scraps of mangled fabric were valuable in Xhonura. They'd even collected a good pile of shoes.

Once stripped naked the bodies were left on the rocky beach for the gulls, crabs, and demons.

Their next body was in better shape than most, as the demons had missed feasting on this one somehow. Whatever had killed him wasn't apparent at first glance, but he was as gray and frozen solid as the rest.

"Come on, that's quality silk and padded cloth he's got on." This was a great day for the workshop, for they made no silk on the island at all and produced very little wool. The collectors would be honored tonight! "Help me cut it free."

The two of them went to work with their shears. Whoever this man was he'd lived a harsh life, for there was hardly any of his muscular form that wasn't covered in scars.

"What do you think they were fighting over this time?"

"Who knows? Whatever nonsense infidels find important. As long as they don't bring their evil here, I don't care. Now hurry up and cut before a demon shows—"

The dead man suddenly grabbed him by the neck.

Terrified, he tried to stab the dead man with his shears, but that wrist was swiftly caught in the dead man's other hand. The flesh was cold as ice, his grip hard as iron.

His companion screamed, dropped his shears, and ran down the beach.

The dead man was staring at him, dark, bloodshot eyes obviously confused. He slowly raised his head, looked around, took in the black rocks of the beach and the wheeling gulls. Then the dead man realized he was choking someone to death, and his grip relaxed a bit.

The collector gasped for air. "Please don't kill me, dead man!"

"Who are you?" the dead man demanded. It was difficult to understand him, because his voice was so raspy, probably from the fresh white scar across this neck, and because he spoke with the strange accent of the mainlander, but mostly because dead men shouldn't speak!

"I'm Moyo of the Collectors Guild."

The dead man looked suspicious but he let go. Moyo rubbed the spreading bruises on his sore neck. He was terrified and wanted to run after his companion, but something made him stay, for this reminded him of a story his mother used to tell him.

"You're not a dead man at all, are you?"

"No."

"You were in the ice water! A man can only survive a few minutes in the ice water! How are you alive?"

"I'm beginning to suspect I can't die."

That was impossible. Only a moment ago he had been frozen. That was a miracle. Unless... Moyo's mouth fell open. *It could not be.* But it had to be! The saga had been passed down through the generations. There was only one Warrior Who Could Not Die, and it was said that he would return to his workshop *someday.* Was *someday* upon them?

Even though he was terrified and wanted to run

away like his companion had, Moyo stayed put, because it wasn't every day that you got to meet a god.

"I thirst," the Avatar of Ramrowan said. "Do you have drink?"

"Yes!" Moyo hurried and took the gourd from inside his seal-fur coat. "I present you this gift. Keep it!"

Avatara took it, looked at it funny, but then drank deep of the water. His skin was beginning to look alive again, and as his color returned, he began to shiver uncontrollably. Moyo had not known the incarnation of a deity could *shiver*.

"Where am I?"

"You're in Xhonura."

"An odd name. I'm unfamiliar with it." Avatara frowned. "I do not know how long I was out. How far did the river carry me?"

The collector pointed at the water. "That is not river. That is sea." Then he pointed at the rocks beneath them. "This is Xhonura."

"I floated all the way to Hell? I don't remember." Avatara seemed very surprised—and a little angry— when he realized it was saltwater he'd been freezing in. "That must be Akara Bay then. Are we on the Akershan side or the Devakula side?"

Moyo did not know those names. "Have patience upon your humble collector, Avatara. I forgot Xhonura is our name for it. You named this land *Fortress*."